The ~~Great~~ American Novel

A Convoluted History of Cannabis Legalization in the United States

---

J.A. LaPaix

Copyright © April 2020 by J.A. LaPaix

Wicker Park Publishing House, Chicago
www.wickerparkpublishing.com

All Rights Reserved. No part of this publication may be reproduced, or stored in a retrieval system, or transmitted in any form or by any means, electronical, mechanical, photocopying, recording, or otherwise, without written permission of the publisher. For information regarding permission, write to info@wickerparkpublishing.com.

ISBN: 978-1-7348604-2-9

Printed in the U.S.A.
First edition, April 2020

This book is a work of fiction. All names, characters, places, and incidents are either the product of the author's imagination or used fictitiously. Any resemblance to actual events, locales, or persons, living or dead, is coincidental.

For the patient souls.

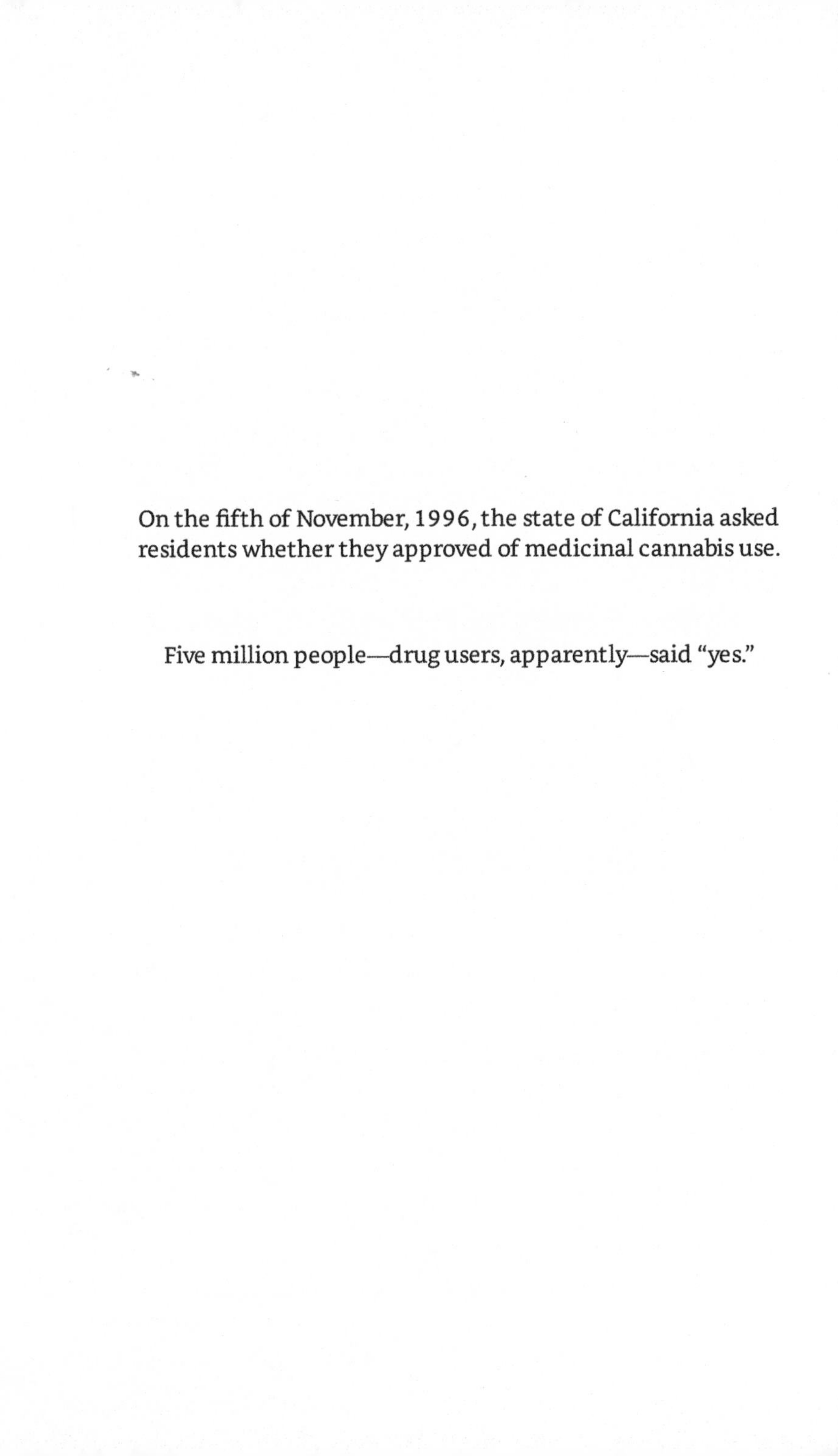

On the fifth of November, 1996, the state of California asked residents whether they approved of medicinal cannabis use.

Five million people—drug users, apparently—said "yes."

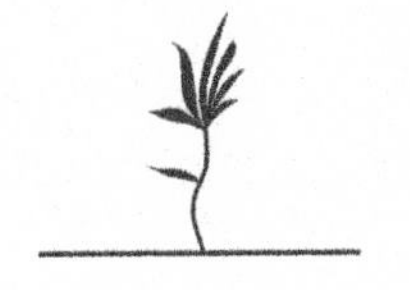

PART I: 1996

ONE

Somewhere in the Pacific Ocean

In the beginning, there was nothing. Nothing of relevance, at least, for a few billion years. Then a tectonic shift triggered an eruption of magma in the middle of the ocean. For days, smoke billowed high into the clouds, and lava sizzled for miles atop the water. When the smoke cleared and the lava cooled, a small volcanic island rose from the endless blue waves of the Pacific.

The volcano went dormant, and for a while the island sat in the middle of the water, appearing to wayward sailors as nothing more than a chunk of black rock simmering in the sun. But over time, the fierce ocean waves eroded the island's volcanic rock, and prevailing winds from the east brought fresh seeds. Add in the surrounding water and sunshine, both plentiful, and the recipe for life found its key ingredients.

At first, a single sprout appeared out of place as it dared defy the surrounding darkness of the volcanic soil. Then that sprout grew leaves, and a second sprout followed. Those sprouts grew into plants, as sprouts tend to do, and those plants multiplied, their descendants slowly covering the island until the black rock disappeared beneath a sea of vibrant colors.

Yet the island stood untouched—a seeming mirage reflecting off the endless blue waves—until a wealthy businessman, alone on his spacious yacht, drifted off course on a windy afternoon. The businessman had never paid attention to coordinates, let alone read a nautical map, so pure chance played a part as he happened upon this secret paradise under the sun. His eyes—a golden shade to those who looked past the powdery white beard framing his face—had never observed something so pure.

So what did he do?

He did what anyone with countless wealth would do: he ran his yacht aground at the shore and stepped his designer boots onto the volcanic soil.

For a moment, the businessman lost his voice. From up close, the island appeared even more impressive than from afar. Giant palm trees shaded black sand beaches. Fallen coconuts surrounded bright yellow pineapples bursting from the soil. Tall prairie grasses and gaudy sunflowers and exotically twisted shrubbery soaked up fresh water from streams running down to the coast. And amidst all that, one particular plant species dominated the landscape: its jagged green leaves visible in every direction, its fresh herbal scent filling the air.

"This is dope," the businessman said.

He referred not only to the island's relaxed ambiance, but also to the slang term for the herbal-scented plants shrouding the landscape. To most of the world, "cannabis" would've been more readily understood than "dope," but he'd never much cared for the opinions of others.

Dope covered the landscape as far as he could see. Then again, he could only see half of the island from the shoreline, so he hiked his designer boots as far as the island went to the sky: to the peak of the retired volcano in its center, where he stood on top of the world in more than one sense. With the sun beaming down on his face, and the fresh ocean breeze gusting through his beard, he couldn't imagine a better place to be as he gazed over the horizon.

"I can't imagine it getting any better than this," he even said aloud.

But then the situation improved even more so, at least temporarily. With a curious eye, he knelt on one knee next to the closest herbal-scented plant and admired a budding flower which looked more like a clump of green fuzz than an artistic display of colorful petals circling a pistil. And he did what many would do in the presence of such natural beauty: he plucked the flower from its stem, tightly wound the flower into a cigarette, and puffed the cigarette until his lungs became as full as he was of himself.

Stroking his thick white beard, deep into thought as he puffed on his cigarette, he spent quite some time peering down at the land below. Before his golden eyes lay a natural paradise teeming with life from coast to coast. Although the island appeared small in terms of acreage, it offered room for at least a dozen people to live peacefully; or alternatively, room for a wealthy businessman to have paradise all to himself.

That's when the mass of neurons in his head lit up his sparkling golden eyes with his best idea yet: certainly an obtainable idea, because in 1996, the purchase of an isolated island by a bright-eyed millionaire took little more than a quick phone call to his attorney.

"I've decided to buy an island," he told his attorney in lieu of a greeting. Coincidentally, the top of a mountain in the middle of the ocean was the best place to receive a clear signal on a satellite phone.

"Finally retiring?" The attorney understood the sentiment.

The attorney should've known better than to ask that question. Under no circumstance would the businessman seek to purchase the island without a plan to profit. His success had always relied on his smarts—his brilliance, actually, according to him. He could spot a lucrative opportunity from over a nautical mile away. The island displayed the potential to make him more money than he could count in a lifetime. He already owned more money than he could count in his lifetime, to be clear, but even more money sounded better than that.

"What's your brilliant idea?" his attorney asked.

Well that should've been obvious by this point, according to the businessman. He planned to enable others to be as high as he stood at that moment: not high from standing at the tallest point of an island, but high from the dope growing in every direction.

"I understand that California is on the verge of legalizing cannabis for medical patients," the businessman said, "which would create a hungry new market in the United States."

That issue fell outside the realm of the attorney's expertise, though he'd gladly research the legal complexities for as long as it took to find out the answer—at his typical hourly fee, of course.

"First," the businessman said, "find out how much this island will cost me."

He ended the call and returned his golden gaze to the sea of life flourishing in every direction to the coastline. The view was such a treat that he lost his head in the clouds as he slowly reduced his cigarette to smoke and ash. And with his head, so went his sense of time—after what seemed like only a moment, his satellite phone buzzed with an update from his attorney.

The purchase of the island turned out to be far less complicated than expected. Neighboring Mexico held the most legitimate claim to the land, and Mexico's Minister of Land Administration was a reasonable negotiator: the island could be purchased for the precise cost of the Minister's immediate retirement in Fiji.

"How soon does the Minister wish to leave?" was the businessman's only question.

"How soon can you get to Mexico?" was his attorney's only reply.

The businessman decided to get moving, before the Minister realized the advantages of Bora Bora over Fiji. Having vacationed in both, he fully appreciated the difference in cost. The sooner he arrived in Mexico and signed the land transfer papers, the sooner he could figure out the rest of the details of his new business.

Of course, once he signed those land transfer papers, he'd be a nameless businessman no more. He'd even be forced to learn a few other names as he built a team to spread his dope across the budding new market in the United States. But all those names could wait. A more pressing task required his attention at the moment.

He needed to pick more dope to puff until he returned.

TWO

Mexico

The unadulterated innocence in María La Virgen's deep blue irises was apparent the moment her eyes peeked open. Her long black hair splashed across her pillowcase, the shimmering waves recently settled from the throes of a sleepless night, her active mind having thrashed helplessly in the darkness until dawn calmed the tide.

Not by chance, the rooster across the street had just signaled the start of the day with an overenthusiastic cock-a-doodle-doo. On a normal day, María would've waited until the third or fourth crow to rise out of bed, but the cock overslept that morning, leaving her slightly behind schedule. In hindsight, it made sense to invest in a battery-powered alarm clock if she truly cared about punctuality.[1]

María glanced across the bed to find an empty space where her boyfriend, José, would typically be lying. On this morning, however, José had yet to return home from a late night's work. Not that his absence raised any alarms. A carpenter by trade, he often found himself working irregular hours. For that sole reason, according to him, he'd warned María not to worry on any given evening if he failed to sleep at the colorful, two-story adobe home she'd inherited, also known by the address of 11 Calle Principal.

José's absence didn't mean María slept alone. Her young Chihuahua, Perrita, scrambled into the bedroom and leapt onto the bed, furiously licking her face in the most genuine show of affection the puppy could muster.

"Good morning, Perrita." María gently stroked the puppy's neck. "I guess José worked late last night."

"Bark," said Perrita, also without knowledge of José's whereabouts.

As much as María wished to linger in bed, she had no time to waste. The tired young woman had a full day ahead, highlighted by her first day on a new job. Since her full day required her full attention, she swallowed an energy pill from a bottle sitting on her nightstand. Suddenly, she didn't feel so tired anymore, just underslept.

With a newfound liveliness, María attacked the day. Breakfast offered the first challenge. She had no idea when José would return, but she knew he'd be hungry when he did. Plus, her energy pill caused mild discomfort when taken on an empty stomach.

"Bark," said Perrita, also hungry.

Perrita wasn't a picky eater, easily satisfied by dry kibbles from a tin can. José, on the other hand, preferred fried bacon and scrambled eggs to start his day. Too bad those ingredients were absent from the house; and even if present, she had neither a fire to fry the meal, nor a clean pan for doing so: the local gas and water companies deserved at least part of the blame.

José promised to pay the gas and water bills in the coming days. Until then, María made do with what she had. That meant breakfast would include a few overripe mangoes from the tree standing tall in the middle of their backyard.

As María picked her mangoes, her next-door neighbor, Vecína, slid open her window and leaned on the sill. Still dressed in her nightgown from the previous evening, the elderly woman looked the same as always, the smile on her face barely contained by her withered cheeks.

"Buenos días, María," Vecína greeted, and asked if María needed any help.

María appreciated the thought, but picking a few mangoes from a tree proved to be far from an exhausting endeavor. As much as she loved to chat, she had to prepare for her first day on a new job. She suggested they share a cup of tea and catch up once her work schedule calmed down.

Vecína agreed, and smiled, and wished María a pleasant day.

With breakfast on the table, María turned to the laundry. José would need a fresh pair of knickers when he returned. Had she not been so forward-thinking the night before, placing a large bucket outside to collect rainwater for the laundry, she would've been in a bind. But since she was a resourceful woman, José's clothes hung from a clothesline before his mangoes began to spoil. She even found time to change the bedsheets so he could comfortably nap after breakfast.

With José and Perrita taken care of, María focused her remaining energy on herself. Not that José drifted far from her thoughts as she readied for work. What a wonderful boyfriend, she believed, who worked so hard through the night and into the morning earning money to put toward their overdue bills. She wished she could afford to pay all of their bills, but she already spent every peso she earned to support the pair, so she was unsure what more she could do.

Determined not to be late for her new job, María had no time to wait for José to return home before heading for the bus station. But the phone rang as she opened the door to leave, and she knew before answering that it was her boyfriend calling to express his love.

"I'll be home soon," José said with a tired voice. "I've been working all night."

"Breakfast is on the table," María replied, "and your underpants are hanging outside on the clothesline. I'll see you after work!"

◊ ◊ ◊

"Work?" José whispered as he hung up the phone. He failed to recall María mentioning any work. Then again, he hardly remembered anything his girlfriend ever mentioned, so the absence of this particular information drew no concern. Rather than put any more thought into the matter, he rolled over and placed his arm around an unclothed woman lying next to him. He failed to recall the unclothed woman's name, but like with María's plans, he found the lack of information unconcerning.

◊ ◊ ◊

María was no stranger to first days on new jobs. She began a new job almost every day. A woman of many skills, she remained consistently employed by Temporary Staffing Agency (or "TSA"), which told her where she needed to be, in return for a portion of a fee collected on her behalf. But since the details of her jobs changed as often as the locations, almost every day seemed like a first day on a new job in some sense.

On this particular afternoon, TSA summoned María to the best hotel in Los Aburridos. It was also the worst hotel in Los Aburridos, since it was the only hotel in Los Aburridos, but resourceful women like María tend not to complain about such minor details. Apparently, the hotel's janitorial staff had just begun to strike. As luck would have it, TSA offered lower rates than the janitorial staff's wages, so the hotel manager felt no urge to rush the striking employees back to work. All the hotel needed was a hardworking young woman, paid at an unbelievably low hourly rate, to do the jobs of a half-dozen protesters.

As punctual as she was resourceful, María arrived on time for her shift—a detail appreciated by the hotel manager, who handed her a mop as soon as they met. Before introducing himself, the manager sent María to scrub the floor of the hotel's bar, which had been dirtied at least a decade earlier, and not properly mopped since. The men's room would be next. After that, she'd attend to the ladies' room, which the manager expected to require the least soap of the three.

At the best hotel in Los Aburridos, tourism accounted for many of the daily patrons, so the television hanging above the bar played a foreign news channel as María worked her mop over the hardwood. The broadcast focused on the United States election, fully underway, with millions of votes being cast every hour. Two news anchors—a smooth-talking man and an equally smooth-looking woman, both with heads as full as their hair—sat behind a long desk as they discussed the issues awaiting the next President. The national narcotics policy would surely be affected by the election, the anchorwoman explained, since the candidates disagreed about how to tackle the drug epidemic sweeping the country. Of course, the unrelated topic of the federal deficit needed to be addressed, as well as unemployment numbers surging out of control.

"And don't forget about immigration!" the anchorman said. (The anchorwoman hadn't.)

The anchorwoman thanked the anchorman for his insight and opined on the importance of the election. The United States found itself caught in a spiral, with only one candidate capable of correcting the downward trajectory. For the sake of transparency, the anchorman noted their status as unbiased reporters; they simply presented the facts, so be it if the facts lined up neatly with the values shared by the likely winner of the election (if the American public voted properly!).

María tended to ignore foreign politics, so she knew little about either candidate. With respect to the United States, she cared about only one issue: immigration. It had long been her goal to move to the U.S., where she hoped to raise a family—an American dream she'd been sleeping on, so to speak. If only she received the chance—even the smallest opportunity—she'd do anything to convert her dream to reality.

"Almost anything," she clarified.

Anyway, María had no time to daydream. With the floor around the bar now sparkling, her attention turned to the men's room—an odious task, assuming the hotel's male guests treated the space similar to her boyfriend, José.

◊ ◊ ◊

José Carpentero revealed his dark brown eyes for the second time that morning, just as he heard a rooster letting out an unimpressive cock-a-doo (and forgetting to doodle). The rooster wasn't his regular neighborhood cock, since he wasn't waking up in his regular neighborhood, but all crows serve the same effect to a certain extent. Like José, the rooster stayed up late the previous evening, so the noise failed to coincide with the sunrise.

Although long overdue to return to the home he shared with his girlfriend, José felt no rush to get back. Across the bed lay another woman whose company he also enjoyed. He could never remember the other woman's name, though that resulted more from intentional amnesia than earnest absentmindedness: he could find out her name if he tried, but he preferred not to know, lest it accidentally escape his lips within earshot of his girlfriend.

Nursing the aches and pains of a late night, José felt in no shape to stand from his comfortable mattress. Nor did he rush to stand, with plenty of time to return home. Earlier in the morning, he learned that María would be working a new job that afternoon. She neglected to mention what the new job involved, or how long it would take, not that either of those details would've plagued his mind one way or another.

The woman across the bed woke from her slumber shortly after José. She felt the same pain as him, which made sense: they spent the same late night together, with the same brand of tequila cascading down the same pipes, leading to the same messy hair covering the same morning headaches.

According to José, they had two options: (1) to linger in bed a short while, doing the same activity they always did in bed; or (2) to get dressed and move to another more upright location, sharing another round of tequila, just as they always did when lounging vertically. Or, José suggested, a third option allowed them to do both, in either order, as he found each activity equally enjoyable.

The problem, noted the woman whose name was only known to herself, involved the only tequila bottle in her apartment sitting empty in the trash can, thanks to the previous evening's party-for-two.

"Then let's do the first thing," José said. "After that, we can get dressed and go to a bar for the second thing."

"Shouldn't you get home to your girlfriend?"

"She's working a new job today," José replied. "Besides, she doesn't do the first thing or the second thing. The first thing she won't do until we're married; the second thing, I'm not sure even then, because she seems disgusted by the taste of tequila."

"Sounds like a bore," the woman opined with a yawn. "Where should we go for the tequila?"

"To the bar at the best hotel in town," José said, as if the answer was obvious.

"That's the worst hotel in town," the woman replied.

José didn't care if the hotel was the best or the worst, as long as it had a bar with a bottle of tequila—preferably two bottles, if the unnamed woman wanted some too.

◊ ◊ ◊

Mopping the men's room at the best and worst hotel in town took a generous dose of elbow grease, despite the lack of visitors that day.[2] But María still finished the task in a fraction of the time it took the regular janitors. Understandably, she worked up a thirst with the effort.

With a few minutes to spare, María stopped back at the hotel bar for a glass of water to wash down another energy pill intended to get her through the rest of the day. And it was lucky she returned, because while she mopped the men's room, someone vomited on the hardwood around the bar. As a resourceful woman with a newfound surge of energy, she returned the floor around the bar to its previous glory—the glory, that is, from earlier in the day, not earlier in the decade.

Thanks in no small part to the extra surge of energy from her trusty pill, María also felt comfortable striking up conversation with hotel patrons. Too bad the bar had only one patron, who failed to share her energized tone, instead preferring to sit silently, stroking his powdery white beard while focusing his sparkling golden eyes on the news broadcasting over the bartender's shoulder. Not that he meant to ignore María; he found her beauty quite striking minus the grimy mop in her hand and the hair net covering her shimmering black tresses. He just had more important things on his mind, so the only words he bothered to muster as an introduction were:

"Hi, I'm Guy."

"Just Guy?" María wrinkled her eyebrows in puzzlement.

That's it: just Guy. One word held enough weight for a man of his importance. Plus, a three-letter word seemed easy to remember, he reasoned, and catchy too.

María introduced herself as well, before moving on to every other topic entering her mind, with her lips being the only impediment slowing the pace of the conversation. Her name was María. She worked for TSA. She liked his white beard, not to mention his golden eyes. The news was interesting, wasn't it? It had always been her dream to move to the United States and raise a family. She wondered whether he'd ever visited the country; and if so, whether he favored a specific candidate in the ongoing election.

As it turned out, Guy cared less about the candidates, and more about the results of a lesser-publicized proposition on the ballot in the U.S. state of California. As a businessman, his business interests took precedent over his personal feelings. The California proposition would have a direct effect on a new business opportunity: if it passed, there'd be no time to lose setting his business plan in motion, because change would be swift across the other 49 states. But rather than explain all of that to María, he asked:

"Can I order a sandwich?"

Regrettably, María didn't serve sandwiches. She mopped floors, and needed to get back to work. Although the hardwood around the bar now sparkled, and the tiles in the men's room looked closer to their original color than earlier that day, the ladies' room still demanded her attention. So she wished well to her new acquaintance, and added that he was a lucky Guy, because he happened to be staying at the best hotel in town; although some people also considered it the worst hotel in town. She enjoyed speaking with him, even if not too many words came out of his mouth. Perhaps she'd see him again before the day's end.

Perhaps she would, the quiet Guy agreed with a nod of his head as the words stuck in his throat before reaching his lips.

◊ ◊ ◊

Guy ordered his sandwich, eventually, though service proved especially slow despite the lack of other customers. Not that his appetite demanded immediate attention. He found plenty to occupy his mind in the meantime.

Step One (1. Buy an Island) of his plan was now complete, and Mexico's newly retired Minister of Land Administration had boarded a flight to Fiji. If the upcoming U.S. election went as planned, and California passed its ballot measure to legalize cannabis for medical patients, then there'd be no time to lose moving on to Step Two.

Step Two (2. Perfect the Product) would require more creativity than Step One. He could make money off his island's natural supply of cannabis, surely, but the quality needed improvement if he wished to maximize his profits. Any competent businessman knows that profits aren't maximized by adding an average product to an overcrowded market, and the cannabis growing on his island seemed to be rather average indeed.

"It's not bad dope," he conceded, "but it's not great dope either."

He needed more than an average product. He needed a hot new product—hot enough to grab the attention of the next generation. From what he could tell, the next generation's attention span seemed rather limited, so a lukewarm product would be insufficient. The product needed to be hot.

On second thought, not just hot, but blazing!

With that in mind, Guy spent the afternoon educating himself about the state of the cannabis industry. He had no trouble finding reading materials on the subject: despite being illegal in the United States, cannabis was the focus of a surprising amount of research. In one article, doctors reported the results of an extensive study of cancer patients who felt immediate pain relief after use of the illegal narcotic; another study dealt with chronic discomfort; yet another addressed social anxiety and depression; still another even hypothesized that the use of cannabis could combat other addictions.

"This is all great," Guy said, "but it doesn't help with Step Two of my plan."

The businessman was right. It certainly helped his business that his product resulted in so many positive effects. But those effects appeared universal to all forms of cannabis; they failed to distinguish his dope from that of his competition. Once again, only a hot new product would grab the attention of the next generation.

And that's when suddenly, as if destiny played a part in the matter, his golden eyes glanced to the top of his stack of reading materials at an article titled *Designer Cannabis for the Next Generation*. According to the author of the article, the future of the cannabis industry relied on the concept of crossbreeding.

"Crossbreeding?"

Guy possessed no grasp of the term. He was a businessman, not a botanist. Fortunately, the article—written by an American botanist named Moses Staffman—provided a basic description of the crossbreeding process. By breeding different strains of cannabis together, the article suggested that the effects of each of the strains could be combined into a single, more potent strain. The author even postulated that designer cannabis could be programmed to provoke distinct personality traits in users, possibly by crossbreeding cannabis with other plant species entirely.

"Interesting," Guy said, stroking his thick white beard, deep into thought as he considered whether crossbreeding might be right for his hot new product. Sadly, brilliant ideas escaped his mind at the moment. No matter how intensely he thought, or how aggressively he stroked his beard, genius refused to strike the mass of neurons located directly behind his sparkling golden eyes.

"Eh," he said. His focus waned, with the leftover dope from his island at least partially to blame. "I'll figure that out later."

Besides, the bartender finally served his long-overdue sandwich, and he wished to devour his meal before it cooled. On his plate sat an Italian hoagie: crisp, soft-middled bread, lightly soaked with oil and vinegar; neatly layered with thinly sliced, dry-cured meats ordered from ham to capicola with soppressata, prosciutto and mortadella between; topped with not only provolone cheese, but sprinkled with chopped onions amidst toasted mozzarella. Of course, no hoagie would be complete, in his mind, without the spicy kick of a few hot peppers tucked in, tying the intense collection of flavors together.

Well it turned out that this sandwich included a local variety of particularly potent hot peppers. The spicy kick enflamed his taste buds more than usual, and the fire on his tongue brought tears to his eyes. The feeling proved more than he could take, quite frankly.

"Yowzah!" he said. "That's hot!"

Unfortunately for him, specifically his tongue, his water glass sat empty on the bar. He possessed nothing to extinguish the firestorm on his taste buds. It was just him, his sandwich, and a stack of recently perused articles about the most controversial narcotic of the California election cycle.

And that's when genius struck him right upside the noggin. Or rather, nothing physically struck him, but his golden eyes locked on the article still sitting at the top of his stack—*Designer Cannabis for the Next Generation*.

"That's it!" He slammed his fist on the bar. "The hot product for the next generation!"

Vague as he was, his intentions became clear as soon as he waved at the bartender and shouted:

"I need more of these peppers!"

Too bad the bartender was busy with two new customers: a man named José, and a woman whose name he failed to catch in the midst of his excitement.

◊ ◊ ◊

José and his unidentified female acquaintance, both fully clothed, arrived at the best and/or worst hotel in Los Aburridos in plenty of time for the bar's happy hour. The floor around the bar sparkled brighter than José ever recalled. The men's room appeared almost spotless as well, though not cozy enough to keep him away from his companion, whose name he began to wonder if he should find out after all. To top it all off, the pair had almost the entire bar to themselves. The only other customer was a man with a white beard intensely studying a magazine across the room.

"Tequila," José said to the bartender, before realizing his error.

"A double, actually," he corrected, smiling at his companion.

"And one for her too," he corrected again.

While the bartender poured the drinks, José and his companion received a chance to catch up. For her this was a good thing, because she hoped to talk to José about their relationship. She tired of him spending one night with María and the next night with her. She wanted him all to herself.

"I don't want it to be José and María," she said. Apparently, she knew far more about her counterpart than he did of her. "I want it to be José and—"

"Here you go," interrupted the bartender with the first glass filled to the brim with José's favorite beverage.

"Why are you with her?" the still unnamed woman asked. "Especially when she doesn't—"

"And here's the other one," interrupted the bartender with the second glass, intended for the lady.

It was difficult to explain José's relationship with María, at least for him (though María could provide a description). The unnamed woman failed to understand that José's job as a carpenter was practically nonexistent (with the term "practically" being practically unnecessary). María's income from TSA kept them afloat from a financial perspective. He assumed that the woman across from him couldn't substitute the same value, since she spent most of her time drinking tequila with him when she could've been working instead.

"Can I ask you something?" wondered the woman.

José agreed, noting that in fact she'd be asking something *else* if she continued with another question.

"Do you love me?"

Rather than answer her question directly, José used a trick he'd learned for these types of occasions. After stroking the hair along her face, he placed his fingers on her chin and pulled her close, leaning in and planting a kiss on her lips in lieu of further conversation.

As it turned out, the woman at the bar wasn't the only person in the vicinity who knew the name of the man at the bar. The number of people in the bar increased by one when a mop-bearing TSA employee emerged from the ladies' room as José leaned in for his kiss.

"José!" María screamed, her face frozen as if a ghost appeared. "Who is she?"

José was unsure what to say, for more reasons than one. He tried to stop María as she sprinted out the door in tears, still with her mop in her hand. He would've run after her, but his tequila had just been served, and he felt uncomfortable leaving the bar before he emptied his glass.

◊ ◊ ◊

María didn't run far. She couldn't. The energy from her pill provided more of a short-term burst than a lasting source of endurance. Besides, she remained on the clock with the hotel, and she wished to be paid for the entire workday. The bar, the men's room, and the ladies' room—she'd completed each task. But she needed a moment to clear her eyes before she turned her mop in to the hotel manager, so she dashed around the corner of the hotel and into the alley to dry out the waterworks cascading down her cheeks.

María couldn't believe what she just witnessed. Or rather, she could believe it, because she saw it with her own eyes, but certain parts of what she witnessed made no sense. Her boyfriend at a bar ordering a glass of tequila—a double, actually—that was normal. But kissing a woman whose name she didn't know? That was abnormal, from what she did know.

María felt conflicted. Part of her wanted to march back into the hotel and face José, but the other part couldn't bear to look him in the eyes. That is to say, part of her didn't want to be alone, and part of her did.

Either way, María wasn't alone. Slowly and predictably emerging from the shadows of the alley came a guy from her recent past—more specifically, Guy, with a capital G—holding a lit cigarette with a stream of smoke wafting from the tip. Though sheepish when they first met at the bar, there appeared a noticeable change in his demeanor, not to mention an arrogant tone to every word he spoke.

"Hello again, beautiful," Guy greeted. Unfortunately, her name eluded him: the dope burning in his cigarette certainly wasn't doing his memory any favors.

María attempted her own greeting, but she failed to get the words out between alternating sobs.

"Try this," Guy said, and offered his cigarette. "It's called a doobie."

Apparently, Guy learned about more than just crossbreeding while sitting at the bar. His new company's budding industry offered a few fun terms: "doobie" was his recent favorite; "dope" remained close behind.

María had no interest in puffing the doobie. She didn't *do* drugs. She never had. Always a hard worker, she needed to retain her work ethic. From what she understood, cannabis tended to rob users of their motivation.

"I don't have time to be a lazy bum," she said, and waved off the offer.

"This isn't your typical dope." Guy squirted a drop of pepper juice on the tip of his doobie. "It'll be the hottest new dope on the market in no time at all."

María didn't care about the drug's temperature, or its age. Her mind remained stuck on her living situation after witnessing her boyfriend in an act of infidelity.

"I can't return home right now." María's tears showed no sign of letting up. "José might go there."

"I have a room here at the hotel." Guy winked.

María noticed the wink, and politely declined the invitation.

"Didn't you say that you've always dreamed of moving to the United States?" Guy must have remembered something about their earlier conversation. "Stay with me tonight, and in the morning, I'll take you with me to the United States."

Until then, María had only dreamed of traveling to the United States. Suddenly, her dream became a possibility, thanks to the strange Guy in the alley. All she needed to do was keep him happy until they left Mexico the following morning, which apparently began with puffing the doobie extending from his hand.

Always the resourceful woman, María made the only reasonable choice and took a few puffs of the doobie. Incredibly, her eyes cleared right up, even drying out to a certain extent. And the pain she felt from José's betrayal slowly melted away, albeit failed to exit her thoughts entirely. But that wasn't all. The cannabis had a strange kick to it, and caused her to feel something she'd never felt before.

Against her better judgment, María accepted the strange Guy's invitation. Given the circumstances, what other decision could a resourceful woman make? She'd always dreamed of moving to the United States; that much had been established. She didn't even care where in the United States they went.

"Where in the United States will we be going?" she asked anyway.

Guy held up his new favorite article—*Designer Cannabis for the Next Generation*, authored by Moses Staffman—and spoke as if the answer to María's question was obvious.

"We're going to California, of course, to meet Mr. Staffman."

THREE

California

The renowned botanist, Moses Staffman, couldn't believe his eyes as he opened his front door to a dizzying display of flames dancing across his doorstep. Nor did he recognize the pungent smell wafting from the fiery tango. Though ages had passed since his prime, his nasal acumen had at one time earned him a full scholarship to the prestigious University of Miasma, where he majored in liberal odors, and minored in molecular biology with a focus on genetic recombination.[3]

Darting to the kitchen in search of a fire extinguisher, Moses found a bucket beneath his sink. Unfortunately, on his way back to the front door, he tripped over a package which fell off his coffee table. The package had been delivered a day earlier, but he'd been too busy to open it. Had he opened it, he would've been in a better mood. It contained a copy of the movie *Happy Gilmore*, which he looked forward to watching, even though he'd seen it twice.[4] Unaware of the contents, he angrily picked himself off the floor and leapt to the front door, slamming his bucket over the flames.

"Damn vandals!"

Moses waved his fist in the general direction of the street, though nary a soul stood in sight. It was only 5:30 a.m., and most of the neighborhood still slept. The block would likely remain silent for another hour, until a forty-something named

Richard Dickens jogged northward, followed by a few chatty housewives. Around 7:00 a.m., a nimble Mexican-American seventh-grader named Manny Hernandez usually sprinted south toward the border, and then the paperboy cycled through to deliver the *Dullsville Times*. Moses knew the neighborhood routine all too well, having lived in the same whitewashed, two-story ranch at 11 Main Street for longer than he cared to remember.

Mentally, he formed a list of potential pyromaniacs and began crossing off names until only one remained.

"The Fernandez boy did this," he concluded. He lacked proof, but recognized the feeling of truth in his gastrointestinal tract.

Moses failed to spot Manny Hernandez in the vicinity, however, so all he could do at the moment was pat himself on the back for averting a crisis. Had he not acted so swiftly to extinguish the fire, his entire home-grown garden of *titan arums* could've gone up in flames. To non-botanists, that might not sound like much, but Moses' *titan arums* were far from the typical decorative flowers bedded around residential homes. Commonly referred to as the "corpse flower" due to an odor likened to a rotting carcass, most people consider the *titan arum* among the most nauseating plants on the planet. But Moses differed from most people, and appreciated that the pungent smell kept his neighbors at a distance. He was so fond of the natural repellent that he'd spread an imported, nutrient-rich soil around his house to promote the unique flowers' growth.

Moses was, after all, an expert botanist above all else.

The smell of the *titan arums* was only one of the benefits. With an inflorescence reaching ten feet in height, and a fragrant spadix wrapped by sheath stretching two feet in diameter, the *titan arums* looked more like trees than flowers. They grew side-by-side so densely across Moses' front yard, thanks to the imported, nutrient-rich soil covering their roots, that neighbors found it difficult to see his house through the flowers without looking carefully. And nobody looked carefully, since nobody dared approach the source of the neighborhood's most notorious stench.

Moses cocked his arm to shut his front door. But before he sealed his house shut, his next-door neighbor, Gabby Blabber, slid open her window and poked her head through the frame. To Moses, she looked the same as always, her worn-out expression unsuccessfully obscured by a coat of colorful makeup. She wore some type of silky orange nightgown, closely matching her makeup, but he only saw as far down as her shoulders. He considered himself lucky.

In an ear-piercing tone, Gabby asked Moses what happened. He'd startled her quite a bit, so much so that she spilled a drop of coffee on the carpet. She'd hustled to the window as quickly as she could, but her creaky knees only allowed her to move so fast.

"You scared me half to death," she said, and massaged her creaky knees.

Moses wished he'd scared Gabby the whole way. He'd never been a fan of his neighbor, not that he'd taken time to get to know her. Then again, perhaps she could be of assistance, he wondered, knowing that she spied on unsuspecting neighbors through her blinds.

"Did you see anyone outside my house this morning?" he asked.

A dangerous fire had threatened his porch. The precise smell of the fumes confused his famous fourth sense, but he likened the stench to rotten flesh (or a bad steak, to the layman's nose).

Unfortunately for Moses, Gabby had been sitting on her couch, watching television, minding her own business during the time in question. Yet she still offered her opinion on the matter.

"I bet Richard Dickens lit the fire," she supposed, brow raised.

Moses wondered whether Gabby saw Richard in the vicinity that morning.

"Well, no," she replied, brow lowered.

Moses rarely became confused, but it happened on occasion. To Moses, Richard seemed to be a pleasant man, always waving and smiling as he jogged by, sometimes saying hello, sometimes adding a well-intended joke. Moses knew little about Richard besides the colorful jogging outfits he chose and the cheery mood he presented at dawn, but Richard sure didn't seem like a pyromaniac. Besides, why would he target Moses' doorstep?

"The more likely suspect is that rascal Manny Menendez," Moses maintained, "or Rodriguez, or whatever his name."

Gabby dismissed the thought. Already having convinced herself of Richard's guilt, she sought the same conviction for her neighbor.

"I heard that Richard is a homosexual." Gabby lowered her voice and glanced over her shoulder toward nobody in particular. When Moses failed to infer the connection, she clarified in an even lower tone:

"He's a *gay*."

An experienced mystery solver, Gabby knew when to provide further explanation. She touched her index fingers together to begin counting on her hand, explaining that (index finger) the fire was dangerous according to Moses' account of the incident, and (middle finger) she read an article the other day, which said that homosexuals typically partake in risky behavior. Plus, (ring finger) on a *different* day, she read a *different* article, which explained what homosexuals do for fun; one of those things involved lighting themselves on fire, which (pinkie finger) explained the smell of rotten flesh.

"And Richard," she concluded with the nod of her head, "well, I heard he's a homosexual."

"You don't know what you're talking about," Moses grumbled. Already a long morning, he'd dealt with enough of Gabby's nonsense. If Richard *was* a homosexual, he'd certainly know. But Richard never demonstrated any attraction to him, so Gabby's hypothesis contained at least one flaw, possibly more.

"He's in his forties," Gabby rambled, "he's always well-dressed; he's in great shape; I've never seen him jogging with a woman—"

Moses slammed his front door. He didn't give a damn how Richard dressed, or what he did with his time, or who he spent it with. Besides, he'd never judge a man by such details. Maybe a woman, but not a man; that much remained certain.

Moses plodded to his bathroom in search of cleaning supplies. He glanced down at his shirt; it appeared clean, but he knew it smelled worse than a *titan arum* (yikes!). Good thing he owned a closet full of shirts, each one nearly identical to the others.

Moses splashed a handful of water on his face and stared at his reflection in the bathroom mirror. Simply put, he looked old: his swollen eyelids evidencing years of missing the minimum amount of nightly shut-eye recommended by the NSA;[5] his sagging nose the victim of an unholy union between heredity and gravity; what still lingered of his once dark brown hair having been choked of its hue over the years; his sun-damaged skin reminiscent of wreckage from a tropical cyclone. He'd certainly seen better days from a physical standpoint, though his mind remained sharp as a knife.[6]

Why would someone torture an old man with this nonsense? Moses wondered, but failed to come up with an answer. He'd now been confused twice in one day—an even rarer occurrence than a single instance. He badly needed a drink, preferably of the alcoholic variety. But it was still early, and he tried not to imbibe before work—only afterwards, or on off-days, or special occasions, or under special circumstances.

Well, a fire on his doorstep probably qualified as a special circumstance, he reasoned. Plus, he was about to find out who won the previous evening's presidential election, so it was a special occasion indeed.

◊ ◊ ◊

Fortunately for Moses, the morning's hullabaloo failed to disrupt his schedule by more than a few minutes. He still found plenty of time to prepare the day's most important meal ahead of his favorite morning news show. Per his usual routine, he dropped two slices of white bread into the toaster and poured himself a glass of orange juice. After slathering butter on the newly heated bread, and adding whiskey to the previously concentrated orange juice, he felt ready to hear what other people had to say about the day ahead.

Moses sank into his recliner and flipped his television to Channel 1, just as his favorite news anchors greeted the country. As they sat behind a futuristic table adorned with mugs presumably filled with coffee, the anchors wasted no time addressing the previous evening's election results. Despite the vote Moses placed on his way home from work, his preferred candidate still fell short by about 8,000,000 more.

"Every vote matters," Moses mumbled, "what a load of crap."

The anchors seemed just as disappointed with the election results, and jumped straight into their confusion and regret.

"I can't believe it," the anchorwoman lamented.

"Why didn't the American public vote properly?" was the anchorman's question for the country.

Rather than dwell on the presidential portion of the ballot, the anchors abruptly shifted their focus to another newsworthy development: the state of California's passage of Proposition 215 with a 55% majority. Otherwise known as the Compassionate Use Act, Proposition 215 exempted certain medical patients from criminal laws for possessing or cultivating cannabis—the first such measure to pass in an individual state. Opposers denounced Proposition 215 as a setback in the country's war on drugs, while supporters celebrated a victory in the country's war on behalf of drugs. Pundits on both sides of the issue forecast a cascade of similar initiatives all over the country.

In case of any confusion, the anchors left no doubt where they stood on the issue.

"What is this country coming to?" the anchorwoman asked.

"This is a dark day for our nation," the anchorman agreed.

Moses rarely disagreed with the anchors, but in this case, his feelings were mixed. On one hand, he despised the use of drugs: a collegiate miscue with an illegal narcotic cost him a promising future, and he swore after that incident to never use drugs again. On the other hand, his employer, Plant Incorporated (or "Plant Inc"), stood at the forefront of the cannabis industry thanks to a friendly government grant, positioning the company to take the emerging cannabis market by storm as the nation's lawmakers eased restrictions. According to the rumors running rampant through Plant Inc's corridors, the passage of Proposition 215 would be accompanied by sky-high bonuses for the company's most integral employees: namely, him.

Regardless, Moses had no time to revel in the thought of impending riches, because he needed to get to work if he wanted his money. To celebrate his inevitable financial windfall, he poured another shot of whiskey into his juice. His first few sips of the orange stuff barely gave him a buzz.

◊ ◊ ◊

To anyone who knew Moses, his fame in the plant industry came as no surprise. His vegetation infatuation became apparent the first time he uttered the word "photosynthesis," which much to his parents' dismay, came before "Mama" and "Dada." Though disappointed, they embraced his passion, gifting him his first greenery: a pair of chias, which he named Bush Reynolds and Loni Planterson. From there, his love affair spread like a controlled burn. Like most plant-loving adolescents, he went through a short-lived xerophytes stage before experimenting with different types of moss, then moving on to creepers and climbers. He even had a serious bond with a fern for a while, followed by a fling with a conifer (the fern's own cousin!). After that, he avoided limiting himself to one species at a time.

In other words: Moses liked plants, a lot.

Despite his overwhelming interest, a teenaged Moses dismissed any thought of a career in botany. There existed plenty of plant lovers in the world, he recognized, and only so many jobs to go around. Besides, his true gift resulted from a condition called hyperosmia, which bestowed him with a heightened sense of smell, placing his nose's sensitivity among the top 1% in the world.[7] For precisely that reason, as a teenager, Moses left his heart in the grass and followed his nose to the University of Miasma on a nasal scholarship.

At the top of his class initially, Moses positioned himself for a high-paying job at one of the smelliest firms in the country upon graduation. Then he suffered a debilitating nasopharynx injury during an ill-advised inhalation of white powder at a late-night celebration. His naturally endowed fourth sense never fully recovered. Before his scholarship voided, he obtained an academic minor in molecular biology, with a focus on genetic recombination, placing him right back in the situation he would've been in to begin with if he followed his heart instead of his nose.

After graduation, Moses found employment peddling gardening supplies to the elderly. Though far from the job he hoped for out of college, he needed experience in the sector. He put his (damaged) nose to the grindstone and proved himself a capable salesman, in his free time experimenting with plant breeding, while also monitoring the *Dullsville Times* for exciting vegetation opportunities with fair salaries.

Eventually, a botany position opened up at Plant Inc, whose company motto—"*Take your hands out of your pants and plant some plants!*"—was as well-known across the country as the greenery they sold. Three applicants applied for the job, with the other two instantly disqualified due to hiring technicalities which severely limited the employment prospects of ex-felons. With a passion for growing all things green, Moses rose through the ranks at Plant Inc faster than any other botanist in the company's history, most notably for his award-winning crossbreeds.

Alas, even the most heartwarming stories include negative footnotes.[8] Moses loathed the politics involved with serving an agricultural behemoth like Plant Inc. Worse, he strongly disagreed with the company directors regarding the monetary value of his labor. But at least that second part was about to change. Thanks to the passage of Proposition 215, his specific expertise had suddenly risen in value.

◊ ◊ ◊

It was business as usual as Moses punched his time card to clock into work. He had plenty to do, from what he told himself, so he wasted little time stopping in his office to drop off his briefcase —his custom-made, gold-monogrammed, patent leather briefcase—before heading straight for the greenhouse. The slight detour to stow his fancy carryall lasted so briefly that he overlooked the freshly printed memorandum sitting on his desk.

Plant Inc's greenhouse spanned several acres of land, all littered with the early development of every plant species pegged for distribution within the next few years. The greenhouse was divided by function: The north end, *Nutritional*, showcased fruits and vegetables ripening to perfection before wetting the tongues of the country's most health-conscious consumers. The east end, *Aesthetical*, fine-tuned nature's most beautiful creations for placement as high-end decorations. The west end, *Functional*, contained timber perfect for building walls and grasses to form the finest natural crafts that money could buy. And the south end, *Illegal*, was in some sense improperly titled, with the products therein being legally developed with the government's permission.

Moses sought out the *Illegal* section, then found the cannabis subsection amongst the various rows of tall stalks and plump flowers and mangled mushrooms and inconspicuous bushes. As one of Plant Inc's top botanists for over a decade, he'd earned the honor of directing the company's Cannabis Development Team. Based on his personal feelings, one might think Moses to be an unlikely choice for the lead role. But his opposition to drug use made him perfect for the job. He was the only botanist certain not to steal the product for personal use, or as some on the Cannabis Development Team might say: "get high on his own supply."

Under Moses' watch, the Cannabis Development Team stood out as a bright spot for Plant Inc, and the future glowed even brighter thanks to the passage of Proposition 215. At his direction, his team discovered that, by crossbreeding cannabis in unorthodox combinations, the plant could be programmed to evoke specific emotions in consumers.

In layman's terms, Moses' team stood at the forefront of the development of designer brands of cannabis.

Of course, Moses' success relied on far more than the simple concept of crossbreeding. Crossbreeding remained well-known across the world, and no self-respecting botanist would claim to have invented the procedure. Moses' notoriety stemmed from a specific strain of cannabis, which he personally bioengineered for the crossbreeding process by neutralizing all but the basic effects felt by a consumer. Internally referred to as *Zerojuana* by Moses' team, this bioengineered strain bore flowers of the purest form from an emotion-evoking standpoint—neutral in this effect: not a depressant, not a stimulant, not a hallucinogen of any kind. As understood by any decent botanist, something so pure could be crossbred with limitless potential, without the risk of substantial, unintended side effects.

"It's the diet cola of cannabis" was how those on the Cannabis Development Team would often explain the bioengineered strain to the layperson. The only side effect of puffing *Zerojuana* directly, from what anyone on the team observed, proved to be a bit of self-reflection and an occasional smile.

Once Moses perfected the *Zerojuana* plant, the rest of the crossbreeding process was fairly straightforward. With surgical precision, he transplanted *Zerojuana* cuttings onto mother plants of other varieties, creating a hybrid of the two. As the hybrids grew, the mothers' nutrients seeped into the *Zerojuana* flowers, programming the flowers with the specific effect intended by the design.

To Moses' knowledge, no competing horticultural company was as far along in the development of designer cannabis. He even published an article on the subject: *Designer Cannabis for the Next Generation*. In unreproducible details, the article described how cannabis could be programmed to evoke specific effects by crossing a neutral strain with another plant species. The article neglected to mention *Zerojuana* by name, obviously, because Plant Inc kept that little detail as a proprietary secret.

Only the time constraints involved with crossbreeding held Moses' team back from a greater level of success. There existed a lot of plants in the world, after all, which Moses understood just as well as the next botanist.[9] It took time to figure out which crossbreeds thrived and which caused negative side effects in consumers. Fortunately for the hourly worker, time in this sense directly correlated with money, irrespective of whether the total amount fell far short of what he felt he deserved.

According to company policy, Moses' time needed to be accounted for, his samples inventoried, and his paperwork written up—at least if he enjoyed his biweekly paychecks. So with a trowel in one hand and a deft touch from the other, he spent the morning digging *Zerojuana* seedlings and harvesting every seed he found. Oh, and he labeled everything, lest he be chastised by Plant Inc's inventory manager, a man by the name of Thutmond Mose III.

◊ ◊ ◊

Thutmond Mose III was a Company Man. Although every male employee could in some sense be considered a company man, Thutmond exemplified what the title meant with the first letters capitalized. Though not the sharpest employee, he stood out as the most loyal: the type who treated coworkers as family, for good or bad; who saw crime against the company as crime against every employee; who risked everything to keep his employer afloat; and who obeyed company policy in every situation, most importantly. Undoubtedly, Plant Inc was fortunate to have Thutmond aboard, running the repository for as long as anyone cared to remember.

The repository stood as Thutmond's kingdom: the heartbeat of the company, in his opinion. Seeds, tools, soil—behind the repository door he kept everything a botanist could ask for. And if a botanist asked for something else, then he denied the request, because he couldn't give what he didn't have in storage to begin with.

Thutmond felt fantastic that afternoon, though his mood arose independently of the results of the election. He'd just taken inventory of the repository, and not a single item was out of place. Every trowel, every rake, every hoe was accounted for; every documented sprout sprung; every registered seed sacked. The seeds took longest to count, so seeing the numbers match with what he expected felt particularly gratifying.

Thutmond sat behind his desk, reviewing the markings on his forms with an eye for accuracy, when his least-favorite botanist, Moses Staffman, strolled into his office. The inventory manager had a reason for disliking the botanist: (he refrained from discussing his reason at the office, in accordance with company policy).

"What do you want?" Thutmond greeted.

Moses pointed toward the repository door, indicating his desire to deposit his *Zerojuana* seeds into Plant Inc's expensive cryochamber.[10] He never needed anything besides access to the repository, so Thutmond understood the nonverbal cue and handed him the necessary paperwork.

"I double check everything," Thutmond said, "so make sure the forms are filled out correctly."

Moses briefly questioned the necessity of the paperwork, but Thutmond refused to change his mind. The inventory manager bent the rules in certain cases, for certain individuals. This wasn't one of those cases, however, and Moses certainly wasn't one of those individuals.

"Also, make sure you label everything." Thutmond lacked any other way of identifying his goods. He was an inventory manager, not a botanist. If improperly labeled, he could mistake a tomato for a cherry, for example, with potentially disastrous consequences if the juicy red berry ended up in a homemade pie.

The paperwork took Moses an extra fifteen minutes, but that meant nothing to Thutmond, who rather enjoyed his coworker's inconvenience and took pleasure each time the botanist groaned at the flip of a page.

"Won't you be late for the announcement?" Thutmond asked when Moses finally handed over the signed forms.

"What announcement?"

"Didn't you see *the memo* this morning?" Thutmond assumed everyone to be as diligent with paperwork as him.

Unfortunately, *the memo* still sat on Moses' desk, next to the fancy briefcase he dropped off earlier in the morning.

"I assumed that you of all people would've seen *the memo*."

Thutmond delighted in Moses' lack of knowledge as he handed over his own freshly printed copy. In crisp black ink, *the memo* announced a meeting in the auditorium at precisely 12:00 p.m., and recommended that all members of the Cannabis Development Team attend, because the CEO would be discussing Plant Inc's plans in the wake of California's passage of Proposition 215.

Moses looked at his watch. It was 12:10 p.m.

"You forgot to label your seeds!" Thutmond shouted as the botanist dashed out the door.

◊ ◊ ◊

Moses' mind raced almost as quickly as his feet as he weaved through the corridors to the auditorium for the CEO's announcement. He could barely contain his excitement, even high-fiving a few unnamed coworkers as he passed them in the hallway. His only question involved how much his salary would increase.

"I should get a bigger bonus than everyone else on the team," he reasoned of his value.

Indeed, in the botanist's mind, no member of the Cannabis Development Team outweighed his importance. He was the father of the *Zerojuana* plant, the architect of Plant Inc's designer cannabis program, and the most instrumental effort in the program's implementation. (Of course, with the development process now underway, the company could simply hire someone of similar capability to continue the project.)

Moses made it to the auditorium just as the CEO finished his introduction and began to discuss the significance of Proposition 215. According to the CEO:

> "The Passage of Proposition 215 is only the beginning. We expect a flurry of legalization measures across the country. It won't be long until cannabis is legal on a national level, and Plant Inc is well-positioned for that day, thanks to your hard work."

The CEO still had plenty more to say, and continued to praise the team:

> "Congratulations, from all of us at Plant Inc, on a job well done on the Cannabis Development Team. I trust that the satisfaction you feel for your job well done is all the bonus you need. If you need more bonus than that, then you're out of luck, because Plant Inc won't be handing out additional monetary compensation for simply doing your contractually obligated job in the first place."

Moses couldn't believe that last part. Or rather, he could believe it if he tried, but he chose not to do so. He badly needed a drink, preferably of the alcoholic variety. But he still had half a day's work to accomplish, and he tried not to imbibe on the job.

"I'm going home." Moses decided to eliminate both obstacles to a glass of whiskey.

◊ ◊ ◊

Main Street was quiet as Moses pulled his Chevy up the street and pulled into the driveway of the whitewashed, two-story ranch marked as #11. Not that he expected Main Street to be noisy. His neighbor to the left, Gabby Blabber at #13, was certainly chatty, annoying in even her best moments, and a threat to his sanity perhaps, but she rarely left the confines of her home. On the other side, Richard Dickens at #9 was pleasant enough, full of friendly hand waves and light banter, but he knew when to keep to himself. And then there was that rascal Manny Hernandez across the street at #12, the most untrustworthy seventh-grader on the block, and the only resident worth watching (for the safety of the neighborhood). That pretty much summed up everything Moses knew about his neighbors, thanks to his motto:

"Mind your own damn business."

Moses sure minded his own damn business. That's why never so much as a controversy arose outside his front door. There had been plenty of controversies inside his house, all the fault of his ex-wife, Cleopatra. But outside his front door, well, folks tended not to loiter in that location, with the *titan arums* just as responsible as his attitude.

So everything appeared normal, at first, as Moses shut off his car and stepped up his walkway. The sun was out, the neighbors were absent, and the rancid odor of the *titan arums* pierced the air. Everything appeared normal, except:

"What the heck?"

Something felt off. Worse than that, something stunk! And for once, his *titan arums* deserved no blame: culpability went to a man with sparkling golden eyes and a powdery white beard, sitting on Moses' porch swing, hand-rolling a cigarette.

"Moses!" the man greeted. "I didn't expect you back so soon."

"Who are you?" Moses wanted to know.

"I'm Guy," the man said, and smiled as he held out his hand.

Moses declined the greeting as rudely as he could, stepping past his visitor and unlocking his front door without saying another word.

"Don't you want to know why I'm here?"

Moses was in no mood for visitors, so he stepped through his doorway and cocked his arm to slam the front door. If Guy insisted on sticking around, he'd fetch his favorite pistol—a Colt single-action revolver—for a true introduction.

"But I can offer you a lot of money," Guy insisted. "A *lot* of money."

Well that last emphasis on "lot" sure caught Moses' attention, and his mood shifted as abruptly as his interest in the conversation. Suddenly, he welcomed his guest inside. Since he'd finished working for the day, he poured a glass of whiskey to sip while they spoke. He offered to pour a glass for Guy, but apparently not everyone enjoys a cocktail in the middle of the afternoon.

"So, what do you want?" Moses asked with his first sip of whiskey.

Guy wasted no time. He needed to hire a botanist, and Moses fit the role perfectly. His new company offered a significant salary, with the potential for a bonus if everything went well. Plus, the position included an excellent medical package, with unlimited access to the company's products. On top of all that, Moses would be exempt from paying taxes on his salary due to a loophole which allowed United States citizens to avoid filing a wage statement.

That sure sounded like a good deal to Moses. Almost too good to be true. But what was the tax loophole?

"The loophole," Guy clarified, "is that the U.S. government can't collect taxes on wages they don't know about."

"How would the government not know about my wages?" Moses scratched his head.

"I have an island." Guy placed his hand-rolled cigarette on the table. "Where you'll be growing this."

Moses knew what hid in the cigarette without being told, because his famous nose immediately picked up the herbal scent.

"Cannabis!" he said. "I knew it!"

"Duh," Guy said. "But we're calling it dope, and the cigarette is a doobie."

He asked Moses to commit to the terms for consistency. Also, this wasn't just any dope. This was a new version, laced with a hot spice, sure to be the hottest new dope on the market in no time at all.

"Try it," Guy insisted, and offered a lighter.

Moses didn't *do* drugs. Not since college, when they cost him his scholarship and derailed his career prospects. Guy obviously knew nothing of that: how would he know Moses' backstory? But Moses swore off drugs after college. Growing them was one thing, but *doing* them?

"Yes, I understand that you're a man of high morals," Guy said. "But you can't just lump different drugs together."

Moses could indeed, and he just did.

"But you drink?" Guy pointed to Moses' mid-afternoon glass of whiskey. "Fairly often, from what I can tell."

That was different, Moses noted.

"Your loss." Guy shrugged as he lit the doobie for himself.

Though ages had passed since Moses' prime, his sensitive nostrils picked up a strange scent from the doobie's fumes: not the scent of any particular type of cannabis, but the distinct aroma of burning capsaicin.

"Did you dip your doobie in pepper juice?"

"Jalapeño juice," Guy replied, fully impressed by the botanist's famous nose. "I call the product, *Cannapeñis*. I crossbred the strain myself after reading your article, *Designer Cannabis for the Next Generation*."

There existed so many problems with Guy's hot new product that Moses hardly knew where to start.

First, Moses explained, the cannabis couldn't simply be dipped in jalapeño juice. No respectable botanist would call that crossbreeding. To properly crossbreed *Cannapeñis*, a jalapeño plant needed to be transplanted with a pure strain of cannabis such as Moses' creation, *Zerojuana*. (Mentioning *Zerojuana* was a mistake—he remained under strict orders not to discuss the details of Plant Inc's proprietary secrets—but his mouth tended to open too wide when a glass of whiskey balanced in his hand.)

Second, Moses began, again sniffing Guy's doobie with his naturally endowed schnoz. Well, on second thought, why reveal all his insights just then? He merely asked:

"How carefully did you examine these peppers?"

Regardless of the answer, Moses could easily perfect *Cannapeñis* with a few minor tweaks to the method of production. Until then, he warned of possible unintended side effects caused by puffing Guy's current version.

"What kind of side effects?" Guy asked.

"I suspect that puffing *Cannapeñis* may make you act like a dick," Moses said.

"And you can fix that?" was Guy's only reply.

Not so fast. Moses wasn't born yesterday, or even the day before that; quite some time passed since he emerged from the comfort of his mother's womb. He retrieved an atlas from a bookshelf in his den and rifled through the pages until he found a detailed map of North America. Now, where was this island?

Unfortunately, the atlas proved incomplete: less the fault of the publisher, and more because nobody knew of the island besides a former Mexican administrator turned Fijian immigrant. Nevertheless, Guy accepted the atlas and drew a bright yellow star in the middle of the Pacific Ocean, labeling the star as "TH Corp" to be clear.

"TH Corp?" Moses asked.

"Tropical Horticultural Corporation," Guy clarified, "unless you can think of a better name for my new business."

Moses cared more about the company's geography than its moniker. The island floated fairly close to the U.S. border—only a half-inch away according to the atlas—so how bad could it be?

Then again, the American felt no desire to leave the country of his birth. The election proved disappointing, sure, but there'd be another election in four years, and then again four years after that. He remained confident in the long-term prospects of the good ol' U.S. of A, and he wished to be around when the country got back on track.

"I'll pay you $1,000,000 when you get to the island," Guy promised, and welcomed Moses to return to the U.S. once he perfected *Cannapeñis* for sale by TH Corp. He also meant to offer a signing bonus of $1,000, if he could figure out what happened to his wallet; he found his pocket unexpectedly empty besides his passport.

With this additional information, the offer suddenly sounded much better than a few minutes prior; and with a few more sips of whiskey, the offer sounded even better than that—more money than Moses made at Plant Inc, medical benefits, and no taxes!

Except, of course, there existed one problem.

"My ex-wife!" Moses shook his fist in the air. "By the terms of my divorce agreement, I can't leave the country."

Whatever the legal issue, Guy felt certain his attorney could handle it. He wondered if Moses could find a way to pass the time until they sorted out his travel arrangements.

If all Moses needed to do was pass time, he supposed that another glass of whiskey would be a fine place to start.

FOUR

Mexico

The unfamiliar surroundings of the penthouse suite at the worst hotel in Los Aburridos explained only part of the reason María La Virgen felt out of sorts on the morning after her confrontation with José. Without a rooster crowing next door, nothing urged her awake until a beam of sunshine peeked through the curtains and crept across her eyes; and without an energy pill already in her body, her ambition lagged significantly behind where it otherwise would've been by that time of day.

María felt a mix of emotions as she lay in bed recalling her history with José—a mental exercise which took a while, considering she'd known him since adolescence. Until the previous evening, a life apart would've been unimaginable. Their relationship had never been easy, but life in general had never been easy for the young woman from Los Aburridos, so why would her romance be any different?

Only through María's persistent effort did her relationship with José survive for all those years. Though that was no revelation to anyone who knew her. Without hard work, she would've been another poor girl in Los Aburridos needing a lover's good favor to survive; but through her labors, María not only survived, but took care of her lover instead of the other way around.

As any determined woman like María understands, such a

sustained effort comes at a price, most notably in the calories burned on any given day. It took a significant exertion to work from morning until night. She needed to sleep at some point; as much as she would've preferred to forgo the energy-building exercise, her body wouldn't allow the omission. That's where her pills came in. Her natural liveliness fell short of what she needed, and the artificial oomph from her pills allowed her to survive the typical day.

María encouraged José to try the energy pills too, in an attempt to jolt him into a state of determination. But he felt content with her as the only over-energized partner in the relationship. Besides, the energy pills didn't mix so well with tequila, and he sure as heck refused to give that up.

Looking back, María questioned when her relationship with José went wrong. Her role as a giver, and his role as a taker, set them up for the ideal give-and-take relationship. Perhaps she went too far as a giver, driving her boyfriend away with her overzealous work ethic; or perhaps he went too far as a taker, exploiting her generosity.

Either way, there was no going back. She'd already found a new Guy, who was full of promises, beginning with a trip to the United States.

It was a new feeling for María: to rely on someone else, instead of shouldering every semblance of responsibility herself. If things went as planned, she could even give up her energy pills. Though on this morning, she still needed an energy pill: not because she required a push to start another day of work, but because her body relied on the early jolt to the point that she doubted she could function otherwise. So she rose out of bed and wandered around the room until she found her purse, and after swallowing her first pill of the day, found the rest of her clothes too.

With that, María had everything she needed except her promising new Guy. He was awake, most likely, since he no longer lay in bed. But he was nowhere to be seen. Though he must have been close, she thought, because his wallet sat on the nightstand. Perhaps he left to fetch breakfast, or to obtain their tickets for the trip north? She couldn't fathom what type of effort went into crossing the border into the United States, never having done so herself, though she imagined the journey as quite the exhausting endeavor.

On the television, María bypassed the local channels to learn more about the current state of affairs in the United States. Instead of finding an attractive couple of newspersons sitting behind a desk, she turned the channel to a live broadcast from the Old State Capitol in Little Rock, Arkansas, where the newly elected President prepared to deliver his victory speech.

The President looked handsome, his full hair overshadowing his tired eyes. Smiling with pride, he began by thanking his wife for her support. Apparently, his wife had been quite understanding of his absence at home while he campaigned for the highest office in the land.

María sure understood the First Lady's perspective, though their situations differed considerably. For one thing, the President seemed like such a decent man—nothing like her ex-boyfriend, José. Surely, the President's wife never found her husband passionately locking lips with another woman at a hotel bar. The President of the United States had no time for such shenanigans.

The President did more than just thank his wife, of course. He also thanked his daughter for her love, his associates for their work, his pastor for his prayers, and even the Lord Almighty for making him an American citizen in the first place. He thanked the American people for some 47,000,000 votes of confidence that he was leading the country in the right direction, and he guaranteed a bridge to the next century by the end of his term. America would continue to be a place where everyone could live free and equal, he promised, where anyone could succeed.

"Four more years!" the President shouted, his promises apparently only valid for a limited time.

María could barely contain her excitement as the President's words echoed off the walls of the penthouse suite. She certainly hoped for more than four years of sustained success, but she'd take what she could get. Four years of success was still four more years than she'd experienced up to then. Though if she'd be limited to four years, she might as well get moving.

"Where the heck is he?" she wondered of the missing Guy as

she surveyed the room for clues.

Although her precise question as to where the heck he *was* would go unanswered in the coming moments, she found an answer to where the heck Guy *wasn't* when she finally noticed a small note, written on the hotel's letterhead, sitting on the desk next to the television. The note read:

> *María,*
>
> *I'm sorry, but I won't be able to take you to the United States with me. I had a wonderful time last night though.*
>
> *Sincerely,*
> *Guy*

"What a dick," María said, noticeably displeased by the broken promise, particularly in view of what she gave in return.

The good news, if any existed: the wallet on the nightstand contained $1,000, not to mention an identification card for the promise-breaking Guy, along with a second note written on the hotel's letterhead. The second note read:

> *Tropical Horticultural Corporation's Secret Recipe:*
> *Cannabis + Jalapeño = Cannapeñis*

"At least something came of this disappointment," María supposed of the $1,000, which would immediately pay a few overdue bills.

◊ ◊ ◊

José Carpentero gained little sleep the night after unexpectedly encountering María at the best hotel in Los Aburridos. Not only did he feel restless from the guilt of upsetting his girlfriend, but the woman whose name he still didn't know had kept him up late into the evening to polish off another bottle of tequila. Understandably, dawn had long cracked by the time José finally opened his eyes the next morning.

The previous evening, José declined to chase after María as she sprinted away from the hotel in tears. He knew better than to approach her when she looked upset. He preferred to talk to María while she worked, when she could barely pay attention to his words. When she wept over something he did, on the other hand, that became a time for avoidance.

According to José, he knew María better than she knew herself. Evidently, that's what happens when two people spend most of their lives together. When they first met, she was a young girl caring for her ailing mother, and he was a foster child looking for a friend. But their relationship grew quicker than their heights, and before long they'd shared most of life's pleasures. (Though not *every* pleasure, to be clear.)

María introduced José to a new world. She became the first person to show him compassion, the first to care for his feelings, and the first to spend her hard-earned salary making sure he had everything he needed. Oh, and she was also the first to love him. Others said they loved him, sure, but nobody in his life took care of him quite like María. His foster parents did the best they could; his birth parents did a bit less than that; but only María made him a top priority.

Nevertheless, José supposed that the events of the previous evening happened for the best. Their relationship had been fun for a while, sure, but lately María kept wanting to have conversations: not the good conversations either, but the more serious type involving the direction of their lives. María sought a lifelong commitment from José, which seemed significantly longer than he wished to pursue.

The woman lying next to him avoided asking for the same level of commitment. She seemed content to let him sleep in her bed and eat the bacon in her fridge and drink the tequila in her cabinet. He failed to grasp how she paid for any of those items, not that it mattered: like with her name, the details held less importance than the outcome.

To his credit, José realized he should probably learn the name of the woman with whom he'd now be living. For one thing, he no longer risked having her name accidentally escape his lips in front of María. For another thing, it seemed like a good idea to know at least the first name of the person he lived with, if not the rest of her name as well. Unfortunately, the pair had now slept in the same bed for several months, which he deemed too long to ask for her name without seeming insensitive.

José quietly rose out of bed and found his new roommate's purse. Sifting through the contents—lipstick (a seductively deep red), earrings (sparkly but not too flashy), hair brush (filled with dead protein filaments), prophylactics (good to know!)—he failed to find anything with her name. Even her wallet contained nothing besides a few pesos, which he repossessed for safe keeping; she'd likely forget about the pesos to begin with, he presumed.

Creeping across the bedroom, José searched in vain for clues: old forms filled out or signed, mail addressed to her apartment, something monogrammed with initials at least. Nothing helped, as if destiny meant for his task to be difficult.

As José shuffled around the room, he made barely enough noise to awaken the woman still lying in bed. Once she opened her eyes, the naked man wandering around her bedroom had some explaining to do.

"What are you doing?" she asked upon seeing José slide open her dresser drawer.

"Looking for my wallet," José replied, instinctively.

She pointed to the bulging pocket of the tequila-stained trousers on the floor next to the bed. "Check your pants."

José thanked the woman and retrieved his wallet from his trousers, folding her pesos inside before removing his driver's license from one of the slots. After staring at his own picture for a moment, he handed the card to the woman in bed.

"Aren't ID cards interesting?" he asked. "Now that I've shown you mine, can I see yours too?"

His questions confused the woman. Why would he want to see her picture on a card? Her smiling face was directly in front of him.

Frustrated, but not defeated, José refused to give up. Too bad his next idea involved outsmarting his counterpart—not his finest skill.

"Do you remember what we talked about at the bar yesterday before María interrupted us?" he asked.

Of course the woman remembered. She started the conversation. It shocked her to hear José raise the subject, but perhaps the confrontation with María the previous evening had been for the best.

"You said you don't want it to be José and María." José pointed to himself, then to his bedmate. "You said you want it to be José and—"

"That's right," the woman agreed, and wondered why José stopped in the middle of his sentence, since she certainly hadn't interrupted. She could say their names together over and over, but their relationship would only flourish if he also committed to the idea. She wanted to hear him say their names in the same sentence.

"Well," José said, "I want that too."

If José wanted what he said he wanted, then she insisted he finish his sentence.

"I want it to be me and you," José said, and stepped to the side. By no means a wordsmith, the alleged carpenter still understood the importance of pronouns in circumstances like his own. "Just like you said yesterday."

The woman, elated to hear the confirmation, threw her arms around José and planted a kiss on his cheek.

José, frustrated by another failure, still had one idea: "How do you spell your name?"

"How do you think it's spelled?" she replied, and insisted that the spelling matched the way her name sounded out loud.

José didn't know where to begin. He didn't know where to end either, or where to go in the middle. But by this point she wanted an answer, so he guessed the first letter.

"B?"

The expression on her face quickly changed as she failed to recall the last time José spoke her name. Actually, she failed to recall any time he'd spoken her name.

"C?"

José guessed again, to which she responded that unless he said her name right then and there, he should put on his trousers and walk out the door.

"D?"

"Get out!"

Well this certainly wasn't the turn of events José hoped for—being banned from two homes in less than 24 hours.

◊ ◊ ◊

The janitorial strike at the worst hotel in Los Aburridos dragged on for the second consecutive day, leading the hotel manager to ask for María by name when he phoned TSA for assistance. Apparently, her efforts the previous afternoon left the hotel sparkling as brightly as he'd ever seen. Though to be fair, he'd only managed the hotel for a decade.

The elevator ride from the penthouse suite to the manager's office was the shortest commute of María's life. According to the manager, her spotless floors from the previous afternoon failed to make it through the night in the same condition. And he added both the lobby and the kitchen to her workload as he handed her a mop. Rather than complain, she got straight to work. She no longer had a boyfriend or a wealthy Guy in her life —but she had a job, and that was all she needed to take care of herself.

After another long day depleting the grease in her elbows, María felt anxious to return home. Yet she still found time to stop by the local marketplace—across from the only dock in Los Aburridos—where dozens of tables stood stacked to the sky with local meats and produce. With $1,000 in her pocket, she found every reason to splurge. She hadn't eaten all day. Plus, her favorite puppy would be hungry. She expected to find an open mouth waiting at the door of her colorful, two-story adobe home.

María's assumption about the mouth at her door proved accurate. Though the mouth belonged not to a Chihuahua, but to a lover from her past: not the promise-breaking Guy from the night before, but the promise-breaking boyfriend from the time before that.

"Hello, María," José greeted from the doorstep.

María felt no desire to speak with her ex-boyfriend. But that failed to deter José. According to him, the woman from the hotel bar was a potential carpentry client, and his apparent kiss with the woman was an attempt to save her from choking on a peanut.

"Have you seen the size of the nuts they serve at that bar?"

José would've explained all of this the night before, but María disappeared before he had the chance.

María remained unconvinced, and asked her ex-boyfriend to step out of the way of her door.

"I don't even know that woman's name," José said, honestly, and reminded María of their lengthy history. María always forgave him in the past, for almost every indiscretion imaginable. Presuming this time to be no different, he begged for forgiveness again, hoping to return to their previous arrangement.

María reached into her pocket and fingered the note from her formerly promising Guy. She fully understood that mistakes could be made—even by her, in theory. She refused to discuss any of her own mistakes, specifically on one ill-advised overnight stay at the best and/or worst hotel in Los Aburridos, but she understood nonetheless that mistakes happened. Even still, she felt no desire to return to their previous arrangement. If she forgave José, then their relationship would have to be better than that.

With all of his heart, José promised to be better. He'd never betray María again, he said. He'd chip in with the bills too. And he'd never miss a night away from home—not only because the woman whose name he didn't know forbade him from returning, but also because he wished to spend more time with the woman whose name he *did* know.

That all sounded wonderful, but how could María trust him to keep his promises? He'd never kept his word before. Why would this time be any different?

"Because, this time—" José took María's hand and lowered himself to one knee. "—I want to marry you."

A day earlier, María would've been elated by the surprise. Despite his seeming worthlessness, José had his better moments too. He stood as a bastion of support at the lowest point of her life. When her mother died, he extended the shoulder she cried on, and she never forgot that one instance of comfort. But the past 24 hours involved a roller coaster of emotions, with a betrayal, followed by a promise, followed by a betrayal again. Earlier in the morning, she expected to be halfway to her dream of moving to the United States and starting a family.

Well, José wouldn't be taking her to the United States; she remained certain of that much. Though he could help with the other half of her dream, she supposed, so she answered the proposal with an unenthusiastic:

"Sure, what the heck."

FIVE

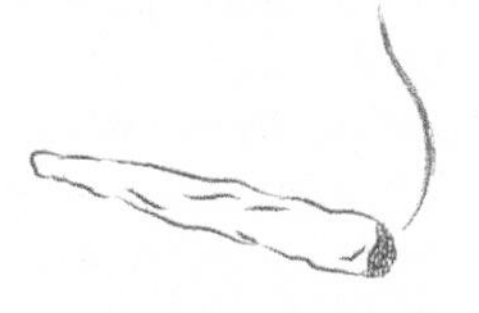

California

Engagement, marriage, and divorce—Moses Staffman had experienced all three. His engagement had been defined by optimism for the future; his marriage by boredom with the present; and his divorce by his presence at Dullsville's only courthouse, a constant reminder of the mistakes in his past.

A portrait hung on the wall outside the main door to the courtroom of The Honorable Judge Judith Solowoman, where Moses stood as he waited to meet his attorney. Regrettably, his ex-wife arrived before his legal advisor. At Moses' summons, she'd come to discuss an amendment to their divorce agreement to allow him to travel abroad. A few minutes remained before their hearing—plenty of time for the former lovers to catch up.

"Fuck you," greeted Cleopatra Spiter as she and her attorney walked straight past Moses and entered the courtroom.

Moses shrugged and turned back to the portrait on the wall. In it, a black-robed Judge Solowoman posed judiciously at her bench, gavel in one hand, some type of legal scripture in the other. The portrait was new: placed on the wall a few days earlier as the courthouse hurried to keep up with the rapid pace at which she replaced her predecessor, Judge Kingsley Solomon, who abruptly retired in the wake of allegations of impropriety.

"Beautiful woman, isn't she?" asked a gangly man in an expensive suit, implying his fetish for a scholar of the law. The gangly man then forced a handshake and introduced himself as:

"Howie Spirit, Esq."[11]

"You must be my lawyer," Moses guessed.

"Sort of," Howie replied.

A practicing attorney for more years than indicated by his law license, Howie Spirit, Esq., maintained a small book of clients for whom he provided legal assistance, 24 hours a day, seven days a week, as needed. One of those clients—a golden-eyed, white-bearded businessman—requested assistance with Moses' case. Howie argued on Moses' behalf, to be certain, but his undying loyalty went to whoever paid the bills.

"Regardless of semantics," Moses said, "you'll get me permission to travel to this secret island?"

"Absolutely," assured his sort-of attorney. "I've reviewed your case, and I believe there's a pretty good chance we can perhaps obtain some-or-other type of alteration to your divorce agreement, if all goes as planned."

"That sounds promising," Moses replied.

For the first time, Moses felt a semblance of confidence at the courthouse. He'd long sought to shed the burden of his previous marriage, impulsively entered during the folly of his youth under the assumption that the torch of love would only burn brighter as he aged. How foolish he'd been, he realized, though he forgave himself for the youthful indiscretion, hoping he might finally gain reprieve for the biggest mistake of his life.

Looking back to the portrait of Judge Solowoman on the wall, Moses considered how quickly circumstances could change. When he signed his divorce agreement, it failed to occur to him that he'd ever wish to leave the United States, even temporarily. Yet now, his desire to travel had shifted faster than Judge Solowoman replaced Judge Solomon. He wondered what else might change in the coming days, or months, or even years.

"Are you ready?" asked the attorney.

Moses felt ready, though not enthusiastically so.

◊ ◊ ◊

Judge Solowoman, who preferred to be addressed as "Judge Judi" for the sake of notoriety, slouched behind her bench as Moses entered the courtroom with his sort-of attorney by his side. Her Honor was in a poor mood, already behind schedule, not yet halfway through her case docket for the day. She hoped to leave the courthouse early for her weekly jazz-dancing lesson, but she needed to pick up the pace to depart her chambers in time to boogie.

Judge Judi banged her gavel on the bench. "Next up we have Staffman v. Spiter. Are the parties present?"

"Yes, Your Honor." Howie motioned Moses to make his way toward the front of the courtroom. "Howie Spirit, Esq., on behalf of the petitioner, Moses Staffman."

"We're all here, Your Honor," the other attorney also answered as she and Cleopatra followed their counterparts up the center aisle. "Laurie Lawler, Esq., on behalf of the respondent, Cleopatra Spiter."

"Can you remind me what's going on?" Judge Judi had read the court pleadings on file, but since she was new to the case, she required a full explanation of the stakes. Who better to provide the explanation than a pair of state-licensed legal professionals?

"Well, Your Honor," began Howie as he stepped to the podium facing the judge, "Mr. Staffman is petitioning to have the No Travel Clause removed from his divorce agreement with Ms. Spiter. Quite frankly, Your Honor, the No Travel Clause impinges on Mr. Staffman's constitutionally guaranteed freedom of travel—a liberty of which a citizen cannot be deprived without due process of law under the Fifth Amendment."[12]

"You're getting due process right now, aren't you?" Judge Judi asked.

"Thank you, Your Honor," continued Howie. "As I was saying, the No Travel Clause in Mr. Staffman's divorce agreement prevents him from traveling outside of the United States. He's essentially being held as a prisoner in his own country. Now I realize, Your Honor, that there are specific cases in which citizens should be prevented from fleeing the country: citizens accused of a crime, for example. But Mr. Staffman is only guilty of unrequited love. Is that a crime worthy of taking away a man's fundamental right to travel? This is supposed to be the land of the free? It doesn't sound like he's free if that's the case."

Judge Judi got the gist of Moses' dilemma.

"I'd like to hear what the other party has to say," Her Honor requested, and turned to Cleopatra's side.

"Your Honor." Laurie nudged Howie sideways to overtake the podium in the center of the courtroom. "This isn't the case of a forlorn man cursed with unrequited love. Mr. Staffman signed his divorce agreement knowing full well of the No Travel Clause, which we included because he couldn't afford the entire divorce verdict at the time of the separation. The parties agreed to allow Mr. Staffman to avoid an upfront fee in exchange for larger alimony payments over time and the loss of his right to flee the Court's reach."

"Your Honor." Howie grabbed the podium back from his verbose counterpart. "The divorce verdict was unfair. Mr. Staffman surrendered almost everything he owned to Ms. Spiter. Even now, Ms. Spiter still receives half of his paycheck. From what I can tell, she's made no attempt to find a job to relieve Mr. Staffman's burden. She's forcing Mr. Staffman to remain here in the country so he can pay her expenses."

"Your Honor." Laurie slid in front of Howie at the podium and pushed his body backward with her protruding derriere. "As you know, Mr. Staffman took on a duty to support Ms. Spiter when he married her. Like many young women, she became dependent on Mr. Staffman during their marriage. She sacrificed her own future so he could achieve an illustrious career growing plants, or whatever it is he does. It's too late for her to begin a new career."

"She's only thirty-six!" Moses shouted as he jumped up from his seat.

Judge Judi glared at Moses. She hated interruptions, and instructed him to only speak when spoken to.

"Thank you, Your Honor," said Laurie, relieved.

Judge Judi glanced down and shuffled the papers in front of her, furrowing her brow as she studied the top sheet. "I must say, I've been reviewing the numbers, and these are some of the highest alimony payments I've ever seen, especially when you consider how low Mr. Staffman's salary is in comparison."

Yet despite Her Honor's concern, she needed to wrap things up—the jazz music already played in her head—so she continued:

"That being said, the divorce agreement says what it says, and Mr. Staffman agreed to it. I'm sorry, Mr. Staffman, the No Travel Clause in your divorce agreement is valid as far as I can tell."

Judge Judi banged her gavel and looked for the next case on her docket. Perhaps she'd make her jazz-dancing lesson after all.

"Your Honor," Howie interjected. "If that's your decision, then there's one more minor issue. Mr. Staffman would like to petition this Court to leave the country for a brief period. By the terms of his divorce agreement, section two, subsection D, subsubsection three-point-four, trisubsection alpha-sigma-sigma, you have the power to allow Mr. Staffman to temporarily leave the country for *any* reason at *any* time."

"How long would he like to leave?" asked Judge Judi.

"The time period is undetermined." Howie smiled, expecting a victory. "Mr. Staffman needs time to care for a terminally ill friend living in Mexico. His friend is only expected to live for a few months, but it's difficult to say with these types of affairs."

"That seems like a reasonable request." Judge Judi turned her head toward Laurie and Cleopatra. "Wouldn't you say?"

Laurie whispered back and forth with Cleopatra before returning to the Judge.

"Your Honor," Laurie said, "we have some doubts as to the veracity of Mr. Staffman's reason for leaving the country."

Judge Judi turned back to Moses. "Do you have proof of this illness?"

"Your Honor," begged Howie, "we accelerated this hearing so Mr. Staffman could get to Mexico before his dear friend dies. It's not easy to obtain this type of proof outside the United States; there's a lot of red tape. And—"

"What's his name?" Judge Judi interrupted.

Howie needed the question repeated.

"The friend who's terminally ill," Judge Judi clarified. "What's his name?"

Howie stood helpless, silent for the first time, and turned to Moses for an answer.

Moses looked back at Howie, then down to his feet, then over at Cleopatra, and then up at the Judge. Then he looked back over at Cleopatra, then down to his feet, and then back at his sort-of attorney again. Impulsively, he said:

"Adam."

"Adam?" the Judge asked, implying that there must be more to the friend's name than a single word.

"Adam Sandler," Moses said.

"Adam Sandler," Judge Judi repeated. "Okay, Mr. Staffman, I'll give you permission to leave the country for two weeks. That should give you enough time to see Mr. Sandler and obtain proof of his illness from a licensed medical care facility. Send something back here, and I'll give you permission to stay abroad until he croaks. Does that work?"

"Yes, Your Honor." Howie jumped in to save the day. "Thank you, Your Honor."

◊ ◊ ◊

Howie waited until he and Moses left the courtroom to express his excitement, since he always kept his emotions in check in the presence of a judge. But once he and Moses stood alone in the hallway, he could contain himself no more, and burst with pride as he said:

"Congratulations on the win in there!"

Moses needed clarification of two details: (1) who won, and (2) when the win took place.

"I got you two weeks out of the country!" The boastful attorney answered both inquiries at once. He would've patted himself on the back for his role in the victory, but his fancy suitcoat kept his free arm from stretching all the way around his body.

Moses felt as elated as one would expect. He noted that the original request included a term of months, not weeks, with even that being a compromise on the failure to eliminate the No Travel Clause in its entirety, despite his sort-of attorney's confidence going into the hearing.

"The precise time period is irrelevant," Howie assured. "Don't focus so much on that."

"Eh," Moses decided after thinking it over, "as long as I'm paid $1,000,000, what do I care?"

"That's the spirit," Howie agreed.

Moses shrugged. "So, what now?"

Howie was glad he asked. Prior to the hearing, he'd spoken to TH Corp's owner to discuss the legal complexities of the botanist's responsibilities. Now that Moses could leave the U.S., his $1,000,000 paycheck hinged on the completion of three simple tasks: (1) stealing *Zerojuana* from Plant Inc, (2) bringing the stolen *Zerojuana* to Mexico, and (3) developing *Cannapeñis* for TH Corp.

"Um, what?" Moses paused to unpack the additional information. Surely, these three details had been omitted from his handshake agreement with Guy.

First, he was a botanist, not a thief.

Second, when did Mexico become involved?

And third, he wished to discuss the name of the new product, or as he put it:

"I don't want my name attached to something called *Cannapeñis*."

Howie ran the legal department, not the marketing department, so he carried no sway in the naming process. But Moses' legal concerns lined up neatly with his expertise. As far as thievery, Howie argued that Moses had every right to use his own work.

"Didn't you create *Zerojuana*?" Howie asked.

Moses supposed the attorney made a convincing argument. Still, he asked, "What about Mexico?"

Mexico was never part of the deal, and Moses could prove it. An atlas at his house marked the location of the secret island with a yellow star, and he remained certain that the island floated at least a half-inch from Mexico. He felt no desire to set foot in the forsaken land of the Mexicans, filled with thieves, and murders, and worse!

"That wasn't part of the deal!" he even shouted.

To that, the attorney explained that Mexico held no control over the island. The island simply existed *near* Mexico, just like the United States, and the only route to the island twisted through Mexico.

"And in any case," the attorney concluded his argument, "you have to complete each of these tasks to get your $1,000,000."

Moses grunted to show his displeasure. Then again, he supposed it would be easy to swipe a few seeds from Plant Inc. With plants being easy to reproduce, the missing seeds would likely go unnoticed.

Ugh, and he supposed he could stomach Mexico as long as his stay was brief.

◊ ◊ ◊

Howie rode the high of his courtroom victory as he left the halls of justice, gleefully tossing his briefcase into his trunk and then firing up his favorite tune—*I Fought the Law*—for the drive back to his office.[13] His job rarely proved easy, but nothing matched the feeling of remedying his clients' problems; or even if he failed to remedy their problems, billing them for the time he spent trying. That feeling was the reason he dedicated his life to the practice of law.

Despite being credentialed as a Doctor of Law, Howie served as more than a mere expert in jurisprudence. He'd been trained to solve legal issues, sure, but his problem-solving abilities went far beyond writing briefs and arguing to judges. He was even better at managing conflicts, legal or otherwise, to minimize the probability of disaster. Or more simply, as Howie liked to say:

"I'm a fixer."

A darn fine fixer he was. That's the way it had been for as long as he'd known the golden-eyed businessman. Nobody knew how long that had been, with that information falling under the attorney-client privilege, but Howie's gray hair and withered skin told the story of a career spanning decades.

In any case, and particularly in any legal case, an attorney must keep his client fully informed of the judge's major decisions. In this particular legal case, that turned out to be easy for Howie, because his client already sat in his office, waiting for that precise information.

"How'd it go in court?" Guy kept his head down as the attorney walked through the door, more focused on twisting a doobie with his island's finest dope.

"Couldn't have gone better," Howie replied, implying that his statement was in view of the circumstances without saying as much. The judge declared Moses to be free to leave the United States. As soon as Moses took possession of Plant Inc's *Zerojuana* seeds, per Guy's instructions, he'd be on his way to Mexico.

"Fantastic," Guy summarized of his plan's progress. His attorney never let him down. That's why he always paid the exorbitant fees Howie charged for each minute of his time.

"And I round up," Howie reminded, and checked his watch.

"As long as the clock is running," Guy segued, "where do we stand on cannabis legalization as a whole?"

"Funny you should ask," Howie replied, because that was another matter entirely. Moses' issues were trivial compared to the legal hurdles involved with the sale of cannabis in the United States. As it turned out, the legalization of cannabis would take more time to navigate than the attorney cared to spend.

"I have full confidence in your ability to sort out the legal issues," Guy said.

Howie could handle the task, certainly, and failure remained his least concern. He simply felt no desire to work forever, despite his love for the practice of law. And even if he desired to work forever, Father Time would surely deny the proposal, no matter how hard he argued in its favor.

"I'm retiring," Howie insisted. "I'm too old for this."

"Retiring?" Guy asked. "But this is easy money."

Howie had accumulated enough wealth over the course of his lengthy legal career. He wished to retire to a cabin by the beach, and spend the rest of his days watching the waves crash into the coast, sipping fruity drinks as his pasty skin soaked in the sun for the first time in more than half a century.

"Can't you just help me with this?" Guy asked. "And then retire?"

If only it was that easy, according to the attorney. His client failed to grasp the extent of the legal complexities involved with the new business. Although California legalized medicinal cannabis use, Guy couldn't simply walk into the state and start selling the crops from his island. He needed registrations and permits, none guaranteed. There'd be complicated questions involved with testing and distribution, and standards which could change at any time.

"And don't get me started on figuring out the tax situation," the attorney added.

Even then, they had more than state laws to consider. California's Proposition 215 conflicted with federal law, since cannabis remained a Schedule I narcotic under the Controlled Substances Act (with a high potential for abuse, no medical use, and significant safety concerns). Nobody knew whether the President of the United States would support Proposition 215, and without support from the highest office in the country, California's new law could fail just as quickly as it passed.

"This will be a lot of work," Howie predicted, "and sorting out these issues will take longer than I have left in my career."

"Nonsense!" Guy disagreed. "The current President could address the issue any day now. He's admitted to smoking dope in the past."

"But he didn't inhale," Howie pointed out.[14]

Regardless, Guy strongly disagreed with his legal advisor—a difficult feat when all his recent doobies rendered him generally agreeable to begin with. Not only did he disagree, he came to the opposite conclusion. In his mind, they had no time to lose. More states would follow California's lead in no time at all. TH Corp needed to be the first company to enter the budding market as legalization measures passed across the nation.

"Even if you rush development, TH Corp still won't be the first to market," Howie argued. "Other companies like Moses' employer, Plant Inc, are ready to launch their products, and they're better positioned than TH Corp."

"Can't we sabotage Plant Inc?"

"I just don't have time for this," Howie explained. "As far as it seems we've already come, this is still only the beginning. We'll have to put up with a lot of nonsense before this is all said and done, and I'd rather spend my remaining days lounging on the beach."

"What can I do to change your mind?" Guy felt certain that TH Corp would fail without Howie advising him how to navigate the inevitable legal hurdles.

Howie grinned: no teeth, only lips. After decades of employment, he knew his client would ask that precise question.

"From your grin," Guy observed, "it seems like you know exactly what you want to get out of this."

Guy inferred correctly. Howie always had a plan; and typically, his plan was already in progress by the time he revealed its existence.

"As I mentioned, I wish to spend my remaining days lounging on the beach," Howie reminded. "And it just occurred to me that you recently acquired an entire island with vacant beachfront."

"Oh," Guy said, "I see where this is going."

There was only one problem: Guy hated to share. He'd purchased the island with his own hard-earned money. Why should anyone besides him enjoy the land?

"You're going to need me." Howie nodded confidently.

"Fine," Guy agreed with a groan. "You can retire to the island once TH Corp reaches $100,000,000 in profits. By then, we'll have made enough money to fund both of our retirements."

Howie frowned, shook his head, and insisted: "No."

"C'mon," Guy urged, undeterred by rejection. With Moses now ready to kick off Step Two (2. Perfect the Product) of the plan, Step Three (3. Reap the Profits) would begin in no time at all. Once Step Three began, $100,000,000 would accumulate faster than they could count.

Howie thought there might be something missing between Steps Two and Three. Even once perfected, *Cannapeñis* wouldn't magically turn into profits. TH Corp still needed someone to sell the stuff.

"What if," Guy suggested, "you retire as soon as we start selling *Cannapeñis* in the United States."

That was earlier than Guy wished for the attorney's retirement to begin. Then again, he supposed it would be nice to have Howie nearby, since his retirement could be reversed if a problem arose. Of course, this advantage went without saying to the attorney, which is why Guy refrained from mentioning it aloud.

Howie pinched one eye and opened the other, puckering his lips as he caressed his chin: he found the offer intriguing. Yet despite his interest, he agreed to nothing. His first lesson in law school dealt with the emptiness of a vague oral promise.

"I want the deal in writing," Howie negotiated, "and I want to retire after the *first* sale of *Cannapeñis*."

"Done," Guy agreed without further thought. "Since that's now settled, who should we hire to sell the product?"

Regrettably, Howie knew nothing about selling a Schedule I narcotic, besides the legal ramifications of doing so. TH Corp needed more of a do-it-all laborer to sell the product, he supposed.

"What we need is a hot young saleswoman," Guy said, "since we're selling a hot new product."

"What about a hot young saleswoman with experience as a do-it-all laborer?" Howie compromised.

"And she has to be willing to work for low wages," Guy insisted.

Those were all fine thoughts, they agreed. Too bad nobody fitting the description came to mind, at least not from what Guy recalled with his woefully deficient short-term memory.

"Eh." Guy's focus waned. "I'll figure that out later."

Besides, he needed to hit the road. His rental car was due back in Mexico by the end of the day, and he detested paying late fees.

SIX

Mexico

A vague recollection of the details of María La Virgen's relationship with José Carpentero steered the smart money away from their engagement lasting until their wedding day. Yet the smart bet was a losing bet, because in almost no time at all, the couple commenced their nuptials at the old county courthouse in downtown Los Aburridos.

With the only judge in town presiding, the fiancé and fiancée exchanged vows in front of their neighbor, Vecína, and pet Chihuahua, Perrita. They would've welcomed additional guests, but with the ceremony hastily arranged on a weekday, only the retired old woman and unemployed young canine were available on short notice.

The ceremony made an impression, according to the audience of two. Draped in an airy white dress hand-stitched by the bride herself, María certainly looked the part as she stood in front of the judge with her shimmering black hair cascading down her back. José looked like José, his mangled hair and pungent body odor evidencing a late wedding's eve; though he wore a suit, so he fit in for the occasion. Vecína and Perrita also did their best to dress up, but they had little notice or ability to truly splurge for the event.

María felt nauseous, but deemed her wedding day important enough to put up with a few cramps. She simply needed an energy pill to get through the ceremony. Correct to some extent, she made it through the ceremony. She found the energy to say "yes" when the judge wondered of her sound mind to enter into the arrangement, and she even smiled when she said it, to imply that her dreams were coming true.

José felt just as pleased as his bride, though not because of any dream in particular. María agreed to take him "for richer or poorer," and half of her net worth significantly raised his own. More importantly, they could finally consummate their union in a way he only previously experienced with women who remained nameless.

So the newlywed couple stood in front of the judge, with their elderly neighbor and young Chihuahua as witnesses, and swore the most sacred vows either of them thought to say. The lovers impressed the judge so much that he concluded the ceremony:

"By the power vested in me by the Los Aburridos Chamber of Commerce, I now pronounce you husband and wife."

"¡Felicidades!" congratulated Vecína.

"Bark!" congratulated Perrita.

The bride and groom puckered their lips and sealed their pact in front of the audience of two. Of course, with no marriage being perfect, they were bound to experience bumps down the road.[15] The first bump occurred before the newlyweds had a chance to thank their guests for attending—through no fault of José as one would expect—when María leaned over and covered the leather on her husband's shoes with her breakfast.

"Are you alright?" José asked, more concerned with his wife's health than that of his loafers, much to everyone's surprise. (Unbeknownst to them, the loafers weren't even his to begin with.)

"Bark!" Perrita agreed with the sentiment.

"I'll be fine." María assured of her fine health. "I have to work today. It's my first day on a new job."

"Then I'm making a doctor's appointment for when you're finished," José insisted, in case his wife suffered from something contagious.

María couldn't argue with her husband, at least not on their wedding day. Besides, they had no time to argue. A few minutes remained before her latest job began, so she suggested that they rush home and make their marriage official. Or as she put it:

"Let's hurry up and consummate!"

José couldn't argue with his wife, irrespective of their wedding day. Nor would he, even if he could. He'd waited a long time for this day, and nothing could keep the excited groom from taking his wife back to her bed—not the vomitus on his shoes, nor the minor weight she gained during their brief engagement.

◊ ◊ ◊

María's failure to stomach an energy pill made her first day on her new job tougher than usual. Fortunately, not much energy was required to sit behind an elongated counter and punch the keys of an old computer owned by the only car rental company in Los Aburridos.

The day dragged for the janitor-turned-receptionist as she gave customer after customer whatever car became available in the lot. Yet she welcomed the slow pace, particularly with how fast the past few weeks had flown by. First José disappeared, then he returned, then they married—as if barely any time passed. As appreciative as she was resourceful, María understood the need to slow down when life seemed to be passing her by in the blink of an eye.

As for her relationship with José, María felt satisfied with the general direction. He may not have been the model husband, sure, but every day he took another step forward. Although he drank tequila to the excess here or there (or both here and there), at least he'd spent more time at home than usual. To her surprise, he hadn't missed a night at home since their engagement; and he wouldn't miss a night at home, she warned, or he'd find himself out on the street.

As for María's own well-being, she felt good, emotionally speaking. Physically speaking was another matter entirely. Shortly after drinking a glass of water, she found herself bending down behind her computer, out of sight from the customers, with her face buried in a small trash bin, releasing more of whatever bile still remained inside her. So not only was she in an extremely poor mood when she lifted her head and accepted the next customer, but the next customer also failed to identify her until that precise moment.

This proved important because her next customer would've avoided the counter if he saw her before then. But he stood next in line, so once they locked eyes, his only choice was to approach. Reeking of some combination of cannabis and pepper juice, he strode up to the counter and greeted:

"Hello again, beautiful. It's me, Guy, remember?"

Of course María remembered. Although the only response she mustered was:

"What are you doing here?"

"I heard that this is the best car rental company in Los Aburridos." Guy smiled at what he thought to be a clever quip.

"It's the worst," María groaned. "Are we really doing this again?"

Guy apologized for the tired joke. He needed something to break the ice after his disappearance following their night shared in the same hotel room.[16]

"What are *you* doing here?" Guy asked, the ice now broken, or at least chipped. "I thought you worked at the hotel?"

María explained her employment situation, which she thought she previously made clear. She worked for neither the hotel nor the car rental company. Temporary Staffing Agency (or "TSA") operated as her direct employer. Anyone who contacted TSA could procure her services for a reasonable fee. She'd explained everything to Guy at the hotel. Apparently, he'd failed to pay attention.

"Understand this time?"

Guy did, undoubtedly.

"So, I ask again," María said, "what are *you* doing here?"

"I'm here to drop off my car."

Guy jingled the keys to his Ford Ranchero.[17] He noted, however, that he'd enjoy taking the vehicle for one more ride if María wished to join him, citing the Ranchero's private cab with room for two seated passengers, combined with its roomy cargo bed with space to lie down. Perhaps they could pick up where they left off?

"I'm married to José now," María snapped, leaving no ambiguity as to her loyalties.

"But he's a dick," Guy reminded, only to receive a carefully designed look that clearly meant:

"So are you."

Guy was unsure what to say.

"You promised to take me to California," María recalled, "and then you left without saying anything."

"I left you a note." Guy shrugged.

"José is fully committed to me," María insisted. "He's been home every night, whereas you've been missing since the hotel. Are you willing to spend every day with me?"

"Oh, jeez." Guy noted the time on his nonexistent watch. "I wish I could, but I have business to attend to. José is a lucky man."

That's what María thought.

◊ ◊ ◊

Before returning to his secret island, the border-hopping Guy made a quick call, and wasted no time as soon as his attorney answered on the other end.

"I found the hot young saleswoman we discussed," he boasted.

Specifically, he found an attractive, do-it-all laborer available at an affordable price, just as they discussed before he left California. This woman worked for a company called TSA, and anyone could procure her services for a reasonable fee.

"Great!" said Howie. "We can talk about her once I arrive at the island."

"Actually—" Guy needed Howie to act as the contact between TH Corp and TSA. "—it's best if she doesn't know of my involvement."

"But you said—"

"And once she's set up in the United States and selling *Cannapeñis*," Guy interrupted, "then you can retire on the island as promised."

Howie sighed into the phone, exaggerating his frustration as only an attorney could. Then he hung up and got to work. If he hurried, he felt certain he could still retire without further delay.

◊ ◊ ◊

María sat in the waiting room at the only doctor's office in Los Aburridos, watching the news on a twenty-inch television mounted near the ceiling in the corner of the room. The news anchors, neither Mexican, focused on the President of the United States being sworn into office after already holding his position for the past four years. According to the President's Oath, he swore (solemnly!) to faithfully execute his duties, and to do his best to preserve, protect, and defend the Constitution.

"Seems like a pretty broad oath," María observed, though she hadn't read this alleged Constitution.

The newspersons lauded the President's past accomplishments. Under the President's leadership over the previous four years, the U.S. improved by leaps and bounds: the economy grew; the unemployment rate shrank; home ownership increased; the crime rate decreased; and families received new protections. And they saw no reason to expect these trends to reverse any time soon.

"Seems like a great time to be an American." María thought so, at least, and wished to hear more of the last part about family protections.

But the newspersons had no time to go into detail, because they found too many accomplishments to rattle off, including the President's signing of the North American Free Trade Agreement (or "NAFTA"), which created the world's largest free trade zone by eliminating almost every trade barrier between the United States and Mexico (and Canada too, as if they mattered).[18] According to the newspersons, NAFTA made it easier to move freely across the borders between countries.

"That's interesting," María noted, unsure what the barriers were to begin with, or how this tidbit might apply to her own situation.

María thought about the golden-eyed Guy as she followed the news—partly because she saw him earlier in the day, and partly because she would've been living in the United States by then if he kept his promise. But since he broke his promise, she took no pleasure in the foreign news, with the talking points having no impact on her life.

José was equally displeased. Someone also broke a promise to him. Though for him, a medical professional made the promise, and he'd yet to give anything valuable in return.

"Can you believe this?" José asked. "I checked us in ten minutes early for our appointment, and we're still waiting here twenty minutes later!"

If José had known the doctor would be running behind schedule, he would've served himself another shot of tequila to prepare for the delay.

María minded the wait less than the chatter on the television, so she changed the channel to something arguably more pleasant: the local premiere of an American movie, *Billy Madison*, dubbed as a courtesy for the foreign audience.[19]

"Who's that actor?" José wondered of the lead role in the film. Even if María knew the answer, she had no time to reply.

"María La Virgen," called out the receptionist with a manufactured smile. "The doctor is ready to see you."

After navigating a few hallways to a small room in the back of the office, the receptionist instructed María and her husband to make themselves comfortable. The doctor would be with them shortly, she explained as she closed the door. José asked for context on "shortly," but the receptionist declined to provide further details besides "when the doctor is ready."

"But you just said that the doctor is ready to see her," José protested, to no avail.

So they waited, with María content to relax on the examination chair while José nervously paced around the room examining the medical gadgets scattered about. He questioned the cost of the blood pressure machine mounted to the wall. Or what about the ultrasound machine in the corner? Or the tongue depressors on the counter? How would they pay for all this?

They probably wouldn't pay for any of it, María noted, since their wallets remained empty, her words calming José's mind for the moment.

Finally, someone knocked on the door.

"Finally!" José's patience ran thinner with each passing moment. He opened the door expecting to see a doctor, but found only the receptionist, who again greeted the pair with a smile on her face. Unfortunately, a problem arose regarding María's medical insurance through her employer, TSA.

"What's the problem with my insurance?" María asked.

"It doesn't exist," replied the receptionist.

María suspected as much. "What if I pay with cash?"

She barely finished her sentence when a doctorly fellow in a white lab coat popped his head into the doorway and greeted:

"How may I help you?"

María took it from there. She'd felt ill for a few weeks, she said, which surprised José, who only noticed her sickness a few days earlier. Perhaps she hid her symptoms effectively, or perhaps José should've paid more attention to the love of his life. He found it tough to pay attention after a glass of tequila, anyway. Apparently, María had been feeling bloated, and urinating more than usual.

She'd also been moodier than usual, José thought, but refrained from saying aloud. He blamed a viral infection for her symptoms.

The doctor had a hunch. But before he offered his opinion, he ran the normal tests, taking María's height and weight and temperature and blood pressure with a few overpriced gadgets scattered about the room.

"Is there any reason to think that you might be pregnant?" the doctor asked once he deemed her vitals to be normal.

"Impossible," José replied. According to him, María steadfastly refused a certain horizontal activity until earlier that day.

"What about oral?" asked the doctor. "The throat is indirectly connected to the uterus by the gastrointestinal tract. Or aural? The ear canal is indirectly connected to the throat by the Eustachian tube."

María assured the doctor that neither possibility existed. Prior to their wedding, she and José had kissed on more than one occasion, sometimes rather passionately, but hardly any saliva passed between them.

José supported her statement, unenthusiastically.

The doctor massaged his temples as he thought carefully. He'd never heard of a case of mouth-to-mouth pregnancy. Though he'd never heard of aural pregnancy either. Not that he kept up to date with medical journals. Anything remained possible, he supposed. He might as well run a few more tests.

"You're paying with cash, right?"

"Yes," María said, "after the tests."

With that guarantee in place, the doctor raised María's seat, stretched a pair of latex gloves over his hands, lifted her skirt, spread her legs, pulled her knickers to the side, and looked directly through her cervix.

"Yup," the doctor immediately concluded. "I can see it."

"What do you see?" wondered María, and José equally so.

"The baby," the doctor replied. "You're pregnant."

José failed to understand how María could be pregnant. María appeared less surprised than her husband, but neglected to share why.

"Nobody is going to believe this!" the doctor said. He marveled at two possibilities: (1) mouth-to-mouth conception, or (2) impossibly rapid growth within the womb. No other plausible explanation came to mind.

María shrugged; José buried his face in his hands.

"Are you taking any drugs?" The doctor still intended to explain the situation in scientific terms.

María didn't *do* drugs. The only medication she took were her energy pills, which reminded her to take another, because the visit to the doctor's office had been exhausting.

"You should stop taking those." The doctor cautioned that all drugs cause side effects. The energy pills may have accelerated her pregnancy, for example, or could even be responsible for other unintended complications as time passed.

Even though the doctor's opinion held less weight after his aural pregnancy hypothesis, María supposed that his advice made sense. But she needed her energy pills to work, and she needed to work to pay her bills. Rather than explain all that, she simply smiled, nodded, and thanked the doctor for the advice.

After a brief moment marveling over the medical miracle, the doctor asked:

"May I have that cash now?"

SEVEN

California

Moses Staffman's last day of gainful employment at Plant Inc stood out as abnormal. Abnormal, that is, for a last day of work. Normally, departing employees spent their final hours saying goodbyes to coworkers—wishing well to some, subtly dissing others. His case differed in that he intended to leave with as few people noticing as possible. After all, he still hadn't told anyone he was quitting.

With no time to lose, Moses punched his time card and went straight to the greenhouse, where the *Zerojuana* plants flourished under his care. He would've dug up the plants and taken them with, but they stood too tall to fit in his custom-made, gold-monogrammed, patent leather briefcase. Instead, he doused each plant with a desiccant intended to cause withering death within a week. He hoped to leave the impression that no other botanist could care for the plants.

"Screw 'em," Moses reasoned, his hard feelings outwardly apparent regarding Plant Inc's failure to pay him more than his contractually owed salary.

After that, Moses made his way to the repository, where Thutmond Mose III kept close track of the company's transportable inventory. Knowing all too well of Thutmond's tendency to make matters difficult, Moses made an out-of-character decision to be cordial with the inventory manager. Based on his understanding, that began with a healthy smile and a demonstrated interest in his coworker's well-being.

"Hi, Thut!" Moses greeted the inventory manager with his best attempt at a grin. "How are you doing today?"

Thutmond felt quite well, until then. To him, something seemed off: not only had Moses never asked about his well-being, he'd never seen a smile on his coworker's face.

"I thought we might bury the hatchet," Moses offered.[20] The coworkers should at least be courteous, according to his suddenly optimistic opinion.

Thutmond felt no desire to bury anything. It wasn't his job to plant items in the ground—biological or otherwise. That was Moses' job as a botanist. Moses could bury as many hatchets as he desired. Thutmond's job involved keeping Plant Inc's repository secure.

"In that case," Moses said, "I need access to the repository to retrieve avocado seeds for a new project."

By this point, Thutmond stood on full alert: eyes wide, ears perked. He kept himself apprised of every project at Plant Inc —his job required knowledge of when and where the inventory went—and he hadn't heard of any project requiring avocado seeds. Nor did he trust Moses' word on the matter. Unfortunately for Thutmond (and for Plant Inc, in hindsight), botanists ranked above inventory managers in the complicated company hierarchy, and Moses needed nothing more than his word to gain access to the repository. Thutmond had been previously warned not to refuse entry to the botanist, so he reluctantly handed over the required paperwork with simple instructions.

"Detail everything you're taking."

Moses briefly questioned the necessity of the paperwork, but he failed to change Thutmond's mind. The inventory manager bent the rules in certain cases, for certain individuals. This wasn't one of those cases, however, and Moses certainly wasn't one of those individuals.

With no choice but to fill out the forms, Moses did as told. Whether he filled out the forms correctly was another matter entirely. It's not like Plant Inc could fire an employee who no longer worked there. Once he signed and dated the papers, he received a key to the repository, accompanied by a final warning.

"Remember," Thutmond reminded, per company guidelines, "you're not allowed to remove anything from company grounds."

◊ ◊ ◊

Plant Inc's repository looked impressive, at least from a plant lover's perspective. Thousands of samples at all stages of growth covered hundreds of square feet of warehouse space. In other words, the inventory took up far more space than Moses possessed in his custom-made, gold-monogrammed, patent leather briefcase.

First, Moses sought out the section of the inventory he mentioned to Thutmond, and gathered every avocado seed he could find. But the avocado seeds remained outside his briefcase, because he had no intention of wasting the valuable space in his carryall. Instead, he brought the avocado seeds to an expensive cryochamber housing the *Zerojuana* seeds. After a quick swap of the labels, he relocated the *Zerojuana* seeds, labeled as avocado seeds, into his briefcase; and he placed the avocado seeds, labeled as *Zerojuana* seeds, into the newly empty space in cryostorage.

Then he returned to his office for the electronic data. Although Plant Inc kept its physical merchandise under lock and key, they made the virtual information easily accessible. Moses plugged a hard drive into his computer, logged on to the company network, and downloaded the entirety of a file marked, "Research and Development." He even backed-up the data on a second hard drive to be safe.

Moses' phone rang as he sat at his desk downloading the files. He let the call go to voicemail. Once he walked out the door, nothing related to Plant Inc would matter. Why lie to whoever decided that the precise moment he sat stealing files from his company would be the best time to chat?

Moses felt (some) regret over the way he was leaving his faithful employer of so many years. At the same time, the items he took resulted from his own blood and sweat (no tears), so he felt like he possessed just as much right to the work as his employer (logically, not legally). Besides, even if his employer possessed more of a right to his work than he did, his $1,000,000 signing bonus with TH Corp dwarfed his career earnings at Plant Inc, so there existed few (if any) doubts in his mind that he made the right choice.

Moses' phone rang for the second time as he finished pulling the back-up hard drive from his computer and squeezing it into his briefcase next to the *Zerojuana* seeds. He remained as uninterested as the first time, his feelings unchanged over the course of a few minutes. Instead of answering, he shut his briefcase and stood from his desk, ready to walk out the door and never return.

Regrettably, the doorway was blocked by none other than Thutmond Mose III.

"You forgot to sign out." Thutmond handed Moses the official sign-out form. "Please confirm that you took exactly what you indicated on your sign-in form."

Thutmond was right, according to company policy; Moses knew it. So just like on the way into the repository, Moses filled out the forms with no regard for accuracy, and handed them back to his counterpart, expecting their interaction to be complete.

Thutmond had other ideas, which became evident as he lingered in the doorway after receiving Moses' signed forms. He apologized for his rudeness earlier. Perhaps the hatchet should indeed be buried between the two rivals, he supposed. He was no expert in burying anything, let alone a weapon, but he knew exactly where to find the tools needed to dig up the earth. Trowels hung at the top of the third shelf in the sixteenth row of the repository, and planter's soil could be found seven rows over in the organic section.

"Ugh," Moses groaned. "That again?"

Fortunately, Moses' phone rang yet again. This time, he felt the need to answer. "Sorry, I have to take this."

Thutmond understood, and needed to return to the repository anyway. He nodded and showed himself out the door.

Relieved to be rid of his coworker, Moses picked up the phone with optimism, no longer bothered by the distraction. Though as they say in the plant world: "When one problem wilts, a new problem sprouts."

"Moses! It's Howie Spirit, Esq."

"Can this wait? I'm about to leave for Mexico."

"That's why I'm calling," Howie explained. "I just got off the phone with Judge Judi's clerk. Your ex-wife obtained an emergency injunction to prevent you from leaving the country. She called every hospital in Mexico and couldn't locate a terminally ill Adam Sandler to corroborate your story. Her attorney is on her way to Plant Inc to serve you with the injunction."

"So I can't leave?"

"Once you're served with the injunction," the attorney advised, "your ex-wife's attorney will notify the government that you're not allowed to leave the country."

All Moses heard was "Once you're served with the injunction—"

He had an idea: it involved not being served with the injunction.

◊ ◊ ◊

Moses grabbed his briefcase full of company merchandise—biological and otherwise—and ducked through the hallway toward the parking lot. Unfortunately, the exit to the parking lot was past the reception desk, where he found his ex-wife's attorney chatting with the receptionist.

"Listen here, you blonde bimbo!" shouted Laurie Lawler, Esq.

If not clear from the attorney's tone, she questioned whether she should be permitted to deliver a message to one of Plant Inc's botanists. Up to then, the receptionist had dutifully followed company policy by refusing to allow the attorney to pass without authorization from the recipient of her message. For safety reasons, the company prohibited uninvited visitors from roaming through the corridors, the receptionist explained.

"Nevermind," Laurie said after locking eyes with Moses just as he turned the corner. It appeared, at least for a moment, that her job would be easy. "Moses Staffman, I'm here on behalf—"

"La-la-la!" Moses covered his ears to drown out her voice. "I can't hear you!"

Laurie doubted Moses' sincerity. With a toddler of her own, she was used to such infantile behavior. Regardless, her words held less weight than an envelope with an urgent order from Judge Judi. As soon as Moses accepted the envelope, she'd be on her way.

Quickly assessing the room's geometry, Moses calculated his escape route: (1) his ex-wife's attorney stood directly in front of him, and (2) the door to the parking lot stood directly behind her, (3) which meant that the only path to the exit led straight through the legal expert. Although he believed he could outmuscle her slender frame, he also needed to avoid her envelope in the process.

Moses tucked his briefcase under his arm and shuffled to his right, positioning himself to spring around his adversary. Laurie countered by moving to her left, of course. So Moses shuffled back to his left, at which point she countered by moving to her right, again blocking his path. He went back to the right, her to the left. Him left, her right, yet again.

This went on for several minutes.

"We can do this all day," the attorney advised.

Frustrated, but not discouraged, Moses shuffled left and right a few more times; the attorney countered his every move.

"Enough!" Laurie finally instructed of Moses' nonsense. She stopped shuffling side-to-side and approached Moses directly, extending her hand with an unmarked envelope.

Time was up. Moses faked left, spun right, and leapt to the side, landing just outside of her reach with a direct path for the exit. Realizing her misstep, the attorney flung the envelope in his direction, though he nimbly dove underneath the flying parcel, which almost grazed his shoulder, but failed to make contact.

"Gotcha!" Laurie called.

"No, you didn't!" Moses replied as he sprang to his feet and dashed out the door.

◊ ◊ ◊

Laurie tracked Moses as best she could, but he was surprisingly spry for an old man. His Chevy had already peeled out of the parking lot by the time she gathered herself. She could've followed in her luxury sedan, but she found no need to exert the extra effort.

The attorney picked her unmarked envelope off the floor and checked it for evidence: a strand of hair, a speck of sweat, anything tying Moses to the parcel. Finding nothing to her liking, she decided that a DNA test would've been overkill. Besides, she had something arguably better than DNA: an eyewitness. The dutiful receptionist saw the entirety of the events unfold, from Moses' arrival until his exit out the door.

"You saw what happened, right?"

The receptionist certainly saw what happened. Despite being blonde, she exhibited an exceptional memory. She not only remembered what happened with Moses, she also recalled her interaction with the attorney immediately preceding the incident. Someone called someone else a "bimbo," according to her memory.

The attorney groaned. She'd get back to the receptionist later. Despite the absence of DNA evidence or a reliable witness, she did have one important thing: her word as a licensed attorney-at-law.

She needed to make two calls: first to Judge Judi's chambers to report what happened, then to her client to explain the same incident in different terms. She simply needed to be careful with what she said so she wouldn't later be called a liar. That being considered, her client received the message:

"He ran out the door and drove away!"

◊ ◊ ◊

With infuriated veins swelling across her temples, Cleopatra Spiter jammed her gas pedal to the floor, peeling her tires as she pulled her red coupe out of her garage and onto the street. Although her attorney advised that the situation remained under control, she took no chances with her primary income at risk.

Cleopatra's destination was 11 Main Street, where she assumed Moses would go following the confrontation at Plant Inc. The whitewashed, two-story ranch stood only a few blocks away from where she began, so she peeled into Moses' driveway shortly after leaving her own. With fire in her eyes, she hopped out of her car without bothering to shut off the engine, leaving the driver's door open as she raced to his front porch, threw her fists against the door, and screamed:

"I know you're in there!"

She lied about what she knew, but Moses wouldn't have known the difference if he happened to be in the house at the time.

When no one answered, Cleopatra crept around the house, peering through the windows, investigating for clues as to where her ex-husband might hide. The lights remained off for the most part, along with the major appliances, so she found no visible signs of his presence. And she heard nothing, so she found no audible signs either. As for olfactible signs, well, she couldn't smell anything over the stench of Moses' damn *titan arums*!

Eventually, Cleopatra discovered an important detail: Moses' mailbox stood full of mail, yet to be emptied since the previous day. From that detail, she deduced that she beat him home—a sensible theory, since Moses' house was a twenty minute drive from Plant Inc, and her attorney saw Moses at Plant Inc only ten minutes prior.

With time to spare, Cleopatra adjusted her strategy. Rather than confront Moses with a tirade of expletives when he expected it (her usual strategy), she'd surprise him when he least expected, and then unleash the tirade of expletives. So she hopped back into her car, drove down the street, and parked out of sight. Then she trotted back to Moses' house and found a hiding spot behind his *titan arums*, where she lay in wait for her ex-husband to return.

◊ ◊ ◊

The relationship between Moses and Cleopatra hadn't always been so strained. They once existed as a happy couple, save for a few disagreements here and there. Then again, that was a different time: an actor served as President of the United States, as silly as that sounded.[21]

The pair met at a holiday celebration thrown by Moses' employer, Plant Inc. Attendance was mandatory for all employees, with every employee allowed to bring a guest. Moses arrived alone, sans guest. Cleopatra's invitation came from Plant Inc's inventory manager—a man by the name of Thutmond Mose III.

The evening went as expected, with the invitees mingling over cocktails before taking their seats for the main course. Moses sat at a table with Cleopatra, who appeared less than enthralled with the initial conversation. Not that she disliked Moses in particular, but she lacked any interest in plants or other photosynthetic-related matters. The meat in her main course stood out as her only concern.

Plant Inc's CEO kicked off the meal by holding a microphone and thanking his employees for their hard work. No company-sponsored dinner would be complete, he said, without a few made-up awards. The Perfect Attendance Prize, the Top Newcomer, the Safety Star—every honor garnered a round of applause as the recipient accepted recognition with a brief speech. Yet nothing the CEO said proved more impactful than his announcement of Plant Inc's Botanist of the Year.

"Congratulations, Moses Staffman!"

The award came as no surprise. Each year, the Botanist of the Year Award went to Plant Inc's most profitable botanist. This particular year, the most profitable botanist turned out to be Moses, based on the company's complicated algorithm for determining value.

For the rest of the night, the compliments flowed as freely as the whiskey. Some of Moses' coworkers shook his hand; some patted him on the back; some rubbed his head. All showered him with praise: Moses this, and Moses that.

With Cleopatra sitting at the same table as the Botanist of the Year, nothing kept her from overhearing the accolades—not even the inventory manager doing his best to divert her attention. By the end of the night, she forgot who invited her to the dinner in the first place. When the celebration came to an end, she received a ride home from the only name stuck in her mind —Moses Staffman I, the future of Plant Inc and undoubtedly the future of the industry, according to the night's conversation.

From there, the story of Moses and Cleopatra progressed just as it does with most love stories. Lust turned to love, leading to a wedding creating a marriage with endless possibilities. And as the story typically goes, then came a husband who drank excessively to cope with boredom or whatever other excuse he mustered, followed by a wife seeking intimacy outside the marital household, ending in a contemptuous divorce which generated two enemies rife with anger and resentment.

Well, not just *two* enemies, depending on who was asked. The events also generated a *third* enemy, if Thutmond Mose III counted for anything.

◊ ◊ ◊

Word of Moses' abrupt exit from company grounds traveled quickly through the corridors of Plant Inc. The receptionist relayed her version of the events to the mailman as he swung through for his daily deliveries, complete with a description of some unkind words spoken by the attorney. The mailman relayed the story to the human resources manager as he dropped off a package, although in his version of the events, it remained unclear who called whom a "bimbo." The human resources manager relayed her version of the events to the rest of the botanists in an emergency meeting to find out about any other instances of derogatory language. And eventually, a discussion of the occurrence caught the ear of Plant Inc's inventory manager, a man by the name of Thutmond Mose III, if anyone forgot.

According to what Thutmond overheard, Moses screamed the word "bimbo" at a female visitor as he shoved her to the ground before sprinting to the parking lot—by all means, a disturbing account. The physical abuse aspect of the story bothered him less than Moses' disappearance. With Moses having visited the repository earlier in the day, and now having left company grounds, there stood a nonzero chance that the inventory went with him. Certainly, nothing had been checked back into the repository after his coworker received the key.

Thutmond sprinted to the last place he saw his adversary. But in Moses' office, he found no sign of life—either of the human or plant variety. Had it not been for the unimportant detail of a computer screen displaying the words "Data Deleted," one wouldn't have suspected that the botanist came into the office that day.

Thutmond dashed back to the repository to reexamine Moses' incoming and outgoing forms for discrepancies, of which he found one. Moses' check-in form requested the removal of only one species: avocado seeds. Conversely, Moses' check-out form confirmed the removal of a similar but slightly larger group: (1) avocado seeds, and (2) one large *Fuck-off Flower*. The inventory manager had never heard of the second variety, and found no record of its keeping in the repository.

Despite Thutmond's confusion, the discrepancy between forms meant that Moses undoubtedly broke company policy, with the potential for a serious offense.

◊ ◊ ◊

Cleopatra grew angrier with each passing minute as she waited at Moses' house for over an hour. What she initially assumed would be ten minutes with the *titan arums* slowly dragged on to twenty, then thirty, forty, fifty minutes and so on. Her legs certainly tired from squatting for so long, but the majority of the pain concentrated at her nostrils.

The smell was as insufferable as her ex-husband!

Only Cleopatra knew why she hated Moses so much, though understanding her reasons required no imagination. She'd wasted the best years of her life married to a man who drank excessively and failed to live up to her expectations from the day they wed. She still recalled his vows as if he just spoke the words:

> "I, Moses Staffman, take you, Cleopatra Spiter, to be my lawfully wedded wife. I promise to love and honor you, and to support you from this day forward, for better, for worse, for richer, for poorer, in sickness and health, until death do us part."

That's exactly what Moses promised so many years earlier. Yet he failed to live up to his words. He sure didn't "love and honor" Cleopatra after a few glasses of whiskey. Instead, he pounded his fist on the table and shouted about his job or his neighbors or the government or whatever else bothered him at the time. Then he fell asleep before she got the "love" she needed, which he promised equally with the "honor" she desired.

Cleopatra spoke the same vows as Moses. And she stuck by those vows to the best of her ability. Although she vowed to take Moses "in sickness and in health," she questioned whether alcoholism truly qualified as a sickness. Besides, Moses vehemently denied having a problem with whiskey. One way or the other, she excused herself on that clause. As for any other portion of the vows she failed to follow, well, she reasoned that Moses broke his vows first.

Regardless, none of that mattered anymore. Moses wronged her. He owed her. From her perspective, he promised "support...from this day forward...until death do us part." The broad definition of "support" included monetary support, so Moses owed her money at least until he died. If need be, she'd spend every last breath to make him comply with his obligation.

Just when Cleopatra reached her wits' end with the smell of the *titan arums*, she glimpsed through the plants to see the grille of a car curve around the corner. The car slowly pulled into Moses' driveway and came to a stop, the engine idling as the driver examined his surroundings with the utmost caution.

Wary of being seen, Cleopatra quietly crouched farther back into the foliage to conceal her position. She desperately craved the satisfaction of jumping out of the bushes and ruining Moses' day. She deserved that satisfaction, she reasoned, after spending over an hour with the damn *titan arums*!

Finally, the car's engine shut off, followed by the slam of a door, and footsteps trailing up the driveway toward the front door. She shifted her body ever so slightly to position herself for a fierce leap into view.

"This is it," she whispered. "I've got you now."

Just as the footsteps turned the corner, Cleopatra leapt from behind the *titan arums* and said:

"Thutmond?"

"You remembered my name this time," noticed Thutmond Mose III.

◊ ◊ ◊

Gabby Blabber sat on her couch with a cup of hot coffee, watching her favorite daytime soap opera, *The Interesting & The Attractive*, when she heard a car pull into Moses' driveway next door. Normally, she would've peeked out the window to watch Moses walk from his driveway to his front door, but this particular episode of *TI&TA* was moments from its climax. One of the male leads just revealed an infidelity with his wife's sister. Gabby wondered how the husband would excuse his behavior, and how the wife would retaliate.

Gabby wished her own life was as interesting as the wife or her sister on *TI&TA*, but nothing interesting ever happened in Dullsville. If it did, she'd certainly know, either through personal observations or secondhand knowledge traded at her local salon.

Back on *TI&TA*, the husband revealed that he suffered from periodic bouts of amnesia, one of which prevented him from remembering his marriage during the adulterous misdeed with his wife's sister. Not only that, his wife's sister also suffered from amnesia, which prevented her from remembering she had a sister, let alone knowing whether her actions with her sister's husband crossed a line of decency.

Gabby couldn't believe it. Or rather, she could believe it, because it happened on an earlier episode to another set of characters. But she couldn't believe amnesia happened *again*. How could the same drama happen twice? In the earlier instance, an intoxicating substance caused the amnesia. She wondered what caused the loss of memory this time around.

Gabby remained so focused on *TI&TA* that she resisted the urge to shuffle to the window as a conversation began next door. The walls of her house stood so thin that she heard almost every word moderately spoken within a small radius. On most days, any conversation would've piqued her interest, but she needed to know how *TI&TA* turned out. Surely, the ladies at the salon would be discussing the crazy twist sure to come in the final moments of the episode.

"Dammit!" screamed a woman just past Gabby's wall.

The scream came so suddenly that Gabby spilled a drop of coffee on her carpet. Well now she had no choice but to leap from her seat, shuffle to the window, and rip her curtains to the side. As interesting as *TI&TA* played out, the drama unfolding outside offered more potential. The last time she heard a scream from next door, a raging inferno on the porch practically brought down the neighborhood.

Outside the window, Gabby found two individuals having a discussion. She knew one of them: Moses' ex-wife, a woman named Cleopatra Spiter. She'd never seen the other: a man by the name of Thutmond Mose III, though his name would've been a mystery at that point, because he'd yet to introduce himself. Rest assured, she'd remember his name after the first time she heard it, along with whatever gossip came with it.

In an ear-piercing tone, Gabby asked what happened. They'd startled her quite a bit, so much so that she spilled a drop of coffee. She'd hustled to the window as quickly as she could, but her creaky knees only allowed her to move so fast.

"You scared me half to death," she said, and massaged her creaky knees.

Cleopatra wished she could scare Moses in the same manner, and Thutmond volunteered to provide the other half of the equation.

"Have you seen Moses?" Cleopatra asked.

Gabby hadn't seen Moses since he left for work earlier that morning, when she watched him walk from his house to his car, carrying his fancy briefcase, no different from any other day.

"I'm worried about him," Cleopatra fibbed. "Do you have any idea where he might be?"

Gabby thought, and thought, and thought some more. From what she could tell, a mystery needed to be solved. Who better to solve the mystery than the most knowledgeable woman in the neighborhood? To no surprise, she already had a suspect in mind.

"I bet Richard Dickens is involved," Gabby said.

Cleopatra furrowed her brow. Thutmond scratched his head. Neither recognized the name. Naturally, they needed more of an explanation, which Gabby gladly provided.

"Richard is a homosexual." Gabby lowered her voice and glanced over her shoulder as she spoke.

Cleopatra turned to Thutmond, who mirrored her confusion.

"He's a *gay*," Gabby clarified in an even lower tone.

"Have you seen this Richard fellow with Moses lately?"

"Well, no."

Gabby realized that they required further explanation. Not everyone could keep up with the logic of an experienced mystery solver. She touched her index fingers together to begin counting on her hand, explaining that (index finger) Moses—a man—went missing according to his ex-wife's account, and (middle finger) Richard happened to be a man who liked men. Plus, (ring finger) she read an article the other day about two men who fell in love and moved to San Francisco together, and (pinkie finger) she hadn't seen Richard since his morning run—about the same time she last saw Moses.

Gabby connected the dots to her satisfaction.

"Did you see them talk to each other earlier today?" Cleopatra asked.

Well, Gabby explained, Moses waived as Richard jogged past, and they both smiled at the time. Though if Cleopatra wanted to know about Moses' recent discussions, another more eccentric man with golden eyes and a white beard had visited Moses' house in recent history.

"Go on," Cleopatra urged.

Well, from what Gabby thought she heard, the golden-eyed man promised Moses a significant amount of cash, and then they came to some type of agreement.

"Incoming money!" Cleopatra's eyes lit up. "That's mine!" (She was partially correct: approximately 50% legally belonged to her.)

"What was the agreement?" Thutmond asked.

Regrettably, Gabby found it difficult to hear exactly what they said. Despite the thin walls of her house, not every word spoken next door made it all the way to her ears. She remembered hearing something about plants. Though again, she sometimes found it difficult to hear exact sentences.

"Plants!" Thutmond's eyes lit up. "Those are mine!" (He was partially correct: his employer owned the plants, legally speaking, though he assumed responsibility for their keeping.)

"Do you think we should check for clues in Moses' house?" Gabby wondered. "I've seen him tuck a spare key underneath the welcome mat."

◊ ◊ ◊

The newly formed team of sleuths—consisting of a bitter ex-wife, a jealous coworker, and a curious neighbor—slowly opened the front door of 11 Main Street under the guise of a worried group of friends. At first glance, nothing appeared out of the ordinary.

"Let's check the bedroom," Gabby suggested. She presumed the most scandalous—and thus most interesting—evidence to be located where Moses lay to rest each night. If Moses moved to San Francisco with Richard Dickens, which remained her best explanation for his disappearance, then she suspected there'd be some type of clue where the two men likely spent the most time together.

Unfortunately, upon closer examination: Moses' sheets lay flat on his bed; his room looked tidy besides a few clothes in the hamper; and his closet stood full of shirts, minus the one he wore that day.

After thirty minutes in the bedroom searching for clues, Cleopatra grew frustrated. "Did you ever see the man with the white beard in Moses' bedroom?"

"Oh, him? No, I can't see into the bedroom from my house. He smoked a cigarette in the living room, from what I saw."

With the additional information, Cleopatra and Thutmond agreed that the living room seemed like a better place to check for clues.

And clues they did find!

On the coffee table sat the first clue: a used cannabis cigarette extinguished in an empty glass lined with whiskey residue.

"Illicit substances!" Thutmond exclaimed.

On the recliner sat the next clue: an atlas opened to a page showing North America, with a bright yellow star drawn in the Pacific Ocean next to the phrase "TH Corp."

"International intrigue!" Gabby exclaimed.

On the side table sat the third and final clue: a recently watched copy of the movie *Happy Gilmore*.

"Adam-fucking-Sandler!" Cleopatra exclaimed.

EIGHT

Mexico

María La Virgen's blue eyes burst open as the battery-powered alarm clock on her nightstand shot out a high-pitched siren at precisely the time she intended to wake. Without delay, she leapt from her bed to silence the noise, glad that she no longer relied on the undependable rooster across the street to signal the start of her morning. How foolish she'd been to trust a cock for so long, when society's advancements allowed for such an appealing alternative.

Ignoring her doctor's advice, María wasted no time swallowing an energy pill to invigorate herself for her first day on a new job. On a normal day, she may have heeded the doctor's opinion, but this wasn't just any first day on any first job. This was the opportunity of a lifetime: she happened to be the first TSA employee approved for international travel.

That's right: she was going to the United States!

Her dream of raising a family in the United States was finally coming true. She had a husband, not to mention a baby on the way, and a trip to the U.S. checked off the final detail on her list.

The plans were all set. She had a temporary worker's visa to allow her to travel to the United States, plus a used Ford Ranchero to get her there and back. If she impressed on her first day, then there'd be a second day, and a third, and so on, until she impressed no more. A representative from TSA told her to prepare for a lengthy stay assuming all went well.

The only problem involved the man still lying across the bed. Her husband, José, had spent every night with her for as long as she cared to remember. If she stayed overnight in the United States, his streak would be broken.

Unless José came with on the adventure.

"Wake up, my love." María nudged José's shoulder. "We're starting a new life today."

José felt no rush to rise from his slumber, his brain rhythmically pulsing to the tune of a violent morning lullaby induced by his favorite spirit.

"What's going on again?" José kept his eyes shut as he mumbled.

María's plan was simple. Although she'd already told José everything he needed to know, she didn't mind repeating the details to make sure he understood the situation. She had a temporary worker's visa to travel to the United States, and a Ford Ranchero to get there. Of course, the pregnant woman wouldn't think about making such a lengthy trip alone. Without his own visa, her husband would curl up in the trunk of her Ranchero while she drove across the border. Once they arrived safely in the U.S., he could sit up front for the rest of the ride. She knew he'd stay close once they made it to their destination, particularly because he'd have nowhere to go.

"So get ready," María instructed. "I'm going to walk next door to ask Vecína to check in on Perrita while we're gone. We'll be leaving when I get back."

José wondered if his wife would be gone long enough to take a shot of tequila. What a dumb question: he found time for two shots before she even walked out the door.

◊ ◊ ◊

The Ford Ranchero wasn't what María expected. Though in hindsight, her expectation seemed unreasonable, considering she'd never seen a Ranchero up close. She supposed she could've paid more attention while working for the car rental company, but she saw no point to revisiting the past.

Of noteworthy importance, this particular make and model proved ill-suited for smuggling a drunk husband across the border. At least two people fit in the cab, maybe three or four. But an open cargo bed replaced the trunk, leaving nowhere for her husband to hide.

"Duh," José said. "Haven't you ever seen a Ford Ranchero?"[22]

"What a stupid car to choose," María replied. "Well, get in."

José could ride up front. Always the resourceful woman, she'd figure out a solution by the time they reached the border. She refused to leave behind such a vital part of her dream.

◊ ◊ ◊

To no surprise, María found an extended line of cars at the border, each waiting patiently to cross the invisible line between countries. She thought of countless reasons to journey northward: some cars, she assumed, contained Mexican nationalists, like her, traveling to the United States to make a living; others, perhaps, only planned to visit for a day; others could've been northern residents on their way home from vacation. No matter the reason, a line was a line, and she had no choice but to wait her turn for entry.

José sat silently in the passenger seat, unsure of what would happen when they reached the front of the line. María said she had a plan, and he was in no position to question his wife. Or rather, he was positioned to question his wife, since he sat next to her, but his mind lacked the ability to form the right inquiry. He needed another glass of tequila as soon as possible, and hoped they might make a quick stop as soon as they crossed the border.

As much as María told herself not to worry—countless others made the same journey every day—she couldn't stop her knees from shaking as she slowly pulled closer to the border. Part of her restlessness came from the amphetamines in her energy pill. The other part involved her nerves.

At the front of the line, an overhead sign reminded all travelers to have their passports in hand. José, unusually attentive, informed María that he lacked a passport to hold. To which she responded for him to be silent until told to speak. She had too much on her mind, and a patrolman was already waving their car forward.

"Hello," the patrolman greeted with a healthy smile. "Welcome to the United States."

To some extent, the greeting put María at ease. Not that she expected anything different, but it felt good to be welcomed into the foreign land. The smile helped too.

"How long are you visiting?" the patrolman asked as he perused her passport, holding the photograph up to her face to confirm at least that part to be accurate. "Less than a week?"

María shook her head. She had a temporary worker's visa, which she promptly handed over. Oh, and she was pregnant, by the way, she noted as she gently caressed her bulging midsection. That's why her husband sat in the passenger seat, in case the patrolman cared to know.

José smiled in agreement, but kept his mouth shut, lest he ruin the plan that he didn't know was already in progress.

"Congratulations, ma'am," the patrolman replied. "Are you traveling with any pork, beef or poultry products?"

María shook her head. From what she understood, the meat available in the United States tasted absolutely delectable. She could hardly wait to devour a juicy red T-bone steak—the biggest, juiciest, reddest T-bone steak she could get her hands on. She ate for two, after all, if the patrolman ignored her the first time.

"What about any fruits, vegetables or dairy products?" the patrolman asked. "Or any seeds, seedlings or fresh plants?"

María shook her head. She possessed none of those items. The car contained just her, her husband, and her unborn child, along with the bare necessities to survive. Her baby needed nothing more than a pair of supportive parents.

"I'll need to see your husband's passport," the patrolman noted as his final request. "Your child is fine without a passport until after the birth."

"Absolutely," María replied before turning to José and saying, "give him your passport, dear."

At this point, poor José found himself in a bind. Should he tell the truth, or should he lie? If he told the truth—that he possessed no passport—how would the patrolman react? If he lied about having a passport, surely the patrolman would notice when he failed to produce the document. He sure wished

María had given him more instructions, and began to wonder if his wife's plan even existed in the first place.

"I don't have it," José finally answered after much contemplation.

"You need your passport—" the patrolman said.

"José!" María shouted before the patrolman finished his sentence. "How could you forget your passport? You know we can't turn back now!"

"If you don't have your passport—" the patrolman continued.

"Aah!" María screamed, and clutched her stomach with a look of pure agony on her face. "The baby!"

"The baby?" wondered José.

"The baby?" wondered the patrolman as well.

"You'll have to deliver my baby!" María screamed at the patrolman, before providing an alternative. "Unless there's a hospital nearby."

The patrolman wished to turn María back toward Mexico, but he had no idea how close a hospital might be in the direction she came from. He'd never paid much attention to anything south of the border. There also remained a line of cars behind her—a hassle, to be certain. And he was no expert in the birthing procedure, nor did he wish to become an expert that day.

"There's a hospital five minutes up the road," the patrolman said, and raised the gate.

That was easy, María supposed, and pulled her car through the gate, waiting to be out of range of the patrolman before allowing a smile to grow across her face.

Americans are so dumb, she thought.

"I can't believe the baby is coming!" José said.

"Shut up," María replied, calmly, and hit the open road.

◊ ◊ ◊

Howie Spirit, Esq., was so close to retirement that he felt the excitement building deep inside his abdomen. With his first sort-of client on the move, and his second sort-of client on the way, his plan neared completion. Or if not completion, he'd at least reached the point of picking out furniture for his seaside retirement home.

The attorney had no sooner hung up on his first sort-of client, the botanist from Plant Inc, when his second sort-of client, the woman from Los Aburridos, walked through the door of his office. The botanist's complicated situation had set his plan behind schedule, so he would've welcomed a delay on her part. But rather than complain about her punctuality, he held out his hand and greeted:

"Howie Spirit, Esq."

"María," greeted the woman.

"And I'm José," added her companion, refusing to be left out of the conversation.

At this point, a few details confused the attorney.

First, he thought he requested, from TSA, a woman named María, allegedly as beautiful as she was resourceful. The woman standing in front of him looked attractive, sure, but not as stunningly beautiful as her reputation suggested. Indeed, she appeared a bit overweight in the midsection.

Second, he thought he requested, from TSA, only the woman named María, without a man named José. Plus, did he smell tequila?

"I'm pregnant." María answered the first question.

"And I'm the father." José partially answered the second question.

"Well those are a few interesting developments," noted Howie. Even still, what did those interesting developments matter to him? His contract guaranteed his retirement after the first sale of *Cannapeñis*, regardless of the salesperson or any baggage she carried.

"How was the drive?" Howie made small talk, unable to stomach even the briefest silence.

The drive proved surprisingly easy, according to María. Far easier than she'd imagined. If she'd known she could simply drive across the border, she would've moved to the United States a long time ago.

"It wasn't always so easy." Howie credited the President for signing NAFTA a few years prior. Because of NAFTA, she'd been granted a three-year stay in the United States based on the representation that she worked as a teacher. If the attorney knew about José, he would've also obtained a visa for her husband, because NAFTA allowed for spouses to travel as well.

"That's great," María said, "but I'm not a teacher."

"You'll be teaching people about a new product while you're here," the attorney argued, "so the title is appropriate, in my mind."

María was in no position to argue with the attorney, nor was she trained to dispute such a master of linguistics. Instead, she asked:

"What now?"

"I'm still awaiting word on your housing accommodations." Howie offered a glass of water while they waited. "Have a seat. It may take a while."

If anything would take a while, then José needed more than a glass of water, which he signaled with a loud groan. The attorney recommended Dullsville's finest tavern, conveniently located around the corner.

"Go on," María urged. She understood the stress felt by her husband. "I'll come get you when we're ready."

◊ ◊ ◊

Moses Staffman may not have returned to the whitewashed, two-story ranch at 11 Main Street, where a team of acquaintances searched for clues of his disappearance, but he hadn't crossed into Mexico yet. Amidst the excitement, he sought a moment to relax, not to mention bid farewell to his closest friend in town: Barney, the bartender at Dullsville's finest tavern. He would've hated for Barney to get the wrong idea about his temporary absence, lest it affect his bar tab when he returned.

"The usual," Moses told Barney as he sidled up to the bar and placed his briefcase next to his stool. With not only the *Zerojuana* seeds to worry about, but also the R&D data and backup data, he preferred to keep his briefcase within an arm's reach until he handed the stolen merchandise off to his new employer.

Moses scanned the bar for anything out of the ordinary. He recognized almost every one of the unsavory characters sitting around the room as regular clientele known to frequent the establishment most weekday afternoons. The only unfamiliar face belonged to a man attempting to order a glass of tequila without any identification, excusing the deficiency on a hurried trip across the border with his pregnant wife.

"What do I care?" Barney finally asked himself, and poured the cheapest tequila he could find.

Moses' first glass of whiskey went down smoothly, and relaxed him enough for a second. After his second glass, he felt friendly enough to converse with his fellow patrons, though "friendly" differed from "nice."

"I don't know how you can drink that Mexican swill," Moses said to the unidentified tequila-sipping man on the next barstool.

"I'm Mexican," the man replied, and held out his hand. "José, to be specific."

Ugh, just Moses' luck. About to enter an entire country full of Mexicans, he was now stuck with one before even crossing the border. He'd hoped for some good ol' American conversation before he left, unsure when he'd hear such witty banter again. Unfortunately, his lack of desire to speak with the Mexican failed to prevent the Mexican from speaking to him.

"Nice briefcase," José said. "Is that patent leather? And a gold monogram? It must have been a custom order, I presume?"

Moses slid his briefcase between his legs and extended his pointy knees for protection, knowing full well that most Mexicans were criminals, presumably thieves at the very least.

"Have you ever tasted tequila?" José immediately forgot about the briefcase as he slid his glass toward Moses. "Here, try a sip of mine."

Moses appreciated the offer, but respectfully declined. Though the more he thought about it, he didn't even appreciate the offer so much, and decided that his declination had been too respectful. But by then, it was too late to retract his regard for the Mexican's feelings.

Well if Moses couldn't show proper disdain for the Mexican, he sure could leave. With that, he picked up his briefcase, stood from his barstool, slapped a few dollars on the bar, and wished good health on Barney until he returned.

"I don't suppose you could pay for my drink too?" José asked.

"No way, José," Moses replied, and patted himself on the back for his cleverness.

◊ ◊ ◊

Moses sidled up to a payphone outside the tavern, with the intention of contacting his sort-of attorney before leaving the country. Without knowing how phone systems worked south of the border, or if phones existed in the same capacity, he thought it might be their last chance to catch up.

"Where are you?" asked Howie Spirit, Esq.

"I'm about to cross into Mexico," Moses replied. "I avoided being served by Cleopatra's lawyer."

The update surprised Howie, who'd heard the opposite from Judge Judi's chambers a short while earlier. According to the judge's clerk, Cleopatra's attorney properly served Moses and then notified all relevant border security of his plans.

"She's a liar!" Moses shouted into the phone. "She didn't serve me!"

Unfortunately, she said she did, Howie explained.

"The envelope didn't touch me!" Moses argued. "I ducked underneath her throw!"

Too bad Moses failed to previously ask his sort-of attorney for clarification as to what constituted proper service under the law. For a meager fee, he could've avoided the mess he now found himself in. As explained by Howie:

"Direct contact with the document doesn't matter, as long as the document comes within close vicinity of your body."

"Oh," said Moses.

"How close did the document get?"

"An inch?" Moses supposed. "Maybe two?"

"I'd say that qualifies," the attorney advised, "and I'd say that you're fucked, legally speaking."

"What am I supposed to do now?"

"You can't go back to your house, so just move on to Mexico. The U.S. border security doesn't check cars *leaving* the country, only cars *coming in*."

Moses' mind raced faster than his blood pressure. He needed another drink, preferably of the alcoholic variety. Good thing he still stood next to an establishment offering just that.

◊ ◊ ◊

Moses sidled up to the same barstool he occupied a short while prior, placing his briefcase next to his stool in the same arm's length manner as before, and ordering the same beverage previously consumed twice over.

"One more." Moses motioned to Barney, unnecessarily, with Barney already sliding a glass of whiskey across the bar.

"You're back," José greeted.

"You're still here?" Moses kicked his briefcase between his legs, carefully guarding the attaché by extending his pointy knees once again.

"I thought you left." José felt especially friendly after knocking back another glass of tequila in Moses' absence. "What happened?"

Moses found no reason to explain himself to the Mexican. And even if he found a reason to explain himself, he refused to give the Mexican such satisfaction. Besides, something bothered him about this José fellow: though José called himself a Mexican, he sure didn't look like one.

"Why aren't you dressed like a Mexican?" Moses pointed to José's lack of a serape,[23] or a sombrero at the very least.[24] Instead, José wore a simple button-down shirt, similar to the garments made in the United States. If other Mexicans dressed the same way, how would Moses tell a foreigner from a national once he crossed the border?

"These are my normal clothes." José noted the similarity between their outfits, the two men both with shirts on their backs and shoes on their feet.

Moses heard enough. How dare the Mexican suggest that they had anything in common. They were as different as whiskey and tequila.

"Maybe you can give me some tips about living here in the United States?" José sipped his tequila. "I may be staying for a while."

"Drink whiskey" was Moses' only advice.

With that, Moses stood from his barstool, slapped a few dollars on the bar, and once again wished good health on Barney until he returned. He'd be proceeding directly to the border.

◊ ◊ ◊

Several vehicles formed a line at the Mexican border when Moses pulled up. That was several more vehicles than he expected to see. They all traveled in the wrong direction. Why would so many Americans drive south? Even for a short vacation, why risk one's life for warm weather and cheap medication?

Moses told himself not to worry as he inched closer to the border. Yet his palms perspired all over the steering wheel. There was no telling what lay to the south, besides an assortment of criminals (perhaps a few good people too, though probably not many). He wished he took one more drink at the bar to calm his nerves, but it was too late to turn back once another car pulled up behind his Chevy.

Moses swiveled his head in every direction in search of someone to turn to if anything went awry. But the American patrol officers guarded the other direction, paying no attention to the cars traveling south. He supposed it made sense for them to focus in this manner, though it would've been comforting to see a few friendly faces.

Never having ventured across the border, Moses examined the other cars for some hint of the exit procedure. To no surprise, Mexico's guardians gave no effort besides reading passports and asking a few questions. And why should they give more effort? The real concern involved their own citizens traveling in the other direction.

As Moses pulled closer to the border, an overhead sign reminded all travelers to have their passports ready. Glad to have remembered the document, he rolled down his window and held out his traveling papers as a Mexican border patrolman waved him forward for his turn to proceed.

"Hello," the patrolman greeted with a friendly smile. "Welcome to Mexico."

Moses scratched his head: he found the greeting confusing. Not that he misunderstood the patrolman. He just expected to be greeted with "Hola, bienvenido a Mexico." Not that he understood the Mexican language to begin with.

"How long are you visiting?" the patrolman asked as he perused the passport, holding the photograph next to Moses' face to confirm at least that part to be accurate. "Less than a week?"

Moses nodded. He expected to spend less than 24 hours in the godforsaken country. If his new employer expected him to be there any longer, he'd turn his car right back around and drive home; he assured the patrolman of that much.

"Are you traveling with any pork, beef or poultry products?"

Moses shook his head, and wondered why the patrolman would restrict the entry of meat, especially with the juicy red T-bones in America being so delectable.

"Are you traveling with any fruits, vegetables or dairy products?"

Moses shook his head, and wondered why food remained the focus of the patrolman's attention. Shouldn't Mexico be more worried about drugs and weapons? Then again, the country contained so many drugs and weapons already that a few more probably made no difference. Besides, the criminals traveled in the opposite direction.

"Last question," the patrolman claimed. "Are you traveling with any seeds, seedlings or fresh plants?"

Moses froze. Seeds happened to be precisely what the attorney instructed him to carry across the border. Surely his employer must have known what the border patrol would be looking for. He wondered what would happen if the Mexicans found the illegal contraband in his vehicle.

"Why does that matter?"

Suspicious beads of sweat dripped from Moses' forehead. Partly from the hot Mexican sun directly ahead, partly from the anxiety of his crime—he poorly concealed his guilt by both tone and action. If only he kept his mouth shut and shook his head, the patrolman would've waived him through to the south. But his question, combined with the sweat trickling down his nervous face, gave enough cause to pique the patrolman's interest.

"Do I need to search your car?" the patrolman asked.

Moses shook his head, indicating that he did *not* have any seeds, seedlings or fresh plants in the vehicle, or any other illegal substances for that matter; and therefore, *no* reason existed for the patrolman to waste his time searching for any of those items.

The patrolman stepped out of his booth and flipped on his flashlight, shining the light into Moses' eyes before slowly pacing around the car. At each door, he pressed his cheek against the window and illuminated the Chevy's interior, paying just as much attention to the contents as to Moses' hands nervously squeezing the wheel. Only once he circled the car completely did he stop back at the driver's side door with one last instruction.

"Enjoy Mexico." The patrolman clicked off his flashlight and waved Moses through.

Moses slowly pulled past the gate, carefully concealing his excitement until out of view. It was so damn easy to trick a Mexican, who would've caught Moses in a lie had he paid any attention to the briefcase tucked into the back seat of his Chevy. Custom-made, gold-monogrammed, patent leather—his fancy luggage was tough to miss.

What a dummy!

Speaking of such, Moses turned his head toward the back seat in search of his briefcase. It must be in his trunk, he supposed, though he needn't retrieve it until he arrived in Los Aburridos.

◊ ◊ ◊

Back on the northern side of the border, José sat at the bar, finishing off the last drops of his third glass of tequila, more than ready to end this chapter of his life. His wife's pregnancy had been especially tough on him. Sure, he wasn't carrying the child, so he didn't have to deal with the aches and pains and cramps and nausea; and he didn't have to deal with the hormonal imbalances or mood swings either; but he had to deal with María while she dealt with those issues, and she was quite a handful. He eagerly awaited the baby's birth so his life could get back to normal.

María felt equally eager to end this chapter of her life, though her reasoning differed from that of her husband. Not a fan of the spirits, she felt no desire to linger at Dullsville's finest tavern any longer than necessary.

"Let's go," ordered María just a moment after setting foot in the tavern.

Barney the bartender appeared in no such hurry. Fortunately, María found enough cash to pay José's tab.

"Where are we going?" José asked.

"11 Main Street," said María of the whitewashed, two-story ranch where they'd be living for the time being.

José shrugged and stood up, politely thanking Barney for the tequila before noticing the fancy briefcase tucked underneath the empty barstool next to his. Without thinking, per usual, he bent down and grabbed the briefcase as if he owned it.

"Where did you get that?" María asked.

"I guess the last guy forgot it." José shrugged. "He probably thinks it's in the trunk of his car, or something dumb like that."

NINE

California

María La Virgen awoke early on her first morning in the United States, though not because a gallinaceous bird crowed through her window, nor because an alarm buzzed next to her bed, nor even because she had so much to do. Rather, she intended to discover what her new life had in store. With her husband by her side and her baby on the way, her American dream had come true, at least temporarily. Not one to complain about the time, she'd bask in the dream for as long as she could.

As for her darling husband, José lay still on the other side of the bed, sleeping off the previous evening's consumption. María let him be, knowing what little chance of success existed even if she tried waking him. Besides, he had nothing to do besides drink more tequila, so a few extra minutes in bed probably benefited his health, she reasoned.

The young couple found themselves in a holding pattern. As explained to María by her sort-of attorney, she needed to sit tight and wait for further instructions. Her latest employer, still unnamed, would have a hot new product ready for sale in the near future. Once ready for sale, she'd coordinate its distribution from 11 Main Street. That was the plan, or at least what she knew of it.

With little to occupy her time, the energy pills María popped on a daily basis became unnecessary. Yet she took an energy pill anyway, because she'd become so accustomed to the buzz that she doubted she could get by without it.

"The doctor said to stop taking those pills," José somehow muttered from his sleep, apparently awake enough to monitor his wife's behavior.

"Shut up," María replied, and threw her pillow across the bed.

Moving through the house, María surveyed the living space. Clearly, it had been a while since a woman lived on the premises. Her husband could enjoy the clothes in the closet, but she'd need to shop for herself. Although baby clothes were the first priority, even if a few months remained until her due date.

The kitchen appeared acceptable, tidy enough, with gas flowing from the stove and water running through the pipes. How much easier it would be to cook breakfast, she thought. Plus, fresh bacon and eggs chilled in the refrigerator. Not to mention the liquor supply in the cupboard next to the sink; at least her husband would be pleased.

The living room felt cozy, albeit a complete mess—as if the previous resident found no chance to clean up. María didn't mind tidying the space: tossing a used cigarette in the garbage, placing an empty glass in the dishwasher, relocating an open atlas onto the bookshelf in the den, tucking a movie into the entertainment center. Pregnant or otherwise, she made no excuse for living in filth.

As she cleaned the room, María turned on the television to catch up on the most breaking news in her new country. Perhaps broken, the knob remained stuck on Channel 1. At least Channel 1 gave her exactly what she sought: two news anchors with hair as full as their heads.

The news anchors greeted the country just as María tuned in, but wasted no time with pleasantries after a quick, "Hello America." There had been no shortage of scandals during the President's first term in office, and they remained shocked, months after the election, that the American public would support such an immoral man.

"Doesn't the American public remember the President's illegal real estate deal?" the anchorman asked.

"Or what about the sexual harassment lawsuit filed against him?" the anchorwoman wondered.

In no mood for negativity, María shut off the television. She'd finished cleaning anyway. With the house in decent order, she stepped outside to the porch and attempted to inhale her first fresh breath of the day.

But all she smelled were the *titan arums*!

María didn't know the name of the plants, of course, just that they required immediate removal—a perfect job for her husband, the carpenter—lest her unborn child be poisoned by the odor. Though for the time being, she pinched her nose as she examined her new property: circling the house, crisscrossing the yard, glancing up and down the street. When her energy dwindled, she took a seat on a swing hanging from the front porch.

Leaning back in the swing, María took a moment to appreciate the neighborhood. A sense of calmness surrounded her house. Main Street stretched through just the type of community she'd always imagined north of the border, where nothing extraordinary occurred.

The neighbors seemed nice. First, a man wearing a red windsuit jogged past with a welcoming smile accompanied by a gentle wave. Then, a young child sprinted up the street, without a smile on his face, though María recognized his solemn expression to be more due to his intense focus than a bad attitude. There were a few other random men and woman in all sorts of moods, scurrying to and from wherever, not to mention the paperboy who hurled her a copy of the *Dullsville Times* as he bicycled by.

What interesting neighbors, María thought. She hoped to meet each of them.

The *Dullsville Times* arrived hot off the press. The day's top story alerted the community of a local man who stole from his employer and then disappeared without a trace. Apparently, he only stole a small supply of avocado seeds, so the employer put little effort into finding the thief besides supplying a number to call with any information. María knew nothing of the man or the company, so she flipped the page.

In national news, the President of the United States spent the previous afternoon kissing babies at a hospital in Washington, D.C., to celebrate the four-year anniversary of the Family and Medical Leave Act (or "FMLA"). Under the FMLA, each of the working mothers of those newborns would receive twelve weeks of unpaid leave as they cared for their new children.

María felt relieved to again confirm the President to be such a family man. Mexico first enacted a similar measure about eight decades prior, but at least the United States wasn't too far behind.[25] Regardless, she remained months away from her delivery date, so she simply filed away the information for later use.

◊ ◊ ◊

Gabby Blabber had barely taken her first sip of morning coffee when she heard the door to Moses' house crack open. On a normal day, the noise may have gone unnoticed, since Moses usually stepped outside around that time. But as anyone who read that morning's edition of the *Dullsville Times* would know, this wasn't a normal day of any sort. Scurrying to the window as fast as her creaky knees carried her, she threw open the curtains to find, not Moses, but instead a tan young woman with shimmering black hair.

Gabby had never seen the woman. She'd remember if she had. She never forgot a face, or a name for that matter. Rather than opening the window and learning that new name, she watched in silence, examining the woman's movements for clues.

Was the woman Moses' new lover?

No, that made little sense: Gabby's working theory of Moses' disappearance involved a scandalous tryst with Richard Dickens. Then again, perhaps her working theory required a tweak or two, since Richard Dickens appeared to be jogging down the street at that precise moment, smiling and waving to the new woman, wishing her a pleasant morning.

"What the heck is going on?" Gabby wondered. "Why is Richard Dickens interested in *her* now?"

Keeping a low profile in the window after adjusting the curtains so only a sliver of viewing space remained, Gabby crouched back and observed the woman next door with a keen eye for detail. As she watched, the woman crisscrossed Moses' front yard and peered around the house, paying close attention to the bed of *titan arums* lining the front yard. Clearly, Moses' unusual plants caught her attention. How could they not? The flowers smelled horrendous from up close! Though from behind Gabby's closed window, the *titan arums* looked beautiful, she supposed.

The new woman appeared to be either pregnant or fat. Or, a third option involved a hearty breakfast. Every possibility warranted consideration, because any less could lead to an inaccurate conclusion. With most of the woman's added weight concentrated just above her waist, it seemed that the third option, breakfast, stood out as the most likely source of her lumpy figure. Moses kept his refrigerator stocked with bacon and eggs, after all, which Gabby knew after scouring his house the previous day.

The evidence was adding up.

Gabby thought to call Cleopatra Spiter and Thutmond Mose III to report her findings, but she remained unsure what to make of the situation. Better to hold off until she understood the extent of the crime. For now, the only report went in her trusty journal.

But before Gabby could log one clue in her journal, another clue would be revealed, even more interesting than the last. The woman sitting on Moses' porch lifted up her skirt and screamed:

"José!"

And now a naked man ran out of the front door!

"What the heck is going on?" Gabby wondered for the second time in one morning.

The good news: if ever someone could solve the mystery, she was already on the case.

◊ ◊ ◊

José leapt out of bed at the shriek of María's voice, and raced through the house just a moment later, in such a rush that he overlooked a key aspect of his outfit. Fortunately, María pointed out the discrepancy once he found her on the front porch, sitting on a swing near a cluster of strange flowers.

"Put on some pants!" María said. "We need to get to the hospital, so I can deliver the baby."

Understandably confused, José noted that his wife remained a few months short of her due date. Although he realized that her precise due date could vary, he expected the gestation period to take a bit longer, even if he failed to understand what the word "gestation" meant in this context.

María had no time for a vocabulary lesson. She lifted her skirt to reveal four tiny fingers dangling from between her legs.

Well that proved enough of an explanation for her husband, who responded by rolling his eyes back into his head and fainting to the ground. Though a slap in the face from his wife got him back on his feet.

"Hurry up!" María said. "And get me a change of clothes!"

Without hesitation, José dashed back into the house and found a clean pair of trousers in the closet. Then, he ruffled through a few of María's clothes until he found her a dress. Besides that, one item remained missing. He searched in the obvious places where tequila might hide, but he only found a bottle of whiskey in the kitchen.

"Let's go!" María shouted from the car, and laid on the horn.

José shrugged, and grabbed the bottle. But he still needed to conceal the spirit, preferably in something easy to carry around for the rest of the day, perhaps with room for María's dress too.

That's when José remembered the fancy new briefcase nestled next to the front door, still untouched from a day earlier, when he found it just after the angry gentleman at the bar lost it in front of his eyes. Had he examined the contents of the briefcase, he would've found six dozen seeds, labeled as avocados, and two computer hard drives loaded with a girth of information.

"What's taking so long?" María shouted from the car, her hand glued to the horn.

With no time to lose, José stepped outside and dumped the contents of the briefcase into an imported, nutrient-rich soil hidden behind the smelly *titan arums* lining the front of the house. He didn't know the name of the smelly plants, of course, nor that the soil was so special, not that either of those tidbits would've caused him to act one way or another.

◊ ◊ ◊

Gabby didn't see everything next door. She did her best to take notes in her journal while watching her neighbors through the window, but she found it difficult to do two tasks at once, especially with her favorite soap opera playing in the background. She saw the naked man fall to the ground, only to be slapped by the fat woman, followed by both dashing off in a bizarre vehicle, which she failed to positively identify as either a car or a truck.

"What the heck is going on?" wondered the curious neighbor.

◊ ◊ ◊

Understaffed and overused, Dullsville General Hospital never stopped accepting patients. Had María not been ready to burst, it would've been a lengthy wait to see a doctor. But the hospital did its best to accommodate with María yelling like a lunatic as José carried her through the door. Between alternating gasps, she attempted "A baby is coming out of me!"; though her words sounded like "Blah blah blah!"; which her husband then translated to the nurse as:

"She's pregnant."

"Come with me," the nurse instructed as she led the pair through a few hallways to a cozy room in the maternity ward, where she helped María onto a bed. After filling out a few forms, the nurse explained that the doctor would be there shortly. José asked for context on "shortly," but the nurse declined to provide any further details besides "when the doctor is ready."

"Oh, this again," José said. "Different country, same shit."

María lay back on the bed and clutched her stomach, breathing heavily in short bursts as she focused her eyes on the ceiling. She attempted to speak, but made no sense; not that José listened to his wife even when she spoke clearly.

"Just hold in the baby until the doctor gets here," José recommended.

A lengthy wait followed—then finally, a knock on the door.

"Finally!" José's patience ran thinner with each passing moment. He opened the door expecting a doctor, but only found the nurse, who greeted the pair with a smile on her face. A problem arose with María's insurance through her employer, Temporary Staffing Agency.

"What's the problem with her insurance?" José wondered, with María too out of sorts to ask the question.

"It doesn't exist," replied the nurse.

José suspected as much, and should've known better.

"I also see that you're not an American citizen?"

That was correct, María noted, although she possessed a valid temporary worker's visa, which she explained by screaming:

"Work visa!"

Regrettably, under the hospital's policy, uninsured immigrants could only be treated in emergency situations. As long as she appeared stable, policy required the nurse to turn her away.

"Does she look stable to you?" José asked, rather unstably.

"Let's see how far along you are." The nurse lifted María's skirt to reveal the palm of a tiny hand, with four fingers and a thumb, waving from between her legs.

José peeked under María's skirt before fainting to the floor.

"What an aggressive baby," observed the nurse. "You haven't been taking any drugs during your pregnancy, have you?"

While María denied any wrongdoing, José regained his bearings and picked himself up from the floor. As he stood up, he switched places with the doctor, who insisted that José excuse himself to the waiting room unless he showed some type of identification.

"I guess I'll wait outside then," José agreed. He needed a swig of the whiskey in his briefcase anyway, after what he just saw.

"Let's see how far along you are," the doctor said, and lifted María's skirt to reveal not only a tiny hand, but also the majority of a forearm. Before he had a chance to say "Yikes!", a second hand emerged. With no more time to wait, he instructed María to use all of her remaining energy to push.

Unfortunately, María had burned through most of the energy in her body by that point, so she asked the doctor to hand her the bottle of energy pills from her purse.

"Energy pills?" The doctor paused and crinkled his brow. "Have you been taking energy pills during the entire pregnancy?"

Before María could respond, her baby's two tiny hands clutched her inner thighs and began to tug. First came a bald head, with bright golden eyes open wider than the toothless grin that came next. Then the neck pulled through, up to the shoulders, enabling those eyes to tilt toward the doctor before turning back to María. Distracted, not to mention covered in fluid, the child struggled to retain the grip on María's thighs as most of an upper torso emerged, so the doctor grabbed the child's hands, slowly pulling the newborn into the world. Once free, the child fell backward between María's legs, for the first time revealing himself to be a boy. The only remaining connection between the boy and María was an umbilical cord, which the newborn then grasped with his hands and chewed in half.

"Wow," the doctor said, and wrapped the babe in cloth. "This kid is special."

"Is it normal for the baby to chew through the umbilical cord?" María asked, although reasonably certain that she already knew the answer.

"You shouldn't have been taking those energy pills," the doctor advised. "I'm surprised nobody told you that."

María shrugged. She had no idea the pills could cause such a strange side effect.

"All drugs cause side effects," the doctor said, "that's why people take them."

The boy seemed fine though, with normal vitals and a healthy smile, so the doctor simply smacked the baby's behind and congratulated the new mother, before letting José back in the room and congratulating him as well.

Taking note of José's brown eyes, and María's blue eyes, the doctor found it unusual for the baby's eyes to be gold. Though the birth hadn't been normal in any sense, so he raised no concern with the parents. Instead, he wished them well and moved on to his next patient.

After that, the nurse returned to discharge María and her baby so that the hospital could focus on the insured patients. Once María filled out the necessary form for a birth certificate, she'd be free to leave.

"What will you name the boy?" the nurse asked.

María had yet to decide on a name. Until that day, she thought another few months remained before she needed to decide on the arbitrary moniker.

Regardless, the nurse's paperwork contained one detail much more important than the baby's name. The bottom of the form included a finely printed note about the baby's status as a natural born citizen of the United States of America.

"*This* is an important detail," María realized as she filled out the paperwork.

Oh, and as for the arbitrary moniker, she decided to name the baby:

"Jesús," which meant, "to deliver."

Because, why not? The name seemed appropriate, since her son essentially delivered himself. Perhaps he'd even make other deliveries in the future, though that may have been a bit presumptuous with the boy still only a few minutes old.

TEN

Mexico

The runaway botanist, Moses Staffman, had no idea what to expect in Mexico. His only knowledge of the country came from his most terrifying nightmares. Needless to say, the doors of his Chevy remained locked at all times as he made his way from the border to the coastline.

Only once did Moses dare leave the safety of his car. How else could he phone Dullsville's finest tavern to find out if anyone turned in a custom-made, gold-monogrammed, patent leather briefcase? To no surprise, Barney the bartender failed to locate any lost luggage—let alone one matching his lengthy description—and suggested that Moses should've kept a better eye on the fancy briefcase if it was as valuable as he claimed.

"Duh," Moses agreed.

It didn't take a genius to figure out what happened back in Dullsville: that tequila-sipping Mexican was a thief, just as Moses suspected as they sat at the bar.

Without the briefcase, Moses found himself in a $1,000,000 bind, with no guarantee of payment once he reached the secret island. But he was a smart man, right? He was competent, at least. Surely, he could solve his present dilemma.

Quite the dilemma though.

Yet the solution seemed obvious: he could bioengineer more *Zerojuana* from scratch.[26] After all, he invented the original

Zerojuana plant with nothing more than a few cannabis relatives and his deep understanding of molecular biology. *Zerojuana* took almost ten years to perfect the first time around—by no means a simple task—but he didn't need specialized seeds for the original strain. He even saved his R&D data on a hard drive. If he followed his own directions, he could produce another strain of *Zerojuana* in no time at all.

Unfortunately, there remained one problem: the hard drive sat in his missing briefcase, next to the *Zerojuana* seeds.

"Drat," Moses mumbled.

But wait—he'd downloaded a backup copy on a separate hard drive. Even without the original data, he could use the backup data. Now where did he place the backup data again?

"Drat," Moses mumbled again. Perhaps the backup data should've been kept separately from the initial data, though the benefit of hindsight made that conclusion easier now than before he crossed the border.

Distraught, but not defeated, Moses searched his pockets for whatever he could find. With merely a single *Zerojuana* seed, he could produce an entire stock, which he could then crossbreed with jalapeño plants to create the *Cannapeñis* for which his new employer would pay a seven-figure price. Alas, his pockets held nothing of value besides $20.

As an obvious target with $20 in his pocket, Moses parked his Chevy at the only dock in Los Aburridos—the designated meeting point—and kept his doors locked and his windows rolled up as he awaited further instructions. He had no intention of leaving the comfort of his car. Besides, even if he stepped outside of his Chevy, it's not as if he understood the Mexican language to begin with, so what would be the point?

Fortunately, Moses' wait turned out to be relatively short. Before he knew it, he spotted a familiar face, covered in a white beard, belonging to a man tapping on the window of his Chevy, speaking a tongue he understood, reeking of some combination of cannabis and pepper juice.

"Sorry I'm late," Guy greeted.

Moses just felt relieved that the agonizing wait had ended.

"Are you hungry?" Guy pointed to the marketplace across the street. "We have a lengthy voyage ahead."

Moses felt no desire to spend any longer in Mexico than necessary, which he thought he already made clear. But Guy's stomach growled, and he held the keys to the yacht which would bring them to their final destination, so the question turned out to be more rhetorical than earnest. Besides, it made no sense to leave the country before their legal counselor arrived, since he'd be joining their voyage to the island.

With no say in the matter, Moses shrugged and followed his new boss to a fruit stand barely monitored by a sunburnt hombre wearing a sombrero and leaning back in his chair as carelessly as the botanist dared to imagine possible. The hombre must have been an acquaintance, because he greeted the hungry Guy with a friendly "Hola" the moment the two men made eye contact.

At the fruit stand, Moses observed a lazy attempt by a local to make a few pesos, presumably selling whatever produce he found by the side of the road. The fruits and veggies on display in crates lining the front of the stand weren't half as bad as Moses expected; not that they were half as good as he expected either (though the math said otherwise).

Moses pitied the sunburnt man, though his pity only went so far, since nobody could be forced to wear a sombrero, or to bask in the sun for that matter. If only the hombre put in the smallest effort, he could distinguish himself from the rest of the pathetic stands in the marketplace; but instead, he leaned back in his chair and took in the sun, while his produce suffered the same fate as his darkened skin.

"Mango?" Guy held out the juiciest piece of fruit he found.

"I can wait," Moses insisted. He spoke of his desire to eat, not his desire to leave the country, thankful for the bowl of pretzels he gobbled down at the bar before crossing the border.

The most interesting items sold at the marketplace, in Moses' opinion, fell outside the realm of edibles. Directly across the aisle from the fruit vendor stood a merchant of bootleg movies. One of the movies, *Bulletproof*, starred none other than Adam Sandler. Back in the United States, a licensed copy of the same movie likely sat on his doorstep thanks to his membership in the esteemed Adam Sandler Fan Club.

"Well, I'll be!" Moses picked up the movie and rejoiced for

the first time since crossing the border. "I guess some Mexicans do have good taste."

Too bad some trickster dubbed the movie in the Mexican language for the local audience. Even if Moses understood the vernacular, much of Adam Sandler's comedy relied on his voice inflection.

"Just another thing the U.S. does better." Moses tossed the movie back onto the vendor's table. "I guess I'll wait until I'm back home to watch this one."

Guy noted the time on his nonexistent watch. His attorney ran late. With a lengthy voyage ahead, he hoped to be floating on the ocean before the setting sun drew out the waves. Plus, the botanist could begin growing *Cannapeñis* the moment they returned to the island.

"As long as we're waiting," Guy said, "can I see these *Zerojuana* seeds?"

"About that—" Moses gently scratched the back of his neck. "—there was a minor setback."

Not a major setback, Moses assured, merely a minor setback. He'd have to create *Zerojuana* from scratch once they reached the island, which would be easy, considering he invented the process to begin with. He simply needed a fertile landscape along with a bit of patience on the part of his employer.

"I just need some time," Moses said.

"How much time?" Guy wondered.

Moses hemmed and hawed, and hemmed some more, mumbling of the variables factoring into the equation. The exact climate would affect growth, for example, not to mention the condition of the soil. If he needed to mineralize the island, that would also extend the timeline. If forced to estimate, he supposed that five to ten years served as a suitable assumption.

"The sooner I get my $1,000,000," Moses reminded, implying that the lower end of the timeline remained attainable, "the sooner I can get started."

"We don't have that long!" Guy had his reasons for thinking as much. "With California now leading the way on cannabis reform, the rest of the United States will follow in no time at all. Even the President has puffed dope."

"But he didn't inhale," Moses pointed out.

Guy meant that they had no time to lose if they wished to be among the first to market once nationwide legalization measures took effect in the U.S. Now that California broke the first barrier, the legalization of cannabis appeared imminent, and would be arriving in a hurry.

"We probably have a year or two to prepare," Guy guessed. "Four years at most, because the President is sure to address the issue before the end of his term."

"Then we better get started," Moses said, "which I'll do as soon as I'm paid."

This created quite a standoff, and not only because both men stood on their feet. Neither man possessed any patience, and since each man was as stubborn as he was avaricious, the result came as no surprise.

"I'm not paying until I have a product to sell," Guy said.

"I'm not working until I get paid," Moses said.

"Hi Guys!" greeted Howie Spirit, Esq., who just arrived.

"I mean, hi Guy and Moses," Howie corrected himself. "Are you ready to go?"

◊ ◊ ◊

Howie could barely contain his excitement as he pulled south across the border from the United States into Mexico. Although honest when he told the border patrolman that his visit would be short, he failed to explain what he meant by "short." In truth, he planned to leave almost as soon as he arrived. An attorney for longer than he cared to recall, decades had passed since he last worried about the omission of relevant information from his statements.

The attorney's retirement was so close he could smell it; it smelled like a buffalo-style chicken wrap, with a side of French fries and ketchup, from Pepe's Fried Chicken, the finest fried chicken joint in Dullsville.[27] And he meant that as a positive statement, because he enjoyed nothing more than precisely that meal. Coincidentally, he'd stopped at Pepe's Fried Chicken and purchased a buffalo-style chicken wrap, with a side of crispy fries and more ketchup packets than he needed. The food sat in a plastic bag on his passenger seat, so the pleasant smell may have been more due to the wrap itself than the excitement he felt as he crept closer to retirement, but by that point all of his emotions blended together.

The attorney's plan required everyone to be on the same page. He knew his client as well as anyone, and as long as all went according to plan, he'd be left to himself to enjoy island life to its fullest extent. Guy felt no desire to spend his free time with Howie, any more than the other way around. Heck, Howie remained shocked that Guy agreed to share the island to begin with. Perhaps all his doobies resulted in a positive effect after all.

As for the island life, Howie's mind swirled with visions of blue waves crashing onto white sandy beaches and green palm trees swaying in the salty ocean breeze—an image based more on movies than anything else, since he'd never seen the island. Regardless, he'd see the island soon enough. A boat floated at the edge of Los Aburridos, ready to leave as soon as he arrived. (His client preferred for the boat to be called a "yacht," but "boat" held a broad definition, legally speaking.)

As expected, Howie found Moses' car parked next to the coast. But the Chevy sat idle under the sun, seemingly abandoned, leaving the attorney to wonder whether he missed the boat. Fortunately, as soon as he glanced across the street, he spotted both the golden-eyed businessman and the green-thumbed botanist in the midst of a heated discussion at the local marketplace.

"Hi Guys!" greeted the attorney, before his legal mind realized that the proper noun in his introduction rendered its plural status improper.

"I mean, hi Guy and Moses," he corrected. "Are you ready to go?"

◊ ◊ ◊

To answer the pending question, both Guy and Moses were ready to go when Howie arrived. But they weren't ready to go where Howie hoped. They were ready to go their separate ways, because each man refused to give in to the other's demands.

"I'm not paying until I have a product to sell," Guy said.

"I'm not working until I get paid," Moses said.

It didn't take a brilliant attorney to understand both arguments—a good thing, because the only person available to negotiate the dispute was Howie Spirit, Esq.

Howie was no stranger to controversy. He'd resolved far more complex disputes over the course of his lengthy career. To him, it seemed obvious that everyone's best interests favored a compromise. Yet neither Guy nor Moses had their common interest as the utmost concern.

"I've witnessed this kind of stubbornness from donkeys," Howie said, "but not from men."

The polite insult slipped through without effect. Not only did neither Guy nor Moses understand the attorney's convoluted metaphor, neither man intended to negotiate. Of the two men, Guy showed his resistance in a more animated display, turning his back to Moses and walking away.

"Wait!" Howie shouted to his client, who responded not by turning around, but by raising the longest finger on his hand as he continued across the street toward the dock.

"He's being such a dick," Howie told Moses, without attributing legal significance to his use of the term.

Moses fully understood the root of the problem: a side effect of *Cannapeñis* caused Guy's unfortunate personality trait. He began to convey the problem to Guy back when he caught his first whiff of *Cannapeñis*, but he held back his advice at the time, which he now believed wise in view of the events unfolding.

"I can fix *Cannapeñis*," Moses said, "but if I'm not paid, then I'll let him keep acting like a dick."

"But if you fix the product," Howie pointed out, "then he'll stop acting like a dick, and we can move the story along."

What a conundrum.

"I'm going home," Moses decided. He intended to resume his old life since his $1,000,000 island adventure failed to work out as planned. He'd accept his ex-wife's court order to remain in the United States. After this awful experience, he felt no desire to leave again anyway. Surely, he could explain the situation to his superiors at Plant Inc, if they even noticed his sudden absence in the first place.

"They've noticed," Howie confirmed. He spoke to Judge Judi's clerk before crossing the border. Apparently, someone at Plant Inc believed that Moses stole an entire supply of avocado seeds.

"So what?" Moses asked.

That was a good question, according to the attorney. Legally speaking, the theft of trade secrets within the United States earned offenders up to ten years in prison. If Moses returned to Dullsville, he'd be arrested and prosecuted to the fullest extent of the law. (He'd also find a Mexican family living at his house, but that went without saying, so the attorney avoided the topic.)

"Then what am I supposed to do?"

To no surprise, Howie had a plan. Although he intended to retire momentarily, he'd make a few calls and find someone in the U.S. to sort out the botanist's legal issues. In the meantime, he'd also talk to the stubborn Guy about payment of the $1,000,000. Until then, he recommended that Moses keep a low profile in Mexico.

"Where am I supposed to go?"

For the first time since crossing the border, luck was on Moses' side. A colorful, two-story adobe home at 11 Calle Principal just became vacant. Howie neglected to mention why the previous residents left, or where they went, and simply handed over the key.

"11 Calle Principal?" Moses wondered what the heck that meant.

◊ ◊ ◊

Howie sprinted to get to the dock before he missed the boat—a task easier said than done for someone who detested physical exertion. At the edge of the coast, he found Guy preparing to disappear into the vast Pacific Ocean: not preparing his yacht, but preparing himself by lighting a pepper-infused doobie ahead of the windy voyage.

Howie begged his client to reconsider. Why throw away all the work up to that point? There had to be an acceptable compromise. Perhaps he could pay half of the botanist's money up front? It's not as if he lacked the funds.

"We don't have ten years to wait for Moses to develop the product," Guy said. "We'll move forward with *Cannapeñis* in its current form. Is our hot young saleswoman in place?"

"María is ready to distribute," Howie replied. "Did you know she's pregnant?"

"It's not mine" was Guy's quick answer.

"She said her husband is the father," Howie clarified. "I believe his name is José."

"Good," Guy agreed, and nodded.

Howie knew when to refrain from a follow-up question, so he returned to the botanist. Step Two of TH Corp's business plan, according to what he understood, was specifically titled "2. Perfect the Product."

"You can't distribute the product if it's not perfected." Howie threw up his arms. "It'll turn people into dicks, like it's doing to you."

Guy disagreed with the first part. He also disagreed with the second part. In his opinion, 1997 seemed like the perfect time to begin the distribution of *Cannapeñis* in the United States. In other words:

"Americans love being dicks. Haven't you been watching the news?"

Howie sighed, and buried his face in his hands. But he didn't stay upset for long, because after a moment of self-pity, he realized something important: if he wouldn't be puffing any *Cannapeñis* himself, then what did he care?

"Fine," Howie agreed. "Let's just get to the island."

Well that's where Howie received some unfortunate news. Guy felt hesitant to share his island to begin with, and now he had an excuse to keep his attorney on the mainland. Without Moses involved, distribution became of the utmost importance. Someone needed to stay in California to guide the young woman from Los Aburridos through the legal hurdles involved with the distribution process. Only once she sold the product would Howie be granted access to the island to begin his retirement.

"Remember," Guy reminded, "our contract says you can't retire until TH Corp starts selling *Cannapeñis*."

"You're such a dick," Howie replied, and now understood why.

Guy missed that last part, because his yacht's engine fired up just as the attorney attempted the insult. So rather than reply, he throttled onward out to sea.

◊ ◊ ◊

Back at the colorful, two-story adobe home at 11 Calle Principal, Moses' arrival gained immediate attention. His new neighbor peered out of the window next door as soon as his Chevy pulled into the driveway. She even smiled and waved as he stepped out of the car.

Moses had no idea what the woman could be so happy about. He assumed her bliss to be rooted in ignorance. At least she couldn't harass him like Gabby Blabber: even if she slid open her window and opened her mouth, he failed to grasp the Mexican language to begin with. Perhaps Mexico came with an upside after all.

Moses soon found out that his new neighbor differed from Gabby Blabber for another reason: Gabby never left the comfort of her own home to harass Moses; whereas this Mexican woman had the gall to open her front door, walk across her yard, and greet Moses with an open palm ready to be shaken.

"Hola," the woman greeted. "Soy Vecína."

"Ugh," Moses groaned, and wondered what the heck she said.

"¿Donde esta María?" the woman asked.

"Yeah, María," Moses said with a shrug as he unlocked the door. The woman saw his key, so she simply smiled as he shut the door in her face.

"When will this nightmare end?" Moses wanted to know.

Unfortunately, the nightmare would get worse.

Without warning, a Chihuahua named Perrita scrambled into the front room at the sound of the door slamming shut. Though without a tag, the canine's name remained a mystery to Moses. The only clue provided by the Chihuahua was:

"Bark."

Moses preferred plants, of course. To him, animal life slotted in at a distant second place. And even if he could tolerate animals, a dog—a damn Chihuahua, as a matter of fact—would've been lowest on his list. But the dog was far from the worst part of his new residence, he'd discover as soon as he found the liquor supply—or the lack of a liquor supply, in his words—because:

"There's nothing but tequila!"

The liquor supply consisted of only a single bottle of tequila, more specifically.

"How the heck am I supposed to survive?"

Luckily, he needn't survive for long: a licensed attorney promised to remedy his situation with the utmost haste, and a professional of that stature wouldn't tell a lie.

ELEVEN

California

The new family living at 11 Main Street had everything they needed to live a pleasant life. With a loving mother, a healthy baby boy, and a father figure-of-sorts, the pieces were in place for a wholesome All-American experience, nevermind that only the boy was American from a legal perspective.

María was simply thankful for her son's full bill of health. And since health was the only bill she paid attention to, the hospital found no reason to keep the uninsured mother in the maternity ward. So just like that, the family of three found themselves back at their home away from home, waking up a few hours after sunrise, ready to start a new life.

A new life indeed, the morning after Jesús' birthday began like no other, with María forgoing her energy pill for the first time she recalled. After watching Jesús rip himself from her body—thanks to an abundance of energy, according to the doctor—she now appreciated the aggregate effect of the tiny powder-filled capsules.

"All drugs cause side effects," she kept hearing the doctor say, over and over in her overactive mind.

Most new mothers tend to be a bit overprotective, and María was no different. Sure, Dullsville seemed safe enough; but she knew full well of the dangers lurking in the world around her, with even the brightest locales experiencing darkness.[28] She'd do whatever she could to protect her son: climb any mountain, swim any river, even cut down any tree.

Heck, if need be, she'd cut down oversized, tree-like flowers —her precise intention as she stood in her front yard and stared at a home-grown bed of the finest *titan arums* in the state. The plants looked beautiful—no doubt about that—but their smell overshadowed the aesthetic appeal, in her opinion.

"These stinky plants need to go," she decided. "If not for my sake, then for Jesús."

Cutting down the *titan arums* would've been a suitable chore for a strapping young man like José, but María came to realize that her husband wasn't much of a handyman. Though he called himself a carpenter, she questioned how much hands-on experience he truly possessed. Besides, he remained in bed after a late evening.

Hacksaw in hand, María attacked the *titan arums*, which grew much taller than one would think without having seen them in person. And the daunting size was the lesser challenge. Not only did María lack the arm strength to saw through the stems, even more so she lacked the patience to put up with the damn smell for long enough to do so.

Apparently, at least one of the neighbors also had his doubts.

"You're not getting those plants down," advised a man in a red windbreaker and matching pants, sweaty from his morning jog. His name was Richard Dickens, and he lived next door at 9 Main Street. María's attempt to cut down the neighborhood's most infamous vegetation caught his attention, since the previous resident would've opposed the destruction.

"You knew the previous resident?" María hoped to hear more about the house's history, including the story of how it came to be her own.

Richard wouldn't go so far as to say he *knew* the previous resident, at least not in any deep sense. He often wished the previous resident a friendly "hello," sometimes offering a well-intended joke, but he never received much of a reply. The previous resident seemed like a nice enough man, from what Richard could tell. Then again, he tended not to judge others too harshly.

"It's a pleasure to meet you," María said. "I'd hoped to get to know my neighbors. What's your story?"

Richard stepped backward in shock. Her predecessor at 11 Main Street never shared more than a wave and a greeting, let alone asked a personal question. "You want to know my story?"

"Of course," María replied. "We're neighbors, aren't we?"

◊ ◊ ◊

Richard Dickens had quite the history, and would elaborate for anyone who cared to listen. The only detail he kept secret was his exact age. Not that the number embarrassed him; he simply preferred to leave something to the imagination.

Born and raised in Dullsville, Richard was the son of an Irish Catholic father and a Scottish Catholic mother, and expectations soared from the day he arrived. And when he said "from the day he arrived," he meant the very first day he entered the world. His father immediately deemed him a superstar athlete, his thick baby thighs destined for sporting stardom; his mother saw more of a scholarly calling, noting the intellectual look in his eyes the first time they opened. Understandably, he found multiple ways to disappoint from the start.

Growing up with such promise proved difficult, particularly from a time management perspective, with the Irishman and Scottishwoman urging Richard in opposite directions. His mother pushed him to focus on his schoolwork. To her, nothing outweighed his next B+. Schoolwork led to a profession, she reasoned, and a profession then led to success. In a sense, she remained fairly close-minded about how he spent his time.

His father possessed more of an open mind. The sport he played proved less important than being exceptional at whatever it was. It's just too bad he failed to be exceptional at anything, at least from a sporting perspective. He tried golf, but par always seemed to be a difficult score for a first-grader. He tried football, but his feet failed to strike the ball as hard as other second-graders. He even tried the American version of football in third grade, but his slender stature proved ill-suited for crashing into his peers.

For years, Richard did as told. He studied for his mother in the morning, then practiced for his father in the afternoon, then studied for his mother again in the evening. Yet he never felt fulfilled. His real passion lay in the performing arts, though he hid his true feelings from the Irishman and Scottishwoman. For the sake of appearance, he kept up with his studies and sports; but in his spare time, although scarce, he behaved truly dramatically.

His parents sensed that something was amiss. But they remained unaware of the particulars until he came out with the truth.

"I want to be an actor," he finally told them one day in his teens.

The news shocked his parents to their cores. His mother cried in denial; his father accused him of throwing his life away. They refused to support his passion. How could their only son—with his above-average grades and almost-exceptional athletic ability—choose a profession for the overly dramatic?

"It's hardly a choice," Richard explained at the time. "It's what I'm meant to do."

So be it—Richard needed to be true to himself, so he left home to follow his heart to a prestigious performing arts university, where he studied all forms of dramatic interpretation in the company of like-minded individuals. To his excitement, he wasn't graded with capital letters or scored by balls through a hoop, but evaluated by the subjective opinions of his peers.

Upon graduation, Richard held high expectations for the future. First, he moved to New York to make a name for himself in live theater; unfortunately for the transplanted New Yorker, his talent failed to separate him from his competition. So then, he moved to Los Angeles, where the bright lights tended to overshadow the lack of talent; unfortunately for the transplanted Angelino, the bright lights also highlighted the physical imperfections absent from his attractive counterparts.

"It's a tough industry," Richard explained, "no matter where you go."

After not one, but two failed attempts, the thespian wondered whether he made the right choice by following his heart. Perhaps his parents had been right all along, he supposed in a moment of anguish, on the verge of leaving his dream behind.

Then again, perhaps he set his sights too high. In New York

and Los Angeles, he'd competed against the best actors in the industry. Why be a small fish thrashing in two of the deepest lakes in the country, when he was better suited as a big fish ruling over a home aquarium?[29] So he moved back to Dullsville, where mediocrity was not only appreciated, but celebrated as special. As the only thespian in town, he immediately landed a role as Bystander #2 in a commercial for Pepe's Fried Chicken, followed by a guest role on a soap opera, *The Interesting & The Attractive*, during a locally filmed episode.

Local stardom also suffered a downside, of course. With his focus on his career, he had no time to attend to the other areas of his life. The lack of thespians in town meant more roles for him, but also the lack of like-minded individuals for socialization. Though he couldn't complain too much, mostly because he had nobody to complain to.

"Wow," María said, "that's more information than I expected for an introduction."

It was indeed more than she needed to know, Richard agreed, but he found his new neighbor so welcoming that he could hardly contain himself.

"So, basically," María summarized, "you're an actor."

"Basically," Richard agreed.

◊ ◊ ◊

Gabby Blabber hid behind her curtains, watching intently as Richard spoke to María for quite some time. She wished he spoke louder, but the level of his voice failed to match the pace of his lips. He'd always been a soft-spoken man, from what she could tell through her window, so his quiet tone came as no surprise.

No matter. Gabby didn't need her ears to gather clues: her eyes also worked.

The conversation at 11 Main Street was the first evidence of a possible collaboration having to do with the disappearance of Moses Staffman. María and Richard appeared full of smiles and laughs as they traded stories on the front lawn, which told Gabby that they weren't enemies.

"And the opposite of an enemy is a friend," she realized.

Gabby remained unsure what to make of the situation. The

evidence didn't add up, even if she counted on her hand: (index finger) first, Moses and Richard seemed chummy; (middle finger) then, Moses disappeared without a trace, after making off with his company's merchandise; (ring finger) but before she got through a storyline of her favorite soap opera, Moses' house acquired a new woman, who went from fat to skinny in only one day; and (pinkie finger) now the woman seemed chummier with Richard than her predecessor.

"What the heck is going on?" Gabby wondered.

There had to be an obvious answer, though darned if she knew it. Not that she lacked the power of deduction; she simply had yet to find every clue.

She needed more time.

More patience wouldn't hurt either.

Gabby thought about phoning Cleopatra Spiter and Thutmond Mose III with an update. But if she still hadn't solved the mystery, neither would they. No, it was best for everyone that she continue to collect evidence. There'd come a time for her to act, and she'd be ready when that time came.

◊ ◊ ◊

José sprawled across the couch as María stepped back inside after speaking with Richard. He should've been watching Jesús while she cleaned the yard, but that proved difficult with his attention focused on the television. He'd found a movie called *Happy Gilmore*, starring someone named Adam Sandler. And another Adam Sandler movie, *Bulletproof*, just arrived in the mail. Not to mention that *Billy Madison* sat on the shelf. Apparently, the former resident signed up for some type of fan club.

"And this whiskey from the cupboard isn't half bad either," he added.

María sighed and went to check on Jesús. Although she wished for the boy to spend the morning bonding with José, the elder man of the house appeared in no shape to be a role model. She didn't know if this Adam Sandler fellow was appropriate either. So instead of handing Jesús over to José, she cradled her boy in her arms, instantly losing herself in his golden eyes as she stroked his bald head with a gentle touch. The boy remained silent as he lay in her arms, but he'd yet to speak a single word, so her expectations remained low to begin with.

Finally at ease, María took a moment to reflect. Before Jesús' birth, her life involved a nonstop series of tiring activities, none of which ultimately mattered much to anyone. But as she stood next to the crib with Jesús in her arms, she felt like she mattered to someone. For the first time, she enjoyed that precise moment, with no concern for what would happen in an hour or a day or a year, simply relishing the presence of such a beautiful, innocent child.

"The doctor was right." María ignored the boy's capacity to understand her words. "You're special."

Jesús certainly began his life on the right foot, even if he'd yet to stand on his toes.[30] Born several months premature, he was ahead of schedule from a time management perspective.

The town where he'd spend the first years of his life sure seemed nice. If Richard Dickens provided any indication of the general population of Dullsville, Jesús could expect a lovely childhood as long as they lived at 11 Main Street. María had no idea how long that would be, of course, but she hoped for enough time to meet a few more locals.

At that precise moment, the doorbell rang.

María wondered whether that might be another local already, if not Richard Dickens returning for another chat. Yet with Jesús cooing gently against her chest, she lacked a free hand to answer the door.

"Can you see who's at the door?" María called to José, wishing for him to get to know the neighbors as well.

"I'm in the middle of something," José called back, then let out a hearty laugh as he watched Adam Sandler take a knee to the groin.

◊ ◊ ◊

Gabby Blabber barely had time to move from the window for another cup of coffee. Because only a few minutes after Richard Dickens left the house next door, before she recorded the visit in her journal, a car pulled up to the curb outside 11 Main Street.

Gabby failed to recognize the new visitor. All she knew about him involved what she saw and heard from the window. He appeared intelligent, with an expensive-looking suit draped over his gangly frame, and she thought she heard something about a "next hire" in the tone of his squeaky voice.

"Next hire?" Gabby wondered if her ears made sense. "What could that mean?"

Perhaps she was mistaken. Maybe he said, "just fired"?

Or, "best squire"?

In times like this, she regretted the thickness of her walls.

◊ ◊ ◊

"It's Esquire," Howie Spirit, Esq., reminded as María answered the door. "Howie Spirit, Esq."

"That was quick," María observed. Although it may have seemed like quite some time passed since she last saw the attorney, it had only been two days according to the calendar on her refrigerator. Based on their last conversation, she expected several months to elapse before another meeting.

In Howie's mind, time hadn't passed rapidly enough. If all went well with María right then and there, however, he'd be retiring momentarily. Their meeting was last on his to-do list before he departed the country for a secret island in the Pacific Ocean. Though he avoided telling María all that; instead, he broke the ice by asking:

"How was your first day in the United States?"

Always willing to chat, María thanked him for asking. As he may have noticed, she'd lost weight since they first met. Well, she'd expelled a baby boy's worth of mass. Had her son not been lying in his crib right then, she would've introduced the two.

"Congratulations." Howie hoped the birth went smoothly.

Smooth enough, María agreed, though it would've been smoother if she knew the specifics of her medical insurance plan. Since the attorney operated on behalf of her employer, attending to the legal details of her employment, she wondered if he might clarify the situation from this perspective.

Howie was glad she asked: he loved nothing more than to clarify legal details. He represented a company named TH Corp, which contracted with TSA for María's services. Officially speaking, María was employed by TSA, not TH Corp, though she would perform her upcoming job responsibilities on TH Corp's behalf. Insurance therefore remained a question for someone at TSA; he could only answer questions related to TH Corp.

"That doesn't make any sense," María said.

"Welcome to America," Howie replied.

Since that seemed to be her only question, Howie got straight to business—TH Corp business, to be certain. He now possessed the company's hot new product, if she wished to see it.

"No thanks," María said, surprising the attorney. She saw no point in continuing the discussion. She'd be happy to start selling this hot new product—whatever it was—in about three months, if he came back then.

"Three months?"

"Twelve weeks to be exact." María handed the attorney the previous morning's edition of the *Dullsville Times*. "I've just started my maternity leave."

"Maternity leave?"

A crease in the *Dullsville Times* marked an article detailing the President's dedication to family life with his signing of the Family and Medical Leave Act. According to the article, as interpreted by María, the law guaranteed her up to twelve weeks of maternity leave as (1) a new mother, (2) residing in the United States, (3) who worked for an employer having fifty employees or more.

María's legal acumen impressed Howie. How could it not? Unfortunately for her, TH Corp employed nowhere near fifty people. Even under the most generous interpretation of the term "employee," Howie counted no more than three, including himself.

"But you said that TH Corp isn't my employer," María pointed out. "TSA is."

TSA employed plenty more than fifty people, from what María knew, though she welcomed the attorney to investigate the matter himself.

Although displeased, Howie showed no emotion. He couldn't retire until María sold TH Corp's product. Yet he also realized that TH Corp would be better off without María bringing attention to the company's business practices. So despite his irritation, he smiled and nodded his head.

"I'll be back in twelve weeks," Howie agreed, and delayed his retirement once again. "Not a day later."

As María watched Howie pull his car away from the curb, she realized the impact of the President's decisions. Evidently, the President possessed significant power, which he could yield as he wished. Going forward, she'd have to pay closer attention to the news coming out of Washington, D.C.

"I wonder if anyone else is paying attention to the President?" she even thought aloud.

TWELVE

Washington, D.C.

In the capital city, an office full of Secretaries paid attention to the President. The walls of the office formed the shape of an oval, and the Secretaries tended to agree with their leader, and that's pretty much the way the White House operated for as long as anyone cared to remember.

The Oval Office—iconic not only for its geometry, but for the influential leaders who signed their names across the enormous oak desk in the center—had seen a flurry of activity in recent months.[31] Not that anything noteworthy had been accomplished. But ask anyone in the room, and he'd say he was busy.

On this day, the President prepared for his State of the Union Address.[32] It would be his fifth consecutive speech of this type. Yet he took no comfort in his speechwriters' familiarity with the occasion, instead fretting over what the nation's most popular newspersons might say if he failed to impress. The citizens who reelected him held high expectations when he spoke into a microphone.

"So what should I talk about during this State of the Union thing?" asked the President from behind his desk, with his most trusted advisors standing shoulder-to-shoulder in an oblong line matching the shape of the room.

"You should talk about the economy," advised the Secretary

of Commerce, "and how unemployment numbers decreased during your first term."

"And then mention crime," advised the Secretary of Housing and Urban Development, "and how crime rates have gone down too."

"And don't forget about improvements to the public school system," advised the Secretary of Education, "and your investment in the minds of the future."

"And make sure to say '*God bless America*' at the end of your speech," added the Secretary of Energy, "because that kind of statement really energizes people."

Those remained fine suggestions, agreed the President, but the American people already heard those bullet points during his reelection campaign. Now that he'd won the election for the second time, thanks to some 47,000,000 votes of confidence that he was guiding the country in the right direction, his supporters deserved a new reason to shower him with praise.

"Isn't there anything else I can talk about?" the President asked the oval audience. "There must be an issue I haven't addressed?"

The Secretaries hemmed and hawed for a bit, though not a single advisor dared make a concrete suggestion until the Secretary of Defense wisecracked that the President had yet to address rumors of his sultry affair with a White House intern. An uncomfortable laugh preceded an awkward pause, with the Secretary of Health and Human Services finally breaking the silence by suggesting:

"What about California's passage of Proposition 215?"

Logically, since California was the first U.S. state to pass a medicinal cannabis initiative, not a single President received the chance to address the issue until then.

The Oval Office returned to silence as the Secretaries braced for the President's opinion, sure to be brilliant, or forward-thinking at the very least. Even in the midst of the President's silence, not one Cabinet member dared speak until their leader's thoughts became clear. Not one Cabinet member dared speak, that is, until the Secretary of Defense once again broke the silence.

"Mr. President, haven't you admitted to smoking cannabis?"

"That happened in England," the President said, "where it was legal at the time."

"But what effect did you feel?" asked the Secretary of Health and Human Services. "Is cannabis dangerous?"

"As I've said before," the President chose his words carefully, "I didn't inhale, so I felt no effect."

But what about the Secretaries? According to the country's latest survey, 33% of American citizens had sampled the Schedule I narcotic. Well, every single one of the Secretaries standing around the President's desk was an American citizen, so the math suggested that someone in the room must have tried the stuff.

"Nope," said the Secretary of Commerce.

"Not me," said the Secretary of Education.

"Me neither," said the Secretary of Energy.

"Maybe that survey occurred in an urban environment," suggested the Secretary of Housing and Urban Development, to which no other Secretary could argue.

"Drat," the President muttered in disappointment. "How are we supposed to decide my position if nobody has tried the stuff?"

Another good question from the President. Yet again, his Secretaries stood unprepared to answer. Fortunately, his Cabinet contained more than mere Secretaries; an Attorney General knew what to say.

"I advise you to stick with the current laws," the Attorney General recommended. "Regardless of what those Californians think, cannabis is still a Schedule I narcotic under federal law. As the head of the federal government, you have no other option but to follow federal law."

"What about changing the federal law?" wondered the President.

The Attorney General was far from the only person in the room who advised the President to forget his question. This was no time to pass a controversial measure involving a dangerous narcotic. The President already stood at risk of impeachment, thanks to the alleged affair regrettably mentioned by the Secretary of Defense.

"There aren't enough votes to impeach you right now," the Secretary of the Interior advised, "but if you do something controversial, that could change."

The President hoped to avoid impeachment. Four years' worth of work lay ahead, and then the rest of his life would be filled with book deals and speaking fees. Why jeopardize that bright future?

"I'll instruct the Press Secretary how to deal with the cannabis issue," the Attorney General said. "You can stick to your talking points."

"Like the economy," said the Secretary of Commerce.

"And crime," said the Secretary of Housing and Urban Development.

"And don't forget about education," said the Secretary of Education.

"And say '*God bless America*' as much as you can," reminded the Secretary of Energy.

They'd let the next President deal with the cannabis issue, or perhaps the President after that. Eventually someone would have to decide something, right?

THIRTEEN

California

For twelve weeks, María La Virgen enjoyed every moment with her son. The feeding, the burping, the peek-a-boos, the lullabies, even the diaper changing—every milestone offered a new delight. Not that taking care of Jesús was easy. No mother would admit as much, let alone one living in a foreign country and caring for her husband at the same time. But without overdue bills to fret over, she finally dedicated her time to something she believed in: keeping her child alive and healthy.

Jesús wasn't the only one feeling healthy. Three months without an energy pill turned out to be exactly what María needed. Not only was her natural supply of energy more than enough to survive, she also felt more at ease without an unnatural oomph urging her forward at every moment of the day—two shocking revelations, to be certain. She never realized how easy enjoying oneself could be.

Although María spent most of her waking hours looking after Jesús, she still caught up on the news whenever she could. And that's precisely what she found herself doing as Jesús napped on a quiet afternoon near the end of her maternity leave, when she turned the television to Channel 1 to find the White House's Press Secretary preparing to address California's newly passed Proposition 215.

"This should be interesting," María whispered to Jesús, who

neither agreed nor disagreed in the midst of his nap.

The Press Secretary avoided mincing his words. Regardless of California's passage of Proposition 215, cannabis remained an illegal narcotic according to the federal laws that the President swore to uphold. Those who broke federal laws would still face consequences: doctors who prescribed cannabis could have their licenses revoked; companies which made cannabis publicly available could be sued; and immigrants found in possession of cannabis could be deported under the IIRIRA.

"Deported?" María wondered about that last part. "The IIRIRA?"

The Press Secretary failed to elaborate, but the broadcast then cut to the news studio for a breakdown. According to the station's most popular anchors, the newly enacted IIRIRA—also known as the Illegal Immigration Reform and Immigrant Responsibility Act—not only expanded eligibility for deportation, but also gave the Attorney General the authority to construct barriers along the border between the United States and Mexico. Not typically fans of the President, the anchors praised their elected leader for signing the legislation.

"Finally," the anchorman cheered, "a wall to keep the Mexicans out."

"How has nobody thought of this before?" the anchorwoman wondered, shocked at her country's obvious security flaw.

Importantly, the legislation also protected American citizens from the immigrants who already crossed the border. Under the IIRIRA, legal immigrants could be deported if they committed a minor theft or trafficked an illegal drug.

"And they've all got drugs on them," the anchorman opined of the immigrants.

"Right you are," agreed the anchorwoman.

María had heard enough from the newspersons for one morning, so she shut off the television and took a seat on the porch to enjoy the morning sun until Jesús woke. Although glad to be up to date on the news, she hated even hearing the word "deported," which represented the greatest threat to her American dream. Then again, there was no need to worry: she had no intention of doing anything illegal.

◊ ◊ ◊

For twelve weeks, Howie Spirit, Esq., began each morning by drawing an X on a calendar tacked to the wall of his office, with each X marking the passage of another night. He did more than that over those twelve weeks, obviously, but there existed no better visual representation of his desire for time to pass. Finally, one morning, he looked at the calendar and realized that his countdown had reached zero, with that day's square obscured by a sticker showing sunshine and palm trees, staples of the retirement life.

"Finally!" Howie pumped his fist. "It's time to retire!"

After a quick stop at Pepe's Fried Chicken to pick up one last buffalo-style chicken wrap, with a side of French fries and ketchup, the attorney made his way to 11 Main Street. If all went according to plan at the house, and he avoided traffic after that, there remained plenty of time to make it to Mexico, board his client's yacht, and retire in paradise by the end of the day. As luck would have it, he avoided wasting time knocking on the door at 11 Main Street, because María already sat outside on the porch when he arrived.

"Hello, María," Howie greeted, and hoped her son had been well.

"Hello, Mr. Squire," María returned, and thanked the attorney for his concern. Her son slept peacefully, or she would've introduced the pair.

"It's Esquire," Howie corrected, "or Esq. if you abbreviate."

Whatever his title, María cared more about why he returned to her house so soon, since three months had yet to pass.

"Actually," the legal expert pointed out, "according to the law, you get twelve weeks, not three months, and yesterday was the last day."

María shrugged. She was in no position to argue. Besides, even if she properly positioned herself, she spoke to a master of quarrels. She enjoyed maternity leave while it lasted, but she expected to get back to work at some point, so that day seemed as good as any.

Howie wished to get straight to business: TH Corp business, to be clear. Though he suggested that they move inside the house to speak further. Peering through the curtains next door lurked a strange woman unauthorized to view TH Corp's proprietary secrets.

María noticed the woman next door. She'd noticed the woman more than once since moving in. But her neighbor would know about the product once she started selling it, so why did it matter if her neighbor saw the product right then?

"It's cannabis," Howie whispered, and winked.

"Cannabis?" María jerked her head back in shock. "You want me to sell cannabis?"

She couldn't sell cannabis. According to what the Press Secretary said on the news that morning, cannabis remained illegal under federal law, regardless of what Californians voted. Under the IIRIRA, she could be deported for trafficking cannabis, even in small amounts.

As always, her legal acumen impressed the expert. Howie understood her argument, of course; arguing was part of his job. Yet he faulted her logic. Sure, she could be deported for possession of the illegal narcotic. Under federal law, even an American citizen could get in trouble for holding a Schedule I narcotic. Alternatively, she'd be back in Mexico if TH Corp stopped paying TSA for her services.

"It's quite a conundrum," Howie noted.

Despite switching countries, María remained the hardest-working woman imaginable. She fully intended to earn her paycheck, but not if that meant risking deportation.

"What can I do instead?" she asked.

"There's nothing else to do," Howie said. "TH Corp only has one product, *Cannapeñis*. You've been hired to sell *Cannapeñis*."

"*Cannapeñis*?" María swore she'd heard the same term before the attorney just said it, and even before he said the term prior to that.

"Impossible," the attorney said. "TH Corp's owner came up with the name himself."

Actually, María knew more than just the name; she knew the precise recipe for making the product. She excused herself for a brief moment to retrieve a certain wallet found in the penthouse suite of the worst hotel in Los Aburridos less than a year earlier. Initially, the wallet contained $1,000, an identification card, and a note—written on hotel letterhead—which read:

> *Tropical Horticultural Corporation's Secret Recipe:*
> *Cannabis + Jalapeño = Cannapeñis*

The $1,000 had long disappeared, but the other two items remained. She gave the attorney what she had, knowing that a professional of his stature could be trusted to hold the important documents in confidence.

"I've also made copies," María revealed.

"I see," the attorney said, though he hadn't actually seen what he said he saw.

"I assume that TH Corp stands for Tropical Horticultural Corporation," María guessed, with her sudden and unexpected trip to Dullsville finally making some semblance of sense, "and that TH Corp's owner is the Guy on the ID card."

The attorney would neither confirm nor deny the charges. Nor did he care whether she knew TH Corp's proprietary secrets, let alone the owner. Once he retired to his island getaway, it wouldn't matter to him who knew what about whom. Then again, he received another surprise momentarily, because when he offered María a small amount of *Cannapeñis* to hold, she simply said:

"No thanks," and respectfully declined.

"Come again?"

"I told you," María said. "I'll only perform work that doesn't place my family at risk of deportation."

"You'll be going back to Mexico anyway when Guy stops paying TSA," Howie reiterated.

"I don't think Guy would stop paying my salary."

"He would," the attorney argued. "He's a dick."

María already knew what to call the promise-breaking Guy who abandoned her at the worst hotel in Los Aburridos. Speaking of that incident, she wondered:

"You still haven't met my baby, Jesús, have you?"

No, the attorney hadn't? Of course he hadn't met Jesús: the boy had been napping that entire time.

"It's time to wake him from his nap," María decided.

The attorney didn't particularly care to meet the child, but he received no choice in the matter. So he sat on the porch and waited patiently as María retrieved her son, and received quite a surprise when she returned. With the boy's eyes now open, it became perfectly clear that their golden hue matched only one man he knew.

"Do you understand the situation now?" María asked. And just in case any uncertainty remained, she clarified: "Guy can either pay child support, or he can pay my TSA wages and give me a lawful job. His choice."

◊ ◊ ◊

Howie slammed his door shut as he returned to his office. Not only did his retirement plan seem to be falling apart at the seams, he spent so much time at 11 Main Street that his chicken wrap was cold and his French fries were stale. The ketchup looked fine, and he had plenty of spare packets in his desk drawer, but who needs ketchup without the rest?

Regardless of the answer, the reliable counselor would never dig into his lunch before phoning his client to report the latest development.

"How'd it go?" was the first detail Guy wanted to know.

With no reason to delay the inevitable, Howie relayed the issues troubling the young woman from TSA. Apparently, she'd educated herself about recent legislation—especially the newly implemented IIRIRA—and understood the risk involved with selling TH Corp's not-quite-legal product, *Cannapeñis*.

"Duh," Guy said. "Of course there's risk. What's the problem?"

The attorney spoke directly this time, explaining that María refused to risk her family's new home in the United States. Under the IIRIRA, possession of even relatively small amounts of *Cannapeñis* rendered her susceptible to deportation.

"And she doesn't want to return to Mexico," Howie advised. "She'll only work for TH Corp if there's no risk involved."

Guy failed to grasp the problem. María risked deportation by distributing *Cannapeñis*, sure, but her only alternative led to the same result.

"Just tell her to do what she's told," Guy said, "or she's going back to Mexico anyway."

Howie already thought of that, of course, and suggested as much to María in a more eloquently phrased manner. She appreciated TH Corp's options, but she now had a baby boy to consider. Interestingly, the baby boy's golden eyes matched only one man Howie knew. Also interestingly, she possessed a copy of Guy's ID card, useful if she ever sought to serve a court order or locate assets.

Guy groaned, and slapped himself on the forehead.

"Her rates with TSA are easily affordable," Howie advised, "cheaper than child support, at least."

"Fine," Guy agreed after a second slap.

The attorney wasn't satisfied with the outcome, not that he was unsatisfied either. At least they reached some type of outcome. He supposed he should finally see the island in person, since he did everything Guy asked.

"Not so fast," Guy said. "Did she say that she's willing to sell *Cannapeñis* once it's legal to do so?"

Well then luck was on their side, according to Guy, because *Cannapeñis* would be legal in no time at all. California's Proposition 215 was only the beginning of the legalization movement—he felt certain of that much—with other states and the federal government certain to follow in short order. Even the President admitted to puffing dope, and would undoubtedly support the legalization of cannabis before the end of his term, regardless of what his Press Secretary said at the moment.

"The President didn't inhale," Howie said.

"My point," Guy clarified, "is that María will be able to legally sell dope in the very near future."

"But—"

"And per our written contract, you'll remain in Dullsville until she makes a sale."

◊ ◊ ◊

María's mind filled with optimism as she sat on the front porch, cradling Jesús in her arms, enjoying the sunny afternoon in anticipation of many more to come. Her conversation with Howie went about as well as she could've hoped: her American dream remained intact, at least temporarily.

Still, she felt guilty over the ultimatum presented to her

sort-of attorney. She wasn't a freeloader. She'd gladly perform any task with minimal risk of deportation. But she'd also do whatever it took to protect her golden-eyed, all-American boy, who could expect a lovely childhood as long as they lived at 11 Main Street. Perhaps he'd even make a few friends, such as the Mexican-American seventh-grader standing in her yard.

"Hi," greeted Manny Hernandez.

Manny lived across the street at 12 Main Street. He meant to inform María of his babysitting potential, that is, if she ever needed help watching the child in her arms.

María smiled and invited Manny to join her on the porch. Her own schedule appeared to be wide open for the foreseeable future. But she'd keep him in mind if she needed a break.

"This is Jesús," she introduced.

"It's nice to meet you, Jesús," Manny greeted, and shook the baby's tiny hand, oblivious to what the child understood.

María and Manny spoke for a bit, though the middle-schooler from across the street was far too young for a lengthy life story. Still, his short-lived experience proved worth hearing. Not only was Manny earning money to support his ailing mother after the loss of his father, he'd also taken an interest in promoting good health. He sprinted up and down the street every morning to stay in shape, and he hoped to become a doctor when he grew older.

"I'm sure you can do it," encouraged María. Now living out her own dream, she wished for everyone to experience the same satisfaction.

To no surprise, Manny possessed a mischievous side too; he was a seventh-grader, after all. He'd once set fire to a bag of excrement on the doorstep of her house, back when a grumpy old man named Moses inhabited the premises.

"But he deserved it." Manny defended his actions. "I got in trouble when he told my mother that I ran across his lawn."

Anyway, Manny's mother called from across the street, so he smiled and disappeared as quickly as he arrived.

At this point, María had one neighbor left to meet. After introducing herself to Richard Dickens of 9 Main Street and Manny Hernandez of 12 Main Street, only the strange woman of 13 Main Street remained in need of a greeting. As luck would have it, the strange woman sat at the window at that precise moment, gazing at María as Manny walked away.

◊ ◊ ◊

Gabby Blabber's journal had a busy morning. First, the gangly man in the expensive suit returned to 11 Main Street for the first time in almost three months. Then, Manny Hernandez from across the street stopped by for a visit of his own.

"Now the Hernandez boy is involved?" Gabby observed from behind her curtains. "What the heck is going on?"

The situation would become even stranger, because suddenly the tan woman next door was waving in Gabby's direction. No, wait, the tan woman wasn't just waving in Gabby's direction; she was waving *at* Gabby, and saying:

"Hello there, neighbor."

Busted.

Gabby could hide no more, so she threw her curtains to the side, opened the window, and said:

"Hello, yourself."

It seemed awkward, at first, as the two women exchanged names, neither having much in common with the other. María introduced herself as a TSA employee, new to town on company business. She wondered if her neighbor knew anything about the previous resident of her home.

"You don't know Moses?" Gabby made a mental note.

Gabby could speak of Moses' daily routine and the people who visited on a regular basis. But that's all she could say. For one thing, that's all she knew, since Moses kept to himself, much to her constant chagrin. For another thing, her favorite soap opera was about to start, so she needed to shuffle her creaky knees back to the couch.

"Well, it's nice to meet you," María said.

"You too," Gabby agreed, and shut the window to quietly supplement her journal with two new pieces of information: (1) that María denied knowing Moses, and (2) that María worked for a company called TSA. And when she finished scribbling, all she could do was sit back and say:

"What the heck is going on?"

◊ ◊ ◊

There remained one detail which nobody in Dullsville had yet to realize—not the curious neighbor, or the unenergetic mother, or the tequila-filled father, or even the young baby boy. Hidden behind the *titan arums* lining the front façade of the whitewashed, two-story ranch at 11 Main Street, several discarded seeds—improperly labeled as avocados—began to root in the imported, nutrient-rich soil layered over the ground by the previous resident.

PART I½: 1997 - 2016

FOURTEEN

California, Alaska, Oregon, Washington, Maine, Hawaii, Colorado, Nevada, Vermont, Montana, Rhode Island, New Mexico, Michigan, Arizona, New Jersey, Delaware, Connecticut, Massachusetts, Illinois, New Hampshire, Minnesota, New York, and Washington, D.C.

Jesús' brief childhood progressed similarly to most American boys, at least in that he accomplished nothing that mattered. Some considered him an annoying child, born with an abundance of energy, but most tolerated his presence, the same as anything else. Regardless, his growth deserved no fuss, and could be summed up rather briefly, with relevant news wedged into the timeline.

Between one day and two months of age, Jesús did little more than smile and coo—cute from a visual standpoint, but useless from a utility perspective. At six months, the coos turned into babbles. And at one year, María felt certain that one of those babbles turned into "Mama," though all José heard was a bunch of nonsense. Whatever the boy said, it caused his mother countless sleepless nights; José slept through the noise, but only thanks to an extra glass of tequila each evening.

In the news, a midterm election occurred around the twentieth month of Jesús' life. The states of Alaska, Oregon and Washington joined California in permitting medicinal cannabis use—a detail noted by María, who paid close attention to the news.[33] She fully intended to stand by her promise to distribute TH Corp's product once safe under federal law, though it quickly became apparent that plenty of time remained until then. The newly seated House of Representatives, fresh off the midterm election, voted to impeach the President on charges related to an improper relationship with a subordinate. According to the official charges, the President not only lied under oath about his illicit affair, but also obstructed justice in the process.

"Considering the President's situation," María told Howie when he stopped by for a visit, "I don't think he'll have time to deal with the issue of cannabis before he leaves office."

"I'll check in again soon," Howie promised after a lengthy groan, anxious as ever to begin his retirement.

Between two and four years of age, Jesús calmed down a bit with the incessant babbling, as the states of Maine and Hawaii decided to permit medical patients to ease their pain with cannabis products.[34] Jesús began to walk, and learned how to dress himself, though the highlight of this time of his life, at least from his mother's perspective, involved his mastery of the toilet.

"Cleanliness is next to godliness," María would always say.[35] The comparison may not have been entirely accurate, but it motivated Jesús nonetheless.

Just before Jesús' fourth birthday, there was a new presidential debate, followed by a new presidential election, followed by a new President with new presidential ideals. The new President admitted to being a merrymaker in his youth, and was even rumored to have once sniffed a federally banned white powder.[36]

"And who knows what else?" according to some on the news.

His optimism replenished, Howie believed that the time was right for María to begin selling TH Corp's hot new product. The President had used far worse drugs over the course of his lifetime. Plus, the states of Colorado and Nevada joined their predecessors in allowing cannabis to be sold as a medication, if only the President would allow it.[37]

"This President is our guy," Howie told María after the election. "He's done worse drugs than cannabis, so he understands the relative harm."

"Well, until he acts," María replied, and kept her household free of the federally prohibited narcotic, "I'll pass on selling your grass."

Ages four to twelve in Jesús' life were somewhat of a blur for most members of the family. María possessed the only functioning memory, with Jesús being a child, and José drinking tequila the majority of the time. To his credit, Jesús felt certain that he did something during this portion of his life, but looking back later he never quite remembered what that was. He began attending school, and made a few friends, though none seemed much smarter than him, or any more memorable. The only acquaintance worth mentioning by name was Manny Hernandez, who was more of a babysitter than a friend, initially; though as time passed, the line blurred between those two titles.

Jesús began to develop a personality during this period. Equal parts confident and charismatic, with a pinch of sassiness mixed in, he was smart as a whip from what his mother could tell.[38] But even those traits paled in comparison with his ability to connect and communicate, making the boy a natural salesman.

"He could sell water to the ocean," María would always say. The sentiment probably rang false for a variety of reasons, but since his mother believed what she said, when she said it, she wasn't necessarily lying.

As Jesús' age approached a dozen years, the current President of the United States reached the end of his term, to the delight of half the country and the sadness of the other half. Like his predecessor, the President spent his term too embroiled in controversy to directly address cannabis legalization. Though this time around, an overseas war kept the President busy, as opposed to an in-house affair. That didn't mean the cannabis issue went entirely ignored, however, with the states of Vermont, Montana, Rhode Island and New Mexico joining their predecessors in permitting the sale of the country's most herbal narcotic to those in pain.[39]

Even as the leader of the free world departed from his post, the United States retained competent leadership, because yet another presidential election yielded yet another new President to rule over his compatriots. This time, the President came from Hawaii (supposedly), and his election marked a historic first event—he became the first President elected from a state that had previously legalized the sale of medicinal cannabis!

Howie showed more optimism than ever that the nationwide legalization of cannabis lurked just around the corner. He deemed the new President a sure bet to remove federal restrictions against TH Corp's budding product.

"Why is he a sure bet?" María asked.

"Just look at him," Howie said.

"What do you mean?"

"Well, he's—"

"He's what?"

"C'mon, don't make me say it, he's, you know, he's—"

"Hawaiian?"

"Yes." Howie stopped himself. "And Hawaii legalized medicinal cannabis eight years ago."

In a sense, Howie presumed correctly. The nation's top newspersons subsequently confirmed that the President from Hawaii flat-out admitted to puffing cannabis as a youth, and even inhaling the smoke.[40] Never had a President made such a glaring public acknowledgment.

So it seemed somewhat foreseeable, only a year into the new administration, when the Justice Department issued a memorandum advising U.S. attorneys to respect state law when dealing with the issue of cannabis.[41] With this news, Howie insisted that María should begin her sales career.

"The memo only *advises* not to prosecute cannabis providers," María told Howie. "It doesn't *prohibit* prosecution."

Right she was, leaving the attorney just as impressed by her attention to legal significance as he was disappointed by her refusal to work. The Justice Department's memo proved to be more of an opinion piece than actual legislature. The nation's top news anchors reported that raids on cannabis providers actually increased after the Justice Department's memorandum. Those responsible for the raids argued that the President's recommendation only applied to individual medical patients, not providers of their federally banned narcotics. Until the President used the word "prohibit," or a reasonable synonym, neither María nor her family would be safe if she sold the stuff.

So they waited.

And Jesús grew older as they waited. Now almost thirteen, his personality continued to form—a dry sense of humor coupled with genuine curiosity, he became at least mildly interesting to talk to, even if his opinions remained undeveloped. More interesting than a conversation with Jesús during this time was that Michigan, New Jersey, Arizona, Delaware and Connecticut decided to join the growing faction of states to allow medical patients to calm their aches and pains with one of nature's most herbal remedies.[42] Heck, even the capital city joined the party after a dozen years of effort.[43]

"What about now?" Howie asked. "With Washington, D.C., permitting the sale of medicinal cannabis, even the President is living in a legal territory."

"As nonsensical as it sounds," María replied, "cannabis is still a Schedule I narcotic according to federal law."

Between thirteen and sixteen, Jesús entered those dreaded teenage years, which coincided with puberty. Better not to focus on the boy during this period. Safe to mention was that Colorado and Washington became the first states to legalize recreational cannabis as Jesús quietly progressed to adulthood.[44]

"Now will you sell it?" Howie asked. "I mean, now it's being legalized for recreational use in some states."

"It's still not safe to sell," María insisted, "until the President guarantees it."

Around sixteen, Jesús' hormones seemed to stabilize, making it safe to continue his history. But before returning to the boy, more important to note was that the President finally made a statement strong enough to convince María to get to work. After Massachusetts, Illinois, New Hampshire, Minnesota and New York joined the growing list of states to allow limited cannabis sales to the sick,[45] and Alaska, Oregon and Washington, D.C., decided to let their citizens have some fun,[46] Congress issued an Amendment *prohibiting* the Justice Department from spending funds to interfere with the implementation of state cannabis laws.[47] Not only that, but the President gave his seal of approval.[48]

"C'mon, now?" Howie asked. "They used the word *prohibit* and the President gave his guarantee."

"Fine," María reluctantly agreed, finally satisfied by the seemingly minimal risk. A reasonable woman, she expected to earn her keep at some point. Plus, with Jesús approaching adulthood, her leverage over her employer waned with each passing year.

◊ ◊ ◊

Guy pumped his fist when he heard that his employee of sixteen years was ready to get to work. He'd shouldered TH Corp's sales burden himself in the meantime, and only abject disappointment resulted from his efforts. Not that he could be blamed: he was a businessman, not a salesperson. The strength of his voice came from the fear created by his tone, not the crafty way he strung his sentences together. And fear was one thing his potential clients lacked, mostly because they puffed too many doobies to feel the emotion.

Despite one failed sales call after another, Guy never gave up on his company. He crisscrossed the country again and again, determined to find buyers appreciative of TH Corp's flagship product.

He started in California, shortly after the passage of Proposition 215. Then he moved up the west coast to Oregon, Washington, and Alaska. But none of those states showed any interest in *Cannapeñis*, even with it being as hot as he claimed.

"Medical patients don't want a hot product," said potential vendors and investors alike, "they simply wish to relax and relieve their pain."

"I suppose you're right," Guy generally responded, "but they may find that they enjoy my dope's extra spice."

"It's more likely that they'll be turned off by the experience" was the typical reply.

Undeterred, Guy traveled to Colorado, Nevada, Vermont, Montana, Rhode Island, New Mexico, Michigan, New Jersey, Arizona, Delaware and Connecticut—sure that someone, somewhere, would appreciate his ingenuity. Yet even the spicy southwestern states of Arizona and New Mexico lacked interest in *Cannapeñis*. They told him the same thing: medical patients needed pain relief, not a zesty night of fun.

"Plus," someone in New Mexico asked, "can we see your business records?"

"Nevermind," the wise Guy replied. "I don't have them with me."

So he moved on, and made his case to anyone who listened. When Colorado and Washington legalized cannabis for recreational use, he felt certain that his hot product would sell. A recreational user himself—he sure enjoyed the *Cannapeñis* kick.

The good news was that recreational users in Colorado and Washington tended to be more open-minded than their medical counterparts in other states: at least they sampled *Cannapeñis* after his pitch. The bad news involved the actual reviews coming out of the two states.

"It's not a fun high," they told him. "We can't figure out why, but puffing it makes you act like a dick."

"No" was his initial response, "that's just my personality."

Regardless, even amongst recreational dispensers, Guy found no interest in *Cannapeñis*. One bad experience with cannabis could turn off a potential customer, they all said.

"Generally, people don't enjoy being dicks," one Coloradan explained, "at least not in our community."

Alaska and Oregon gave the same general response, but worded their statements more gently, simply saying:

"No thanks."

Dejected after sixteen years of failure, Guy returned to his island to consider shutting down TH Corp for good. He tired of traveling the country to market the hot new product which nobody seemed to appreciate. Perhaps the critics were right, he supposed in a moment of doubt, and *Cannapeñis* had always been destined to fail.

Clearly, this became the perfect time to receive an unexpected call from his longtime attorney.

"María is finally ready to sell," reported Howie Spirit, Esq.

The sudden news changed everything. Of course *Cannapeñis* wasn't the problem; the problem was that he—the ruthless businessman—happened to be an ill-suited salesman. That's why the original plan called for a hot young saleswoman.

"Well," Howie supposed of the hot young saleswoman, "she's now in her forties, and she's the mother of a teenager."

She remained hotter and younger than Guy, according to him. Plus, she seemed more educated on the relevant laws, which many of TH Corp's potential customers appeared to follow.

"So can I come to the island now?"

"In due course," Guy said. "María still needs to make a sale."

Howie sighed. Somehow, he felt certain that would take longer than he wished.

◊ ◊ ◊

María may have been the first member of her household to educate herself about the laws surrounding the United States' most well-known narcotic, but she wasn't the only one in the family to learn about the stuff. Because Dullsville Middle School, in partnership with the U.S. Drug Enforcement Administration (or "DEA"), required every twelve-year-old in the district to complete an educational program titled "Drug Abuse Resistance Education."

"Or DARE, for short," the teacher would often clarify, "as in, I DARE you *not* to use drugs."

If the motto confused some people, who suggested that the word "not" might become lost in the shuffle, the teacher would further clarify that clever acronyms are difficult to come up with. Besides, the teacher wasn't a linguist, but a specialist: an Agent with the DEA, trained in the art of psychoactive substances.

"Agent Stan DeVille, to be specific," the teacher and DEA Agent introduced to the class on his first day. He'd just transferred to the Dullsville branch of the DEA with a plan to clean up the streets in town. But upon arrival, he found the streets fairly tidy to begin with. Instead, his primary responsibility involved teaching a class of middle-schoolers everything he knew about some of the greatest dangers facing the country.

In many ways, Jesús' drug education proved more thorough than his mother's self-taught course, because the DEA Agent gifted each twelve-year-old in Dullsville with an in-depth look at every type of drug in existence. From flowers and powders, to rocks and lumps, to spore-bearing fungi and manufactured pharmaceuticals—the DEA Agent considered no substance too obscure. In minute detail, each student learned (1) to identify each drug by its scientific and slang terms, (2) to recite the mind-altering effects of consumption, and (3) to calculate the street price for a personal stash. If education is power, the DEA placed the students in a powerful position.

"Cannabis," DEA Agent Stan DeVille introduced to the class the first day, beginning the curriculum with the most common drug of them all, "also called dope or weed or pot or grass or reefer, is the first drug you should avoid."

That was good for the students to know: most of them had never heard any of those names to begin with. Of course, the young minds required a reason to avoid the drug. For the DARE program to truly get through to them, they needed to understand the consequences of their poor decisions.

"Excess relaxation is the most common negative side effect," Stan explained, "but other negative side effects include excess pain relief, both physical and mental, or even excess creativity or excess euphoria."

That was also good for the students to know: most of them had no idea that those traits could be enhanced so easily. Of course, to avoid those debilitating effects, the students needed to know how *not* to consume cannabis. They couldn't avoid the stuff if they remained clueless as to how it got into their bodies in the first place.

"The most common use is to light the cannabis flowers on fire and inhale the smoke," Stan explained. "People use pipes or bongs, or they grind up the flowers and sprinkle the grounds into tightly wound flax paper to form a cigarette, which is typically referred to as a *joint*."

The DEA Agent then demonstrated the cigarette-rolling process using non-toxic tobacco as a substitute. He even took a puff of the cigarette to demonstrate how *not* to inhale smoke into the lungs.

"Eww," the class collectively moaned, disgusted by the act of smoking. They learned in health class that any type of smoke could damage their lungs.

"There are other ways to consume cannabis which don't involve smoke," Stan clarified. The children also needed to be careful with what they ate, since cannabis flowers could be ground up and baked into foods of all sorts. "Chocolate brownies, as one example, are often used to digest cannabis."

The last part of the DEA Agent's suggestion caught the ear of one particular middle-school student, because Jesús avoided chocolate to begin with. Not that he hated the taste—an allergy prevented him from enjoying the dark ingredient.

"What about people with chocolate allergies?" the innocent twelve-year-old wondered.

"Cannabis can also be baked into other edible goods." According to Stan, the key step involved heating cannabis flowers in oil or butter, which could then be used in any recipe calling for either ingredient.

"What about blondies?" wondered Jesús, the allergenic twelve-year-old understanding relatively little about cooking besides what tasted delicious. "My mother makes butterscotch blondies instead of chocolate brownies."

"That should do the trick," Stan agreed, and continued to explain to the class what they could expect to pay on the street for various quantities of the drug.

Jesús certainly took that DARE class seriously, paying close attention to the facts about cannabis and the DEA Agent's instructions surrounding its use. The reason he paid such close attention resulted less from the Agent's engaging speaking style, however, and more from his knowledge of the same plant growing behind the *titan arums* lining the front façade of his house. Nobody besides him knew about the secret garden, given that only an adolescent boy could stand the smell of the *titan arums* for long enough to find what lay in their shadows.

And this is where Jesús' life took its first turn. Remember, Jesús became a curious boy at a young age, and his curiosity grew in proportion to his height over the years. So Jesús did what any curious boy would do after his DARE education. When school got out, he snuck behind the *titan arums* lining the front of his house, picked one of the cannabis flowers from its stem, and rolled it into a *joint* as he'd been taught. Then, despite his resistance to smoke, he lit the *joint* on fire and inhaled, just as the Agent demonstrated in class.

"This is pretty good," Jesús observed, and continued to puff until his attitude became as relaxed as the fit of his baggy jeans.[49]

He felt so good that he momentarily lost his voice. So rather than say anything, he dug his hands into the soil behind the *titan arums* to see what else he could find, which turned out to be two sixteen-year-old hard drives along with broken packaging that said, "Avocado seeds, property of Plant Inc."

Jesús decided to keep his discovery a secret, at least for a while. Not only was he unsure how his parents would react, he also hoped to puff a few more *joints* in the meantime.

◊ ◊ ◊

Not to be forgotten, José was there too over the course of Jesús' childhood. His level of activity failed to match that of his wife, but he was still there. For the most part, he relaxed and enjoyed himself, with tequila being the most important element in this regard, followed by the Adam Sandler movies which kept showing up at the door. Without the movies, he would've been stuck watching the boring Channel 1 news all day.

Apparently Adam Sandler kept busy, just like everyone else José knew. By Jesús' sixteenth birthday, José owned copies of *Billy Madison, Happy Gilmore, Bulletproof, The Wedding Singer, The Waterboy, Big Daddy, Little Nicky, Punch Drunk Love, Mr. Deeds, Eight Crazy Nights, Anger Management, 50 First Dates, Spanglish, The Longest Yard, Click, Rein Over Me, I Now Pronounce You Chuck & Larry, You Don't Mess with the Zohan, Bedtime Stories, Funny People, Grown Ups, Just Go with It, Jack and Jill, That's My Boy, Hotel Transylvania, Grown Ups 2, Blended, Men, Women & Children*, and *The Cobbler*. On top of those, another film seemed to arrive at the door every few months, with *Pixels, Hotel Transylvania 2*, and *The Ridiculous 6* still on the way.

"When does Adam Sandler have free time?" José often asked, and wondered if his favorite actor should place more focus on the quality of his films as opposed to the sheer quantity of theatrical releases. Yet without much to do besides drink tequila, he avoided complaining about the free entertainment.

On a weekday morning, right around Jesús' sixteenth birthday, José finally regained relevancy. Waking up with his brain rhythmically pulsing to the tune of a violent morning lullaby —the predictable result of a late night with a strong bottle of tequila—José was in no mood to greet the sun. Instead, he kept the lights down and turned the television to a movie from his collection, *Jack and Jill*, planning to spend the rest of the day on the couch in an endless fit of laughter.

Yet somehow, Adam Sandler failed to distract from the throbbing pain between his ears. Although José had dealt with such cerebral tremors before—on numerous occasions—he'd never found it so difficult to quiet the noise. Usually, a glass of tequila would do the trick, but on this particular morning, his body denied all liquid deposits. All he could do was sprawl across the couch and moan of his sobriety, which is how he gained Jesús' attention as the teenager returned home from school.

"Are you okay?" Jesús asked as he walked in the door.

José assured his son that he would be fine. He simply needed to rest. His head hurt so badly that he hadn't laughed once during *Jack and Jill*, even though Adam Sandler played the twin sister of himself in the flick.

"Maybe it's not funny," Jesús suggested.

José assured his son that Adam Sandler remained innocent in the matter; no need to drag the actor's name through the mud. Surely, his headache deserved the blame. He just hoped he could rid himself of the throbbing pain before it killed him. (He exaggerated his impending death, of course, though to his teenage son the embellishment seemed less obvious.)

"If you really need to cure your headache, a bit of cannabis might do the trick." Jesús recalled the first lesson he learned from his favorite DEA Agent. "It may also make the movie funnier."

José's first laugh of the day came at his son's suggestion. He didn't *do* drugs. Not that he morally opposed cannabis use, but he needed nothing more than tequila to feel good. Unfortunately, his stomach refused to cooperate at the moment, or everything would've been fine. Besides, he lacked any cannabis to begin with.

Well that's when Jesús urged his father to try a puff of the cannabis growing behind the *titan arums* in the front yard.

"Uh, what?"

When Jesús repeated that a garden of cannabis grew behind the neighborhood's most notorious flowers, José pinched his nose to see for himself. That turned out to be easier said than done with tequila sweating through his pores, but he only puked twice as he pushed the *titan arums* to the side.

José stood in disbelief. For over a decade, cannabis grew in his own front yard. He would've known if only he ventured closer to the *titan arums* at any point in time. But he couldn't tolerate the smell for long enough to see the truth. Although in some sense, the smell seemed like a good thing, because it also kept nosy neighbors from discovering the truth.

José then did what any desperately hungover man would do: he picked one of the cannabis flowers clean from its stem. After Jesús showed him how to grind up the flowers and roll a cigarette, he lit a fire and inhaled the fumes, just as his son suggested.

"It's called a *joint*," Jesús said.

"Whatever it's called," José replied as a single puff of the *joint* erased his headache, "I like it."

José felt so good that he momentarily lost his voice. Not only did he feel better than a moment prior when his headache pulsed in full force, he also felt better than when he drank the tequila in the first place.

Rather than say anything further, José allowed his son to take a puff of the *joint* as well. And with that, they became bonded by not only their relaxed attitudes and optimistic outlooks, but also the desire to keep their secret from the last member of the household.

"Don't tell Mom," Jesús said.

"No shit," José agreed, then instructed the teenager not to repeat the last word he said.

◊ ◊ ◊

By the time the first shipment of *Cannapeñis* arrived at 11 Main Street, María was the only member of her household who avoided puffing cannabis for over a decade. She had no interest, recalling the effect on her judgment at the only hotel in Los Aburridos. But she needed to sell the stuff to support her family, so she accepted TH Corp's assignment, as any resourceful woman would.

The first shipment of *Cannapeñis* came with an attorney —Howie Spirit, Esq., to be specific—who remained anxious to begin distribution. Even more so, he remained anxious for María to generate some kind of profit—any kind of profit, really, so he could finally begin his retirement.

"I thought your retirement would've begun by now," María said.

"That makes two of us," Howie agreed.

Well María would do what she could, she assured, as tired of hearing about the attorney's forthcoming retirement as anyone else. Though she wondered how to sell the product. All she knew about cannabis involved which states permitted its sale and what the current President thought of the stuff.

"Just find degenerates, and ask if they wish to get high," suggested the attorney, as unsure of the distribution process as the mother of their cause.

"That's all?" María wondered, to which Howie shrugged.

Before shaking hands with the attorney, María had one final condition, even if she no longer stood in the best position to make demands. She asked that the arrangement be kept quiet from the rest of her family. Neither of the men in her house needed a temptation like cannabis, with her husband already intoxicated enough from tequila, and her son merely an innocent boy.

"If I find either of them doing it," the wife and mother added as she wagged her finger at nothing in particular, "then I won't be happy."

◊ ◊ ◊

Always the resourceful woman, María tried her best to sell TH Corp's *Cannapeñis*-brand cannabis. Too bad her best fell short of acceptable. No matter how hard she tried, she lacked any kind of rapport with her potential customers, who often seemed caught off guard when the middle-aged mother-of-one asked:

"Wanna get high?"

Some were confused by her appearance; others by her lack of a sales pitch; still others by some combination of the two. Once in a while someone took a puff, and promised to buy more *Cannapeñis* if all went well. But all never went well, and María found herself with a customer demanding back the money he hadn't even paid to begin with.

And that wasn't the worst part. As much as María tried to hide *Cannapeñis* from her family, her secrecy proved futile, because they found out all on their own. José came upon a sample in María's purse while searching for her wallet, and he and his closer-than-ever son decided to give the stuff a few puffs. Fortunately, neither her husband nor her son grew more addicted to TH Corp's proprietary product than anyone else in the country. Neither enjoyed *Cannapeñis* one bit, actually, after the stuff led to a strange contest to see who could urinate the farthest.

"Let's never do that again," said José.

"We'll stick to the stuff behind the stinky plants in the front yard," agreed Jesús.

"And let's not tell your mother either," added José.

"No shit," agreed Jesús, by this time a legal adult at eighteen years of age, who could say whatever words he wished.

To her credit, María never gave up. Day after day, month after month, year after year, she endeavored to earn her salary. Not only was she determined to be useful, but she also had a Doctor of Law on her case.

"Have you sold any yet?" Howie constantly asked.

"I'm trying," María always replied, "but nobody likes it."

"Well keep trying," Howie pleaded. "At some point, something has to happen, for crying out loud!"

◊ ◊ ◊

Gabby Blabber never gave up on the mystery of Moses Staffman's disappearance. For two decades, she carefully watched her neighborhood for clues. It was tough at times, especially with her knees only growing creakier as the years passed, but she refused to rest until she figured out what was going on—both on *TI&TA* and in real life.

On *TI&TA*, the past twenty years had been a whirlwind of drama and deceit. The twists and turns, the complicated relationships and unlikely circumstances, the affairs and double-crosses—that's what made *TI&TA* such a must-watch television show.

Dullsville had been fairly boring over the same stretch of time. The boy next door grew into a teenager, but he and his parents never did much to gossip about. Their routine remained consistent from what Gabby could see. The mother left for her TSA job at any and all hours of the day, while the father and son tended to the *titan arums*. Besides that, the family kept relatively quiet, besides friendly conversations with Richard Dickens and Manny Hernandez and any other neighbor who cared to say hello. Gabby herself even conversed with her neighbors on several occasions, though nothing besides pleasantries ever came from their mouths.

But she kept watching.

She knew that if she waited long enough, and paid enough attention, something interesting would happen. It always did, in her experience, if the lessons she learned from *TI&TA* meant anything at all.

Then, one day, on a warm winter afternoon as Gabby sat at her window, Dullsville finally became more interesting than her soap opera.

PART II: 2017

FIFTEEN

California

Jesús' twentieth birthday was always meant to be a day to remember. So in some respect, the occasion lived up to its billing. Then again, the initial expectation called for nothing more than the celebration of a milestone—a single day to pause and appreciate the present as the years passed faster than his mother could count.

"Where did all the time go?" María would often ask, though she never received a suitable answer.

So much changed over the course of twenty years. Not only had Jesús grown in height, he'd also developed a well-rounded personality, even if only appreciated by those living under the same roof. Easygoing, friendly, and always the optimist—he was generally a pleasure to acquaint. And he looked fairly handsome—if appearances mattered to the boy—the wavy mop of thick hair on his head so carelessly perfect, the whiskers on his chin framing the deep dimples of his casual smile. Oh, and he dressed fashionably too, rarely seen without an unwashed hoodie on his back, a pair of baggy jeans sagging from his waist, and his trendy backpack slung over his shoulder.

Yet Jesús' birthday offered the opportunity to celebrate more than physical growth. He'd just finished his first semester at Dullsville Community College. Not only that, he'd paid his tuition by finding part-time employment. His mother beamed with so much pride that she could hardly contain herself when her son's name crossed her lips.

Intentionally or not, Jesús' parents had blessed him with the skills to thrive. Inheriting his mother's resourcefulness, and his father's entrepreneurial spirit, the golden-eyed child could overcome any challenge; he could adapt to any change. Which turned out to be a good thing, because the world around him certainly presented its fair share of challenges, and never seemed to stop changing. Most recently, the citizens of the United States elected yet another new President to rule the country.

Jesús paid no attention to the President, or to politics in general. He stayed busy enough trying to juggle his job with his schoolwork. Besides, his mother paid enough attention for the entire family. To no surprise, his birthday morning began with the sound of Channel 1 blaring in the corner of the kitchen as María prepared breakfast. Though she avoided getting too caught up in the news to spare a moment for her son as soon as he emerged from his bedroom.

"Happy birthday!" she sang.

María kissed her son on the forehead as he sat down at the kitchen table. She'd woken early to ensure a special start to her son's special day, with his favorite breakfast—pancakes, sans chocolate—already hot on the stove.

"Thanks, Mom," Jesús said between oversized gulps of non-chocolate pancakes.

As Jesús devoured his breakfast, María turned her attention back to the television, where the news anchors praised a flurry of Executive Orders signed by the newest President of the United States.[50] In only a short time since taking office, the President had enacted numerous measures seeking to erase the legacy of his predecessor. María could barely keep up with all the Executive Orders: one affected healthcare; another reduced regulations; yet another funded a wall between her birth country and that of her son.

"A wall?" María asked Jesús, his mouth too full to respond. "Haven't we heard that before?"

But on Jesús' birthday morning, the anchors shifted their focus to another issue entirely. The White House Press Secretary had just announced yet another change in policy to roll back the achievements of the previous administration. Apparently, the newly elected President declined to continue his predecessor's permissive approach to drug use. The sale of cannabis still violated federal law, the Press Secretary pointed out, and the President refused to encourage the use of a federally banned substance like cannabis or opioids.

"That's not good," María said, though she failed to grasp the opioid comparison.

As calm as María appeared, the Press Secretary's announcement was the last news she wished to hear. She suffered from enough stress already. Without the extra cash from Jesús' part-time job, she couldn't have afforded his college tuition. The family barely got by, since her TSA salary failed to rise with inflation over the past twenty years. And even her TSA salary fell in jeopardy, she believed, since she'd yet to make a sale of *Cannapeñis*, despite more attempts than she could count. Any day could be her family's last at the whitewashed, two-story ranch at 11 Main Street.

Yet despite all that, most important to María remained for Jesús to be happy, healthy, and poised for the future. She'd do whatever she could to keep it that way, so she had no time to dawdle in the kitchen for any longer.

"I need to run a few errands," María told her son, who seemed too busy finishing his breakfast to listen. "Save room for dinner. I have a special celebration planned for tonight."

◊ ◊ ◊

As much as Jesús loved his mother, he smiled when she left the house to run errands on his birthday morning. Not that he hated having her around; she was the best mother imaginable. But he needed to do something, and he preferred to keep it a secret.

His mother knew little about his part-time job. He wanted it that way. She would've disapproved; he felt certain of that much. So rather than upset his hardworking mother, he left out certain details when they spoke. From what she knew, he worked as a simple flower salesman, which made sense to her considering he'd been a natural salesman since the first time he opened his mouth.

In a literal sense, Jesús was honest with his mother. He worked as a salesman—that much was true—and he sold flowers too. Though he didn't sell roses or lilacs or orchids. He hawked the cannabis flowers growing behind the *titan arums* in his front yard. And he made a darn fine living doing it. Many of his peers at Dullsville Community College remained in a constant state of anxiety over their studies, and paid generous sums to release their stress.

With work to do, Jesús' twentieth birthday began like most other mornings. After his mother walked out the door, he peered through the window as her car disappeared down the street, and he scanned for other eyes in the vicinity. Once certain of his privacy, he slung his trendy backpack over his shoulder, crept over to the *titan arums*, covered his nose, and disappeared between two pungent tree-like flowers planted by his family's predecessor at 11 Main Street.

By this time, the secret garden of cannabis had matured into a breathtaking scene—an oasis-of-sorts, hidden from sight, its brilliant herbal aroma somehow held in check behind the aggressive scent of the surrounding *titan arums*. Over the course of twenty years, the original seeds morphed from a series of small sprouts into a dense sea of green, with clusters of sharp leaves fanning in every direction. The small jungle grew so thick that Jesús found it difficult to tell where one plant ended and another began; not that the difference mattered to him, since each flower smelled roughly the same, and evoked the same feeling when puffed from a *joint*.

It was an unbelievable sight, really, though Jesús never put much thought into the unbelievability of it all. Something about the soil around the *titan arums* allowed the secret garden to flourish. Yet he ignored the science, regardless of whether he planned to enroll in Biology 101 during his next semester. As long as the flowers kept budding, he felt no need to understand the details.

With a delicate touch, Jesús lifted a sharp cluster of jagged leaves to reveal a flower which looked more like a clump of green fuzz than an artistic display of colorful petals circling a pistil. And he did what most in his position would do in the presence of such natural beauty: he plucked the flower from its stem, condemning its life for someone else's pleasure, sure that the sacrifice would prove worthwhile.

By this point, Jesús had sold the cannabis from his front yard for long enough that he knew how many flowers to pick without the need for a scale. That day, his customers needed about seven midsize flowers—so he picked eight, obviously, adding one for himself.

"No, make that two for me," he decided, and placed the flowers in his trendy backpack. "It's my birthday, after all."

With that, the twenty-year-old peeked out from the *titan arums*, making sure his mother hadn't returned. He longed to end the secrecy and tell his mother where his money came from, but she surely wouldn't understand.

◊ ◊ ◊

María would've understood more about her son's business than he realized. She would've understood the general idea, at least, since she meant to sell the same type of product. But she wouldn't have understood how he profited, because she still had yet to sell her first *Cannapeñis* flower, despite years of effort.

María was a poor saleswoman. She could mop floors and rent cars with the best, but convincing a customer to buy a product required another skill entirely. It sure didn't help that nobody enjoyed the actual product, but a decent saleswoman would've overcome the challenge; she felt certain of that much. Yet still, she wondered what to change about her approach. Most times, potential customers refused to give her product a chance when she asked them:

"Wanna get high?"

They grimaced in disgust, or told her to go away, or threatened to call the police. Even when they agreed to give *Cannapeñis* a chance, they coughed and gagged and cursed. They said that puffing *Cannapeñis* stirred an unpleasant feeling, and they never wished to do it again.

Yet despite the struggles, María tried her hardest to keep the promise she made to her sort-of attorney so many years earlier. She hoped that by making the effort, she'd keep earning her salary. Then again, any day could be her last of gainful employment in the United States. When Jesús became a legal adult, she lost her leverage over her employer, whose company—from a business perspective—would realize sooner or later that there was no reason to employ a saleswoman who couldn't make a sale.

So on the morning of Jesús' birthday, María hopped in her car with the intention of selling *Cannapeñis* flowers to a stranger. She needed to be discrete due to the potential risk if anyone found out, especially after the Press Secretary's comments earlier that morning. Which is why she found herself underneath the only bridge in town, seeking out Dullsville's most undesirable residents, who she asked:

"Wanna get high?"

The responses differed in tone, but not outcome.

"Not with that," one man said.

"Who are you?" another man asked.

"Got any real drugs?" was a third man's reply.

Yet another failed effort for the mother-of-one. If the bridge-dwellers were a more thoughtful bunch, they may have given her a chance. But they had no way of understanding her state of mind. Nor could they tell how close she came to her breaking point.

◊ ◊ ◊

José woke up late on Jesús' twentieth birthday, though not due to a hangover. He hadn't suffered a hangover in quite some time; because he hadn't drunk tequila in quite some time; because several years earlier he discovered something better than tequila, when Jesús introduced him to the hidden garden behind the *titan arums* lining the front façade of their whitewashed, two-story ranch at 11 Main Street.

At first, cannabis became the miracle cure that his headaches always needed. He drank tequila at night, puffed cannabis in the morning, and repeated the cycle based on the sun. Though eventually, he decided he felt better with no hangover to cure in the first place, and one night forewent tequila altogether in favor of the green stuff. Much to his surprise, he enjoyed himself even without any liquor involved.

"Wow," he said at the time, "this stuff is good for more than curing hangovers."

From that moment on, tequila was out, and cannabis was in, at least from his body's perspective. Besides that, not much else changed in his life. He remained lazy, so he still slept late each morning, watched Adam Sandler movies all day, and trusted his wife to handle the finances.

By the time José moved about on Jesús' birthday morning, the television in the kitchen blared with the day's breaking news, and remnants of non-chocolate pancakes sat on the stove. He wished his wife cooked more flapjacks. Didn't she know he'd want a taste too?

"María!" he called out, to no reply. "Are there any more pancakes?"

"Jesús!" he then tried, again to no reply. "Why didn't you save any for me?"

With neither wife nor son nearby, José shrugged and poured a bowl of cereal. He could've fired up the stove for a warmer breakfast, but that required effort, and would've cut into his movie-watching time.

Across the kitchen on Channel 1, the news anchors praised the President for his fast actions to correct the country's downward spiral. In no time at all, their great nation had made huge strides. First, the President addressed immigration reform. Then, he went after the poor healthcare plan which had dogged the nation for years. And now, according to what the White House's Press Secretary said earlier that morning, he even sought to fix the drug epidemic plaguing the country.

"He's a mover," the anchorman commented of the President's quick actions.

"And a shaker," the anchorwoman added wholeheartedly.

The newspersons exchanged smiles and laughs as they discussed how much the country had changed over the past twenty or so years. There finally existed the feeling of accountability, the feeling of progress, and most of all, the feeling of power returning to the people thanks to the most honest leader of the free world in quite some time.

"Remember the President twenty years ago?" the anchorman asked. "The one who ran the real estate scam?"

"Don't forget, he was also a sexual deviant," the anchorwoman added. Though he did have a great head of hair, she had to admit.

The United States was far from perfect, of course, and the newspersons realized that too. The main problem involved the Americans who rejected the direction of the country. Some opposed the President, and others opposed those who opposed the President. If everyone stopped opposing each other, the newspersons suggested, then the President could do his job and the country would be better off.

José shrugged and shut off the broadcast, instead focusing on the bowl of cereal in front of his face, slurping his breakfast as rapidly as his throat allowed. He'd never paid much attention to politics, and that morning was no time to start.

Even with the television off, the house only remained silent for so long. As José gargled the last of the milk from his bowl, the front door cracked open, and the birthday boy entered, with the hood of his sweatshirt covering the back of his head, and his trendy backpack slung over his shoulder.

"Why didn't you save me any pancakes?" José asked the moment he spotted Jesús. "Also, happy birthday, son."

Pleased to see his father awake, Jesús already held a freshly rolled *joint* between his fingers. And that wasn't even the best news of the morning. Despite it being one man's birthday, the other received the biggest surprise of all.

"Another Adam Sandler movie came today," Jesús said, and held out his hand with a package from the mailbox.

"*The Do-Over*," José read aloud from the packaging, which displayed a bullet-vested Adam Sandler hugging a small man under a caption that said:

"Dying was their first mistake."

Well that sounded hilarious to José, who looked forward to seeing the duo's subsequent foibles. His only question related to how long Jesús' mother would be gone.

"She's running errands," Jesús replied. "She said she'll be back tonight for a special celebration."

"Then let's smoke that doobie," José suggested.

"It's called a *joint*," Jesús corrected. "I've told you before, only old people call it a doobie."

José shrugged. He'd never been one to quibble over semantics.

And with that, José turned on the movie, and Jesús lit the *joint*, and the two men puffed, and laughed, and repeated the process over and over again. The *joint* wasn't the first, or even the second they shared, with the two men bonding more over *joints* than anything else during the previous few years.

On Jesús' birthday, the two men laughed as hard as ever: the *joint* was a good one, and *The Do-Over* wasn't the worst Adam Sandler movie they'd shared. Indeed, they laughed so hard that they didn't hear the front door open. But they did hear a familiar voice shout:

"José! Jesús! What's going on?"

Well, they knew they were in trouble after that.

◊ ◊ ◊

Despite yet another failed sales attempt, María put on a happy face as she drove home from the grocery store with her son's birthday cake sitting on the passenger seat. There'd be plenty of time to worry about the family's future on another day.

Rather than dwell on her failures, María thought about how far her baby boy had come. To her, the years had flown by since Jesús pulled himself from her womb. In the blink of an eye, he went from an infant, to a toddler, to an adolescent, to an adult, and she could barely remember what happened in between. Or rather, she could remember, but the memories might cause her mascara to run down her cheeks on her son's big day.

"Where did all the time go?" she wondered, so proud of the man her baby boy had quietly become.

In truth, María felt relieved that nothing significant had happened in her son's life up to then, with events of negative significance as likely to occur as the positive version. Her family lived in peace, for twenty years, with few changes in their lives. The same whitewashed, two-story ranch still stood at 11 Main Street, with the same friends running up and down the same street in the morning, and the same strange next-door neighbor peeking through her blinds whenever María looked across the yard. Even that day, as María pulled into her driveway, she spotted Gabby Blabber sitting at the window.

"Doesn't she ever have anything else to do?" María wondered aloud.

Regardless, this was no time to focus on her neighbor. This was a day to spend with her family. And that's precisely what Jesús was busy doing, María came to find out. As soon as she walked through the door, she found him and his father sitting on the couch, puffing a *joint*, laughing off their derrieres as their favorite actor played on the television.

"José! Jesús!" María screamed as she dropped her son's birthday cake onto the floor, where it splattered into a mess of multicolored confection. "What's going on?"

María's question went unanswered. But her intuition told her all she needed to know, and her eyes and nose helped too. José shoved the *joint* in his pocket, but he acted too late to keep the secret from his wife. All he accomplished was to burn a hole in his trousers.

"Are you smoking cannabis?" María asked, already aware of the answer, so furious that her mouth had yet to catch up with her brain.

José attempted to reason with his wife, and Jesús with his mother, but nothing could calm her as she stood at the door with birthday cake covering her feet. She'd fought so hard, for so long, to keep drugs away from her son; and here he was, puffing the stuff with her idiot husband right under her nose!

"Darling," José said, "let's talk about this."

But María was in no mood to talk. She was in the mood to blame, with no doubt who she faulted between her deadbeat husband and her collegiate son. Rather than articulate her disappointment, however, she grabbed the fancy briefcase from the corner of the room, hurled the luggage at José, and screamed:

"Get out!"

Now José may have been dense, but he could tell when his wife felt upset. This wasn't the first fight of their marriage, or even the second. She'd threatened to kick him out before; yet there he remained. He assumed that this time would be no different.

"How could you give drugs to my son?" María asked, aghast at the thought.

José placed his hands on his hips. "He's my son too."

"He's not your son!" María revealed in frustration. "Haven't you ever wondered why he has golden eyes?"

José supposed he'd never looked too closely at the boy's eyes. Even if he did, he tended not to worry about inconsistencies. He idolized Adam Sandler, remember?

"Take your stupid briefcase, and get out!" Finally fed up with her husband's antics, she pointed to the door.

"Where am I supposed to go?"

"You can go back to Mexico for all I care!"

But José refused to leave without his most prized possessions. At least his custom-made, gold-monogrammed, patent leather briefcase fit every Adam Sandler movie in his collection.

◊ ◊ ◊

María should've been relieved by the end of her marriage to José. Yet she felt no relief as she sat on her bed with a flood of uncontrollable tears cascading down her cheeks. She felt like too much of a failure to see the bright side. She'd failed as a saleswoman, as a mother, even as a wife—a seemingly impossible outcome in view of José's limited effort as a husband.

How could she tell José that he wasn't Jesús' father? She certainly lamented the split-second decision.

Worse than that, how could Jesús be doing drugs?

Without a viable alternative, she buried her face in her hands and let the waterworks flow.

Jesús hated to see his mother cry. He blamed her tears on his lapse of judgment. Then again, he wondered whether he actually experienced a lapse of judgment. He still felt pretty good, after all, thanks to the *joint* he shared with José. So he sat down on the bed next to his mother, put his arm around her, and said the most comforting words he could think of.

"Sorry, Mom."

Jesús deserved no blame, his mother explained. José remained mostly at fault: he was a terrible partner and a terrible father. But she also needed to accept her fair share of the guilt: she brought the drugs into the house in the first place.

Jesús knew that José was a terrible father. He'd always known that, and it never bothered him. Nor was he troubled by his inaccurate genealogy, or anything else for that matter. He felt good—or *pretty* good, at least. And he wanted his mother to feel that way too—an achievable goal, because in his hand lay another *joint*, just like the one he shared with José. Well, not *exactly* like the one he shared with José, but better than that one, since the brainy twenty-year-old never stopped improving his skills.

"Try this," Jesús insisted, and offered the *joint* to his mother. "It'll help heal your grief."

"Oh, Jesús," María resisted. "Not another doobie."

"It's called a *joint*," Jesús corrected. "Only old people call it a doobie."

"Well, I'm old," replied María, no longer the twenty-something who first crossed the border.

María had avoided puffing cannabis since that fateful night twenty years earlier at the worst hotel in Los Aburridos. Though in hindsight, perhaps she overreacted to one bad experience. After all, if not for her decisions that night, Jesús wouldn't exist. Certainly, Jesús wouldn't now be twenty years old, offering her the same product that led to his birth, in a coming-full-circle type of moment. Only this wasn't the *exact* same product, because it lacked even a hint of pepper juice.

"Oh, what the heck," María agreed, and puffed until her eyes became as dry as her personality.

"What do you think?" Jesús wondered after a brief silence.

María felt so good that she momentarily lost her voice. Not only did she feel better than a few moments prior when tears flooded from her face, she also felt better than before the unfortunate series of events leading up to that waterfall.

"Where did you get this?" She noted not only the lack of a peppered flavor, but also the lack of *Cannapeñis*' well-known side effect. "I don't feel like a dick."

Feeling honest, Jesús came out with the truth: (1) that he found the cannabis growing behind the *titan arums* out front, (2) that his flowers happened to be far better than her *Cannapeñis*, and (3) that he sold the stuff from the front yard to pay for his tuition.

The last part surprised María the most. "How do you convince people to buy it?"

That was the easiest part, according to Jesús. The use of cannabis resulted in numerous benefits, from what he learned in DARE class. Whenever he met a new customer, he pitched the benefit that they needed most; the precise reason depended on the particular individual.

"Oh," said María. "I've just been asking people if they want to get high."

Jesús chuckled at his mother's silliness. With her, he offered to cure her grief. With José, a throbbing headache needed soothing the first time around.

"You're the one who gave this to José?" María assumed the opposite when she saw her husband and son on the couch a short while earlier.

Jesús admitted the truth: he and José had puffed far more *joints* than the one witnessed by his mother. But hadn't the former alcoholic been all the better for it? José had never been a good father, and probably wouldn't be a good father under any circumstances, but at least he'd become more tolerable on cannabis than the alternative of tequila.

María supposed that Jesús was right. José had gotten better, relatively speaking, even if she glossed over that detail as the years passed. Twenty years earlier, her husband wouldn't have been spending time with Jesús. He would've been waking up in another bed with some nameless woman. At least now, he'd become a better roommate, if nothing else.

"When did you become so wise?" the proud mother wondered, and hugged her son.

Jesús supposed that they might as well attribute his wisdom to another positive effect of the *joint*, as long as they were making correlations.

◊ ◊ ◊

María swung open the front door of her house, expecting to find her husband sitting on the porch. She hoped to apologize for their argument, but he was nowhere to be seen as she stepped outside.

"José!" she called out, to no response.

Oh well, he'd be back soon enough. He'd always returned in the past, and it wasn't as if he had anywhere else to go.

José's disappearance didn't mean María's call went completely unheard. Her next-door neighbor, Gabby Blabber, answered by sliding open her window and poking out her head. In an ear-piercing tone, Gabby asked María if everything was alright. The yelling startled her so much that she spilled a drop of coffee on her carpet.

"You scared me half to death," Gabby said.

María apologized. She'd never wish any fraction of that outcome on anyone. Everything was fine, but she appreciated her neighbor's concern, and wondered:

"Did you see where José went?"

Gabby hadn't seen a thing. During the time in question, she'd been sitting on her couch, watching her favorite soap opera, minding her own business. Unfortunately, her creaky knees kept her from witnessing any of the action. By the time she shuffled to the window, there was nothing left to see. Yet she still felt comfortable offering her opinion on the matter. Although she missed José's exit, she thought she knew where he might be.

"Check Richard Dickens' house," Gabby advised, brow raised.

María wondered whether Gabby saw Richard in the vicinity.

"Well, no," Gabby replied, brow lowered.

Always polite, María thanked her neighbor for the advice. After living next door to Gabby for twenty years, she understood the importance of good manners, not to mention the name of her neighbor's favorite soap opera and the frequency of her chronic knee pain.

Suddenly, a light bulb flickered over María's head. No surprise—her porch light had been malfunctioning for weeks. José repeatedly promised to change the bulb, but her husband had yet to keep a single promise, making the inaction somewhat foreseeable. As the bulb flickered, María thought back to her conversation with Jesús. Her son found success as a salesman by addressing the needs of his customers. So instead of wishing well to her neighbor and shutting her front door, she told Gabby:

"I have something that might help your creaky knees."

Gabby's eyes grew wide, forcing her eyebrows as high as they reached. Her creaky knees had held her back for over twenty years. She'd visited every doctor in Dullsville, and neither cured her chronic pain. The effects of old age, they told her, became inevitable at a certain point.

Before Gabby had the chance to ask what was going on, María reemerged from her house with a smile on her face and a cannabis cigarette in her hand. Approaching Gabby's window with an outstretched arm, she offered the cure-all for a minor fee.

"It's called a doobie." María used the term she felt most comfortable with, and added that more doobies could be purchased if Gabby enjoyed the first one.

"You sell these?" Gabby felt as confused as ever. "I thought you worked for TSA?"

Technically speaking, María worked for TSA. Part of her work involved selling doobies. The main part of her work, actually, or even the only part—if she really wished to get into specifics. Although the doobie she offered to Gabby didn't contain her company's proprietary product; it enclosed a more enjoyable strain discovered by her son.

Gabby didn't know what to think. But she knew what to do. So she accepted the doobie, offered a smile with a nod of the head, and gave María her fee in return.

"Do you need a lighter?" María asked.

No, Gabby had everything she needed. She'd sample the doobie after her soap opera. That's what she said, at least.

SIXTEEN

California

DEA Special Agent Stan DeVille's face appeared as blank as the boxes in the crossword puzzle of the *Dullsville Times*. A mysterious four-letter word for "Medicine" deserved most of the blame. Perplexed by the clue, he'd scratched his head so hard that the bald spot on his crown grew by half an inch. Rather than attempt an answer, he crumpled up the newspaper and threw it into the trash bin, with no explanation other than:

"This is impossible!"

The stack of files on Stan's desk begged for attention. But he was in no mood to work. He hadn't been in the mood for quite some time. When he first started with the DEA, his attitude had been different. Back then, he was just an ordinary Agent, not Special, with a knack for telling people what not to do. Then again, that was back when the DEA stood out as the hottest federal law enforcement agency in the country, with Agents working tirelessly to become the next Earnest Stoppit.[51]

Stan groaned as he reached down and retrieved the *Dullsville Times* from the trash bin, then uncrumpling the newspaper for a clear view of the headlines. The top story involved the U.S. Immigration and Customs Enforcement (or "ICE") arresting fifty Mexicans during the raid of a warehouse in Arizona. Gracing the cover page was a photo of the lead ICE Agent shaking hands with the President of the United States on the front lawn of the White House in Washington, D.C.

Ever frustrated, Stan crumpled the newspaper and threw it back into the trash bin. Everywhere he turned, he heard: (1) immigration this, and (2) immigration that. Nobody cared about the DEA anymore. I, C and E—in that order—were the only letters anyone paid attention to. Sure, the President offered lip service to the nation's drug epidemic. The Press Secretary even spoke on the matter earlier that morning. But since immigrants brought drugs into the country in the first place, locking down the borders solved two problems at once.

Stan had already applied for a transfer to ICE. After all, his experience uniquely qualified him for a position: at the DEA, he told people which drugs not to do; with ICE, it was a matter of telling them where not to go. Though apparently those in charge of ICE felt differently, because they'd yet to return his calls about the transfer.

Stan understood the situation. He'd made a name for himself as an Agent to become a Special Agent. He'd have to make a name for himself as a Special Agent to be seen as even more special than that. He needed a big case: something big enough to get his picture in the paper, shaking hands with the President on the front lawn of the White House.

On second thought, a big case might not be big enough to grab the President's attention; it would have to be huge.

He had only one problem: there wasn't a damn thing to do in Dullsville!

There hadn't been a damn thing to do in years. He spent almost every minute of his valuable time preaching drug resistance to middle-school students, DARE-ing them *not* to use any of the illegal narcotics prohibited by the Controlled Substances Act.

"DARE *not* to use drugs," he repeated, noting—as he always did—the rarity of a truly clever acronym.

Maybe, he conceded, a case with potential hid somewhere in the stack of papers on his desk. But the likelihood of him finding that type of case seemed slim, especially when he felt no urge to sort through the loose files to begin with. No, if he'd be breaking a big case, then the case would have to fall directly into his lap; or if not physically fall from his desk into his lap, then at least find its way to his ear in the form of a phone call.

Just then, the phone rang.

"Is this the Dullsville branch of the U.S. Drug Enforcement Administration?" asked a concerned resident.

The concerned resident then identified herself as Gabby Blabber of 13 Main Street. A developing situation required the full attention of the DEA. Moments earlier, she'd purchased a federally banned Schedule I narcotic from one of her neighbors.

"Drugs?" Stan raised his brow. "In Dullsville?"

Gabby confirmed the accusation. She could testify, if need be. She possessed an incredible memory, and remembered the incident as if it just happened, because it just did. Not only that, she'd saved the evidence.

"Heroin or cocaine?" Stan widened his eyes as if either drug pulsed through his veins. "How much is involved?"

"Cannabis," Gabby clarified. "My neighbor sold me an entire doobie."

His enthusiasm for naught, Stan groaned into the phone. A cannabis arrest wouldn't grab the President's attention. He couldn't even relay the information to his supervisor, since he remained under strict orders to keep to himself unless he had a felony to discuss.

Gabby wondered whether Stan saw the news that morning, when the Press Secretary stood on national television and emphasized the President's commitment to drug control.

"Yes, I saw the news." Stan's interest waned with each passing second. "Is there anything else?"

"Oh, yes," Gabby insisted, and once again bragged of her memory. "Before my neighbor gave me the doobie, I heard her shout at her husband to go back to Mexico."

The Special Agent's ears perked.

"*Back* to Mexico?" Stan paused as he processed the information. "Did you say, *back* to Mexico?"

"Yes," Gabby confirmed, "that's what my neighbor said initially, and then I said it to you after that."

"Which means—" Stan postulated as he fingered his chin. "—that her husband was in Mexico in the first place?"

"Or certainly at some point before now," Gabby agreed.

The Special Agent stood from his desk and stared out the window at nothing in particular as his mind buzzed with excitement. This might be just the case he needed to grab the attention of the Washington elite. Plus, it's not as if he had much else to do besides sort through the paperwork on his desk.

No sooner had Stan hung up on Gabby, than he picked the phone back up and dialed the White House. His request to speak with the President was denied, but an intern promised to leave a message with one of the President's Secretaries. He then dialed his supervisor and reported the developing situation.

"Keep pulling off these types of operations," his superior said, "and soon you'll be shaking hands with the President."

"Precisely," Stan agreed with a devilish grin.

◊ ◊ ◊

11 Main Street seemed normal as Stan pulled up and parked along the curb. Of course, any Special Agent worth his salt knows that not everything is what it seems to be.[52] Plus, with this being his first time on Main Street, he lacked a baseline for determining what fell under the definition of normal.

Normalcy notwithstanding, precautions needed to be taken: the Special Agent strapped on his vest, mostly bulletproof, and checked to make sure his pistol was fully loaded.

Next, he cleared the area of innocent bystanders. Three individuals gathered in the front yard directly across the street from 11 Main Street, and a strange woman peered through the window of the house next door. With the woman next door already secured in her home, he crossed the street and warned the other three bystanders to hurry inside for their own safety. As he spoke, he flashed his loaded pistol to demonstrate his seriousness. The pistol's safety remained on, but they failed to notice that minor detail as they scurried out of the way.

With his eyes focused on the whitewashed, two-story ranch, the Special Agent crossed the front lawn of 11 Main Street, slowly and carefully, slightly crouched, taking half-steps, the sum of his movements adding legitimacy to the raid. He drew his pistol, but pointed it at the ground, ready to be raised in a moment's notice. Known within the DEA for his twitchy trigger finger, he never raised his pistol unless he intended to fire. He'd learned that the hard way: (he preferred not to talk about it).

With a quick lap around the house, Stan surveyed the possible entry points. A lock bolted the back door shut; and some type of foul plants blocked the windows; but the front door swung wide open. Evidently, the residents hadn't expected a breach through their primary entrance.

"Idiots," Stan suspected, and quietly entered the house through the front door, with his pistol leading the way as he stepped over the remnants of a birthday cake splattered on the floor.

The house stood quiet. Too quiet. Or, too quiet for comfort, since he preferred some type of white noise in the background of any situation. The sound of crashing waves, perhaps, or birds chirping in the distance, would've lightened the excruciating tension, or at least distracted him from the pounding beat of his heart.

Tiptoeing through the living room, the Special Agent found his first piece of evidence without looking particularly hard. On the table, a used cannabis cigarette rested against the edge of an empty glass. The crime scene was consistent with the neighbor's statement: the cigarette appeared to have been subject to several heavy puffs before being extinguished.

"Drugs. Check."

Stan tightened his grip on his pistol, keeping the safety on, lest his twitchy trigger finger bend farther than he intended.

Down the hall in the master bedroom, the situation would further be revealed. Stan immediately deduced that both a man and a woman lived at the house. The living arrangement came as no surprise, again consistent with the neighbor's report of a woman kicking a man out of the house. The surprise came from underneath the mattress, where he found the second piece of evidence: a Colt single-action revolver.

"Weapons. Check."

Stan tightened his grip on his pistol even more so than before, still keeping the safety on, lest his twitchy trigger finger bend farther than he intended.

Then he moved on to the den, where an oak desk stood in front of a bookshelf filled with all sorts of literary works organized by subject and title. To anyone looking closely, an atlas appeared out of place amongst a row of plant-breeding titles.

"Meh," Stan said after dusting his fingers over the covers. He wasn't much of a reader.

The oak desk looked important: like the type of desk which might hold something valuable. It was made of oak, after all, with a nice cherry brown finish. Not maple; not cedar; but solid oak. And in the oak desk, Stan found the most interesting evidence yet—a piece of paper transcribed with the names of María, José, and Jesús.

"Immigrants. Bingo."

Stan gripped his pistol as tightly as he could, flipping the safety off to be ready to fire. If someone had to die that day, it sure as heck wouldn't be him.

Slowing creeping down the hall, Stan reached the kitchen, where he sidled up to the doorway, with his back to the wall, and attempted to peer around the corner using the reflection on his pistol. Unfortunately, he couldn't see anything, since his pistol wasn't reflective in the least. So he trusted his other senses. First, his nose sniffed a controlled substance, with no accepted medical use and a high likelihood for abuse. Then, his ears heard a loud buzzing noise, which forced him to act with the utmost haste.

The Special Agent cocked his pistol, took a deep breath, jumped into the doorway, and screamed:

"Freeze!"

What followed was three loud bangs—heard throughout the neighborhood, or at least next door and across the street.

◊ ◊ ◊

Just a short while earlier, María made up her mind that nothing would ruin Jesús' birthday. He would only turn twenty once. With her husband now missing, she had to shoulder the full weight of the occasion. Not that much would be different with José present.

"First," she decided, "we need a cake."

A store-bought birthday cake would no longer do. For one thing, the store-bought cake lay splattered all over the foyer. For another thing, the special day called for a special dessert: something prepared by a mother with love, not by an underpaid grocer with stale ingredients.

María decided to bake Jesús the most delectable dessert she could think of. Or rather, she decided to bake him the *second* most delectable dessert she could think of. Her *first* choice would've included chocolate, but her son's allergy was so well-known that she avoided mentioning the option.

"Why don't we bake a batch of blondies?" she asked her son.

Jesús liked the idea, and added a thought of his own. According to his former DARE instructor, cannabis could be added to baked goods with little effort.

María agreed, and smiled, with her only question involving how much cannabis they should use with her recipe, since her cookbook omitted any mention of the ingredient.

"Let's use an eighth." Jesús assumed the amount to be relatively standard.

"An eighth?"

"An eighth of an ounce," Jesús said. "How'd you ever sell this stuff without knowing that?"

"I didn't," María replied, and wondered whether her son recalled their earlier conversation about her failures as a saleswoman, or if he took too many puffs of his doobie since then.

"Please," Jesús said, "call it a *joint*, not a doobie. You're embarrassing me by calling it a doobie."

"Sorry, son." María pinched his cheek. "I'd never want to embarrass you."

Despite the language barrier, the mother and son shared smiles and laughs as they baked the delicious butterscotch dessert. María melted the butter, Jesús ground up the cannabis, and they combined the two over a low flame. Then they added the key ingredient—the brown sugar which put the "blonde" in "blondie"—followed by flour and baking powder and vanilla and eggs. As a bonus, María added a strawberry topping, to which Jesús made no objection. With that, she placed the pan in the oven, adjusted the temperature, and set the timer so the buzzer would ring in exactly one half of an hour.

Long overdue for a few flower deliveries, Jesús welcomed the half-hour hiatus. His customers lived close. He could drop off their orders, collect their payments, and be back in ten minutes.

"Someone has to make some money around here," Jesús joked, showing his mother the cannabis filling his trendy backpack, smiling as they shared a special moment between mother and son. Then he slung his backpack over his shoulder, pulled his hood over his head, and was on his way.

With the blondies in the oven and her son out the door, María found a moment to reflect. Though she needed more than a moment to collect her thoughts. Earlier that morning, she feared that any day could be her last in the United States as she failed at her job time and time again. But now, everything changed.

She'd made her first sale!

Perhaps everything would work out after all, she supposed, optimism creeping through her mind like never before. Even if TH Corp fired her, she and her son could sell the cannabis growing in front of 11 Main Street; the stuff sure beat *Cannapeñis*. It would be so much easier to sell a product that people enjoyed using in the first place.

Finally, after so many years, María understood why TH Corp's potential clients rejected *Cannapeñis* in favor of milder strains. The difference was night and day. How unfair she'd been to equate all strains to the one she tried twenty years earlier at the worst hotel in Los Aburridos.

"Evidently," she supposed, "not all strains of cannabis make people act like dicks."

María made the decision right then and there to destroy the rest of her supply of *Cannapeñis*. Why even keep the stuff around? She grabbed what was left in her purse, dropped it into the toilet, and watched it swirl into the sewer.

"Nobody should be acting like a dick," she reasoned of the destruction.

With that, she returned to her thoughts: pleasant thoughts, thanks to the doobie—er, *joint*—shared with her son. Thoughts so pleasant that she lost track of the time. First five minutes passed; then ten; then fifteen; and before she knew it, the blondies appeared just about ready for tasting. But the birthday boy had yet to return.

"Where the heck is Jesús?" she wondered. Plenty of time had passed: enough time that he should've returned from his deliveries by then.

An investigation ensued. Well, a short investigation ensued. As soon as María opened the front door to her house, she spotted her son across the street, chatting with Manny Hernandez. Normally, she would've left him alone, but the blondies neared perfection in the oven. So instead of waiting, she crossed the street and joined the two young men, forgetting to shut the door behind her.

"Hi Manny," María greeted, "I'm making blondies to celebrate Jesús' birthday. Would you like to join us?"

Manny would've likely agreed, if only he knew what a blondie was to begin with. But before he received an explanation, the strangest event occurred: a dark SUV pulled up to the curb outside 11 Main Street, and a man with a DEA badge scurried over and introduced himself as Special, before asking the threesome to please move inside.

"It might become dangerous out here," warned the Special Agent as he flashed his pistol and pointed across the street.

María nodded; Jesús smiled; Manny opened his front door and let them inside. They understood the gravity of the situation from the way the Special Agent then proceeded to cross the street, slowly and carefully, slightly crouched, taking half-steps with the utmost caution.

"Do you know a good attorney?" Manny asked María once safely inside.

María didn't know a good attorney, but she knew a local man who sort-of practiced the profession.

◊ ◊ ◊

Inside the whitewashed, two-story ranch at 11 Main Street, a bloody mess covered the inside of a previously clean oven. Though upon further examination, the mess wasn't made by blood, but rather a strawberry sauce layered over an underbaked dessert.

"Dammit," Stan DeVille cursed.

His decision to fire his pistol at the oven had been made in haste. He loved brownies, and had never tasted the dessert with a strawberry topping. After scrutinizing the dessert splattered on the side of the oven, he scooped a sample onto his finger and set the evidence on his tongue.

"Wait a second," he said, "are these even brownies?"

Something was off; the Special Agent knew it.

Also, he found no immigrants.

◊ ◊ ◊

If Howie Spirit, Esq., was honest with himself, he would've admitted that he'd long given up on his dream retirement in the tropics. But he was an attorney, so he wasn't honest with himself. He refused to admit defeat until he had nothing left to argue to the contrary. And even then, his response involved more of a lack of opposition than an acknowledgment of truth.

Howie had grown weary over the years. Weary of false promises. The saleswoman from Los Aburridos kept promising to sell that dumb *Cannapeñis*. The businessman kept promising him a seaside retirement home on a secret island. Heck, even the darn cook at Pepe's Fried Chicken kept promising him a free buffalo-style chicken wrap one of these days, since he remained such a loyal customer.

None of them kept their promises, which in Howie's mind, raised a good question:

"Why am I the only one who follows through?"

The attorney always came through when someone fell into trouble. When an alcoholic botanist wished to leave the country despite his divorce agreement, Howie found a loophole. When an overenergized laborer needed a temporary worker's visa and a place to stay in Dullsville, Howie figured out a way. When a wealthy jerk sought to avoid child support for an illegitimate child, Howie made it happen. For once, he wished his life could be about more than getting a bunch of idiots out of trouble.

So it came as no surprise, then, that the attorney received an incoming phone call from a sort-of client, along with the message:

"I'm in trouble."

Howie groaned, covered his face with his hands, and replied:

"I can't do this anymore."

But María begged and begged. She had nobody else to call.

Not to mention nowhere to go. Their whitewashed, two-story ranch was no longer safe, with squad cars of police officers arriving by the minute.

Heart of gold, Howie relented, and agreed to be right there. He sympathized with the mother and her son, but more so than that, his fingerprints happened to be all over 11 Main Street.

◊ ◊ ◊

Howie arrived at Main Street to find two squad cars parked at the curb of the 11th house on the block. The police officers appeared to be scouring every inch of the property for evidence of wrongdoing. The only place they avoided was near the *titan arums* out front. Howie couldn't blame them, knowing darn well of the gut-wrenching stench from his own visits over the years.

Howie parked across the street at 12 Main Street, where he found two of his sort-of clients anxiously waiting to speak. Manny Hernandez would've been happy to join the conversation, but he left them alone to ensure that the attorney-client privilege sort-of applied to the situation.

"What happened?" was the first question Howie asked. More specifically, why were police officers suddenly so interested in their home?

"This is because of the IIRIRA," María insisted. "They've come to deport me for selling cannabis. I told you this would happen."

To María, the raid made perfect sense. For twenty years, she resisted selling cannabis for just this reason. Why didn't she listen when the White House's Press Secretary warned of the outcome that very morning? Now she'd committed a federal crime, and it would cost her an American dream.

"This isn't happening because of the IIRIRA!" Howie shouted in frustration. "You haven't even sold anything."

Well this is where Howie received a surprise.

"Actually," María clarified, "I sold my first doobie about an hour ago. Jesús taught me how to sell cannabis."

Howie's ears perked, his eyes widened, and his jaw dropped. He'd waited twenty years for this moment. According to his contract with TH Corp, his retirement began as soon as the company made its first official sale of *Cannapeñis*, which meant:

"I can finally retire!"

He needed to get to Pepe's Fried Chicken as soon as possible. He possessed plenty of leftover ketchup packets from past meals, but quite some time had passed since he last enjoyed a buffalo-style chicken wrap, not to mention crispy French fries on the side.

"To clarify," María said, "I didn't sell *Cannapeñis*. I sold a much better strain of cannabis that Jesús found, then I flushed the rest of the *Cannapeñis* down the toilet."

Howie's ears returned to normal, and his eyes and mouth proceeded shut as he buried his face in his hands.

"Trust me, I understand." María tapped his shoulder for comfort. "But we can make this work."

Howie refused to trust her. He refused to trust anyone. He felt hopeless, and he couldn't hide it. Even Jesús saw the despair, which is why the freshly minted twenty-year-old removed a *joint* from his pocket and offered to share.

"Try this," Jesús insisted, and held out the *joint*. "It'll give you hope."

Howie sure craved the feeling. But he didn't *do* drugs. Representing a client was one thing, but actually *doing* his client's product? What an outlandish idea. Then again, he felt hopeless, and hopeless men tend to make outlandish decisions.

"Oh, what the heck," Howie agreed, and puffed until his tongue became as numb as his feeling of despair.

Howie found himself at a loss for words—an oddity for the long-winded legal counselor. Yet his mind remained far more active than his voice. Suddenly, he came up with a plan to benefit everyone.

"Even me," he confirmed, the hopelessness having faded from his thoughts.

"What's the plan?" María and Jesús both wondered.

First, they needed to get to Mexico.

Then, they needed to get to the secret island, where the story began.

SEVENTEEN

California

The best attorneys are ready for anything, since most problems tend to arise without warning. So Howie Spirit, Esq., wasn't quite ready to leave the country with his sort-of clients, though he gathered what they needed rather quickly.

First, Howie found a copy of María's long-expired passport; as the only identification she possessed at the moment, it would have to be enough for the border patrol. Jesús' birth certificate remained tucked into an oak desk in the den at 11 Main Street, but Howie's sedan included an enclosed trunk which could remedy that deficiency. As for the attorney, he just needed one last buffalo-style chicken wrap from Pepe's Fried Chicken, with a side of French fries and excess ketchup packets, before he felt ready to leave town and never return.

"I guess we're ready to go." The attorney spoke with a full mouth, after biting into the delicious chicken wrap for hopefully the final time.

Manny Hernandez stayed behind in Dullsville. He would've loved to travel abroad to clear his head, but his job as a paramedic kept him from leaving on such short notice. He was scheduled for a double shift the following day, and the health of his town took precedence over his own mental well-being.

"But if there's anything I can do to help out here in town,"

Manny said as he bid his neighbors goodbye, "don't hesitate to ask."

Without hesitation, Jesús asked: "Can you hide my backpack?"

A wise request by the twenty-year-old as he tucked himself into the trunk of the attorney's sedan—the situation stood out as a poor time to hold such a large quantity of an illegal narcotic. Of course, he still placed a *small* quantity into his pocket: he needed something to puff during the lengthy trip south.

With that, the travelers were on their way to the border, with an American driver, a Mexican passenger, and a dual citizen curled up in the trunk. Most comfortable seemed to be the dual citizen, despite his tight quarters, since he failed to fully grasp the legal consequences if the trip went awry; in this respect, the attorney felt most anxious.

At the border, an extended line kept the attorney's sedan from immediately exiting the country. The line failed to surprise María, who passed that same location some twenty years earlier. What surprised her was the lack of a barrier north of the border, based on what she kept hearing on the news.

"Where's the wall?" María asked.

"That's more of a running joke than a feasible solution to a pressing issue," Howie replied.

With impeccable eyesight, María became the first to notice an overhead sign reminding all travelers to have their passports ready. She hoped her expired identification would suffice, but she didn't ask the attorney for his opinion, because a border patrolman waved the car forward by the time she thought the issue through.

"Hello," greeted the patrolman as the sedan made it to the front of the line. "Welcome to the Mexico."

Howie thanked the patrolman for his greeting; María added a smile; Jesús kept his presence to himself.

"How long are you visiting?" the patrolman asked as he perused Howie's passport, holding the photograph next to the attorney's face to confirm at least that part to be accurate. "Less than a week?"

Howie nodded. His plan remained up in the air, and largely

depended on the unpredictable reaction of a golden-eyed island proprietor once they met in Los Aburridos. But he chose to withhold that information from the patrolman, simply smiling and saying:

"Yes, less than a week."

"Are you traveling with any pork, beef or poultry products?" the patrolman asked, in accordance with his duty.

Howie joked that the remains of a buffalo-style chicken wrap from Pepe's Fried Chicken occupied his stomach, but no pork or beef; and María seemed to be a bit of a chicken sometimes, but he supposed that type of poultry didn't count; and there certainly wasn't anyone else in the car besides the two of them, he added, because he just couldn't stop himself from speaking once his lips started moving.

"If there was someone else," the patrolman noted, "then wouldn't I see them?"

"Exactly," the clever attorney replied.

"What about any fruits, vegetables or dairy products?"

Well, Howie's chicken wrap contained blue cheese, and his French fries came from sliced potatoes. He also assumed that the red color of his ketchup originated with tomatoes. Regardless, the combination of ingredients tasted delectable. He recommended that the patrolman visit Pepe's Fried Chicken if ever in Dullsville.

By this point, the patrolman wished to end the annoying conversation, so he declined to ask whether the sedan contained any plants, afraid that Howie might ramble about the lettuce in his chicken wrap—a smart decision by the patrolman, since the attorney would likely keep his mouth moving as time permitted.

"May I see your passport, ma'am?" the patrolman asked María.

María had no trouble presenting a copy of her passport. Though she found it difficult to explain why she only possessed a copy, and why the original expired seventeen years earlier. At least an experienced arbiter sat in the driver's seat, more than ready with a reasonable excuse.

"I'm taking her back to Mexico to get a new passport," Howie explained. "Or we could stay here with you, and I could tell a few more jokes about my chicken wrap."

The patrolman lifted the gate. Unsure if the attorney's comments even qualified as jokes—enough was enough either way.

"That was easy," María supposed as the sedan pulled through the gate—just as easy as when she crossed the border in the opposite direction two decades earlier. And she could think of so many other ways to cross the border. Based on her experience, a wall would do nothing more than force people to be more creative with how they crossed the line between countries.

"Like I said, the wall is more of a running joke than anything," Howie replied, "and even if the U.S. builds a wall, California will pretty much let anyone in."

María shrugged, and supposed that Howie was right, even if the joke fell flat. Not that his witticisms about the buffalo-style chicken wrap set a particularly hilarious bar to begin with.

Howie agreed, and apologized for his poor humor. He'd been under a fair amount of stress for several decades, and the anxiety had taken its toll.

"Where to now?" María asked once the coast cleared.

"We're meeting Guy at the dock in Los Aburridos," replied Howie, as if the answer seemed obvious. If all went well at the dock, they'd be cruising over the ocean before dusk set in.

"How does he know to meet us at the dock?" María scratched her head.

Because the attorney already arranged the meeting, that's how. Whether the attorney arranged the meeting under false pretenses was another matter entirely.

◊ ◊ ◊

The aging Guy stood at the highest point of his secret island, puffing one of his infamous pepper-infused doobies, when he received a call from his attorney on an idle winter morning. Initially, he chose to ignore the vibrations of his satellite phone and instead enjoy the view. But in the end, curiosity won out over indolence.

"We did it," Howie reported. "We finally sold the product!"

For a moment, the phone line stood silent as Guy gazed out across the horizon. It had been a while since he last spoke to the attorney, regardless of how fast time seemed to pass. Not that their time apart caused his silence; rather, his head floated in the clouds, both in a literal and figurative sense.

"Sorry, I wasn't paying attention," Guy apologized, and took another cloud-sized puff of his doobie. "Can you repeat that?"

"We sold the product," Howie said. "I have a boatload of money to give you."

"A boatload of money?" Guy's golden eyes lit up with excitement. "That's precisely the amount that fits in my yacht!"

"Can you meet me at the dock in Los Aburridos?" Howie asked.

"I'll see you there," Guy replied. "Come alone."

"Sorry—didn't hear you—see you at the dock—bye" was the attorney's rambling response.

◊ ◊ ◊

The attorney, Howie Spirit, Esq., and his sort-of clients, María La Virgen and her son Jesús, arrived in Los Aburridos a few minutes early for their meeting with the owner of TH Corp. Never one to complain about an extra few minutes, María suggested that they grab a quick bite to eat while they waited, since the attorney failed to share any of his chicken wrap before they crossed the border.

"You didn't say you wanted any of my chicken wrap," Howie protested, and threw his hands in the air.

"You still could've offered," María replied with her hands on her hips.

Fortunately, the marketplace across the street offered no shortage of appetizing options. Some vendors offered fruit; some offered vegetables; some offered beef or poultry or pork. One stand even sold stacks of bootleg DVD's, not that the travelers found those to be useful right then.

"What do you want to eat?" Howie wondered on a full stomach.

"I don't know." María shrugged. "Let's look around."

So the American, the Mexican, and the dual citizen perused the marketplace, examining this and that as they wandered up and down the aisles. With so many options, María found it difficult to make a decision. She also found it near impossible to gain the attention of the vendors, who for the most part chose to ignore their customers as they lowered their sombreros over their eyes and leaned back in their chairs. Of course, not every vendor acted the same: some tilted their sombreros to a greater extent; others varied the lean of their chairs.

Suddenly, María heard a familiar sound: not the nasally voice of an attorney as he spoke on and on about his forthcoming retirement, nor the reassuring tone of her son's calm demeanor, nor even the drunken ramblings of her missing husband. The sound, and more specifically the saying, was:

"Bark."

Well María only knew of one canine who sounded like that.

"Perrita?" María called out as she swiveled her head, her eyes darting back and forth across the rows of sunburnt hombres lounging under the sun.

Her companions shrugged off her question, never having met the pooch in question. Twenty years was a long time away, they told her, especially if counted in dog years. It remained highly unlikely that her pet still lived, let alone wandered around the marketplace.

Just then, María heard the sound again, even more exclamatory than the first time.

"Bark!"

Two barks, and María was sure: Perrita may not have been the spry young puppy from twenty years prior, but María would never forget the voice of the second witness at her wedding.[53]

Across the marketplace, Perrita recognized María as well, and vigorously wagged her tail in a show of affection, leaping into the air against the pull of a leash tied to a chair supporting a sunburnt hombre in a sombrero. The hombre leaned back less carelessly than most of the vendors in the marketplace, but in all other respects he blended in seamlessly, with the scorched skin on his face taking refuge beneath his oversized brim as a glass of tequila warmed in his hand.

"Perrita!" María left her attorney and son behind as she rushed across the aisle, dropped to her knees, and scooped the canine into her arms. It may have been twenty years, but there was no mistaking the old bitch. "It is you!"

Now the nearest hombre may not have adjusted his sombrero or leaned forward in his chair, but he certainly took notice of his pooch furiously licking María's face out of the corner of his eye.

"Her name is Mexicandog," the hombre said without moving a muscle.

"This is my dog, Perrita," María told him, ecstatic at the discovery. "Where did you find her?"

"Her name is Mexicandog," the hombre repeated. And María was nutty as a fruitcake if she thought the pooch belonged to her, because he and Mexicandog had sat side-by-side at the same spot in the marketplace for twenty years. Though not much of an animal lover initially, the pooch had been his closest friend ever since the first day they met at his colorful, two-story adobe home at 11 Calle Principal.

"11 Calle Principal?" María's memory kicked in. "That's my house."

"If that's your house," the hombre asked, "then where have you been for the past twenty years?"

María explained that she and her son most recently lived in a whitewashed, two-story ranch in the town of Dullsville, California, at the address of 11 Main Street. To which the hombre responded:

"That's my house!"

With that, the hombre leaned forward and lifted the wide brim of his sombrero to reveal twenty years' worth of sunburn on a face devoid of smile lines. By this time both Howie and Jesús stood next to María, and the attorney noticed that the hombre wasn't an hombre at all, he was:

"Moses!"

He was Moses, alright. Though not the same Moses, who by this time never left home without a sombrero. His sunburn no longer bothered him, having become more of a permanent condition than a sudden rash. But he always wore a sombrero anyway, never missing the opportunity to pair one of the broad-brimmed hats with a matching serape.

"Where have you been?" Moses demanded to know. "I've been waiting for your call for twenty years!"

"My apologies," Howie offered. "If it makes you feel any better, I've also been unhappy with how long this has taken."

◊ ◊ ◊

The once-famous botanist, Moses Staffman, saw his life in Mexico pass along as quickly as everyone else's. Evidently, twenty years in Mexico passed at the same rate as twenty years in the United States, at least according to the Gregorian calendar.[54] Not that he remained as active as his counterparts to the north, mostly because he saw no point to expending the energy.

Twenty years earlier—in fact, beginning on the first day he arrived in Los Aburridos—Mexico's deficiencies were immediately apparent.

—First, he couldn't drink whiskey, since all anyone sold was tequila.

—Second, he couldn't watch Adam Sandler's antics, with every movie in the marketplace dubbed in the Mexican language.

—And converse with his neighbors? What a strange thought. Even if they spoke English, why would he want to hear their voices to begin with? He barely spoke to anyone when he lived in the good ol' U.S. of A., so why would Mexico be any different? His closest neighbor looked like an innocent old woman, sure, but he knew better than to believe his eyes. His nose remained the only sense he trusted, and it told him that the entire country stunk!

Unfortunately, Moses quickly realized that he needed to do something at some point. At the very least, he needed to eat three square meals a day. But what could he do?

"Well," he supposed only a few days into his stay, "I guess I could grow a few plants."

Moses was, after all, an expert botanist above all else.

Yet problems arose. For one thing, he lacked Plant Inc's expensive equipment to work with. For another thing, the damn Mexican sun never let up. So not only did he now need to work harder just to raise his favorite fruits and vegetables, doing so proved to be a pain in the epidermis even besides the extra effort.

A few weeks into his stay, the last of Moses $20 ran out as he waited to hear from his sort-of attorney. This left him in a bind the first time his stomach growled. His crops had yet to mature, and his colorful, two-story adobe home offered nothing but an annoying Chihuahua. So he did what any desperate man would do in his situation: he grabbed the pooch by a leash, found a knife in the kitchen, and trudged to the backyard as an aura of gloom hung in the air.

"I'm sorry, Mexicandog," he told the Chihuahua. "I wish it hadn't come to this."

"Bark," whimpered Perrita, eyes wide with despair.

Surely, it was a sad state of affairs for both the botanist and the canine. But desperate times called for desperate measures. Without action, both man and beast would starve to death.

"Bark," pleaded Perrita, to no effect.

Moses found no point to delaying the inevitable. He tied the leash to the mango tree in the center of the backyard, and withdrew his knife as the canine sat petrified. Good thing he was a plant man, or he wouldn't have been able to bear what came next. With pain in his eyes, he plunged the knife into an overripe mango hanging from the tree, cut a midsize slice, and fed the fruit to the poor Chihuahua.

"Bark," said Perrita after devouring the slice.

"I know," Moses replied, "I don't like mangoes either."

Actually, Moses hated mangoes. Normally, he wouldn't have been able to stomach the Mexican fruit.[55] But this was an abnormal situation, so he cut a few slices for himself after feeding his miniature friend.

"Ugh," he groaned, and choked down the juicy wedges.

Suddenly, something strange happened: Moses enjoyed the mango. Well, "enjoyed" may have been a strong word, but he didn't hate the sweet taste. Neither did Perrita.

"Bark," said Perrita, eager for another slice.

Before Moses could cut another slice, the nosy old woman next door poked her head out of her window and attempted a greeting.

"Hola," said Vecína, pleased to see Moses taking care of the puppy.

"Let's get out of here," Moses whispered to Perrita.

And with that, he plucked the freshest mangoes from the tree, placed them in a bucket, and set off for the only other place in Mexico he'd ever been.

At the marketplace, across the street from the town's only dock, he found an open space next to the same lazy hombre whose overripe fruit he previously declined. Though without a permit to sell his mangoes, the legality of his business appeared questionable at best.

"Am I allowed to set up a stand here?" Moses asked the hombre.

"¿Qué?" the hombre replied, and shrugged in tune with his response.

With nothing to lose besides a bucket of overripe mangoes, Moses sat down on the ground and claimed the space for himself—that day, and the next day, and even the day after that. Strangely, nobody told him to move—not that day, nor the next day, nor even the day after that. Had the roles been reversed, he surely would've opposed having some foreigner show up in the marketplace. But as the foreigner, he avoided complaining about the local hospitality.

Perhaps the lazy hombres in the marketplace tolerated his presence because he posed no threat to their businesses. Although he kept returning to the same spot each day, his sales numbers were far from encouraging. Actually, his sales numbers were as far from encouraging as could be. No matter how long he and his new Chihuahua sat next to his bucket of mangoes, all he accomplished each day was to worsen the sunburn on his forehead.

"How the heck do people survive here?" He wondered the same question each day.

Yet he returned to the marketplace, day after day, desperately hoping to earn enough money to stay alive. Though with his energy waning by the day, he came dangerously close to kicking the bucket. He resisted that grim outcome as best he could, since his mangoes would be worthless if they bruised on the gravel in front of his fruit stand. But he came that close to his breaking point. He kept pacing back and forth, angrily staring at the overripe fruit inside of his bucket, with his feet coming oh so close to ruining the only produce he had to sell.

And that sun!

That damn hot Mexican sun!

Moses didn't know how much more he could take.

One day, with Moses' foot dangling next to his bucket as the sweat rushed down his crisp forehead, the hombre in the next stand noticed Moses' frustration, not to mention his sunburn. It represented a sad fall from grace for a one-time Botanist of the Year; the hombre could only shake his head in pity.

"What are you looking at?" Moses wanted to know.

Without saying a word, the hombre slowly leaned forward in his chair before boosting himself upright to stand as tall as Moses had ever witnessed. Then, after abandoning his chair and ambling around his fruit stand, the hombre made an unexpected gesture: he offered his sombrero to spare Moses' skin of the cruel sun.

Moses' mouth dropped as he stepped backward in shock. His first instinct told him to reject the sombrero. The damn thing looked obnoxious. And it smelled like a Mexican. But with his skin beginning to peel from the sun, he swallowed his pride and accepted the gift, slowly pulling the wide-brimmed hat over his gray hair until the crown nestled against his forehead. Then he surprised himself, because although he expected to hate the awkward piece of headwear, he said:

"This isn't so bad," appreciative of even the smallest reprieve from the hot Mexican sun. He offered his thanks with the tip of his new oversized brim.

Strangely, the hombre's generosity knew no bounds. Now hatless, the hombre stumbled back to his fruit stand and reached under his table to find an extra chair, so Moses could lean back as carelessly as he dared.

Moses smiled at the hombre—his best attempt at a thanks, and first earnest smile of record—as he set the chair next to his Chihuahua and dropped his achy rear on the seat. He dared not lean back as far as the hombre, of course, since this was his first time positioning himself in such a lazy pose. Yet he had to admit, even a partial incline felt pretty damn good under the vast shade of his new sombrero.

Moses attempted light banter: "Got anything else hiding under that table?"

The hombre smiled with more teeth than Moses had ever received. There certainly was something else hidden underneath his table—a distilled beverage made from local agave, or as the hombre said:

"Tequila?"

Moses should've known this day was coming.

"I don't know how you can drink that Mexican swill." Moses negotiated. "Do you have any whiskey instead?"

The hombre only spoke one language, so he poured two glasses of tequila and offered to share.

With Moses now feeling better than a moment prior—in the comfort of his new chair, under the shade of his new sombrero—he owed the hombre a minor debt of gratitude at the very least. The tequila would be disgusting; he felt certain of that much. But considering how close he'd just come to kicking the bucket, he supposed he could stomach the gesture of goodwill.

"Oh, what the heck," Moses agreed, and took a sip.

The tequila sure didn't taste like whiskey. Yet it wasn't as bad as he imagined. The buzz that kicked in after a sip felt pretty close to what he remembered from the brown stuff.

Suddenly, Moses felt good, in a relative sense. He felt better than a moment earlier, at least. So he nodded at the hombre and leaned back in his chair—not as far back as the hombre, but still farther than he previously dared. For the first time, he enjoyed the Mexican sun beneath the shadow of his oversized brim.

And that's how Moses' life went—day after day, week after week, month after month—for twenty long years. Each day he returned to the marketplace with his bucket of mangoes at his feet, and his Chihuahua by his side; and each day his skin burned less from the sun, his throat less from the tequila, and his nose less from the smell of an entire nation.

◊ ◊ ◊

For a while, the marketplace hosted a lively debate as to who had the right to be where. Moses claimed both 11 Main Street and 11 Calle Principal as his own; María felt that at least one of the two should belong to her; and Jesús, the loyal son, stood by his mother in silence. Howie remained the only person with a complete picture of the past twenty years, but he kept his mouth shut for the most part, a difficult undertaking for the verbose legal professional; it would've been a sort-of conflict-of-interest for the attorney to take either side, though neither party seemed like the type to report his conduct to the bar association.

"You stole my house," said Moses.

"You stole *my* house," said María.

"Bark," said Perrita, even more confused than Jesús.

"Let's talk about this," suggested Howie, who could only keep his mouth closed for so long.

Moses was in no mood to talk. He hadn't been in the mood for twenty years. The hombre lounging next to him understood that; so did the dog; that's why they all got along. The last person to attempt a conversation with the botanist was the old Mexican woman living next door to 11 Calle Principal. At least she could take a hint. When he slammed the door in her face, she walked away, precisely what he recommended these new visitors do.

"You mean Vecína?" María wondered about the friendly old woman. "How is she?"

How would Moses know the answers to those questions? He minded his own damn business. So he simply shrugged and said:

"Heck if I know."

(If Moses cared to pay attention, he would've known that the friendly old woman died some time over the previous twenty years. After all, she appeared to be fairly elderly when they first met, and not every character could sustain such fine health over the course of twenty years.[56])

"You're an asshole," María opined of the most recent resident of 11 Calle Principal. Indeed, since Moses chose to ignore Vecína, the friendly woman was never properly introduced; and now that she'd perished, it was too late to find out more about her.

"Just leave me and Mexicandog alone," Moses replied, and began to lean back in his chair.

The old man's disregard for common decency baffled María. But Jesús understood the problem. And he thought he possessed a cure for what ailed the botanist. Coincidentally, it was the same cure he suggested for every ailment: a freshly rolled *joint*.

"Try this," Jesús insisted, and held out a *joint*. "It'll make you friendlier."

"No way," Moses said, crossing his arms, shaking his head. He felt no desire to be friendlier. Besides, even if he sought a change in mood, it would be by watching a funny movie, not by using drugs. He didn't *do* drugs—not since college, when a certain white powder derailed his career prospects and cost him his scholarship. The boy obviously didn't know his backstory, but after college he swore to never *do* drugs again. Growing them was one thing, but *doing* them?

"I can tell that you're a man of high morals," Jesús conceded, "but this stuff is different."

According to Jesús' former DARE instructor, different drugs caused different effects. The white powder differed from the green flowers offered by Jesús. One looked white, for example, and the other looked green.

Moses didn't want white or green. He craved something brown, and asked:

"Do you have any whiskey instead?"

To which Jesús answered: "I thought you didn't *do* drugs?"

Drugs were different, Moses noted.

"How so?"

Because they were, Moses argued, and asked everyone to either purchase a mango or leave him alone.

Ready to give up, Jesús sighed in apparent defeat. He found it difficult to fathom Moses' refusal to give his *joint* a chance. Yet he also forgot the first rule of sales: to appeal to the desires of each customer. Friendliness turned out to be an unwanted benefit. Fortunately, Moses' surliness gave him another idea.

"If you try it," Jesús offered, "then we'll leave you alone."

Well now, that's exactly what Moses wanted in the first place. He certainly wouldn't have changed his mind twenty years earlier, but two decades in Mexico had transformed him. Sombreros hadn't been as bad as he thought; neither had tequila; neither had the dog, or the lazy hombre next to him, or even the country as a whole.

"Fine," Moses agreed, and snatched the *joint* from Jesús' hand. "I'll try it, if that's what it takes to get rid of you."

Jesús shrugged. At this point he didn't particularly care why Moses tried the *joint*, as long as the botanist finally agreed. Rather than say another word, he handed over a lighter and waited in anticipation as Moses lit the *joint* on fire, placed his lips on the tip, and inhaled a puff.

"Huh," Moses said, "this is pretty good."

With that, he continued to puff until his mind opened as wide as the brim of his sombrero. Although he felt no desire to experience the friendliness of which Jesús warned, the positive quality overcame him anyway, and he could suddenly tolerate a bit of conversation. Now on better terms with the border-hoppers, he shared a secret that he recognized with his naturally endowed fourth sense.

"This is *Zerojuana*," Moses pointed out of the flowers within the *joint*. "Where did you get this?"

"I have a source," Jesús said, and reached in his pocket to reveal another small plant. Well, not an entire small plant, but a branch and a flower—precisely the amount needed for a clever botanist to create a clone.

"Can you still get in touch with Guy?" Moses wondered of Howie.

To which Howie pointed across the street, toward the dock, and said:

"Sure, he's right there."

◊ ◊ ◊

The golden-eyed Guy waited patiently at only dock in Los Aburridos, puffing one of his infamous pepper-infused doobies, expecting to meet his longtime attorney at any moment. He arrived a few minutes early for their meeting, so it came as no surprise when his attorney showed up a few minutes later. The surprise involved the attorney being accompanied by a sunburnt botanist in a sombrero, a failure of a saleswoman, and an unacknowledged son.

"What are all these people doing here?" Guy asked Howie.

"We've got some catching up to do," Howie said, with María and Moses nodding their heads in support. Enough was enough, according to them; they wished to tie up loose ends.

First and foremost, Howie shared incredible, plot-moving news. With the botanist by his side, they could finally finish Step Two (2. Perfect the Product) of TH Corp's long-forgotten business plan. In other words:

"We located a sample of *Zerojuana*!"

"*Zero*-what-a?" Guy apologized for his poor memory. Perhaps fewer doobies over the years would've done him some good in this sense, but it was far too late to turn back that clock. And even if he could turn back time, he doubted he would've done so, considering how everything turned out, what with him owning an island and all.

"*Zerojuana*," Moses said. "You promised me $1,000,000 to use *Zerojuana* to create your hot new product. I forget the name of your product, but it sounded unnecessarily phallic."

"*Cannapeñis*," Howie recalled.

"That's it," Moses agreed, "Canna-penis."

"No, no, no," Guy said. "You're saying the name wrong. There's a tilde over the 'n.' It's not supposed to sound sexual."

Suddenly, a light bulb flickered over Guy's head. That light bulb, in turn, sparked the mass of neurons behind his bright eyes. For twenty years, customers said that *Cannapeñis* made them act like "dicks" (their word, not his). He finally understood why: they'd mispronounced the name of his product, and in doing so became psychologically predisposed to acting like "dicks." To think, this entire time, he could've corrected the side effect by renaming *Cannapeñis*. Perhaps he could call his product something like *Happy Plant*? Or what about *Relaxing Stuff*?

"You're wrong," Moses insisted, and suggested that perhaps Guy had puffed too many doobies to make sense. "There's a simple reason your peppered cannabis turns people into dicks."

"Ok then, smarty-pants," Guy replied. "What's the reason?"

"It has to do with the peppers," Moses hinted. "But I'm not telling you what's wrong with it unless I get my damn $1,000,000."

Guy felt no urge to hand $1,000,000 to anyone. Nor did he truly care to change anything about his product. According to him, the timing seemed perfect to sell *Cannapeñis*, with the product's strange side effect at peak popularity in the United

States.

"Nobody wants to be a dick," María interjected.

"Everyone wants to be a dick," Guy insisted, undeterred. "Haven't you been watching the news? *Cannapeñis* was ahead of its time. Twenty years ago, the United States wasn't ready. They were just beginning to be dicks. But now, the country has finally caught up to the product."

If they had nothing else to discuss, Guy would be on his way back to the island. Alone. Oh, once he retrieved the boatload of money promised by Howie.

Howie always had plenty to discuss. Yet he understood that actions sometimes proved louder than words. So rather than say anything, he directed the golden-eyed Guy to look directly into Jesús' matching irises, and reflect on how his stubbornness over the past two decades stripped the pair of men of a potentially enriching relationship.

"We don't even look alike," Guy scowled after glancing at Jesús for a second.

"You're such a dick," said the attorney, the botanist, and the mother-of-one.

Jesús didn't suffer from the same level of denial. His golden-eyes may have been just as dry as his older self, but he saw the truth more clearly (possibly, though not plausibly, due to macular degeneration in the older version). He also came up with an idea for solving Guy's ailment—which by this point, if not obvious, was his same idea for solving every problem. He removed a *joint* from his pocket and offered it to his elder.

"Try this," Jesús insisted, and held out the *joint*. "It'll make you less of a dick."

Guy took no convincing. His lips wrapped around the tip before Jesús finished his sentence, pausing only once between puffs to say:

"This is pretty good dope."

It was so good that he kept puffing until left with nothing but smoke and ash. With nothing left to hold, he used his free hands to hug his son: not because he suddenly loved the boy so much, but because TH Corp was back on track.

"We're officially entering the golden age of *Cannapeñis*!"

With the announcement, Guy threw his fists into the air.

Step Two of his plan was as close to completion as ever. Finally, after so many years, the botanist could use *Zerojuana* to correct the defects in *Cannapeñis*.

But disagreement emerged amongst the crowd, and everyone felt the need to share an opinion.

"*Cannapeñis* sucks," Jesús said. "*Zerojuana* is much better alone, without combining it with other drugs and causing people to be dicks."

"We're only mixing with peppers," Guy argued. "Not another drug."

"Anything can be considered a drug," Howie advised, "depending on the laws."

"And all drugs cause side effects," María repeated the words of her former doctor.

"And in this case," Moses added the final detail, "the peppers are what's causing you to be such a dick. The cannabis isn't to blame."

Normally, the smart Guy wouldn't have been accepting advice from his subordinates, since he would've already known what to do. But after puffing an entire *joint* filled with *Zerojuana*, he felt more open-minded than usual.

"You really think you can sell *Zerojuana*?" he asked Jesús, who nodded his head in reply.

"And you have everything you need to grow *Zerojuana*?" he asked Moses, who nodded his head in reply.

"Alright," Guy agreed. "Let's do it."

"So I can retire?" asked Howie.

"And I'll get my money?" asked Moses.

"And you'll take care of me and Jesús?" asked María, not to be forgotten.

Guy agreed to it all. He couldn't help himself, feeling too darn good to express with mere words.

Suddenly, there was a plan again—a decent plan, everyone agreed. The entire group would return to Guy's secret island, where Moses would reproduce *Zerojuana* to complete Step Two (2. Perfect the Product) of a decades-old plan. Then, once they grew enough *Zerojuana* to sell, TH Corp's best salesman, Jesús, would return to the United States to promote the product, resulting in Step Three (3. Reap the Profits) of the plan, allowing everyone to live in peace on the island—happily ever after, so to speak.

Guy ordered the group to board his yacht and strap on their life jackets. A lengthy journey lay ahead, and they had no time to lose. Dope could be declared completely legal in the United States any day now!

At this point, one detail seemed worth mentioning, at least from Jesús' perspective. And that one detail turned out to be fairly important to the viability of Guy's new plan.

"The last of the *Zerojuana* was in that *joint*," Jesús said, and shrugged.

"Oh," said everyone else.

"I can get more though," Jesús assured. "There's an entire garden full of *Zerojuana* in Dullsville, plus what's left in my backpack at Manny's house."

Guy felt generally agreeable, thanks to the doobie—er, *joint* —now reduced to ash. He'd allow Moses and María to accompany him to the island, he said, while Jesús and Howie returned to the United States to retrieve more *Zerojuana*. Once Jesús and Howie obtained a suitable sample, they too would join Moses and María on the island.

"Fine," agreed Jesús.

"Fine," agreed María.

"Fine," agreed Moses.

"Uh, what?" asked Howie, his attention momentarily lost amidst the excitement of his dream retirement finally coming true.

That was the only way the plan would work, according to Guy. His son couldn't make the trip north alone, and the attorney made the most logical travel companion: of everyone in the group, he had the least risk of arrest upon arrival in the United States.

"How many buffalo-style chicken wraps do I have to eat?" Howie wondered aloud before agreeing to his only option.

"So, we're done with *Cannapeñis*?" asked María. "Just like that?"

"Just like that," Guy confirmed. Though a question remained before they could move on. "But I'd like to know, why did the *Cannapeñis* make people act like dicks?"

"Like I said," Moses repeated, "the peppers made you act like a dick. It wasn't fair to attribute that side effect to the cannabis."

"The jalapeños?" Guy asked.

"Those weren't jalapeño peppers," Moses said. "You've been using peter peppers."

"What are peter peppers?" Guy asked.

"Look it up."[57] Moses was done answering questions.

EIGHTEEN

California

There were questions aplenty in Dullsville, at least from the perspective of DEA Special Agent Stan DeVille, who could hardly contain his excitement as he sat behind his desk reviewing the evidence from his surprise raid of 11 Main Street. He couldn't have asked for a better case. He'd discovered both drugs and immigrants. Or immigrants and drugs—it made no matter which order he said the words, as long as he connected the two.

First question—how many immigrants was he dealing with? From the papers he found in the oak desk at 11 Main Street, his new case appeared to involve at least three. This was an important detail: according to the DEA's official handbook, a case with two immigrants was more important than a case with only one immigrant, and a case with three immigrants was even more important than that.

Second question—where did the immigrants go? Based on the temperature of the drug-infused dessert he found baking in the oven at 11 Main Street, they'd barely escaped ahead of the raid. Although Stan managed to prevent that dessert from baking to perfection, nobody would be shaking his hand for an incomplete task. He needed to make an arrest to bring attention to the case.

And third question—when the heck was the President going to return his call? Over 24 hours had passed since he left a message with the intern who promised to speak to the Secretary.

Stan needed answers. He also needed to fill out a bunch of damn paperwork to justify discharging his pistol at the oven during the raid, since those Washington bureaucrats failed to grasp the challenging nature of his work.

The paperwork could wait.

◊ ◊ ◊

The DEA's Dullsville office held no monopoly over unanswered questions. Back on Main Street, near the scene of the crime, no question had been repeated more often than:

"What the heck is going on?"

Gabby Blabber wanted to know. Not that she found the unanswered question a bother. Her community had finally become more interesting than her favorite soap opera. On *TI&TA*, the highlight of the day involved the reemergence of a major character thought to be dead. Compare that to the multi-generational drug conspiracy brewing in Dullsville.

Gabby hadn't slept for over 24 hours. Eight cups of coffee deserved part of the blame, but the real cause of her restlessness involved her mind's endless race around the illegal activity next door. She'd now found more clues than she could count on one hand. First, (index finger) Moses ran off with Richard Dickens. Then, (middle finger) Richard returned with no sign of Moses. Then, (ring finger) a young family moved into Moses' house and (pinkie finger) lived there for twenty years, culminating with (thumb) illicit drug use and (other thumb) gun violence.

Insomnia aside, Gabby grinned at the satisfaction of having played such an integral role in reviving Dullsville's most interesting story.

On that afternoon, just after the day's episode of *TI&TA* reached a cliffhanging conclusion, Gabby found herself focused sideways as she sat in her favorite spot next to the side window of her house, staring through the curtains in case something important happened at 11 Main Street. With her eyes on the house next door, however, she failed to notice a man approaching her own residence from the front and knocking on her door.

Gabby closed the curtains and scurried to the door as swiftly as her creaky knees allowed. Through the peephole, she recognized a familiar face. Though she'd never spoken directly to the face, so as she opened the door, she asked:

"Who are you?"

◊ ◊ ◊

Who was Stan DeVille?

That was a difficult question to answer. The short version of his story centered around his career at the United States Department of Justice. The long of it turned out to be much more complex.

Of the Generation known only as X, Stan sat in the driver's seat from the start. The first words he heard coming out of the womb were instructions from his father to upgrade his sleeping arrangements in the maternity ward.

"You can always do better," he surely heard his father tell the nurse.

Stan quickly realized the truth of those words. He could always do better, if he tried hard enough. And he found it easier to do better at what he did best to begin with. For him, that was:

Prevention.

Yes, he possessed a knack for prevention; for seeking and stopping; for hindering, and inhibiting, and precluding all the same. If something could be done, then there was also a way to stop it, and that's what Stan did best.

His skills became apparent at a young age. Always the teacher's pet, he began as a meager tattler, telling tales of rules broken to anyone who listened. Teacher's assistant, hall monitor, and even junior security—he rose through the ranks like no student before him. The roles he undertook would limit his meaningful friendships, but he reasoned that a friendship built on broken rules wasn't one worth having in the first place.

Stan paid his way through college as a resident assistant. For ten semesters, he prohibited music after 9:00 p.m., fraternizing after 10:00 p.m., and flammable materials of all sorts, at all times of the day. When off duty, he majored in sociology, learning the ins and outs behind the science of human motivation. If he understood why people behaved in certain ways, then he'd know how to best prevent the behavior in the first place.

Now what would be the best career for someone with a relatively worthless degree and a knack for prevention? Stan asked himself that question over and over upon graduation until the answer became obvious: destiny called for a job with the federal government, with an emphasis on preventing unlawful acts. And he found just that at the United States Bureau of Alcohol, Tobacco, and Firearms (or "ATF"), where he honed his skills preventing three separate categories of criminal behavior.

Time slowed once Stan joined the federal government. His superiors seemed complacent, an annoying truth which limited his upward mobility. Transferring agencies offered the easiest path to advancement. Luckily for him, the DEA expanded at a time when he possessed just the right amount of experience telling people what not to do. The transition seemed natural for the young up-and-comer, from telling his compatriots what not to drink, smoke, or fire at the ATF, to keeping illegal narcotics out of their hands at the DEA.

Stan's career with the DEA took off right from the start, there being no employee more determined to advance. His first-year reviews cited an unprecedented dedication to keeping drugs out of the hands of those who sought them. His future appeared as bright as the jumpsuits of the citizens he arrested.

His future appeared bright, that is, until an undercover mission gone horribly wrong. It was no secret amongst the DEA that Stan possessed a twitchy trigger finger, though nobody foresaw such an unfortunate result: (he preferred not to talk about it). Rather than fire such a dedicated employee and admit fault in a tragedy, the DEA transferred Stan to Dullsville, where his twitchy fingers needn't be anywhere near a trigger.

Stan arrived in Dullsville a mere Agent, not Special. But that simple designation was short-lived, since every action he took openly demonstrated his specialty. Spearheading the local branch of DARE, he taught the town's youth everything he knew about the dangers of drug use. In doing so, he served in Dullsville long enough for a lockstep promotion from a simple Agent to the Special kind.

As much as Stan appreciated arbitrary titles, he craved recognition: for doing his job, for protecting the country, for standing for everything moral and honest and decent and right. And he wasn't getting any damn recognition toiling away in the most boring town in the country. Which meant he wasn't getting any closer to his dream.

Yes, Stan had a dream, and his dream was fairly specific.

He sought to one day shake hands with the President of the United States on the front lawn of the White House. Of course, someone needed to take his picture during the handshake, and print it on the front page of the newspaper, because what would the handshake be worth if nobody knew about it?

◊ ◊ ◊

Stan skipped over most of those details as he introduced himself to Gabby, instead simply extending his palm and greeting:

"I'm Stan DeVille, Special Agent with the U.S. Drug Enforcement Administration."

That's all Gabby needed to know. She never forgot a name, and she knew exactly where and when she last heard that one: over the phone, when she reported the drug use next door. She never forgot a face either, and also recalled the Special Agent raiding the house next door, since her window offered a front row seat for the show.

"Please, come in." Gabby held open the door. "Would you like a cup of coffee?"

Stan preferred to get straight to business. He wished to question Gabby about the call she placed to the DEA's office, prompting the raid on 11 Main Street, which culminated in justified gunfire.

"Completely justified," he insisted.

"Yes, I remember," Gabby said, "you scared me half to death."

There were plenty of people who Stan would've gladly scared to death. Gabby wasn't one of them. Unless she dealt drugs, which he thought unlikely. She wouldn't have reported her neighbors if so. Rather, the Special Agent profiled her as a concerned citizen who kept herself apprised of her neighbors' business for the safety of the neighborhood.

"That's right," Gabby confirmed, and nodded confidently.

Stan appreciated her intentions. He felt the same way. That's why he joined the DEA to begin with. Not only did he keep himself apprised of his neighbors' business, he got right in there and put a stop to their business when the situation called for it. A feeling like no other—he recommended that Gabby pursue the prohibition side of the trade if her passion truly lay in the art of prevention.

"Well," Gabby said, "that's why I called you in the first place."

Stan thanked the thoughtful citizen, and wondered what else she might be able to tell him about her neighbors.

Regrettably, Gabby had yet to piece the puzzle together, as hard as she tried. But she'd certainly answer questions about everything she knew. All he needed to specify was how many decades back the details should go, since she'd spent her entire life training for this moment.

"Your entire life?" Stan asked.

"My entire life," Gabby confirmed.

From what Stan could tell by looking at Gabby, that took a long time. So he asked her to begin with the most recent events and work her way backward. To start, he wondered how long the immigrants lived next door.

"Immigrants?" Had Gabby missed a clue?

"Not just any immigrants," Stan clarified. "Mexicans."

Gabby couldn't believe it at first. But then she could believe it, because Stan explained the subtle clues.

"Each of their names has an acute accent," Stan explained. "The oldest male, José, places his accent over the letter 'e.' The younger male, Jesús, places his accent over the letter 'u.' María's true identity was more difficult to decipher, because her accent hangs over the letter 'í' and blends in with the dot used by Americans."

Gabby had only heard their names spoken out loud; her ears must have missed the accent.

"It's easier to recognize if you read the names on paper," Stan explained, and patted her shoulder to comfort her for the failure. "Although especially with the 'í' in María, you can see how sneaky those Mexicans can be."

With that settled, Gabby recalled the three Mexicans moving into 11 Main Street around the same time the previous owner disappeared. His name was Moses Staffman. The timing sure seemed coincidental—there might have been a connection.

"Let's focus on the Mexicans," Stan said. "When did you say they moved in?"

Gabby recalled the Mexicans arriving about two decades earlier. The precise details of their arrival escaped her memory, but she could fetch her journal if the Special Agent wished to learn more.

"You kept a journal?" asked Stan, ever impressed by her passion for interference.

Gabby smiled and nodded. First, she found her journal; then, she found her reading glasses; and then, after balancing her reading glasses on the tip of her nose, she recalled the particulars of her first conversation with the tan woman next door. At the time, Gabby recorded several details: (1) the woman's name was Maria (scribbled without an accent over the "i"); (2) María claimed not to know Moses; and (3) María worked for a company called TSA.

"TSA?" Stan asked. "You mean the Transportation Security Administration?"

"I suppose so," Gabby said.

From what Stan understood, TSA had only been around for fifteen years. So how could María work for TSA twenty years earlier? Perhaps the journal contained a mistake.

"There's nothing wrong with my journal," Gabby assured, without a doubt in her mind.

"She worked for TSA five years before the agency existed?"

"I'm sure of it."

The Special Agent fingered his chin. The situation was even more serious than he initially thought. "This is what those Mexicans do," he supposed. "They infiltrate and take over."

Gabby had no idea the situation was so dire. Though she supposed Stan was right. On her favorite soap opera, *TI&TA*, there once appeared a Hispanic woman—Sofía or Camílla or Luciána or something like that (an accent must have hung over at least one of the letters, maybe more, based on what she now knew). The Hispanic woman infiltrated one of the wealthiest families in Paradise Cove by gaining employment as the family's maid. She started out doing only menial tasks, sure, but after a couple episodes, the family treated her like a blood relative—joking, laughing, sharing pleasantries, even inviting her to sit down with them at dinner on occasion. Of course, it was all a setup: in no time at all, the Hispanic maid enjoyed improper relations with the family's patriarch, and then disappeared with an expensive family heirloom.

"Interesting," Stan said, even if he didn't mean it.

"She infiltrated and took over," Gabby replied. "Just like you said."

Stan looked at his watch. He wished to wrap up his discussion with the chatty next-door neighbor, and intended just one final question:

"When did you last see any of the Mexicans?"

Gabby watched an episode of *TI&TA* a few hours before Stan arrived, but the maid had been absent from the show for over a month, ever since she stole the expensive heirloom from Paradise Cove's wealthiest family. Surely, the maid would resurface at some point though—the characters on her show always did, even if they looked different the second time around.

"No," Stan said. "When did you last see the Mexicans from next door? María? José? Jesús?"

"Oh, them." Gabby supposed that she hadn't seen any of those Mexicans since Stan's raid. And she'd watched the house next door almost nonstop since then, so she'd know if they returned.

"Nonstop?" Stan asked.

"Nonstop," Gabby confirmed, except that her definition of "nonstop" excluded the hour of her favorite soap opera.

In that case, Stan needed a favor. He asked Gabby to continue to watch 11 Main Street, and notify him if any of the Mexicans returned.

Gabby felt happy to oblige. No, actually, she may have been happy, but that wasn't why she agreed to the favor. She felt obliged to agree, regardless of how happy she felt. Protecting the country was her civic duty, and she felt obliged to do everything she could to help her compatriots fight foreign threats.

Plus, she really wanted to know what the heck was going on.

◊ ◊ ◊

Stan clicked his heels together upon return to his office, giddy at the thought of his hard work finally paying off. Well, there may have been luck involved too, considering that a gem of a case fell directly into his lap. But he deserved the lucky break. He'd worked so hard, for so long, getting people to stop doing the things they wanted to do.

"Good cases come to those who wait," the Special Agent told himself.

Stan understated his luck. This wasn't merely a good case. This was a great case. Not only did it involve drug-slinging Mexicans, it involved Mexicans infiltrating the U.S. government, somehow gaining employment with TSA before the agency existed.

"Those sneaky Mexicans," Stan said. "How do they do it?"

Though in the end, his question proved inconsequential. What was done, was done. His job involved fixing what was done. If he did, he'd be rewarded, most importantly.

Stan picked up the *Dullsville Times* from his desk. The cover story told of another ICE raid, this time in Texas, with dozens of illegal immigrants captured. The immigrants had infiltrated a variety of industries across the state, and in some cases received high marks for their work ethic, loyalty, friendliness, and delicious home cooking—factors which made them endearing, yet highly dangerous, with the ability to blend in and catch others off guard.

"Where are all the Mexicans coming from?" Stan wondered, with the obvious answer being Mexico, though that's not what he meant by the question.

The cover story included yet another photo taken on the front lawn of the White House in Washington, D.C., with the ICE Agent in charge of the raid grasping palms with the President, both smiling and staring into each other's eyes—a harmonious sight to behold, at least for anyone who gave a damn about the country.

Stan set the newspaper back down on his desk and gazed out the window of his office at nothing in particular. A devilish smile grew across his face. Soon he'd be the one standing on the front lawn of the White House, shaking hands with the President.

NINETEEN

California

A triple espresso wasn't how Manny Hernandez preferred to start his morning. Normally, he avoided the dark brew in favor of a sweaty dash around the neighborhood. But some mornings left no time for physical fitness.

It had been a tough month for Manny, in the midst of a tougher year, in the midst of an even tougher life. From the monthly perspective, he'd hardly slept as he struggled to keep up with a demanding work schedule. From the yearly perspective, he approached his first annual review as a paramedic, and the pain and suffering he witnessed could be overwhelming. And from the lifetime perspective, well, suffice to say that life had never been easy for the first-generation American.

Almost everyone in the neighborhood knew Manny's story, mostly because he'd lived there longer than everyone else. His parents arrived amongst the first settlers of Dullsville when the local county board approved the initial housing development. Avocado farmers from a small town in Mexico, they came to the United States in search of a quiet community to grow a loving family for generations.

"And what could be quieter than Dullsville?" Manny's father asked at the time.

The family moved into 12 Main Street the instant that the roof stretched over the walls. With a baby on the way, they couldn't wait for the plumbing. And in an instant came Manuel "Manny" Hernandez VI, a healthy six pounds of joy.

The first few days of Manny's life brought delight to the entire household. Or maybe a week passed, or even a month, before a doctor diagnosed his father with a terminal illness, the specifics unimportant. Before young Manny learned to talk, the family's patriarch left behind nothing but a loving wife, a young son, and a legacy of determination.

Manny's mother carried on, determined not to let the American dream perish with her husband. Working day and night at separate jobs, she earned barely enough money to get by. She did that for as long as she could, until she too received her own terminal diagnosis.

Despite the bleak outlook, Manny persevered, earning money wherever he could to take care of his mother. He studied harder than ever in his classes, aiming to become a doctor and help others in similar medical predicaments. He became obsessed with health: he sprinted up and down Main Street each morning to stay in shape, determined not to suffer the same fate as his parents as he aged into adulthood.

In school, Manny's grades floated just above average. Unfortunately, with his heavy workload, he lacked the free time to raise those grades to exceptional. When it came time to apply to the country's top undergraduate premedical programs, exceptional marks seemed to be a prerequisite, along with the ability to pay a hefty annual tuition.

Fortunately, medical school provided far from the only path to the medical profession. Instead of becoming a doctor, Manny obtained an associate's degree at Dullsville Community College and became a paramedic on the local emergency services team. Paramedic stood out as his perfect occupation for several reasons: he earned a fair salary, at least enough to cover the mortgage at 12 Main Street; he received health insurance, should he find himself in the same predicament as his parents; and, most importantly, he could do what he loved most—care for others' good health.

Manny's job also had a downside, as all professions do. He worked in a tough field—a high stress environment subject to significant emotional breakdowns—with daily reminders of the thin line between life and death, not to mention the pain involved with either condition. Some days, Manny stood on top of the world, with the feeling of saving a life being matched by none other. But he found other days equally depressing, when death proved unavoidable, no matter how hard he fought off the grim reaper.[58]

Without a doubt, Manny's chest housed a heart of gold. But even gold has a breaking point. His parents' deaths, the mounting hours on the job, the high stress work environment—an unstoppable pressure built inside the poor paramedic. Not to mention the policemen and the reporters and the other curious citizens coming and going across the street, day in and day out since María and Jesús left town, asking him questions and demanding answers—he didn't know how much more he could take.

On top of all that, he was late to work!

If even one more stressful event occurred, it might be the last before Manny cracked.

So it came as no surprise that one more event occurred, at that precise moment, when Manny chugged the last drops of espresso and opened his front door to find a local fugitive standing on the porch.

"Hi, Manny," Jesús greeted. "How have you been?"

"Jesús!" Manny yanked his old friend inside and shut the door. "What are you doing here?"

The short answer was that Jesús borrowed his sort-of attorney's sedan to return to the neighborhood and dig up a few plants—which he would've done already except that he spotted several people poking around 11 Main Street as he pulled up the street. The long answer involved a decades-long plan apparently still stuck at Step Two.

"We can talk more when I get off work." Manny warned Jesús not to drive around Dullsville in the daylight. "Stay inside my house until I get back, and don't answer the door."

Jesús agreed without saying as much. 12 Main Street seemed like the perfect place to hide out until he could cross the street to pick more *Zerojuana* plants. Since he now needed to kill some time, he had a single question for Manny.

"Do you still have my backpack?"

The trendy backpack remained hidden in Manny's closet. He'd been eager to get rid of the luggage ever since he caught a whiff of the contents. He even asked:

"With how much that backpack reeks, how do you carry it around unnoticed?"

Jesús shrugged. He'd never noticed much of a smell.

◊ ◊ ◊

Jesús felt no urge to leave Dullsville before Manny returned. Nor did he need to leave; he could spare a few hours before returning to Mexico with his sort-of attorney. But to be safe, he rolled a *joint* with the *Zerojuana* from his backpack, and he puffed until his mind became content to stay put.

Ambition abated, Jesús sunk into the couch and flipped the channels on the television with reckless abandon. First, he turned to a soap opera, *The Interesting & The Attractive*, on Channel 2. Dubbed *TI&TA* for short, the show meant to launch a roller coaster of emotions, though he found it difficult to feel much for any of the characters. To him, the entire show seemed to be more of a vapid set of attractive thespians than a true dramatic tale of heart-wrenching gains and losses. Without a relatable character, he changed the channel.

Channel 3 aired a live-action movie, *50 First Dates*, in which Adam Sandler brought public awareness to anterograde amnesia through the comedic love story of a modern-day Lothario.[59] From what Jesús could tell, the biggest problem any of the characters faced appeared to be showing an emotional range matching the gravity of the issue presented by the film. Without a relatable character, he changed the channel.

Real life far exceeds fantasy, which Jesús understood as much as anyone. Finally, he found something worth watching on Channel 4, where two news anchors, both with incredibly full hair, sat behind a long desk and discussed the despicable conditions imposed on the illegal immigrants discovered during a flurry of recent raids by the U.S. Immigration and Customs Enforcement (or "ICE"). Apparently, the ICE agents treated the immigrants as if they didn't belong in the country. In some cases, the agents separated families, and even threw the immigrants in cages as if they broke the law.

"I've also been told that the detainees aren't receiving the minimum number of servings of whole grains previously recommended by the USDA," the anchorwoman revealed.[60]

"And it's questionable whether they're getting enough dairy," the anchorman added, "though I have yet to confirm exact numbers, and don't want to make an unfair characterization about—"

Suddenly, the newscasters were interrupted: not by a breaking event on the television, or even an occurrence inside Manny's house, but by a deep voice speaking through a megaphone from just outside the front door.

"This is the DEA!" the deep voice announced. "Come out with your hands up!"

Either one of those exclamations would've troubled a fugitive like Jesús, if not for the *joint* now reduced to mostly smoke and ash. But thanks to that *joint*, he took his time rising from the couch to check on the noise. To be safe, he hid his trendy backpack underneath a couch cushion as he shuffled to the window. Someone once told him that the best hiding places are also the most obvious, and he took the advice to heart without much thought thereafter.

At the window, Jesús found relief from his mild anxiety. Or rather, the relief came from what he *didn't* find, since he *didn't* find any action on Manny's doorstep at 12 Main Street.

Across the street told another story entirely. Commingling on the front lawn of 11 Main Street stood at least a dozen people: a DEA Agent with a megaphone, surrounded by a few buff men in black helmets and bulletproof vests; apparent reporters standing in front of cameramen and sound technicians, all angling for the best shot of the residence; and even onlookers relaxing in chairs, seeming to enjoy the entire ordeal.

Before Jesús knew it, the DEA Agent broke down the front door to 11 Main Street and rushed inside; the bulletproof men followed, all waving their pistols in the air. Screaming and crashing and banging and other violent noises rang out, until a man in a bathrobe sprinted out to the front lawn with the Agent chasing closely behind.

Then, as Jesús watched in suspense from across the street, the man in the bathrobe dove behind a car in the driveway, before cocking his gun and firing a bullet at the Agent, who lunged sideways to avoid the shot; the bullet shattered the front window of the house in dramatic fashion, triggering a piercing scream from inside. The Agent fired back at the bathrobed man, shattering the car's front windshield. The rest of the bulletproof men ran out of the house, ducking and diving across the lawn, taking cover wherever they could.

"There's nowhere to go!" the Agent shouted, accurate in some sense.

"There's everywhere to go!" the bathrobed man replied, equally accurate in another sense. With his back to the car, he reloaded his gun's magazine and shoved it back into the handle before firing off two more shots in the general direction of the house. One shot crashed through the window and triggered another scream from inside. The other shot somehow ricocheted off the house and struck a random bulletproof man in the shoulder.

"Ouch!" the random man said. "I've been hit in the shoulder!"

"Step away from the car!" the Agent shouted, taking control by rising from his cover.

The bathrobed man escalated tensions by firing another bullet at the Agent. He missed by a nose—thanks to a quick movement by the Agent to tilt his nose to the side—with the bullet again ricocheting off the house and hitting the random bulletproof man in his other shoulder.

"Ouch!" the random man repeated. "I've been hit again! In the other shoulder!"

"Cover me!" the Agent shouted as somersaulted across the lawn, keeping his pistol focused on the car, firing off two bullets for dramatics, with neither bullet appearing to strike near his target.

Jesús suddenly found himself standing on the porch of 12 Main Street, so caught up in the action that his legs moved outside without warning the rest of his body.

"This is your last chance!" The Agent was serious. He squinted at an exposed section of his adversary's torso, then raised his pistol and focused on the target. (If an onlooker with a video camera zoomed in close enough in slow motion, they would even see the Agent squeeze the trigger of his pistol halfway, coming just short of the precise degree to fire the bullet.) But before the Agent could fire a bullet, an inflatable ball bounced toward the bathrobed man, followed by a diapered toddler chasing his toy.

"A toddler now?" Jesús wondered from across the street. "What's going on?"

"My ball!" The toddler cried out as he reached toward the man in the bathrobe.

The bathrobed man promptly grabbed the toddler around the waist and pressed his gun into a baby-soft cheek. "Put your weapons down," he ordered, "or I'll kill the baby!"

"Okay." The Agent held up his hands before carefully bending over and placing his pistol on the lawn, then motioning for the other vested men to do the same. "Please, let the baby go."

The bathrobed man did as asked, but not before reorienting his gun and firing a bullet at the Agent's sternum, then releasing a hearty laugh as he threw the baby on the pavement and dashed away.

"Now *I've* been hit!" the Agent said, his hands filling with blood as he clutched his left breast, stumbling back and forth across the front lawn, his legs wobbling like gelatin. He stumbled back and forth for quite some time—while the rest of the crowd watched with mouths agape—until he dropped to his knees, then on his stomach, and then, finally, flat on the ground. Somehow still alive, he summoned the last of his energy to tilt his head up to the sky and yell: "God bless America!"

Now something seemed familiar about the Agent's dramatic death, but the *joint* Jesús puffed wasn't doing his memory any favors, so it took him a moment to gather his thoughts. His memory kicked in eventually though, when he realized an important detail: he knew the lead DEA Agent. He knew the Agent pretty well, actually, having lived next door to the fallen hero for the majority of his life. And the Agent's name was Richard Dickens.

"Richard!" Jesús screamed after a short delay. Overcome by emotion, he sprinted across the street, dropped to his knees, and cradled Richard's head in his arms, sobbing and shaking as he released a cascade of tears for his fallen neighbor.

"Cut!" shouted a man in a director's chair, while waving his hands frantically through the air. "Who is that kid?"

Richard suddenly opened his eyes and answered:

"Jesús?"

"Richard!" Jesús cried. "You're alive!"

"Now we have to redo the scene!" screamed the man in the director's chair. "Let's take a fifteen-minute break and then start from the top. And get that fucking kid out of here!"

◊ ◊ ◊

The man in the director's chair wasn't the only one watching as Richard Dickens died and came back to life. Gabby Blabber also saw the drama unfold, including the kid running across the lawn and ruining the theatrical gun battle. The difference between her and the director was that she recognized the kid running across the lawn. And he wasn't a kid, she recalled; he was twenty years of age.

"Also, his name is Jesús," she mumbled, "and he's wanted by the U.S. Drug Enforcement Administration."

◊ ◊ ◊

With fifteen minutes to spare, Richard and Jesús disappeared across the street, back to the twelfth house on the block. Richard was well aware of Jesús' fugitive status and wished to keep his neighbor out of harm's way. Apparently, the only person unaware of Jesús' fugitive status was Jesús.

"What's going on?" Jesús examined Richard's bloodied sternum. "Are you okay?"

"Oh, that?" Richard brushed his hands across his chest, showing himself to be perfectly healthy besides red discoloration. "We're filming a reenactment of the DEA raid on your house. An independent studio is producing the film, and I landed the role of the Agent in charge of the investigation. It's the biggest role of my career!"

"The raid on my house?" Jesús asked. "But it has only been a few days since that happened."

"These indie producers move quick," Richard said, "otherwise the major Hollywood studios buy up the rights to everything."

Jesús thought back to the original incident, which he also witnessed from across the street. He recalled a single DEA Agent, possibly Special, firing the only shots, with the only injuries involving kitchen appliances.

"Hollywood always does some rewriting to make the stories more relatable for the audience," Richard explained. "In the movie version of your story, the DEA Agent takes a bullet from a Mexican drug dealer while saving a baby's life. Don't worry, the Agent survives!"

"Who was the man in the bathrobe?" Jesús asked.

"Didn't you see?" Richard assumed that Jesús recognized the A-list celebrity playing the starring role. "The Mexican drug dealer is being played by Adam Sandler."

"Adam Sandler?" Jesús asked. "I thought he did comedies."

"I don't know," Richard admitted. "I guess he does anything that pays."

Jesús shrugged. He supposed Richard was right.

"You're an amazing actor," Jesús said. Utterly fooled by the death scene, he suggested that Richard deserved an Academy Award for his convincing performance as the victim of a bullet.[61]

Richard appreciated the kind words. Not everyone on the set thought so highly of his dramatic portrayal. Adam Sandler complained about the lack of emotion when Richard clutched his chest and called out in agony. And Adam's opinion carried significant weight with the director. If Adam wanted Richard to be replaced by another actor, all he needed to do was snap his fingers.

"Luckily, Adam has trouble physically snapping his fingers," Richard observed of the actor's strange malady. "He rubs his thumb and middle finger together, but he can't actually make the snapping sound."

Even still, Richard's death scene demanded more creativity. But he wondered what else he could do. He already acted as dramatically as he knew how. Perhaps he wasn't cut out for the movie business, he supposed in a moment of weakness. Perhaps his parents were right about drama being a waste of time.

Attempting comfort, Jesús set his hand on Richard's shoulder and squeezed. He hated to hear so much self-doubt, and wished he could help the struggling thespian. Well, he could indeed help, he realized after a moment of thought. He could help Richard in the same way he helped everyone else. Helping Richard would be no trouble at all, actually, since his trendy backpack still contained enough *Zerojuana* for another perfectly rolled *joint*.

"Try this," offered Jesús, now able to craft a *joint* in a matter of seconds thanks to all the practice. "It'll make you more creative."

Richard didn't *do* drugs. He needed the full range of his wits to die the perfectly dramatic death in front of the camera. From what he understood, cannabis robbed users of their wits, among other side effects.

"You'll be fine," Jesús said, sure that Richard's wits would only disappear to the extent he allowed.

Fortunately, Richard possessed an open mind. He'd try anything once. Perhaps puffing the drug would help him understand his character's motives. Plus, he felt desperate to retain the biggest role of his career, costarring as a DEA Agent beside Adam Sandler's portrayal of a Mexican drug dealer. Adam could learn to snap his fingers at any time; he needed to nail the scene before then. With more reasons to accept Jesús' offer than to refuse, Richard said:

"Oh, what the heck," and inhaled a puff.

"Pretty good, huh?" Jesús asked with a puff for himself.

"This *is* pretty good," Richard observed, emphasizing "is" in a way that only a real actor could pull off, his creative juices flowing freely behind the smile slowly growing across his face, his mind afire with ideas as the smoke escaped his nostrils.

"That's *it*!" After a moment of clarity, Richard understood his biggest mistake with his portrayal of life's ultimate demise. "I think my death scene would be more realistic if I acted *less* dramatic, and straighter to the point."

"Oh," Jesús replied, "good to know."

Richard checked his watch. His fifteen-minute break was almost up. "I have to get back to the set. Where did you get this *Zerojuana* stuff?"

"I have a source," Jesús replied without revealing particulars. "I'll be selling it soon, if you want more."

◊ ◊ ◊

The film crew at 11 Main Street had wrapped up the day's shoot by the time Manny returned home from his shift. He hoped Jesús hadn't been too confused by the circus across the street, since he forgot to warn the fugitive of Hollywood's sudden interest in Dullsville.

That day had been a tough one for Manny—one of the toughest of the young paramedic's career. So when he hung his coat on the rack and Jesús asked how his day went, his answer was:

"Do you really want to know?"

The day started out like any other. His ambulance fired up with the turn of a key, and he and his partner went about their routine, checking the bandages and medicines, ensuring the equipment was charged and ready to save lives. So far, so good, the paramedical partners agreed at the time.

"Are you sure you want to hear the rest?"

Jesús nodded; it was far too late to halt the story by this point.

The first emergency call of Manny's day proved relatively tame—a fender bender at the drive-through of the best fried chicken restaurant in town, a place called Pepe's Fried Chicken. After checking the vitals of the victims, Manny deemed all participants of the collision to be alive and healthy.

"That doesn't sound too bad," Jesús said.

Manny agreed. He preferred those types of calls. Not only was no blood shed, the restaurant manager offered both him and his partner a free meal of their choice. Though with fried chicken so high in sodium, Manny asked for a grilled chicken sandwich instead.

"That was nice of the manager to accommodate you," Jesús said.

Not really, Manny explained, because his second emergency call of the day came in while his chicken still roasted on the grill. The manager promised to set aside the sandwich until Manny returned, but made no guarantee regarding the freshness of the meat until then.

"Oh," Jesús said.

The second emergency call caused slightly more stress. And

Manny meant the term "slightly" in the relative sense—up to that point in the day, that is, not in view of the day as a whole.

"What happened on the second emergency call?" Jesús asked.

The second call brought Manny and his partner to Dullsville's finest nursing home, where an elderly woman felt short of breath. Her husband noticed the minor change in his wife's behavior and alerted the staff. He knew his wife better than anyone, he said, and she needed to get to the hospital with the utmost haste.

Manny and his partner checked the woman's vitals and loaded her into their ambulance; the husband waited behind. But before they left, the husband told his wife, "I love you, darling." His wife returned the sentiment, but used the term "dear" where the husband said "darling." They then shared a brief moment which touched the heart, departing with, "If I don't see you again here on Earth, I'll find you in heaven."

Manny assured the husband that his wife would be fine, and that they'd see each other again at the hospital. With no room in the ambulance for the husband to ride along, someone from the nursing home's staff planned to give him a ride shortly thereafter.

On the way to the hospital, the elderly woman's health took an unexpected turn. Her heartbeat sped up, and she began to cough after she complained of difficulty breathing. Not only that, but when Manny checked her vitals, her blood pressure spiked, and her pulse jumped, and even her temperature suggested a problem.

"Oh my," Jesús said.

Indeed, the situation seemed dire. As a trained paramedic, Manny stabilized his patient to the best of his ability, while his partner drove to the hospital as fast as the ambulance allowed. There existed moments when he thought the woman might not make it, but ultimately, he handed her off to the hospital staff with an assurance from the attending doctor that his quick actions saved her life.

"That's incredible," Jesús said.

Manny found no time to celebrate, however, because his third emergency call came in before he could wish the elderly woman well, let alone accept thanks for saving her life. The third call came from the local shopping mall, where a woman went into labor. With contractions too close for movement, she resigned to crossing her legs on the parking lot pavement to hold her baby inside as she waited for help.

Manny arrived to find the child already breaching, feet-first, a dangerous circumstance requiring quick action to rectify. As a trained paramedic, he knew how to respond, and in short order held a newborn baby in his arms, dripping with fluid, wailing with the first breaths of life.

"That's amazing," Jesús said. "It must be an incredible feeling to deliver a life into the world."

And then, before Manny handed the baby to the mother, the baby died in his arms, the result of an unpredictable birth defect.

"Oh," Jesús said.

And then the mother died of internal bleeding.

"Oh," Jesús said.

And then another call came in from the hospital, informing Manny that the elderly woman fell asleep and failed to wake back up. Although Manny saved her life earlier in the day, she needed saving again at the hospital, and luck stayed away the second time around.

"Oh," Jesús said.

And then the elderly woman's husband arrived at the hospital and received the dreadful news. The husband kept true to his promise to find her in heaven, because only moments after learning of her death, he too passed on to the afterlife, the result of a broken heart.

"Oh," Jesús said.

And then, now with a moment to spare, yet to eat a meal in the midst of such a flurry of activity, Manny returned to the best fried chicken restaurant in town. As if heartbreak knew no limit, his grilled chicken sandwich had been thrown in the trash after spending too much time underneath the warmer. Not only that, but thanks to a shift change, there was a new manager on duty, who lacked any recollection of Manny's heroic actions from earlier in the day. The new manager said he could make Manny another sandwich, but he'd need to charge the paramedic full price, because the previous manager neglected to mention the special offer before leaving for the day.

"Wow," Jesús said. "What a day."

Indeed, the stress overwhelmed poor Manny. And the hospital scheduled him for another shift early the next morning. He wished he could forget the pain he witnessed, even momentarily, but he found it difficult to erase the misery etched into his mind. If only he could relax, just for a few minutes.

Jesús' golden eyes lit up: he had an idea, and he thought it was a fine one too. Manny could relax, he said, because he possessed the stuff to help; it was in his trendy backpack, much depleted from earlier in the day, but still enough in quantity to relieve Manny's pain, at least temporarily.

"Try this," Jesús said, and instantly twirled yet another *joint*. "It'll help you relax."

Manny took a deep breath as he studied the *joint*. He felt tempted by the offer. That day had been one of the toughest of his young career. He wanted nothing more than to forget the pain he witnessed. Then again, as a medical professional, he fully understood the potential health problems commonplace in *joint* puffers.

"C'mon," Jesús insisted.

Manny declined, though not because of the cannabis in particular. Rather, the method of ingestion gave him pause. From a health perspective, he objected to the idea of polluting his airways. He kept his lungs in tiptop shape.

"I've heard it's possible to bake cannabis into brownies though," he said.

Manny had never tried what he suggested, but he believed himself to be a fantastic cook. The worst-case scenario, in his mind, resulted in a batch of a delicious chocolate dessert.

"How about blondies?" Jesús suggested the non-chocolate alternative which used vanilla and brown sugar.

The irony of brown sugar in the blondies notwithstanding, Manny agreed to the idea. He'd never made blondies, but he enjoyed butterscotch flavoring. Who wouldn't? And since he owned all the ingredients for brownies, plus vanilla and brown sugar, they could whip up a batch in no time with the rest of the *Zerojuana* cannabis from Jesús' backpack.

"Is it okay if we use all the cannabis that's left?" Manny asked.

"I'm supposed to pick more fresh plants anyway," Jesús replied. "That's the entire reason I came back to the neighborhood, after all."

◊ ◊ ◊

Out of the oven, the blondies were perfect: from their crisp golden texture, to their savory butterscotch taste, to the relaxing feeling which crept in after consumption. On top of all that, only a small taste of the dessert needed to be eaten to feel the relaxing effect, so the calorie count remained low, if Manny had any further health concerns. (He did.)

Finally, Manny could shed his grief. Although he knew the feeling would return at some point, it felt nice to have a moment of solace—a break from the constant reminders of impending death, to be clear.

Manny felt so good that he thought nothing in particular when his phone rang; and surprisingly, he still felt good after listening to the caller. At another time, on another day, he would've been upset to find out that the fugitive on his couch disobeyed his only house rule.

"You didn't leave the house today, did you?" Manny covered the mouthpiece on the telephone as he spoke.

Jesús shook his head.

"I ask because the call is for you." Manny handed Jesús the telephone. "It's Richard Dickens."

Jesús' memory functioned slower than usual thanks to the blondies. "I forgot to mention that I saw Richard today."

Richard was in a good mood. Apparently, his death performance had improved dramatically upon his return to the set after the fifteen-minute break with Jesús. He'd stunned the entire cast and crew with his sudden creativity. Even Adam Sandler marveled at the way he curled up and pretended to die.

"That's nice," Jesús said.

Richard agreed. That's why he was in such a good mood, with his mood tied to his day. But he'd yet to mention the best part. His performance impressed the rest of the cast and crew enough that they wondered what changed during the fifteen-minute break. When he told them about *Zerojuana*, they all wanted to give the stuff a try.

"Even Adam Sandler is interested!" Richard said.

Most of the cast and crew were at Richard's house, celebrating their final day of filming in Dullsville. Many would return to Hollywood the following morning, so Richard recommended that Jesús bring over more *joints*, right away.

"And when I say 'right away,' I mean 'now,'" Richard advised. "Adam has an early flight tomorrow, so he'll be leaving soon."

Well this presented a problem: Jesús had no *Zerojuana* flowers to twist into *joints*. Instead, he possessed a butterscotch dessert made with vanilla and brown sugar.

"Do actors like blondies?" Jesús looked over the pan of delicious baked goods whipped up by Manny.

"Do you mean brownies?"

"No." Jesús meant blondies. "They're made with vanilla and brown sugar, resulting in a butterscotch taste."

Richard supposed that the actors cared less about the means, and more about the results. They preferred *joints*, due to the carelessly cool image of puffing on a smoking cigarette, but blondies would work just the same.

"Just get over here fast!"

◊ ◊ ◊

The blondies seemed plenty cool, so Jesús cut the dessert into small squares, set the squares on a tray, and covered the tray with clear plastic wrap for transport to Richard's party. He invited Manny along for the walk, but Manny had sunken so deeply into the couch by then that movement was out of the question.

"I'll be right back," Jesús told his host, who strained nary a muscle as Jesús showed himself the door.

For a moment, nothing could erase the ear-to-ear smile across Jesús' face. He knew *Zerojuana* would be easy to sell. And now, in only a half day in Dullsville, he had the chance to make his mark, with a group of individuals already interested—and not just any group of individuals, but a highly influential bunch.

Actors!

How could it get any better than that? There existed no bigger platform than the one given to actors. Nor was there a profession more willing to use their platform. If the actors liked *Zerojuana*, then so would the rest of the country, as long as the actors said to like it.

And a big name like Adam Sandler?

"Wow," Jesús gushed. "This is my chance."

If only he possessed more *joints*, since the actors apparently preferred puffery to ingestion. With actors being such a finicky bunch, he understood the need to appease. He wished he had more *Zerojuana* flowers to give to Richard's friends.

"Hmm," he said.

Gradually, Jesús reached a fairly obvious conclusion. He needed to return to 11 Main Street at some point to pick more *Zerojuana* plants to bring back to the island. Why not pick the plants right then?

The filming equipment had disappeared, and everyone on the crew had either left for the night or made their way to Richard's house for the celebration. The whitewashed, two-story ranch at 11 Main Street sat quiet—so quiet that someone wouldn't have known it stood there if not for the faint glare from the closest streetlight.

Carefully balancing the tray of blondies, Jesús crept across the street, crouching ever so slightly, creating an exaggerated illusion of cautiousness that seemed more show than substance. Though he remained stoic on the outside, his mind raced with excitement. Next door, Richard Dickens' party raged, with music blasting through the walls as the guests rhythmically kicked their feet. There must have been at least thirty people inside, all laughing and singing and dancing and smiling (and in some cases, more than one of those activities at once).

"They're going to love me for this." Jesús assured himself of the adulation of some of Hollywood's finest individuals.

Darkness draped the area around the *titan arums*. Even with the indirect light from the street, Jesús found it difficult to see with absolute clarity. Still, he knew his way around 11 Main Street without lights, having accessed his secret garden at all times of day and night over the years. He walked straight to the *titan arums*, prepared to once again reveal the secret garden of *Zerojuana* like so many times before. But before he moved the *titan arums* to the side, an angry voice made him jump.

"Turn around and put your hands up!"

Jesús turned around to find a flashlight glaring into his eyes and a pistol pointing toward his head, both controlled by his former DARE instructor, DEA Special Agent Stan DeVille. Although he heard Stan's instructions, he kept his arms down: he needed his hands to hold his tray of butterscotch blondies.

"I said to put your hands up!"

Clearly, Stan lacked any recollection of his former student as they stood in the dark more than a half decade after sharing a classroom together.

Jesús deemed himself no match for the pistol. So he slowly stretched his arms upright, and balanced the tray of blondies over his head, all the while careful to avoid sudden movements which might startle the Special Agent, whose trigger finger already appeared to be twitching.

The Special Agent possessed a strong set of windpipes, and his voice echoed far past Jesús, though not everyone who heard the noise felt as nervous as the twenty-year-old with the pistol in his face. Gabby Blabber, at 13 Main Street, had been watching the entire time, and sat on the edge of her seat; Manny Hernandez, across the street at 12 Main Street, had sunken so deeply into the couch that no decibel level could move him.

Then there was the party raging at 9 Main Street, where the music screeched to a halt as the guests scrambled for a view of the standoff next door. Some piled against the windows, others spilled onto the front lawn, most with their smartphone cameras recording as the confrontation escalated.[62]

Neither Jesús nor Stan paid attention to the added presence, each more focused on the pistol pointed toward the former from the shaking hand of the latter.

"Set down the brownies!" Stan stumbled through his words. He was in no mood for games, let alone the type of delicious dessert which someone might consume while playing.

"They're not brownies, they're blondies!" Jesús shouted back. "They're made with vanilla and brown sugar!"

"I said set down the brownies!" Stan repeated himself, unconcerned with the particular flavor. Not that he understood what Jesús said to begin with. Besides, even if he understood the words coming out of his adversary's mouth, he was too caught up in the excitement to process the information.

Jesús found no reason to argue with the man pointing a pistol at his face. He agreed to the Special Agent's terms and began to slowly lower his arms. But before he set the tray on the ground, a crash rang out next door at 9 Main Street as the door slammed behind a particularly obnoxious partygoer just noticing the commotion. And this slam of the door triggered the Special Agent, who triggered his pistol, which shot a bullet straight through the twenty-year-old Mexican-American.

"I've been shot!" Jesús yelled, making clear what happened if there existed any doubt by the onlookers, then collapsing to the ground as a delectable butterscotch dessert rained down on the lawn all around him.

TWENTY

California

An overnight sensation, Jesús became the talk of a nation in no time at all. By sunrise, every news outlet in the country was broadcasting coverage of his arrest, almost every minute of the day besides during the blocks of time allotted for advertisements. There were grainy videos of the incident shot from his neighbor's house; interviews with eyewitnesses recounting wildly varying versions of the event; pundits offering analyses of the social impact; political leaders using the opportunity as a soundboard for their campaigns; and famous entertainers forcing their opinions into the mix.

Needless to say, it was the biggest story of the day.

The closest news station, Channel 4, scored the evening's most anticipated interview: an exclusive one-on-one sit-down with Stan DeVille, the DEA Special Agent involved in the incident which had captured the nation's attention. Jesús, the gunshot victim, was the news station's first choice for an interview. But with Jesús hospitalized, not to mention under arrest, the second option became the first option, and Stan DeVille answered the call.

"Of course I'll do it!"

Stan had never seen the Channel 4 News, but no other station asked for an interview, so he took what he could get. He could only imagine the story Channel 4 would tell about the groundbreaking drug bust twenty years in the making, broken open by a brilliant Special Agent with a thirst for the truth.

With Channel 4's interview set to broadcast live later that day, Stan found himself with a few hours to spare before his free publicity. Not that he could spend the time resting on his laurels. The interview would include questions—he remained certain of that much—and he needed to respond with answers. He'd be forced to explain why he used lethal force during Jesús' arrest. Twenty years ago, shooting an immigrant wouldn't have raised an eyebrow; but these days, the public wanted justification for every shot fired.

That's right, every single shot!

The country had become so damn sensitive.

Stan knew that the Channel 4 reporter would ask why he pulled his pistol on the criminal, Jesús. Fortunately, he had a valid reason: the Colt single-action revolver. Jesús may not have possessed the Colt single-action revolver at the time of the incident, but (1) he found the weapon at 11 Main Street, (2) where Jesús lived for twenty years, (3) meaning that Jesús practically held the Colt single-action revolver in his hand when Stan fired the shot in the video.

"1 + 2 = 3," Stan calculated.

Besides, Stan's bullet struck Jesús in the foot, and nobody could tell which direction he'd aimed based on the grainy video recordings taken from the house next door. According to the doctor, Jesús suffered nothing worse than a lifelong limp.

Interestingly, the Colt single-action revolver was registered to a man named Moses Staffman, who also appeared to be the recorded owner of 11 Main Street.

"Maybe there's a connection," thought the Special Agent.

Only one way to find out: a good old-fashioned investigation.

Since Stan abstained from drug use, he possessed an excellent memory. And thanks to his excellent memory, he recalled the current resident of 13 Main Street mentioning Moses Staffman's name when they last spoke.

◊ ◊ ◊

Gabby Blabber's eyes had been stuck on the circus next door since the incident now making its rounds through the media. Except, that is, when *TI&TA* came on. And even then, she hurried her creaky knees to the window during commercials. Though by this time, she could pause her favorite soap opera when someone knocked on the door, and resume where she left off when she returned.[63]

Coincidentally, that's precisely what happened when a familiar face knocked on Gabby's door just as her soap opera began for the day. By this time, she'd spoken to her visitor over the phone, met him in person, witnessed him fire a bullet at her neighbor, and seen him on the news ever since—so she remembered his name.

"Stan DeVille," she recalled as she answered her door.

"Do you have a minute?" Stan asked. "I have a few questions about Moses Staffman."

Gabby could spare more than a minute, since her television would stay paused for as long as she pleased. Not that she could wait forever to resume *TI&TA*, lest she forget what already happened in the episode.

"I'll make this quick." Stan also operated on a tight schedule. "Tell me everything you know about Moses Staffman."

Golly, was that a lot!

Not only did Gabby have a detailed memory of Moses' daily routine from twenty years prior, she still remembered the names of his ex-wife and ex-coworker, not to mention the reasons they wanted to find him.

"Are they as obsessed with Mr. Staffman as you are?" Stan wondered.

Gabby supposed so—maybe even more so than her, since Moses left both on worse terms. She hadn't spoken to either in quite some time, but their phone numbers remained scribbled in her journal, and she'd been meaning to give them a call.

◊ ◊ ◊

Cleopatra Spiter and Thutmond Mose III were unsure what to think of the situation. Not that Gabby's description sounded confusing, nor that she spoke too fast, but their memories were understandably hazy after two decades of detachment.

"Who are you again?" Cleopatra replied to Gabby's call.

"What do you want?" was how Thutmond phrased it.

But as soon as they heard Moses Staffman's name, both the ex-wife and ex-coworker came knocking on the door of 13 Main Street, anxious to collect their debts. Cleopatra's alimony payments remained twenty years behind schedule, and Thutmond's inventory stood deficient for roughly the same amount of time. Not only that, but the last time they saw Moses, he hurt their feelings as well.

"Where's Moses?" Cleopatra asked the moment she walked through the door.

"And what took so long to find him?" was Thutmond's question.

Special Agent Stan DeVille asked, first of all, for Moses' former acquaintances to have a seat, because he'd be asking the questions. Second of all, he wished to know everything they remembered about Moses, because their former spouse and business associate hadn't been found in any sense.

"And third of all," added Gabby, always the thoughtful host, "would anyone like a cup of coffee while we chat?"

Cleopatra already possessed enough energy to recall the misdeeds of her ex-husband, and she described their awful marriage to the Special Agent in excruciating detail. Moses owed her money, though the exact number eluded her; her attorney held the details.

"Moses stole your money?" Stan asked.

"In a sense, yes," Cleopatra confirmed.

Thutmond filled in the missing information. He portrayed Moses as the worst coworker imaginable when working as a botanist at Plant Inc's Dullsville office. Moses owed him seeds, though the exact number eluded him; his records held the details.

"Moses stole your seeds?" Stan asked.

"In a sense, yes," Thutmond confirmed.

The Special Agent fingered his chin. If Moses was a thief, then why did the evidence suggest the other way around? The Mexicans possessed a Colt single-action revolver registered in Moses' name. That made the Mexicans the thieves, and Moses the victim as the rightful owner of the weapon. Not to mention that the Mexicans appeared to have stolen Moses' home.

"Can anyone confirm that this gun belongs to Moses?" The Special Agent allowed his potential witnesses to pass around the Colt single-action revolver. To be safe, he flipped the safety on; after all, the chamber contained live bullets.

Cleopatra confirmed as much, from what she recalled from their marriage. Moses carried the weapon everywhere he went, and he tucked it underneath his mattress at night. Regardless, there were more important questions to consider.

"Did you find any money?" asked Cleopatra.

"Or seeds?" asked Thutmond.

"Yeah, what else did you find?" asked Gabby, with nothing particular in mind, more to further the conversation.

Stan asked everyone to remain focused on the revolver. The rest of the evidence held lesser importance, and consisted of (1) a spilled tray of a drugged dessert, (2) documents proving the illegal status of a family of Mexicans, and (3) two twenty-year-old hard drives referring to something called *Zerojuana*.

Thutmond's ears perked. From what he recalled, *Zerojuana* was a genetically superior strain of cannabis, free of side effects, created by Moses Staffman. Plant Inc discontinued the production of *Zerojuana* after Moses' disappearance, because all the existing plants withered and died, and when the other botanists planted new seeds, the sprouts came out looking more like avocados than cannabis.

"Interesting," Stan said, and asked Thutmond to continue with whatever else he remembered.

According to Thutmond, suspicious circumstances surrounded Moses' disappearance. Avocado seeds went missing from the repository, with Moses being the obvious culprit. Until then, the inventory had never been deficient under Thutmond's watch.

"Never," Thutmond repeated.

Stan reached into his pocket and dug out yet another piece of previously irrelevant evidence: broken packaging labeled as "Avocado seeds, property of Plant Inc."

"Moses is behind everything," both Cleopatra and Thutmond insisted in unison. "We know it."

The Special Agent wished to focus on the Mexicans. Moses

may have been kidnapped, for example, and held prisoner against his will. That would explain how the Mexicans took over 11 Main Street and blended into the community for decades.

"Let's keep an open mind," Stan said. "It's equally likely, if not more likely, that the Mexicans are behind everything."

Cleopatra and Thutmond agreed to disagree, but promised to reserve judgment until a later time. As for Gabby, she didn't care which direction the story took, as long as some type of conclusion was coming.

◊ ◊ ◊

Stan could barely sit still as he stared into the mirror while Channel 4's makeup artist readied his cheeks with enough blush to glow with the pride of a true American hero. Dressed in his finest suit, with a fresh haircut and a clean shave, he looked as dapper as ever. His first television appearance seemed like as fine a time as any to look his best.

"Are you nervous?" the makeup artist wondered.

Why would Stan be nervous? He was a hero, and once his interview aired, the entire country would know. Not that he needed reassurance, but it would be nice for others to recognize what he'd long known.

On the set, the reporter who would conduct the interview sat in a plush lounge chair, testing her voice ahead of the broadcast. Stan failed to recall her name, except that it began with a C—Christine, or Christian, or Christiane, or Kristen. Not that she mattered. She was there to make him look good. After all, a good-looking Special Agent made for good ratings. Still, it would've been nice to know a few of her questions ahead of time. He also hoped to offer the cameraman advice about the best angle to capture his smile; he'd certainly learned a thing or two during those countless hours staring in the mirror.

"It's nice to meet you," the reporter greeted, and offered a handshake as Stan took a seat. Assuming that Stan already knew her name, she skipped further pleasantries. And after a brief countdown, the cameras began to roll, and the news officially broadcast live.

"Hello, America." The reporter greeted the camera. "Welcome to another edition of the Channel 4 News. I'm Jennifer Smith, and my guest today is Stan DeVille, Special Agent for the U.S. Drug Enforcement Administration. You may recognize Stan from his involvement in a high-profile arrest making the rounds through the media, but we'll get to that later. First, let me welcome Stan to the show."

"Thank you," Stan said.

"Stan." The reporter turned from the camera to Stan. "Welcome to the show."

"Oh, thank you." Stan chided himself for the early slip-up.

"Tell us about yourself," the reporter urged. "How long have you worked for the DEA?"

"About ten years," Stan replied. "I started out as a mere Agent, before the DEA declared me to be Special."

"Great." The reporter moved on from Stan's background. "Now, I'd like to discuss the incident at 11 Main Street in Dullsville."

"Of course." Stan was fully prepared to speak of his heroics.

"Can you lead us up to the incident?" The reporter wanted background to give the audience a full picture of the circumstances surrounding Jesús' arrest. "What brought you to the house at 11 Main Street?"

"The house remained under surveillance." Stan set the stage for his heroism. "On the day of the incident, we spotted a person of interest in the vicinity. Out of an abundance of caution, I dispatched to the house, where I found the suspect carrying a tray of drugs."

"Drugs?" The reporter scrunched her face in confusion. "In the video, he appears to be holding a dessert tray."

"That dessert contained a Schedule I narcotic." Stan wagged his finger. "A strain of cannabis called *Zerojuana*."

"*Zerojuana*?" The reporter had never heard the strange term.

"That's right," Stan confirmed. "That's all I can say at this time, because we're still investigating. But from what I understand, *Zerojuana* is a genetically superior form of cannabis which has never been sold on the open market."

"And can you tell me," the reporter darkened her tone, "why you felt justified—"

"Of course," Stan interrupted. "You want to know why I felt justified discharging my weapon?"

"No." The reporter intended an entirely different question. "I want to know why you felt justified using a racially insensitive term."

"Come again?"

The reporter paused to replay grainy video of the incident for the Special Agent. "Just before you fired your weapon, you can clearly be heard saying: 'Get down you Brownie.'"

"He held a tray of brownies in his hands," Stan explained. "I told him to set the tray down on the ground."

"But we've confirmed that he held a tray of blondies made with vanilla and brown sugar." The reporter replayed the video once again. "The boy can be heard making that distinction in the video."

"I thought they were brownies!"

"But he covered the blondies in clear plastic wrap," the reporter pointed out. "You could see their yellowish color, distinct from the brownish shade of the chocolate version."

"It was tough to see, at night, while he held the tray over his head," Stan said. "They all look the same!"

"They all look the same?" The reporter dropped her jaw in outrage. "They're different, and their differences should be celebrated!"

"I don't even know what we're talking about anymore," Stan admitted.

"Even putting aside what you claim you saw, the boy said that his tray contained blondies before you shot him."

"It all happened so fast," Stan said. "I could barely understand what he said."

"Would you agree that the gunshot victim has dark skin?" The reporter thought it was a relevant question.

"He's Mexican."

"So that gives you the right to use a racial slur?"

"What? No, I—"

"Isn't it true," the reporter aggressively accused, "that you called the boy a Brownie because you're a racist?"

"I'm not racist," Stan said. "I'd much rather eat a chocolate brownie than a butterscotch blondie."

"And you shot the boy," the reporter reminded, ignoring Stan's answer, "because you're so racist that hurtful words weren't enough."

> "This interview is over," Stan declared, and walked off the set after ripping his microphone from his clothes and throwing it at the reporter.

Stan was shocked by the direction of the interview. The reporter forgot to mention the part about how he saved the country from a dangerous immigrant trafficking illegal drugs!

TWENTY-ONE

Washington, D.C.

The vast majority of the country saw Stan DeVille's interview on the Channel 4 News. If not the live broadcast, they saw the replays on other television stations, or the digital clips all over the internet, or the commentary on various social media accounts.[64] The story proved unavoidable for anyone who paid marginal attention to trending topics.

In the nation's capital city, the President of the United States was included in the vast majority. He paid just as much attention to trending topics as his constituents; maybe even more so, he'd argue. He was well aware of the shooting in Dullsville, wherever that was. He missed the live broadcast of Stan DeVille's interview, but he saw a partial replay on Channel 1, followed by a detailed discussion amongst his favorite newspersons. And that was enough to realize he had a potentially volatile situation on his hands.

"Just the way I like it," the President gushed.

The media had been unkind to the President ever since he won the election. Come to think of it, they were unkind to him before that too. But now, even his most ardent opposers would be forced to admit he was right, when he repeatedly warned of the inevitability of this day.

"I've been saying it all along," the President told himself, "immigrants are bringing drugs into the country."

Indeed, the President had been saying that all along, as much as anyone would listen, and then some. It was a major talking point during his election campaign. He'd spoken about the crisis quite a bit since then too.

Yet his opposers doubted him. Some laughed at him. Others called him an idiot. They said he lacked any evidence to back up his claim of a connection between immigration and drug use. But that was before this incident in Dullsville proved him right.

Now, who was laughing, and who was the idiot?

Him, that's who.

"Get me Stan DeVille," the President phoned whichever of his Secretaries appeared first on his speed dial. He wished to congratulate the Special Agent on a job well done. And perhaps award the hero with a medal. What type of medal? He hadn't decided.

"What about the Presidential Medal of Freedom?" the President suggested, and his Secretary ignored.[65]

"Mr. President, have you called back the CEO of Plant Inc yet?" his Secretary asked. "Plant Inc is one of your biggest donors, and the CEO has been calling all morning."

"Just find the Agent," the President ordered, ignoring the Agent's Special status as he hung up.

◊ ◊ ◊

Stan DeVille almost fell out of his chair after picking up the call from the President's Secretary. Luckily for the Special Agent, he wasn't a complete lummox and caught himself as he toppled backward. Though even with the tumble averted, he suffered from a state of shock as he hung up the phone; he couldn't believe what he just heard.

The President wanted to meet *him.*

Could a photographed handshake on the front lawn of the White House be next?

The President's Secretary recommended that Stan catch the next flight to Washington, D.C. Apparently, the President suffered from a short attention span, so although the President wanted to meet the Special Agent right then, Stan received no guarantee that the intention would hold true for any predictable duration.

"Time is of the essence" was how the Secretary put it.

Stan didn't need to be told twice. He didn't even need to be told once. He was standing in the West Wing of the White House, knocking on the door to the Oval Office, before the President could think about anything else.

"Mr. President," Stan greeted at the door. "It's an honor."

"I'm sure it is," the President agreed.

The President may not have smiled, but he was pleased to meet Stan, albeit less honored than his counterpart. He wished to be the first to congratulate the Special Agent on a job well done. The President hated two things above all else, and they happened to be the two greatest threats to the country he swore to serve. One was drugs. The other was immigrants. Between the two, he found it tough to decipher which was worse.

"Do drugs turn immigrants into bad hombres?" the President wondered, in a chicken-or-egg type way.[66] "Or is it because they're bad hombres that they do drugs?"

That was a difficult question to answer, so Stan made no attempt. Besides, even if he tried to answer, the President would've interrupted him.

Whichever came first, both problems needed to stop. The President planned to make an example of the most publicized immigrant in the current news cycle. He asked Stan to return to Dullsville and prosecute Jesús to the fullest extent of the law, or more. Jesús' arrest was of the utmost importance, thanks to all the news coverage, since he'd become a prime example of the connection between immigrants and drugs.

"How'd you figure out that he's a Mexican?" the President asked. "I heard that his family lived undercover in Dullsville for twenty years."

"Accents hung over the names of every person living in his house," Stan explained. "Their names were Jesús, José, and María. María's identity was the trickiest to decipher, because her accent hung over the letter 'i' and blended in with the dot used by Americans. Without looking closely, it's almost impossible to tell the difference."

"Those sneaky Mexicans," the President thought out loud. "This is why we need a wall."

According to Stan, a wall may not have helped in this particular case. He found no record of José or Jesús entering the country, but it appeared that María legally crossed the border with a temporary visa obtained under the provisions of the North American Free Trade Agreement.

"North American Free Trade Agreement?" the President asked.

"NAFTA," Stan shortened.

"Ugh," the President groaned. He'd always known that NAFTA was a bad deal for his country. He'd said it over and over again. How many times did he need to be proved right before his constituents would start to listen?

According to Stan, they had bigger problems than NAFTA. More concerning was that the woman, María, somehow infiltrated the U.S. government, gaining employment with the Transportation Security Administration five years before the Transportation Security Administration existed.

"Transportation Security Administration?" the President asked.

"TSA," Stan shortened.

"God help us all," the President replied once he understood the reference, not to mention the gravity of the situation. "If the Mexicans can infiltrate TSA, then what's next? FBI? CIA? NSA?"

"ICE?" Stan added.

"We've got to stop them!" The President slammed his fist on his desk. "This is a matter of national security!"

That's exactly what Stan had been saying the entire time. He remained baffled that the news reporter at Channel 4—whatever her name—failed to appreciate his heroics.

"Why did you go on Channel 4?" the President asked. "There are nicer reporters on other channels. Have you seen Channel 1?"

Stan shrugged. He wished he knew that much a day earlier. He'd assumed that every channel appreciated American heroes.

Well, the President appreciated Stan's work, even if the media failed to recognize his heroics. He wondered what else the Special Agent knew about the Mexicans.

Stan's investigation uncovered no shortage of interesting

information. Among other findings, it appeared that the Mexicans developed their drug based on an experimental product stolen from an American company, Plant Inc, almost two decades prior. The American company spent years developing the product before the Mexicans stole it.

"American company?" The President heard the phrase twice, and thought back to his earlier message from his Secretary. "Plant Inc?"

"That's right," Stan confirmed, "Plant Inc."

"Would you excuse me for a moment?" the President asked, though it was Stan who excused himself from the room.

◊ ◊ ◊

Plant Inc's CEO answered the President's call after the first ring. Apparently, the leader of the country's largest horticultural company had nothing better to do than sit next to the phone, patiently waiting to hear from the leader of the free world. Or perhaps he knew that the President would only call once.

"Mr. President, my old friend," the CEO greeted.

"Mr. CEO, my old friend," the President replied.

"Have you been watching the news?" The CEO already knew the answer. "This Brownie in Dullsville is the talk of the country."

"Drugs and immigrants are connected," the President said. "It's what I've been saying this entire time. Everyone called me crazy, but now they'll see how smart I am."

The CEO agreed that the President was a smart man—the smartest man he knew, he said, and the best President too. But in this case, it turned out that the particular strain of cannabis discovered in the Brownie's possession had been stolen from Plant Inc's R&D Department.

"Interesting," the President said, regardless of his true feelings.

In other words, the most discussed drug on the airwaves belonged to Plant Inc, creating a unique opportunity for the company. If only the drug became legal to sell, Plant Inc could control its sale. Alternatively, if the drug remained illegal, the Mexicans would gain the upper hand, since the foreigners appeared unconcerned with U.S. legality.

"Interesting," the President repeated, though the conversation dragged for longer than he preferred.

The CEO spoke directly. "I'd like you to remove *Zerojuana* from the list of Schedule I narcotics."

The President doubted he could do that. He'd campaigned on the dangers of drugs, and even more so on the immigrants bringing drugs into the country. This was no time to compromise; this was his chance to prove himself right.

According to the CEO, however, *Zerojuana* posed no danger to anyone. *Zerojuana* was a basic form of cannabis—the safest known form, according to Plant Inc's Marketing Department. The President could carve out an exception for *Zerojuana* in relation to Schedule I of the Controlled Substances Act, with the explanation that Plant Inc had been approved to sell a safe version of cannabis after a complicated safety analysis. Then, since Plant Inc controlled distribution, they'd control the entire marketplace, along with the hefty profits that came with the sale of the most popular drug on the current news cycle.

"I don't know," the President hesitated.

"You'll be asking for more campaign contributions come re-election time, I presume?"

The CEO presumed correctly.

◊ ◊ ◊

Special Agent Stan DeVille stood in the hallway, staring at paintings of his country's past leaders, when the President summoned him back into the Oval Office. He appreciated the former holders of the position, particularly Adams[67] and Nixon,[68] but with all due respect to them, only the current President stood in much of a position to advance his career.

"You've done a tremendous job so far," the President said. He wished to award the Special Agent with the Presidential Medal of Freedom for his work, but he awaited word from his Secretary whether any spares lay around the West Wing.[69]

Although honored, Stan assured the President that satisfaction from a job well done was the only reward he needed.

"Oh, okay," the President said. "If satisfaction is all you need, then nevermind about the medal."

"On second thought," Stan replied, "I'd also like the medal if it's not too much trouble."

In that case, the medal was too much trouble to hand over, the President explained, because any trouble at all was too much trouble to begin with. But if he could honor Stan in another way, he'd be happy to assist.

"How about a handshake?" Stan asked.

"Sure," the President agreed, and held out his hand.

"On the front lawn of the White House?" Stan added before grasping the President's palm. "While a photographer takes a picture for the newspaper?"

Unfortunately, that extra step would take them back into the "too much trouble" category, the President explained as he pulled back his hand. As a busy man, he had no time to round up the entire White House Press Team for a photoshoot on the front lawn. Stan failed to understand how exhaustive the entire process was. They needed makeup artists, speech writers, other high-ranking officials—a lot to put together on short notice.

"What if I give you a promotion instead?" the President suggested. "What's the next rank above DEA Agent?"

Special Agent ranked above Agent, obviously. Though Stan was already a Special Agent, he explained to the President, so a promotion to the same title would be more of a lateral move than career advancement.

"Well, what's higher than Special Agent?"

Stan didn't know what came after Special Agent. Fortunately, he didn't need to know, because the President was an intelligent man, fully capable of answering his own questions when nobody else could.

"I hereby appoint you, Stan DeVille, as a Super Special Agent of the DEA." The President also deemed the appointment to be effective immediately, because that was the only way he knew to be effective.

Stan couldn't help note that such lofty promotions are often accompanied by a photographed handshake in an appropriate location, which would've been the front lawn of the White House in this instance.

"Again with the photo?" The President scowled as he waved off the suggestion. "Finish your new mission, and then we'll talk."

"New mission?"

"There's been a change of plans," the President explained of Stan's first duty as a Super Special Agent. He'd just received new information: the cannabis confiscated from the Mexicans in Dullsville had been stolen from an American company, Plant Inc, which diligently researched and developed the drug for years.

"Yeah," Stan said. "I told you that."

"After giving the issue serious thought," the President continued, "I've realized that this isn't a case of Mexicans bringing drugs into the country."

"It's not?"

"No," the President insisted. "This is a case of Mexicans stealing from the American people, which is much worse. This cannabis is an American-owned product, with American jobs at stake, along with American profits. We need to protect American businesses, first and foremost."

According to the President, they no longer needed to prove that the Mexicans brought illegal drugs into the country. Instead, he asked the newly appointed Super Special Agent to prove that the Mexicans stole their drugs from Plant Inc, so the evidence fit the right narrative.

"You've done a tremendous job so far," the President summarized. "Now I need you to return to Dullsville and prove Jesús to be a thief. Plant Inc plans to start selling *Zerojuana* immediately, so there's no time to lose."

"And then maybe I could get that handshake?" Stan asked.

"Sure," the President agreed, "after you finish the job."

The suddenly-Super Special Agent assured the President that the job was as good as finished. He just had one question, involving how exactly Plant Inc would sell *Zerojuana*, with cannabis listed as a Schedule I narcotic under the Controlled Substances Act.

"Haven't you ever heard of an Executive Order?" asked the President.

TWENTY-TWO

California

The nation's top newspersons were shocked and confused by the President's Executive Order. For one thing, nobody expected such a turn of events. For another thing, nobody understood what the Executive Order said, since the President wrote it himself while his closest Secretary sat in the lavatory. The only detail everyone agreed on was that something called *Zerojuana* became legal under the Controlled Substances Act.

The happiest person in the country seemed to be Plant Inc's CEO, who held a press conference to celebrate the President's decision. According to the CEO, the public's most desired narcotic—Plant Inc's own *Zerojuana*-brand cannabis—would be available for distribution in the near future. Plant Inc had already entered into discussions for distribution in more than half of the U.S. states, and the other half merely needed to tweak a law or two for the same benefit. The CEO went on to thank the President for protecting American businesses, for protecting American jobs, and for protecting American citizens. Overall, it was a great day for America, according to the CEO of the nation's most newsworthy company.

The second happiest person in the country seemed to be Thutmond Mose III, who watched the CEO's press conference with pride, knowing that his diligent recordkeeping allowed

Plant Inc to claim ownership to the country's most talked-about plant. His diligent recordkeeping also allowed the company to locate the twenty-year-old *Zerojuana* seeds in cryostorage. Before long, Plant Inc would be ready to sell the hottest new product in the country, all thanks to Thutmond.

Plant Inc's CEO appeared just as pleased with the inventory manager as he was with himself. He personally congratulated Thutmond on a job well done, even adding a few pats on the back for good measure. That alone would've been enough of a thanks for the dedicated employee, but the CEO also alluded to a potential three-figure bonus at the year's end—a token of appreciation for the company's projected eleven-figure profits. Thutmond, for his part, planned to spend the extra money on a new lawnmower.

Plant Inc suddenly became a hectic place to work. In a rush to bring *Zerojuana*-brand cannabis to market following the President's Executive Order, the top botanists at the company received access to the most advanced equipment money could buy. And that included some darn fine equipment, from what Thutmond understood. He didn't know how the equipment worked, but he knew where to find it in inventory when someone asked for it, and he heard it could begin to germinate a frozen seed in less than 24 hours.

Coincidentally, about 24 hours had passed since the top botanists requested both the fancy equipment and the frozen *Zerojuana* seeds. A few of those botanists had already returned to Thutmond with questions. Mainly, they wished to know why the *Zerojuana* seeds germinated more like avocados than cannabis—an especially curious coincidence, since the same problem occurred twenty years earlier, following Moses' abrupt departure.

"I think these are avocado seeds," one of the botanists even suggested.

The suggestion caused Thutmond to sit down and think. And after he thought for a while, he stood up and searched through his inventory of records. (Yes, the dedicated inventory manager even inventoried his own records of inventory.) Deep in his inventory, he found the records from twenty years prior, taken during the days surrounding Moses' disappearance. But he found more than just the *Zerojuana* documents; he pulled all of his notes from that time.

According to the records, the *Zerojuana* seeds were 100% accounted for after Moses' disappearance. Actually, the *Zerojuana* seeds were *more* than 100% accounted for after Moses' disappearance, since he found more seeds in cryostorage than the records said would be there. Amazingly, he uncovered another coincidence: immediately after Moses disappeared, the number of *Zerojuana* seeds in inventory precisely corresponded to the number of missing avocado seeds.

Two possibilities existed, from what Thutmond could tell. The first possibility involved a mistake in the records. That was an impossibility, of course, since he counted the seeds himself. The second possibility involved Moses pulling the wool over his eyes for twenty years by switching the location of the avocado seeds in the inventory.[70]

◊ ◊ ◊

Jesús' wrist felt extremely sore when he finally awoke in a gurney at Dullsville General Hospital, but not as sore as his foot. The bruise on his wrist came from the handcuffs binding him to the gurney; his foot told another story, though not entirely. Besides that, he found intravenous tubes piercing the veins in his forearms, delivering whatever fluid the doctor deemed worthwhile, and a heart monitor to his left confirmed his health with a rhythmic beep. Oh, and an attorney-at-law sat to his right, waiting for that precise moment when Jesús opened his eyes.

"Jesús!" Howie Spirit, Esq., leapt from his seat. "You're up!"

Jesús may have been awake, but he remained far from standing up. Thanks to the bullet hole through his metatarsals, he'd be unable to walk for several days, at least. But he felt no rush to leave; nor should he feel rushed, according to the attorney.

"You've done it," Howie said, and recapped everything that Jesús slept through. Since being shot in the foot, he missed two important events: first, video of his arrest streamed across every news channel in the country, skyrocketing the public's interest in both Jesús and *Zerojuana*; second, the President declared *Zerojuana* to be legal, opening the door for nationwide distribution—the first step to massive profits for TH Corp. As soon as Jesús' foot healed, they could return to the island, and Howie could finally begin his retirement!

"It's nice to see you too, Howie," Jesús said.

The attorney advised Jesús to relax and allow the hospital staff to nurse him back to full health. He might as well accept the hospital's care, since the island lacked such a fine facility.

"What about these handcuffs?" Jesús wondered of his attachment to the gurney.

"The handcuffs—" began Howie.

"—stay on," finished a voice from the doorway

The voice belonged to an old acquaintance who was merely Special, not Super, the last time he saw Jesús. In view of the promotion, a reintroduction seemed appropriate, so he held out his hand and said:

"Stan DeVille, Super Special Agent with the U.S. Drug Enforcement Administration."

"Howie Spirit, Esq.," Howie greeted as they grasped palms. He'd already familiarized himself with Stan's name and general occupation, not least in part due to the prominent role Stan played in Jesús' arrest.

"I assume you're this young man's attorney?" Stan asked.

"Sort of," Howie replied, and smiled without teeth. "So, when will you be releasing Jesús?"

"Releasing?" Stan laughed from deep within his abdomen. "Why would I release him?"

"Because you have no reason to hold him," Howie answered. "*Zerojuana* is now legal under federal law, pursuant to the President's Executive Order."

"True," Stan agreed. "But that doesn't mean Jesús is innocent. The last time I checked, it's still a crime to steal legal products from their rightful owner."

"Steal?" Howie asked.

"I just spoke with Plant Inc's inventory manager," Stan explained, "and we can prove that *Zerojuana* seeds were stolen from Plant Inc—"

"—by Moses Staffman." Howie interrupted, surprising the Super Special Agent with his inside knowledge of the crime. "Yes, I know."

"You admit that the seeds were stolen?" Stan couldn't believe his luck: never in his career had a criminal confessed to a crime so quickly.

Competent or not, most attorneys don't deny obvious facts. Rather, most attorneys twist the facts to their advantage. Nobody understood this better than Howie Spirit, Esq., who gladly fingered Moses Staffman as the likely culprit of the theft from Plant Inc twenty years prior. And he also admitted to Jesús living in Moses Staffman's house.

"Thanks for verifying all of that," Stan acknowledged, pleased that he wouldn't need additional evidence to prove the charge.

"However," continued Howie, "you can't prove that Jesús conspired with Moses to steal the *Zerojuana* seeds. Nor can you prove that Jesús ever met Moses, since Moses disappeared before Jesús' birth. The most reasonable explanation is that Jesús found a now-legal product, which he innocently baked into a butterscotch dessert." (Note that the attorney carefully avoided asserting that Jesús *hadn't* met Moses, instead stating that the Super Special Agent lacked any proof of such a meeting.)

"Even if that's all true," Stan said with a smile, "Jesús is still an illegal immigrant, and I can hold him until I find more evidence."

Howie smiled, again without teeth. Then he offered a freshly printed copy of Jesús' birth certificate for inspection. "Jesús is an American citizen," he insisted.

Stan's smile disappeared as he grabbed the birth certificate and studied the document, with intense pressure building inside his head as his brain processed the information. He hadn't bothered to check state records for a birth certificate in Jesús' name, not with the rest of his evidence so damning already. From where he stood, Jesús looked every bit the Mexican.

"You can keep that copy," Howie said. "I have more."

Stan's face began to turn red as the pressure between his ears continued to build, forcing his eardrums to pop and his eyes to bulge from his skull.

"As soon as Jesús is cleared by the hospital, we intend to leave the country for a secret island where you have no authority,"

Howie concluded. "Now that *Zerojuana* is legal, TH Corp has urgent business to attend to."

The pressure finally reached its limit: Stan's head exploded.

◊ ◊ ◊

Stan recovered what he could of his shattered psyche and returned to his office, slamming his fist on his desk the moment he walked through the door. He was in a poor mood, to be certain. Yet he refused to give up. He remained so close to shaking hands with the President on the front lawn of the White House that he could imagine the occasion almost as vividly as a photograph on the front page of the newspaper.

Stan could prove that Moses Staffman stole *Zerojuana* seeds from Plant Inc, thanks to the diligent recordkeeping of a loyal inventory manager. And he could prove that Jesús took possession of *Zerojuana* cannabis at some point, thanks to his own brilliant investigation. But there existed a missing link between the two persons-of-interest.

With nowhere else to turn, the Super Special Agent summoned the most dedicated crime-solving team in Dullsville. With Moses Staffman's involvement now confirmed, he thought those closest to the botanist might shed light on the situation. So he invited Cleopatra Spiter and Thutmond Mose III for a sitdown at 13 Main Street, where Gabby Blabber waited to discuss the matter.

"I knew Moses was involved," said Cleopatra.

"I knew it too," said Thutmond.

"I said it first though," said Gabby, brow raised.

According to Stan, the sum of the information outweighed the order of who knew what. They needed to connect Moses to Jesús, or else the entire team of thieves would get away with their crimes. And they needed to make the connection in a hurry, or else Jesús would be on his way to a secret island to reproduce *Zerojuana* for mass distribution by a company called TH Corp.

"A secret island?" asked Cleopatra.

"TH Corp?" asked Thutmond.

"Would anyone like a cup of coffee?" asked Gabby, always the thoughtful host.

"Let's focus on what's important," Stan said. "Did anyone ever see Moses with Jesús?"

Unfortunately, nobody had seen Moses since he disappeared from Plant Inc on that fateful day twenty years prior. Since Jesús resided within his mother's body at the time, there couldn't have been any meeting between the two that gave rise to a conspiracy.

"We must be missing something," Stan insisted.

The foursome spent hours brainstorming, recalling every detail of Moses' life. Gabby pulled out her journal and reviewed her former neighbor's daily schedule, along with every other interaction she witnessed from behind her window. Cleopatra added in the details of her ex-husband's personal habits, and considered who else he might reach out to for distribution. Thutmond scrutinized Plant Inc's records related to the famed botanist, in case he initially missed something in the paperwork. But regardless of how many clues they counted or how much thought they put in, nowhere seemed to be the only place they ended up.

"Dammit!" Stan finally shouted in anger. "Isn't there anything we can do?"

No one knew what to say, let alone what to do. Although after a moment of thought, Gabby came up with an idea, which she thought to be better than nothing at all.

"Maybe we should try puffing *Zerojuana* cannabis," Gabby suggested. "It's legal now, right?"

Gabby was right: *Zerojuana* was now legal. But the drug remained untested.

"Actually," Thutmond said, "*Zerojuana* has been thoroughly tested by Plant Inc." That's why the President legalized the stuff, which caused only mild effects in comparison to other strains of cannabis.

Thutmond was right: *Zerojuana* was rumored to be relatively safe. But even if they wished to sample the drug, they possessed no *Zerojuana* to begin with; the blondies confiscated from Jesús during his arrest remained locked up in evidence.

"Actually," Gabby said, "I still have the doobie from María." That's why she called Stan in the first place. Though it seemed like an eternity since then, in reality only about a week had passed, so the doobie remained fairly fresh.

"Then I guess there's no reason not to try it," Cleopatra supposed.

"And if you lose the double negative," Gabby pointed out, "then there *is* a reason to try it."

Nobody in the room could argue with that.

So the foursome agreed to sample the most popular narcotic in the country. After all, it might help their investigation to understand what they were dealing with, right? And since the drug was now legal, that made it safe to try.

Not one of them knew how to roll cannabis into a cigarette. Good thing María's dexterous son twirled the doobie in advance of its sale. The curious foursome simply needed to light the tip on fire and each take a puff.

Stan puffed first, Cleopatra second, Thutmond third, and Gabby fourth. And once they'd each taken a puff, something strange happened: the foursome enjoyed themselves for the first time on record.

"I feel pretty good," Stan noted as the first to experience the effects. Suddenly, his super special feeling had nothing to do with his important title or his most urgent task, with the title losing its importance, and the task losing its urgency.

Cleopatra, for her part, felt the same way: "pretty good," as she described it. For the first time, Moses' debt disappeared from her thoughts. Actually, Moses disappeared from her thoughts completely. Instead, her mind focused on her growing hunger, so she asked her company:

"Is anyone else craving tacos?"

Now that she mentioned it, Thutmond craved tacos, not to mention tortilla chips with guacamole dip. For some reason, he felt a serious hankering for avocados.

"Also, I feel really good." Thutmond took his companions' observations one step further, supplementing with the type of comment found on his inventory records. "I'm feeling a lack of stress combined with a hint of euphoria."

"And my creaky knees feel better too!" Gabby said, and suggested they puff a bit more, at least until they reduced the entire doobie to ash.

TWENTY-THREE

Washington, D.C.

His displeasure apparent from the scowl on his face and the frustration in his voice, the President of the United States was visibly annoyed to find DEA Super Special Agent Stan DeVille back in the Oval Office so soon after meeting with the illegal immigrant. Though that seemed to be less because he disliked Stan in particular, and more because the immigrant turned out to be not so illegal after all.

"I thought you said he's Mexican," the President recalled.

"I thought so," Stan insisted. "He has a 'ú' in his name, for crying out loud!"

"But he also has an American birth certificate," the President noted.

"Am I supposed to read everything about him?" was Stan's reply.

The President had never been much of a reader himself, so it was difficult to blame Stan for the discrepancy. But he blamed Stan anyway. Someone needed to be held responsible, and it sure as heck wouldn't be the leader of the free world.

"What should we do now?" the President asked.

"I assumed you would know," Stan replied.

The President appreciated the compliment. He typically knew how to fix just about everything, plus a lot more besides that. So much more! In this particular instance, however, he needed more time to think aloud.

"So even though both of Jesús' parents were foreigners, he's a U.S. citizen simply because he was born in California?"

Stan explained that, yes, Jesús achieved a status called "birthright citizenship," which made him a legal U.S. citizen. The Constitution guaranteed automatic citizenship to any person born within the jurisdiction of the United States, which included babies born in Puerto Rico.

"Even Puerto Rico?" the President asked. "What the heck?"

"That's the law." Stan shrugged. "Whether we like it or not."

Well the President had never been a fan of birthright citizenship, ever since he first learned what the phrase meant, right then and there. The entire concept contained inherent flaws which clashed with any semblance of common sense. If born to foreigners, the President reasoned, then the child should be a foreigner; the parents passed down every other gene for goodness' sake. He disliked that Constitution too, and wished everyone would stop bringing up the damn document every time he came up with a brilliant idea.

"So if we get rid of birthright citizenship—" The President prefaced his boldest idea yet. "—then we'll be okay?"

By "okay," the President meant they'd be back to the scenario of an illegal immigrant stealing an American-made product, which product Plant Inc would exploit for profits, which profits Plant Inc would donate to his reelection campaign.

Unfortunately, the President's idea presented far from an ultimate solution. Though Stan wasn't forced to explain that himself, because just then the President received a message from one of his Secretaries that Plant Inc's CEO waited patiently on hold.

"Would you excuse me for a moment?" the President asked, though it was Stan who excused himself from the room.

◊ ◊ ◊

The President wasted no time picking up the call from Plant Inc's CEO. He needed advice. Well, he didn't *need* advice, because he was a genius, and a stable one at that. But he wondered what the CEO thought of the situation, because he respected his old friend's opinion.

"Mr. President, my old friend," the CEO greeted.

"Mr. CEO, my old friend," the President replied.

The CEO got straight to business, knowing full well of the President's busy schedule, not to mention his short attention span. He shared unfortunate news. As it turned out, Plant Inc couldn't produce the newly legal drug, *Zerojuana*. Evidently, the *Zerojuana* seeds found in cryostorage were of the avocado variety instead. His company possessed no *Zerojuana* to sell, even though the President made the sale legal.

"So Plant Inc isn't going to make money off of this whole thing?" asked the President, aghast at the idea.

"Not unless we get our hands on some *Zerojuana* seeds," the CEO replied.

"Hmm," the President hummed out loud to let the CEO know he was thinking. Personally, he avoided drugs: he preferred not to dull his mind. But he promised to ask his Secretaries for ideas. Perhaps one of them knew of a *Zerojuana* source.

"What about Jesús?" the CEO suggested.

"Who?"

"The Brownie."

"Oh, right."

To the CEO, Jesús appeared fully capable of obtaining *Zerojuana*. After all, the young man baked a butterscotch dessert with a sizable amount of the stuff. If they figured out where Jesús' supply came from, Plant Inc could use the supply to regrow *Zerojuana* for sale on the open market. Unfortunately, the cannabis baked into Jesús' butterscotch dessert could no longer be cloned; Plant Inc required a fresh plant to kickstart production.

"I understand," the President said. "So what are you saying?"

The CEO clearly laid out the plan: "We need the Special Agent to find out where Jesús obtained the *Zerojuana* baked into those blondies."

"I knew what you were saying." The President insisted as much, at least. "Also, Stan is a *Super* Special Agent now."

Regardless of title, the CEO suggested that Stan interrogate Jesús until he discovered where to find *Zerojuana*. Of course, the CEO would never tell the President what to do. The President already knew what to do, because he was smart enough to figure that out on his own.

"Got it," said the President, his attention long having shifted. "Anything else?"

Indeed, the CEO wished to discuss something else. According to a recent rumor, Jesús worked for a foreign company called TH Corp. For both their sakes, he suggested that the sale of *Zerojuana* be prohibited in the United States until Plant Inc became ready to sell. A foreign company beating Plant Inc to market served neither of their interests.

"Got it," said the President, ready for the conversation to end.

"Just tell the whatever-type-Agent to wrap this up," the CEO pleaded. "This has all gone on long enough."

The President agreed: "And I haven't even been involved very long."

◊ ◊ ◊

Super Special Agent Stan DeVille stood in the hallway, staring at paintings of his country's past leaders, when the President summoned him back into the Oval Office. Instead of idolizing his favorite leaders, Stan focused on Wilson and Roosevelt, whose nefarious reputations preceded them. From his previous employment at the ATF, he recalled that Woodrow Wilson vetoed the initial act to prohibit alcohol in the United States.[71] Congress overrode the veto (thank goodness), setting the stage for a dozen years of prohibition, until Franklin Roosevelt put his mind to ending the ban.[72]

"Just think how different the country would be if prohibition received more support from our leaders," Stan ruminated.

"I have thought about that," the President said, "but I own an alcohol company, so I'm glad it worked out as it did."

Regardless, why waste time discussing an unrelated subject like alcohol? The President and the Super Special Agent agreed to remain focused on Jesús of Dullsville and his illegal narcotic.

"Actually, it's legal now," the Super Special Agent reminded.

"Change of plans," the President replied.

New information had come to light: Plant Inc needed a fresh sample of *Zerojuana*. The President asked Stan to prove his Super Special title by figuring out where Jesús obtained the narcotic.

"Can you do that?"

Stan could do anything. He wasn't a mere Agent, or a Special Agent for that matter; he was a Super Special Agent, the only one of his kind. If the President wished to know where Jesús obtained his drugs, then Stan would return to Dullsville and figure out as much. But without knowing when he might return, he wondered if the President minded taking a photograph on the front lawn of the White House.

"Shaking hands, perhaps?"

"First, find out where the *Zerojuana* is coming from," the President insisted, "and *don't* shoot Jesús this time."

"What if he won't tell me?" According to Stan, Jesús' status as a legal citizen possessing a legal product left him no leverage to force any type of admission.

"I'll make *Zerojuana* illegal by the time you get back to Dullsville," the President said, "so you can haul him to the courthouse and charge him with possession and intent to distribute."

"Can you do that?" wondered the Super Special Agent.

"Haven't you ever heard of an Executive Order?" asked the President in reply.

TWENTY-FOUR

California

The second Executive Order took less time to write than the first. The only words scribbled on the document were "Executive Order," followed by "*Zerojuana* is illegal again," and finished with the President's oversized signature. That's all the language necessary to achieve the President's goal; and legally speaking, that's all the language necessary for the Executive Order to be effective.

The media enjoyed a field day once word of the second Executive Order made its way outside of the White House. Some blasted the President for issuing Executive Orders with little thought, now using additional Executive Orders to cancel out other Executive Orders. Others lauded the President for recognizing past mistakes, admitting fault, and correcting his errors with the utmost haste. Still others simply laughed and asked:

"What the heck is the President doing?"

But the news struck hardest for one particular group of citizens: cannabis enthusiasts. Some felt sad. Some felt confused. Some felt downright angry. Of course, these feelings rose from their inability to purchase *Zerojuana*-brand cannabis—whatever that was—during the brief period permitted by law. Although the President's first and second Executive Orders provided a window to sample *Zerojuana*, only those already in possession of the then-legal drug could try it during that time.

Thanks to the attention brought to *Zerojuana* by the country's highest office, awareness of the product reached a previously unimaginable level. Legal or illegal, the public became desperate to try the rescheduled Schedule I narcotic, without really understanding what *Zerojuana* was to begin with besides a strain of cannabis held by a young Mexican-American while shot by an arguably bigoted Super Special Agent with the DEA.

And when the public failed to obtain *Zerojuana*, thanks to the second Executive Order, they settled for the Super Special Agent and his Mexican-American detainee.

◊ ◊ ◊

Stan DeVille wasted no time leaving Washington, D.C., albeit without the hero's farewell he felt he deserved. He sure wished to depart the capital city under better circumstances, but his plan kept going wrong where it just as easily could've gone right.

"I'm never getting that damn handshake," he lamented, and accepted his fate.

Regardless, a simple handshake with the leader of the free world no longer drove Stan. For one thing, a handshake with the President may have been special to a Special Agent, but he was now Super Special in this regard. For another thing, he'd seen the President's hands. Either way, the elusive handshake fell secondary to finding more *Zerojuana* cannabis.

"It's my white whale," he decided, comparing himself to Captain Ahab from Moby Dick, a popular novel he never bothered to read.

Stan now believed himself to be the only person in the country with the ability to locate the popular narcotic which for the past few days bounced back and forth across the thin line of legality.

Stan found plenty of time to think during his flight from the nation's capital back to the media's favorite town. He thought about his first time at 11 Main Street, when he fired a bullet through an undercooked butterscotch dessert in a moment of haste. He thought about his second time at 11 Main Street, when he waited for the butterscotch dessert to cool, and then shot the young man holding the tray instead. And mostly, he thought about the mysterious ingredient in the butterscotch dessert—the ingredient which he became one of the few people in the country to sample during its brief legal status—*Zerojuana* cannabis.

"My white whale." Stan—aka Captain Ahab—reiterated his motivation. "I have to find it."

So the Super Special Agent thought long and hard on his flight home from Washington, D.C. Indeed, he thought longer and harder than ever before. And rather than focus on the big picture, he dug into the details, as Super Special Agents tend to do.

The details were plentiful. The first known sale of *Zerojuana* saw a single doobie pass hands from a Mexican mother-of-one to her creaky-kneed neighbor. The creaky-kneed neighbor called Stan, then only a Special Agent, which led him to 11 Main Street, where he discovered an undercooked baked dessert containing what would come to be the nation's most pressing threat—a threat which Stan, at the time, single-handedly eliminated with the bend of his trigger finger.

"Thank goodness I fired before the dessert finished cooking," Stan ruminated.

Undeniably, if not for the now-Super Special Agent, the blondies in the oven would've cooked to perfection. Only thanks to his courage did he avert such an outcome.

After reaching over his shoulder and patting himself on the back, Stan returned to the evidence. 11 Main Street housed more than just that dangerous dessert. He also discovered a revolver registered to a missing American botanist. Presumably, the weapon had been stolen from Moses Staffman when the Mexicans took over the house, demonstrating the danger posed by the unwelcome guests.

When strung together, all of those details led Stan to Jesús.

Or did they?

In one sense, the evidence led Stan to Jesús, since Stan arrested Jesús after he discovered those details. But in another sense, the evidence hadn't led Stan to Jesús; Jesús simply appeared out of nowhere for Stan to arrest, which raised an interesting question.

Why would Jesús return to 11 Main Street?

Why, indeed? The whitewashed, two-story ranch happened to be the riskiest place for the fugitive to show his face. Why would he endanger himself so soon after Stan's initial raid?

Either Jesús was oblivious to the house's surveillance—possible, however unlikely that seemed.

"Or he needed something from the house," the Super Special Agent realized with a devilish grin.

But what would he need?

Of course, only one answer made sense. A drug addict would risk capture for only one thing: the drug of his addiction.

Could a stash of *Zerojuana* cannabis exist somewhere at 11 Main Street?

The Special Agent fingered his chin. The creaky-kneed neighbor at 13 Main Street purchased a freshly ground doobie of the famed drug from Jesús' mother, and he caught Jesús red-handed on the front lawn with a batch of baked goods containing the stuff. Logic suggested that a supply of *Zerojuana* existed somewhere.

Well, 11 Main Street certainly qualified as somewhere.

Stan's theory contained only one flaw: he personally searched the house, on two separate occasions, turning the premises upside-down in a figurative sense of direction. He looked in every closet, under every mattress, and behind every cushion on the couch; every cupboard, every container, every nook and cranny had been uncovered; every pocket fingered, and every drawer pulled. He even checked the lint traps in the dryer.

The only location Stan avoided, for the sake of his nostrils, surrounded the home-grown bed of *titan arums* blooming in the front yard. But c'mon, would the Mexicans really hide an illegal narcotic in such an obvious and accessible place?

◊ ◊ ◊

Jesús remained handcuffed to his hospital gurney when he found out about Executive Order #2. Not only did the news broadcast from a television hanging in the corner of his room, but an attorney sat next to his bed, fully prepared to explain the legal ramifications of the President's decision.

"Now they can throw you in jail," said Howie.

"Oh," said Jesús.

The attorney spoke correctly, not that his legal acumen ever fell in doubt. The intent to distribute *Zerojuana*—like any other Schedule I narcotic—fell subject to fairly serious penalties under federal law, regardless of what the local government thought about the matter.

Nevertheless, the sudden turn of events was for the best, according to Howie. *Zerojuana* had rapidly become the hot new product that Guy always wanted, without needing the jalapeño heat as initially planned. All that the product needed to be popular, apparently, was for a Mexican-American gunshot victim to hold a tray of baked goods of the stuff during an arguably racist incident caught on camera. The attorney was unsure how they failed to realize this earlier, now that it all seemed so obvious, but he reasoned that hindsight proved easier to evaluate than real-time thoughts.

Now that word had spread about *Zerojuana*, the public desperately craved a taste. The drug would sell whether legal or illegal. The President did TH Corp a favor by bringing their flagship product onto the highest stage in the nation. The rest of TH Corp's success relied on getting the product into the marketplace.

"All we need to do now," Howie explained, "is get you back to the island with a *Zerojuana* sample for Moses to reproduce."

"Do you have a plan?" Jesús wondered.

Of course Howie had a plan. To demonstrate his confidence, he dangled a takeout bag from Pepe's Fried Chicken.

"Is that a buffalo-style chicken wrap?" Jesús asked. "With a side of fries, and more ketchup than you need?"

"You know what this means," Howie confirmed. "It's finally time to retire."

That was good to hear, particularly from Jesús' perspective. His wrist felt terribly sore from the constant chafe of the handcuffs. The looming threat of a lengthy stay in a federal penitentiary seemed like no prize either.

"I've requested for you to be transferred to another hospital in the next town over," Howie advised. "Once the paperwork clears, we'll be on our way. An ambulance is preparing to take you right now. Follow my lead, and I'll tell you when you're safe."

Unfortunately, the attorney had no time to explain anything further, because just after he finished saying the word "safe," a man whose job description involved exactly that state of being entered the room. To nobody's surprise, at the door stood Stan DeVille, the Super Special Agent tasked by the President to resolve Jesús' situation in the most nonviolent way possible. He had a loaded pistol tucked into his holster, and two black duffle bags slung over his shoulder.

Stan unlocked Jesús' handcuffs and explained what would happen next. The hospital deemed Jesús fit to be discharged, and now he was officially under arrest for the possession and distribution of a Schedule I narcotic. In a few moments, they'd be leaving for the Dullsville Courthouse, where Dullsville's longest-tenured magistrate waited to hear his indictment. They'd be on the move as soon as Jesús dressed himself. They had no time to lose: Judge Judi tended to grow cranky when anyone made her late for her jazz dancing lessons.

"Right now?" Howie asked. "But he's about to be transferred —"

"Right now." The Super Special Agent tossed one of the black duffle bags onto Jesús' gurney. "Get dressed. We leave at once."

"Perhaps we could make a deal?" Howie wondered. "We can give you more information about *Zerojuana*, if you agree to allow Jesús to be transferred to the other hospital."

At this point, Howie's underexplained plan began to unravel. Stan remained highly interested in the illegal narcotic, *Zerojuana*. But the upper hand now belonged to the Super Special Agent, not the attorney, not least of all because Stan raised his hand in the air and pointed to himself when he said:

"Call me Captain Ahab."

He really should've read Moby Dick.[73]

◊ ◊ ◊

News of Jesús' movement to the courthouse spread quickly, indeed, before the movement began. While he prepared to meet Judge Judi, a crowd filled the street outside the hospital. There were news reporters reporting with cameramen recording; there were protesters protesting, and supporters supporting; and there were even local Dullsville residents simply curious to see some action, not to mention excited to be part of such a lively gathering.

"How long do you think it'll be until he comes out?" Gabby Blabber stood on her toes in a failed attempt to peer over the crowd toward the hospital exit.

"Do you mean the drug dealer?" Cleopatra asked. "Or the Agent?"

"They'll probably be together." Thutmond answered two questions at once. "And it might be a while."

That last part disappointed Gabby. She needed to use the ladies' room as soon as possible. But she also preferred not to miss any action, and her creaky knees only let her move so fast.

"I guess I'll wait," she pouted. "I've already waited this long."

◊ ◊ ◊

Jesús dressed himself, as instructed, though he felt uncomfortable the entire time. Not only did he barely understand the stakes, but the clothes from Stan's black duffle bag were the opposite of his usual unwashed hoodie and baggy jeans. A vested suit with loafers—the new outfit meant to present him as dignified for his appearance in court. His captor, Stan DeVille, could ill afford another televised debacle.

While Jesús dressed, Howie attempted to negotiate a deal. But by the time Howie reentered the room, he had little time to update his sort-of client. This presented a challenge for the long-winded legal expert who struggled to say anything in only a little time. Yet Howie did his best to bring Jesús up to speed, even once again dangling his takeout bag from Pepe's Fried Chicken in another symbolic show of his continued intent to retire immediately.

"We have no choice but to proceed according to plan," Howie said, ignoring Jesús' unfamiliarity with the plan. "Just follow my lead, and I'll tell you when you're safe."

Regrettably, the attorney found no time to say anything else, because once again Stan DeVille stood at the door. The Super Special Agent heard a crowd forming outside. For the safety of everyone, he wished to transport Jesús to the courthouse before the movement gained significant attention.

◊ ◊ ◊

Powerful screams echoed down the street from every direction as soon as the Super Special Agent stepped outside the hospital with his Mexican-American prisoner. Some in the crowd offered support for their hero with shouts of praise and encouragement; others disparaged their villain with bellows of fury and vitriol; still others yelled just for the heck of it, not knowing who the hero was or what he stood for, simply excited to take part in such a newsworthy event.

Stan groaned as he glanced down the street past the horde. From the hospital steps, he could see the courthouse—a light stroll away on a normal day. But between him and his destination stood tens, if not hundreds, if not thousands of angry citizens blocking his path. (It proved difficult to get an accurate count from his perspective.)

Stan's original plan involved loading Jesús into his sleek SUV and driving two blocks to the courthouse, where Jesús would be indicted and then locked away until further notice. Yet plans can change as quickly as they can be made, as every Super Special Agent knows, and that's precisely what happened when Stan found his SUV looking not-so-sleek, covered in overzealous civilians hoping for a bird's eye view of the most popular criminal in the current news cycle.

"I guess we're walking," Stan said.

Stan threw his remaining black duffle bag over his shoulder, shoved Jesús forward, and began forcing his way through the crowd. Jesús offered no resistance, shrugging and continuing on with his captor. Howie began to protest, as attorneys tend to do, but scurried to catch up when he realized Stan and Jesús were already on the move.

The raucous crowd made the journey difficult—screaming insults at some and compliments at others, tugging at shirts and pants and whatever they could grab. Several police officers tried to push the crowd back, but the audience significantly outnumbered the protection. No matter which way Stan turned, he couldn't avoid the various groups of rowdy individuals spilling into the street.

The first group Jesús passed on the street could've been deemed supporters of the golden-eyed Mexican-American. They remained upset from the perceived racial slur in the grainy videos playing across the airwaves. Though most failed to recognize Jesús due to the vested suit and loafers replacing his unwashed hoodie and baggy jeans. They did, however, recognize Stan DeVille, the racist antagonist of those videos, and they made their presence known to him with screams of hate and shrieks of rage and howls of condemnation. To show disapproval beyond the sound of their voices, one man flung a handful of chocolate powder in Stan's face.

"Who's the Brownie now?" the man shouted, which must have made sense to his friends, because the entire group then cheered for the strange insult.

Covered in chocolate, Stan supposed he was now the Brownie, to answer the pending question. Though he pointed out that the powder could've easily been either cocoa or brown sugar to the untrained eye; only because the powder flew directly into his mouth, thus contacting his tongue, could he know for certain.

"It's an easy mistake to make," Stan insisted, and noted his preference for cocoa anyway.

The firing of chocolate powder angered the next group of protesters more than Stan. They supported the Super Special Agent, and fully approved of his actions in the grainy videos. According to them, it was difficult being a Special Agent of any kind, with part of the job involving split-second decisions. This was no time to be overly sensitive about what may have come out of his mouth. Stan was just protecting American citizens.

"Don't listen to them!" one woman urged. "Protect Americans first, then worry about the rest!"

"Thank you," Stan said, and nodded toward the woman.

"Jesús is an American too!" shouted another woman from a third group of protesters. Her words struck a chord with her audience, because the crowd followed with the cheers: "That's right!" and "Shout it!"

Clearly, the third group paid attention to the technical details of Jesús' story. Still, they remained less concerned with Jesús' citizenship, and more focused on making the previous group look silly. Jesús could've been dead for all they cared, as long as he proved their point, which they would've made in clearer terms, if it hadn't already been lost in the shuffle.

A fourth group agreed with the third group as far as the stated fact, but dove deeper into the surrounding circumstances, imploring the third group to consider:

"He's also a drug dealer!"

To them, Jesús' citizenship merely distracted from the real issue: Jesús was a degenerate; a drug dealer; the scourge of whatever nation he happened to be from. Legal or illegal, the real issue involved the lack of morality surrounding him wherever he called home.

Of course, Jesús' drug of choice happened to be the reason that the next group of protesters liked him the most. But they refrained from cheering out loud as he walked past. Instead, they kept silent, smiling and offering moral support for their hero, reeking of some relative of his now-famous narcotic.

"I'm coming for you next," Stan warned a quiet man proudly puffing a doobie in a show of support for the Mexican-American being paraded through the street.

"Isn't the real danger, like, guns, or something?" The doobie-puffing man certainly thought so. "Not, like, the weed, man."

Well that suggestion irked the next group, which pointed out that most of the problems with guns stemmed from the people who held them. When placed in the hands of a trained individual, a gun could be life-saving, as several in the vicinity remained ready to demonstrate.

With the focus on Stan and his prisoner, nobody paid attention to the periphery of the crowd, where an old acquaintance pushed toward the Super Special Agent, the golden-eyed prisoner, and the retiring attorney-at-law. Nobody paid attention, that is, until a shrill voice shouted:

"Look out!"

◊ ◊ ◊

Gabby Blabber was sure glad she delayed her trip to the ladies' room, because it turned out that she didn't have to wait long for the action to start; and boy oh boy, was there action once it started; and the best part was that she already knew most of the people involved.

First was DEA Super Special Agent Stan DeVille, Dullsville's longest-tenured anti-narcotics expert, and apparently the President's new best friend from what she heard on the news. Stan appeared more anxious than the last time she saw him. The screaming crowd probably affected his mood, she presumed, not that Stan stood out as the most pleasant person to begin with.

"Although he seemed fine when we smoked the doobie," Gabby said.

Second was the drug dealer, Jesús, who also appeared anxious. This differed from the Super Special Agent only in that Jesús didn't typically suffer from anxiety to begin with. Gabby had also never seen the boy wearing anything other than an unwashed hoodie, let alone something as fancy as his vested suit.

"Something strange is going on." Gabby lifted her brow. "Why is he dressed that way?"

Third was another familiar face, though the accompanying name escaped Gabby's knowledge. She'd witnessed Jesús' attorney speaking with María on numerous occasions over the years. She could only imagine what they talked about, and she certainly did, imagining quite the diabolical conversations. Perhaps that's why the attorney appeared anxious as he followed behind the other two.

"Everyone is so anxious," Gabby reiterated to anyone who listened.

And then there were the fourth and fifth familiar faces, belonging to Cleopatra Spiter and Thutmond Mose III, who stood directly next to the attentive woman with creaky knees. They'd been there the entire time, doing their best to ignore her.

"What?" asked Cleopatra.

"Did you say something?" asked Thutmond.

"I was just saying that everyone looks anxious," Gabby repeated, this time including her two companions in the generalization.

Oh, wait. There was also a sixth familiar face, attached to a neck extending from the shoulders of a body pushing its way through the crowd. Was that who Gabby thought, holding a custom-made, gold-monogrammed, patent leather briefcase?

"Look out!" Gabby attempted to warn the Super Special Agent, who'd never met the man presumed to be the father of his prisoner.

◊ ◊ ◊

José Carpentero may have walked away from 11 Main Street on Jesús' twentieth birthday, but he didn't walk far. He would've walked far, if he knew where to go; but without a specific destination, he felt no need to put in the requisite effort to get there. Carrying a custom-made, gold-monogrammed, patent leather briefcase filled to the brim with the recorded history of Adam Sandler, he was a man without a home for the first time in two decades.

José briefly considered returning to Mexico to resume the career in late-night carpentry that never really existed, not to mention find a former lover to impose on. Yet one problem remained: the only name he remembered belonged to María. Evidently, that happens when a man spends twenty years with one woman, and also when the man failed to learn any other women's names to begin with. Regardless, why should he return to Mexico? He'd become proud to call the United States his home after twenty years in the country. Sure, he hadn't worked a job or paid taxes, but neither did many of the regulars at Dullsville's finest tavern from what he could tell.

Instead of leaving the country, José trudged to the closest hotel. With no money to pay for a room, he convinced the concierge to trade a night's stay in exchange for a recorded work of art. He chose a movie called *Jack and Jill* because he'd already seen it once, which was one too many times from his perspective. Fortunately, the concierge had yet to see the film.

The good news was that the concierge kept his promises: even after watching *Jack and Jill*, he still allowed José to spend the night. The bad news was that the concierge also learned from his mistakes: the next morning, he promptly informed José that only cash would be accepted from then on.

"How about *You Don't Mess with the Zohan* in exchange for another night?" José asked.

"Get out," the concierge replied.

Disappointed, but not defeated, José learned something: people respected the Adam Sandler brand, meaning that his movies were as valuable as cash, at least until the recipient started watching.

So that's how José survived. *That's My Boy* bought him a good night's sleep at the Dullsville Hotel, and *Funny People* was worth an average night's sleep across the street at the Dullsville Express Hotel. At the Dullsville Motel, he traded *Grown Ups* and *Grown Ups 2* for two nights in advance after convincing the front clerk that he couldn't watch one without the other (though the front clerk disagreed after watching only the first *Grown Ups*). Even better, he stayed three nights at the Dullsville Resort and Spa, because the manager was too busy to watch any of *Just Go with It*, *Click* or *Blended* until the third night. *Bulletproof*, *The Waterboy*, *Big Daddy*, *Little Nicky*, *Punch Drunk Love*, *Eight Crazy Nights* and *Anger Management* bought him another week touring the hotel circuit in the next town over.

For the first time, José appreciated Adam Sandler's emphasis on quantity over quality. Had he been a Daniel Day-Lewis fan, he would've been sleeping on the street by then.

Not every movie in the collection went toward room and board. Falling back into old habits, José traded *The Wedding Singer*, *Mr. Deeds*, *50 First Dates*, *Spanglish*, *The Longest Yard*, *Rein Over Me*, *I Now Pronounce You Chuck & Larry*, *You Don't Mess with the Zohan*, *Bedtime Stories*, *Just Go with It*, *Men, Women & Children*, *The Cobbler*, *Pixels*, and *The Ridiculous 6* for various bottles of tequila. He would've gladly puffed a few doobies instead, but he dared not return to 11 Main Street after María's outburst.

So José hopped from hotel to hotel, sipping tequila, watching the remnants of his movie collection slowly disappear. On one hand, the routine lightened his briefcase, making the luggage easier to transport from one night to the next. On the other hand, each day he possessed less entertainment to occupy his attention. He found spare time to do something he normally abstained from, and that was—

—think.

"No way," José decided.

—watch live television, instead of old movies.

"Fine," José settled.

Alas, the first time José sat down in front of live television, he saw something that made him think anyway: not a soap opera full of confrontations and surprises; or a rerun of a popular movie from decades prior; but a live news broadcast from Dullsville General Hospital, where Channel 4 News' very own Jennifer Smith reported on the famed drug dealer from Dullsville, Jesús with no apparent last name. For anyone just tuning in, the reporter recapped the recent events: the racially charged shooting; the *Zerojuana* possession; the Executive Orders; not to mention Jesús' upcoming transportation from the hospital to the courthouse in only a matter of minutes.

"When did all this happen?" José wondered, having been holed up in various hotel rooms with nothing to do but drink tequila and watch old movies.

Despite his resistance, José had no choice but to continue thinking by this point, with his brain now awake. With a sip of tequila, he wondered how María could've lied to him about being Jesús' father. And with another sip of tequila, he decided he would've been better off staying in Mexico twenty years earlier. He should've stayed with the other woman—whatever her name—instead of marrying María and living a lie.

On the bright side, Jesús introduced José to the pleasure of cannabis—no use at the moment, unfortunately. José hadn't puffed any cannabis since Jesús' twentieth birthday. Of course, his wench of a wife ruined the moment. Not only did she blame him for Jesús' behavior, she also caused him to burn a hole in his trousers when he shoved the doobie inside his pocket in a hurried attempt to hide the evidence.

"Wait a second." José checked the pockets of his pants for the first time in two weeks. "I still have the rest of the doobie."

Clearly, he'd find no better time to finish what he started with Jesús. So he lit up his doobie using the hotel's conveniently placed matchbook, and puffed until his heart was as full as his lungs.

With his first puff, José missed Jesús. He loved puffing doobies with the boy, regardless of their genetic similarities; he simply enjoyed the time shared, conversing and joking and laughing while watching the funniest actor he could imagine.

With his second puff, José dove deeper. He imagined where he'd have ended up without Jesús. The tequila would've killed him eventually. Or perhaps he would've died of another cause, but the likeliest outcome remained the same.

And with his third puff, José concluded that Jesús saved his life.

Now it was time for José to repay the favor.

Besides, José could no longer live the hotel life. For one thing, the concierge had just knocked on the door and informed him of the hotel's policy against smoking indoors. For another thing, his film collection ran thin. Knowing Adam Sandler, another movie would be released within weeks. But José had no time to wait: he could enjoy another two nights, at most, with only *Billy Madison* and *Happy Gilmore* left in his briefcase.

"How far is the hospital?" José asked the concierge.

The concierge pointed across the street, and asked whether José heard the crowd gathered outside. There was something going on with a criminal moving to the courthouse, though the concierge had been too busy to pay attention to the details.

José heard all the details he needed.

"Hold on, Jesús!" José grabbed his briefcase and sprang out the door. "Daddy's coming to save you!"

◊ ◊ ◊

"Look out!"

Stan DeVille recognized the shrill voice behind the exclamation. Unfortunately, he'd never met Jesús' presumed father, so the warning meant nothing without clarification as to what he should be looking out for.

"It's José!"

Gabby further clarified that José was Jesús' father, and also the person clutching a custom-made, gold-monogrammed, patent leather briefcase.

"Gotcha," Stan confirmed, and spotted José pushing through the crowd.

Not that José meant to hide himself from view. He even waved his hands in the air. The entire point of knifing through the crowd was to gain Stan's attention. He pushed his way past the Dullsville police officers, stood directly in front of the Super Special Agent, held out his upright palm, and said:

"Stop!"

Besides that, José didn't know what to do. He'd never been one to think ahead, or even to think in the present.

"Take me instead." José attempted to sacrifice himself. "I'm the reason Jesús had the drugs."

The Super Special Agent wasn't prepared to release his prisoner in the middle of the street. Nor could he, according to the President's orders, or even common sense. Of course, two prisoners seemed better than one, and Stan had hoped to find Jesús' mother and father at some point.

"Thanks for making this easy," Stan said. "José, you're under arrest."

Undeterred, José grabbed Jesús' arm—a curious move, causing a sudden commotion amongst the already-anxious crowd. Some screamed; others cheered; and a few drew their personal firearms, including the DEA Super Special Agent, who unholstered his pistol and flipped off the safety, pointing the weapon at the long-lost character just joining the party.

"You're both under arrest," Stan ordered, his pistol focused on José's nose. Stan felt no desire to shoot José, but his plan was quickly unraveling, and his twitchy trigger finger tended not to act according to plan even when one existed.

Stan wasn't the only person unhappy to see Jesús' presumed father. From the look on Howie's face, José appeared to be ruining his plan as well.

"Get out of here, you idiot," advised Howie. "I have a plan, and you're ruining it."

José stood undeterred. He had his own plan to save Jesús at all costs. "You'll have to shoot me!"

The Super Special Agent shrugged. He appeared fine with the suggestion, and kept his pistol pointed directly at José's nose as he bent his twitchy trigger finger ever so slightly.

"Nevermind," José suddenly reconsidered, releasing his grasp of Jesús and raising his hands in the air.

But before Stan lowered his pistol, he was startled by a buzz in the crowd as a protestor's cellular phone received a spam call from an anonymous number. What followed was a loud bang, then Jesús' head hitting the pavement, and a red mess splattering all over the boy's fancy new vest.

The crowd erupted—some screaming in horror, others squawking with excitement, others just running in circles—all at the sight of Jesús lying on the ground, motionless, with a thick pool of blood slowly growing beneath his body.

TWENTY-FIVE

Washington, D.C.

The President of the United States sat still in the Oval Office, surrounded by Secretaries, stunned by what he witnessed on live television. With the entire nation watching, DEA Super Special Agent Stan DeVille did (1) precisely what the President instructed him not to do, (2) at the precise time the President instructed him not to do it, (3) to the precise person the President instructed him not to do it to.

"What an idiot," the President mumbled.

"And what a mess," he added. By "mess," he meant the criminal who lay on the ground, motionless, with a pool of blood spreading beneath his torso.

As if the blood wasn't messy enough, the President then found out that the situation in Dullsville would become even messier. Breaking news, straight from the lips of a high-profile reporter—who spoke to an attorney, who spoke to an ambulance driver, who spoke to the paramedic attending to the victim—was that:

"Jesús is dead! I repeat, Jesús is dead!"

Yes, it was being repeated, over and over, that Dullsville's most famous resident—Jesús with no other moniker besides "the Brownie"—had succumbed to the gunshot wound delivered to his chest on live television only moments earlier. Reported as the worst tragedy in at least a few days, the news came as no surprise to anyone tuned in for the entire broadcast: the Super Special Agent's bullet appeared to penetrate the victim's fancy vest directly at the heart.

Newspersons across the nation were unrelenting, blaming the President for the entire bloody fiasco, thanks to his hastily issued Executive Orders. And why, they asked, had Jesús been escorted to the courthouse by the same Agent who shot him in the foot? And how could Jesús even walk so soon after being shot in the foot? To make matters worse, someone inside the White House leaked word of the President's multiple meetings with Stan DeVille in the Oval Office. Apparently, the President gave the Super Special Agent specific instructions regarding how to handle his firearm around Jesús.

"I told him *not* to shoot the boy!" the President insisted. Clearly, he wholeheartedly disagreed with the reports that he shouldered any semblance of responsibility for Jesús' death.

Citizens on both sides of the political spectrum remained unhappy. On one side, there were hard feelings about the current President's support of a man who used a racially insensitive term. On the other side, there were hard feelings about the former President's laws which allowed Jesús' family into the country in the first place. And on both sides, there were hard feelings about the other side's hard feelings, not to mention the anger surrounding the President's decision to make *Zerojuana*-brand cannabis illegal before the public received the chance to sample the stuff.

It was time for damage control. The blowback from the incident would be incredulous, from what the Secretaries in the Oval Office advised. That didn't sound bad to the President at first, but then the Secretaries told him what the word "incredulous" meant in this context.

"Oh, that's bad," the President agreed.

Still, they had no reason to overreact. The President had a battle-tested method of avoiding accountability. First, he needed a scapegoat to absorb the blame. Then, he needed a distraction, so the public's attention would shift directions, never to return. By the time the public realized what happened, a new controversy would consume the news circuit.

The scapegoat seemed obvious to everyone in the room. DEA

Super Special Agent Stan DeVille fired the bullet, so he should also absorb the blame, to the full extent of the law. Or if he agreed to take the blame voluntarily, the full extent of the law might be unnecessary. Either way, the Secretaries agreed to point their fingers in the same direction.

"And I'm taking away his Super title," the President added of the Agent who was now merely Special, not Super, with even his specialness in doubt.

The distraction was less obvious than the scapegoat. There were a few different directions they could go, the Secretaries agreed, as long as the distraction was big. Though the President went one step further and insisted that the distraction be, not just big, but bigger than big, or as he called it:

"Huge."

"You're a genius," praised the Secretary of Energy, "and as stable as a noble gas."

"I'd say as stable as a load-bearing wall," said the Secretary of Housing and Urban Development.

"Or as stable as the economy," added the Secretary of Commerce.

Compliments aside, it was time to brainstorm, so the finest thinkers in the nation put their heads together, and considered distractions meeting the President's criteria. There were the old standbys, of course, like starting a trade war or holding a summit or attacking a rival politician. But the Secretaries thought the President should think outside the box for this particular situation, which stood out as unlike any controversy the administration had faced thus far. A unique controversy required a unique solution, they said.

"I still don't understand what the big deal is." The President threw up his hands. "Jesús wasn't even a real American."

The Secretaries in the room hushed the President's suggestion, noting Jesús' legal citizenship for all intents and purposes. With the President repeatedly harping the benefits of legal immigration to his favorite crowds, it would be hypocritical to now carve out a group of legal citizens as undeserving of the designation.

"Hypo-what?" the President asked.

"It's pronounced, hippo—," the Secretary of Education corrected, and the President ignored.

The Secretaries meant that the President needed to be careful. Not a single U.S. citizen, it seemed, felt satisfied with the current outcome. The politically correct wouldn't be satisfied with the now-merely-Special Agent's demotion, and wanted jailtime for his "Brownie" comment alone. The law abiders disagreed with either the use of force or the necessity to use force in the first place, and sought new legislation to curb one issue or the other. And then there were the purveyors of common sense, who questioned the point of anything that happened over the past few weeks.

"Screw that last group," the President decided on the spot.

Even still, with so many angry citizens, the President couldn't make everyone happy.

"That's why we need a huge distraction," the President reminded.

The Secretaries all agreed that the President was correct. The distraction needed to be huge—huge enough to grab the attention of those most interested in Jesús' story. But who made up that group? Who seemed most interested in the news surrounding *Zerojuana*?

"I think it's clear by now that potheads are the audience." The President nodded confidently. "Now, how do we calm the potheads?"

Alas, none of the Secretaries thought of a good answer. Nor did they understand how anxious this group became after *Zerojuana* went from unknown, to illegal, to legal but unavailable, to illegal yet again—quite the emotional explosion for the most easily blown minds in the country.

"It's too bad *Zerojuana* isn't legal anymore," lamented the Secretary of Health and Human Services. "The effects are supposed to be fairly calming."

"Hmm," the President hummed as he considered the suggestion. Part of the reason he made *Zerojuana* illegal with the second Executive Order was to prevent Jesús from fleeing the country. Well, with Jesús now dead, he seemed unlikely to go anywhere.

But the Secretaries advised against legalizing *Zerojuana* once again, which would make the second Executive Order look like a mistake. Such a measure would play into the media's accusations that the President's Executive Orders on *Zerojuana* caused everything now wrong with the entire situation.

"The worst thing you can do is admit a mistake," the Secretary of Labor advised.

"Plus," the Secretary of the Interior noted, "this foreign company, TH Corp, may still control *Zerojuana* production."

The President agreed to avoid admitting any mistakes, not least of all because he made no mistakes to begin with. Besides, walking back on an Executive Order was far from the big action they needed, let alone as huge as they previously discussed. They needed to think bigger than *Zerojuana*. After all, *Zerojuana* was just a made-up word for a specific strain of cannabis. Nobody even seemed to understand the difference between *Zerojuana* and other strains from what he could tell.

"Wait," the President interrupted his own train of thought. "That's *it*!"

The Secretaries wondered what *it* was, or where *it* was, or what the President meant in any respect.

"We won't legalize *Zero*-juana—" The President paused to build anticipation for his huge idea. "—we'll legalize *Mari*-juana."

The Secretaries failed to understand how legalizing cannabis would save the day, so their leader explained his idea in the simplest terms he could think of.

"That's all potheads ever talk about anyway," the President said. "They'd write an entire book about it if they possessed any initiative whatsoever."

The Secretaries debated amongst themselves before reaching the same conclusion as the President who could fire them at any time. The President was a genius, they agreed, and legalizing cannabis was a brilliant idea. The measure would benefit the economy, and the President could take credit. Plus, Jesús' supporters would be so high, they'd forget about their most recognizable advocate being shot in the chest by an arguably racist Super Special Agent. Besides, anyone who paid attention to the trends of the past twenty years understood the inevitability of the nationwide legalization of cannabis. If legalization was inevitable, then why not right then?

Only two questions remained: first from the Secretary of Commerce, then from the President.

"Can we instantly legalize cannabis?" asked the Secretary of Commerce, unsure of procedure.

"Haven't you ever heard of an Executive Order?" was the President's obvious reply.

TWENTY-SIX

Alabama, Alaska, Arizona, Arkansas, California, Colorado, Connecticut, Delaware, Florida, Georgia, Hawaii, Idaho, Illinois, Indiana, Iowa, Kansas, Kentucky, Louisiana, Maine, Maryland, Massachusetts, Michigan, Minnesota, Mississippi, Missouri, Montana, Nebraska, Nevada, New Hampshire, New Jersey, New Mexico, New York, North Carolina, North Dakota, Ohio, Oklahoma, Oregon, Pennsylvania, Rhode Island, South Carolina, South Dakota, Tennessee, Texas, Utah, Vermont, Virginia, Washington, West Virginia, Wisconsin, Wyoming, and even Puerto Rico

Executive Order #3 was clearly written, because the President finally allowed one of his Secretaries to pen the directive. In clear and simple terms, the language of the document removed cannabis from Schedule I of the Controlled Substances Act, making the substance legal across the United States, subject to reasonable state restrictions on sales. The Executive Order was also effective immediately, because that was the only way the President knew to be effective.

The President was right about one thing: his third Executive Order instantly overshadowed any mention of Jesús' name. And even when someone quietly mentioned Jesús' name in afterthought, the reference served in admiration of the greater good coming from his sacrifice, with little thought to the sacrifice itself.

The nation's most popular newspersons differed in opinion, but most appeared generally upbeat. Some applauded the third Executive Order as long overdue; others believed it to be appropriately timed. Some salivated at the economic benefits; others focused on the medical side; still others for the pure enjoyment of the stuff. Some even praised the President's forward thinking with no mention of the Executive Order. There were detractors too, but they could do nothing more than shout their negative opinions on the matter; and when they shouted their negative opinions, they were told to go puff a doobie and relax, now that doobies were legal.

For once, the focus shifted away from the newspersons, or the President, or any one individual. Instead, citizens all over each of the 50 states (and Puerto Rico) united in the streets to celebrate the occasion. Shockingly, even in the states which prohibited cannabis until that day, many of the citizens already had doobies rolled up and ready to be puffed the instant the Executive Order hit the airwaves; and of those without doobies, many held pipes instead; and those who didn't have doobies or pipes, well, they just shared with those who did.

For the first time in as long as anyone cared to remember, there existed solidarity within the good ol' U.S. of A. There existed so much solidarity that a dense cloud of smoke slowly enveloped every state in the country, from the Atlantic to the Pacific, through the Rocky Mountains and across the Great Plains. The fog grew so thick that the nation's most trusted weather service issued a Chill Advisory, recommending that citizens stay in their homes unless they felt prepared to be mellow.

The doobie puffers and the pipe smokers reveled in the herbal fog, as doobie puffers and pipe smokers tend to do. And even those neighbors who previously opposed the drug experienced some semblance of good feelings. After all, they needed to breathe at some point, and it's tough to avoid some type of high if there's enough smoke in the air.

◊ ◊ ◊

It wasn't easy for Jesús' ambulance to get where it needed to be. First, the driver picked up Jesús after weaving through the mobs of people scrambling in every direction, a challenging task even with the emergency siren blaring. Then, the driver dealt with the Dullsville traffic as he tried to leave downtown. And then, once the ambulance hit the countryside, the driver struggled to see through the herbal fog slowly emerging from every direction. To top it all off, this was the first time the driver drove an ambulance, though none of the passengers would've thought so, since he acted like a complete professional the entire time.

Now the obvious question: why would the ambulance drive through the countryside in the first place? The only hospital in Dullsville stood just down the street from Jesús' shooting, and had yet to change his sheets.

"Dullsville is too dangerous for the victim," the ambulance driver radioed to the hospital to explain the situation. "We need to bring Jesús to the next town over."

Not one passenger in the ambulance questioned the decision. Instead, they focused on the health of the unresponsive gunshot victim tightly strapped to a gurney.

"We'll be there soon," Howie whispered into Jesús' ear. By "we," he meant everyone in the ambulance. The attending paramedic, the now-merely-Special Agent, and the ambulance driver were on their way to the same destination. Heck, even José was there—now technically under arrest at the order of Stan DeVille.

Jesús lay still on the gurney. Not that he could move if he tried: that was the point of the tight straps across his chest. His eyes remained closed and his mouth sealed shut, so everyone simply held their breaths in quiet apprehension.

"Will he be alright?" asked Howie, unable to hold his breath for long.

"I hope so," replied Manny Hernandez, the finest paramedic in Dullsville. The steady beeping noise echoing through the ambulance remained evidence of a heartbeat. As long as Jesús maintained a heartbeat, they had a reason to be hopeful, regardless of how hard the bullet struck him in the chest.

Stan said nothing, and took solace in the knowledge that he avoided shouting anything arguably offensive when he fired the bullet that struck Jesús in the chest. He remained certain that the day marked the end of his career as a government official, but at least the worst anyone would think after watching video of the incident was that he was a murderer.

Nobody in the ambulance heard of the President's third Executive Order. Nor did they care at the moment. Their only goal, regardless of the person asked, involved reaching their destination as soon as possible.

So the ambulance zigged and zagged through the streets toward the next town over, as quickly as the driver could handle with all the smoke surrounding the vehicle. But when they reached the next town over, something strange happened: instead of slowing down, the driver shut off his radio and kept driving toward the coast.

◊ ◊ ◊

Guy stood by. Or rather, he sat by, gazing out across the ocean from American soil. His yacht idled on the California coastline, ready to bolt at a moment's notice. Normally he avoided brazenly pulling up to the U.S. coast, but this stood out as an abnormal situation.

Guy hadn't paid attention to the news, so he remained unaware of the gun violence in Dullsville, or the Executive Order out of Washington, D.C., or the doobie sharing everywhere else. For the past few hours, he'd focused on navigating his yacht through the Pacific Ocean, bypassing Mexico on a direct route from his secret island to the United States. During the trip, he'd heard nothing but the radio signals of wayward sailors, warning only of nautical conditions and passing debris. Of course, he saw the fog rising over the mainland, and he smelled the distinct herbal aroma.

"Nice," he said, and lit his own doobie, adding to the western edge of the fog.

Clearly, Guy expected his associates to meet him at the coast. Why else would he be sitting there? Although he didn't expect them to arrive in an ambulance. Nor did he expect to see his bloodied biological son lying on a gurney, accompanied by a paramedic, a government agent, and an unkempt man with a fancy briefcase. Yet that's precisely what happened when the ambulance emerged from the fog and threw open its rear doors.

"What happened?" Guy leapt into the ambulance to be nearer to his son, squeezing the boy's hand in a desperate attempt to find some sign of life.

Howie Spirit, Esq., had never been short on breath, so he took a bit longer to explain the situation than one would expect. He began by describing how he arranged for the ambulance to bring Jesús to the coastline, since the vehicle's siren allowed Jesús to move to his destination quicker than an alternative method of transportation. Then he negotiated a deal with Stan, once it became clear that he had no other option. José wasn't part of the initial plan either, but once he resurfaced, it only made sense to bring him along as opposed to allowing him to speak with the authorities. Oh, and the attorney looked around, and once certain that no one else lingered within earshot, he told Jesús:

"You're safe now."

"Thank goodness," said Jesús, who opened his golden eyes, unstrapped himself from the gurney, and rose up to wrap his arms around each of the other men.

"Thank goodness," said José, who until then knew nothing of any plan and assumed the worst outcome for his son-of-sorts.

"Thank goodness," said Manny, who knew of the plan to smuggle Jesús out of Dullsville in the ambulance, but remained unaware of the DEA's involvement by any means.

"Thank goodness," said Stan, who knew Jesús' vest was bulletproof, even if he led others to believe it was merely a fancy garment. Still, he worried about Jesús' apparent inability to open his eyes after being struck with the bullet, not to mention the blood seeping from his chest.

"Thank goodness," said Howie, still holding his buffalo-style chicken wrap and French fries from Pepe's Fried Chicken. Alas, he now had no sauce for his French fries, because he used all of his ketchup to fake Jesús' blood for the cameras. Though he was sure glad he collected so many ketchup packets, or Jesús' death wouldn't have been such a convincing scene.

"It's not easy to act dead for so long," Jesús admitted, wiping off the ketchup as he removed the bulletproof vest, anxious to change back into his unwashed hoodie and baggy jeans.

"You must have had a great teacher," bragged Richard Dickens from the front of the ambulance. "How was my performance as the ambulance driver?"

"You were very convincing," Manny showered the thespian with much-needed praise.

"Enough chit-chat." Howie was ready to officially retire to the tropics. "Can we get to the island now?"

Only one item remained missing—albeit, an important item. They still needed a sample of *Zerojuana* to reproduce on the secret island. After all, that was the entire reason Jesús returned to Dullsville in the first place—if anyone forgot—setting off the unlikely series of events which followed.

Jesús didn't have the *Zerojuana*: he took a bullet in the foot the last time he tried to retrieve a sample.

José didn't have the *Zerojuana*: his fancy briefcase held nothing but the last of his favorite Adam Sandler movies.

Manny didn't have the *Zerojuana*: his task involved nothing more than procuring an ambulance and finding a trustworthy driver.

Howie didn't have the *Zerojuana*: he was a planner, not an actor.

Even Richard the actor didn't pick up the stuff: *Zerojuana* was unnecessary for his character preparation as an ambulance driver.

And Guy just arrived at the coast.

"Seriously?" asked DEA Agent-of-sorts Stan DeVille. "You guys planned all of that out and forgot to take a sample?"

Nobody responded with more than a shrug. The oversight certainly seemed like an obvious gaffe, in hindsight.

Fortunately for everyone, Stan was an expert in the collection of evidence. In his remaining black duffle bag, which had been inconspicuously slung over his shoulder the entire time, lay several fully grown *Zerojuana* plants—freshly picked from the imported, nutrient-rich soil behind the *titan arums* at 11 Main Street—which he revealed to his associates, followed by a series of cheers and high-fives.

With that, the yacht idling at the shoreline suddenly had seven seamen aboard, all ready to push off the coastline of the now-hazy nation where at least a few of them had been born.

But before they left for good, Guy asked if any questions remained from his passengers, and only Jesús replied.

"Are we in Mexico?" Jesús crinkled his face in confusion. "I thought we could only get to the island through Mexico?"

"Oh, no," Guy explained, "but I save money on gas when I pick up from Mexico, so I like it better that way."

"Please don't mention anything to Moses when you see him back at the island," advised Howie. "He may not be as understanding of that detail as the rest of us."

TWENTY-SEVEN

Paradise

There were high-fives all around as the seafaring Guy arrived at his secret island with a boatload of guests, including: (1) a presumed-dead, twenty-year-old, dual citizen of the United States and Mexico; (2) a once-Super, now-only-Special Agent for the DEA; (3) a thespian with recent experience playing both a narcotics agent and an ambulance driver; (4) a health-conscious paramedic with a history of depression; (5) a newly retired Doctor of Law; and (6) José. First, there were high-fives across the yacht between seamen during the lengthy voyage to the secret island. Then, there were high-fives as the new arrivals came ashore to meet (7) a sunburnt botanist wearing a sombrero, and (8) a hardworking mother eager to reunite with her son.

"Welcome," greeted Moses and María.

"Thank you," replied Jesús, Stan, Richard, Manny, Howie, and José.

"Don't forget about me," added Guy (9), once he finished parking the yacht. He also felt compelled to point out that they were all guests on his island. Not that he meant to complain, pleased to host such a diverse group.

Oh, and a tiny Chihuahua named Perrita kept barking until María told her to be silent.

"Her name is Mexicandog," Moses insisted. "How many

times do I have to explain this?"

Nobody exceeded María's level of excitement. She wrapped her arms around Jesús the moment he stepped on the shore, almost tripping into the ocean in the process. José added a pat on the back, rather than wrestle the boy away from his mother.

Moses seemed to be in just as fine a mood as everyone else. Though he clearly missed a few details: like where the heck Richard Dickens and Manny Hernandez came from. Yet the reemergence of an old handbag confused him more than that of his former neighbors.

"Is that my briefcase?" Moses wondered of the custom-made, gold-monogrammed, patent leather attaché hanging over José's shoulder.

José shrugged, and handed the briefcase to its rightful owner, noting that it only contained two movies: *Billy Madison* and *Happy Gilmore*.

Richard and Manny shook hands with their oldest neighbor, and then hugged their more recent neighbor. It was great seeing everyone in good spirits, Richard commented; and it was good seeing everyone in great health, according to Manny.

"There'll be plenty of time to catch up," Guy said, already tired of all the introductions. A more pressing matter required their immediate attention. In other words, he insisted:

"Let's all smoke a doobie together."

Indeed, the act offered a fitting end to the story, Guy believed, with the highest point of the island's tallest mountain being the best place to enjoy a symbolic toke in the midst of a breathtaking landscape.

Everyone agreed, and followed their self-proclaimed leader as far as the island went to the sky. María and José caught up with Jesús on the way, learning the details of everything from his arrest, to his imprisonment, to his freedom once again. They learned of Richard's ambulance driving, and Manny's blondie baking, and Stan's change of heart. Moses listened too, learning more about his former neighbors than he ever cared to know.

When the hikers reached the top of the mountain, they found the view impossible to describe. Or rather, they could describe the view, because they were right there, looking at it themselves. But they found it impossible to do justice to the view with a mere description of words, so they made no attempt.

With the attention of the island's entire population, Guy twirled a doobie with the *Zerojuana* flowers from Stan's black duffle bag, and held his creation up in the air for all to admire. Before they started puffing, he thanked each person for their contributions. Some contributed more than others (ahem, José), but everyone counted for something. Although everyone agreed that Jesús stood out as the real hero amongst them. Because of him, most U.S. citizens knew about *Zerojuana*. Whether those citizens chose to give the product a chance remained to be seen, but Jesús maintained no control over what people did with his message; all he could do was put them on notice and hope for the best.

So with that, Guy held a lighter up to his doobie, and asked his guests to look around. The world was theirs. Well, not the world, yet. But the island was theirs, at least. There existed nothing but water as far as they could see. Not another soul for miles, except—

"Wait!" María pointed across the horizon. "What's that?"

Well it just so happened that María possessed the best eyesight of the nine islanders standing atop the mountain, so she became the first to see a speck emerge over the water in the distance. She also became the first to realize that the speck was another boat, gliding over the waves at full speed, directly approaching the island from the north.

◊ ◊ ◊

Back in the United States, nonstop coverage of the President's third Executive Order broadcast across every television channel. The news received mixed reactions: some citizens were outraged, others were joyful, and most were stoned thanks to the herbal fog overtaking the country. Oh, and there was one other person, not outraged or joyful or stoned; all she wanted was to figure out how everything fit together, which is why she kept asking:

"What the heck is going on?"

Gabby Blabber refused to rest until she solved the mystery of 11 Main Street. Between her memory and her journal, she possessed all the pieces to the puzzle. She just needed to figure out how the pieces fit together.

The first clue she found—back when Moses initially disappeared—was a hand-rolled cannabis cigarette extinguished in a glass lined with whiskey residue. Twenty years later, the cannabis reappeared in the form of baked blondies, apparently having descended from the same strain, *Zerojuana*, stolen from Plant Inc some two decades prior.

Where had *Zerojuana*-brand cannabis been during those two decades? More importantly, where was it now? With Jesús dead, from what Gabby understood, Moses represented the only remaining connection. Although she also hadn't seen Richard or Manny running down the street that morning, come to think of it.

The curious neighbor thought back to the rest of the clues. The next clue she and her crack team of investigators found —back when they examined 11 Main Street following Moses' disappearance—was an Adam Sandler movie called *Happy Gilmore*. Moses was a fan of Adam Sandler the actor, Gabby came to find out; he also befriended a terminally ill man by the same name, from what she recalled.

But why did Adam Sandler's name keep popping up?

The question haunted Gabby. The second clue seemed to lead nowhere. But there had to be a point to all the attention directed to the actor, right? There had to be a purpose.

Didn't there?

Didn't there? she wondered again.

Just then, Gabby remembered an important detail. Before jumping to a conclusion, she retrieved her journal and her reading glasses. After balancing her reading glasses on the tip of her nose, she confirmed her mistake. The Adam Sandler movie was the *third* clue, not the *second* clue. The *second* clue was an atlas open to a page showing North America, with a bright yellow star drawn in the Pacific Ocean and labeled as "TH Corp."

"TH Corp?"

Suddenly, the puzzle fell into place. With minor research, Gabby discovered that (index finger) only one privately owned island lay in the vicinity of the bright yellow star, and (middle finger) that privately owned island had been purchased about two decades earlier, (ring finger) right around the same time Moses disappeared.

Gabby picked up the phone and dialed Moses' ex-wife and ex-coworker, who—like her—wouldn't find peace until they located the botanist once and for all.

"I think I know where Moses went with the *Zerojuana*," Gabby told them.

"Finally," Cleopatra said.

"It's time for closure," Thutmond agreed.

And that's how (10) the always-curious, creaky-kneed neighbor found herself headed toward a secret island in the middle of the Pacific Ocean, on a boat driven by (11) Plant Inc's angry inventory manager, with (12) a spiteful ex-wife navigating.

◊ ◊ ◊

It felt a bit awkward, at first, as Gabby and the rest of her crew pulled up to the island and parked next to Guy's yacht. There had never been two boats parked at the island at the same time, let alone twelve people of varying degrees of acquaintance clustered at the shore.

"Welcome," greeted María, José, Stan, Jesús, Richard, Manny, and Howie.

"Thank you," replied Gabby, Cleopatra, and Thutmond.

"Don't forget about me," added Guy, who once again hated being left out, particularly when he'd become the presumed person in charge.

"And me," said Moses, completing the group as the last of the initial islanders to make it back down the mountain to the shoreline.

"Moses!" said Cleopatra.

"Moses!" said Thutmond.

"Moses!" said Gabby. "I knew it!"

"Oh jeez," said Moses. He'd always known his past would catch up with him at some point. He could only imagine what they each wanted.

Oh, they had wants. Cleopatra wanted unpaid alimony and an enforcement of Judge Judi's order prohibiting Moses from leaving the country. Thutmond wanted restitution for the stolen plants and an apology for the damage to his reputation as an inventory manager. Gabby simply wanted to know:

"What the heck is going on?"

These wants consumed them for as long as they remembered. The only time they found solace—the one time they felt temporary relief from these obsessions—came after puffing a doobie filled with *Zerojuana* flowers, when it became legal to do so after the President's first Executive Order. Otherwise, they couldn't rid their minds of the notion of debts being owed.

"In that case," Guy interrupted, and waved his previously unpuffed doobie in the air, "can we smoke this now?"

"Yes," said Cleopatra.

"Please," said Thutmond.

"That's why we're here," said Gabby.

Guy also suggested that everyone return to the highest point of the island's tallest mountain to enjoy the doobie, especially since the recently arrived threesome had yet to enjoy the view.

So once again, with three new islanders, everyone trekked as far as the island went to the sky. On the way, Gabby caught everyone up on the U.S. President's third Executive Order, removing cannabis from Schedule I of the Controlled Substances Act once and for all.

When the hikers reached the top of the mountain, they couldn't believe the view. Or rather, they could believe the view, because they were right there, looking at it themselves. But it would've been impossible to convey the landscape to someone not present, so they made no attempt.

With the attention of the island's entire population, Guy once again held his doobie as high as he could reach. And once again, before they began puffing, he thanked everyone for their contributions. Again, some contributed more than others (ahem, José), but everyone counted for something. And again, Jesús was the most important—yada, yada, yada.

"Now let's smoke this dope," Guy concluded, and lit the edge of his doobie on fire before passing to his left, where Gabby Blabber anxiously waited to take the first puff.

Gabby took that first puff, and reveled in the satisfaction of a puzzle completed. She'd connected Moses and María and José and Jesús and Richard and Manny. She'd figured out the meaning of the atlas and the location of the *Zerojuana* and the identity of the golden-eyed man. And although the whole Adam Sandler thing remained a bit mind-boggling, who cared about Adam Sandler anyway? There was just one more detail she'd yet to figure out for certain.

"Are you gay?" she asked Richard Dickens.

"Isn't it obvious?" Richard asked in response.

"Yes," Gabby replied, "I guess it is."

Though now that Gabby knew for sure, she didn't care anymore. Perhaps she should focus on herself, she realized, as opposed to worrying about everyone else. She spent so much time on her neighbors' business that she failed to introduce any of her own interests, besides the name and storyline of her favorite soap opera, which she supposed she'd miss that day, not that she cared anymore; and it felt good not to care what happened on *TI&TA* because, quite frankly, *TI&TA* had a stupid storyline.

Gabby took one more puff of the doobie and then passed it to her left, toward the most recent object of her interest.

"It's not like I've kept my sexuality a secret," Richard said, accepted the doobie from Gabby, and puffed.

Richard was right. He wasn't hiding anything; it was just that nobody asked him the question directly. He lived as an open book, which is how he quietly became a fairly well-developed character in a short amount of time, compared to others in the vicinity who took the opposite approach. He felt proud to put himself out there. And he'd keep putting himself out there. If people wished to pay attention, they would; if not, they could look away, and that seemed fine with him.

After one more puff, Richard passed the doobie to his left, where his favorite paramedic, Manny Hernandez, sat ready and waiting.

With his first puff of the doobie, Manny thought about his family. He thought about the misery experienced by his parents, despite being guilty of nothing more than working hard and seeking a better life; it was the same misery he witnessed from his patients, who didn't deserve some of life's greatest misfortunes. Sometimes, bad things happened to good, hardworking people, he realized. All anyone can do in response is keep their head up and move forward, which is precisely what he'd do—for his parents' sake, for his patients' sake, and for his own sake. But before he moved forward, he'd relax and enjoy the doobie for a few minutes, because in that brief moment, it felt darn good to unwind.

And it felt even better after Manny took one more puff of the doobie.

"You're lucky you entered the legal profession instead of the medical profession," Manny told Howie Spirit, Esq., who waited to the left as Manny relinquished the doobie.

"With greater responsibility, comes greater fulfillment," Howie observed of the paramedic's career choice, having already gained a bit of wisdom with his first puff.

Howie's road stretched just as far as everyone else's, and took roughly the same amount of time to complete. The attorney who could solve anyone's problem except his own finally made it to his destination. There was certainly a lesson to learn about goals, but he wasted no time reflecting on the matter. Now that he'd officially retired, his mind deserved a break. Besides, nobody really cares what an attorney thinks about personal matters. So he took one more puff and remained mostly silent, with only one question before he passed the doobie along.

"How is your lawyer doing?" he asked the ex-wife of his sort-of client of twenty years, "I haven't seen her since we argued against each other in front of Judge Judi."

"She's fine," Cleopatra barked, annoyed by the reminder of her ex-husband's misdeeds. She badly needed a puff of the doobie, so the attorney to her right wasted no more time passing the doobie to his left.

Cleopatra couldn't get her mind off her ex-husband, a circumstance made more difficult with him sitting only steps away. But as she took her first puff of the doobie, she suddenly didn't care where he sat. Her mistake, she realized, involved allowing her divorce to define her. Nobody knew anything about her besides that she once married Moses. Think of how she could've developed by forgetting about her ex-husband at some point over the past twenty years and spending the time on herself instead. She may have even started a new relationship, with a potential mate sitting directly to her left and having once shown interest in the idea.

Cleopatra took one more puff of the doobie before passing it to her left, where the man whose name she now remembered was ready and waiting as she smiled and extended her hand.

Always an afterthought, Thutmond Mose III indeed stood out as the perfect mate for Cleopatra. They both suffered from the same problem. But it wasn't a divorce defining him; it was his marriage to his employer. And as he took his first puff of the doobie, he realized an unfortunate truth: Plant Inc never cared much about their most faithful employee in the first place, and would already be considering a replacement when he failed to show up to work the following morning. He'd fought so obsessively for his employer that Moses' theft became a personal issue. When Moses stole from Plant Inc, it had nothing to do with Thutmond. If only Thutmond realized that sooner, he could've simply moved on. And speaking of moving on:

"Here you go," he told Moses, offering the doobie after one more puff. "You were right about burying the hatchet twenty years ago."

Moses smiled and accepted the doobie, taking a quick puff of his own as soon as it touched his fingers. He agreed with his former coworker, though that wouldn't always have been the case. The bitter alcoholic from Dullsville underwent quite the transformation. Two decades in Mexico was a lengthy sentence in purgatory, but with everything considered, a necessary stay to change his mind about those he once loathed the most. Not only had he learned tolerance, he could now even handle lighthearted conversation with a foreigner.

"So you're an Adam Sandler fan?" he asked José, who sat immediately to his left.

"Arguably," José conceded.

Imagine that, Moses thought, and inhaled another puff of the doobie. Twenty years ago, he would've been appalled by the suggestion of having something in common with a Mexican, what with Americans and Mexicans being as different as whiskey and tequila. Yet here he was, sitting next to a Mexican-born man, discussing their common enjoyment of one of the funniest actors of a generation.

"Are you sure you don't have anything else besides *Billy*

Madison and *Happy Gilmore*?" Moses asked, and offered the doobie to the Mexican version of himself. He'd already seen those two films, and hoped to find out how far Adam Sandler progressed over the past twenty years.

"You didn't miss much," José revealed. "Though he's better if you're high."

As José took his first puff, the truth of his own words became unavoidable. He'd wasted so much time watching Adam Sandler movies and drinking tequila, when he could've been doing so much else instead. He could've spent time with María, or Jesús, or made a few friends of his own. He could've volunteered, or exercised, or developed a hobby, or taken a class, or even just read a good book. He could've started that late-night carpentry business he'd always spoken about.

But he never achieved any of those milestones.

The good news for José: it was never too late to change for the better. A beautiful woman sat to his left, and a son-of-sorts sat just left of her. It didn't matter whether Jesús was his biological offspring or whether María withheld the truth, because José got what he deserved. Actually, he got more than he deserved, in a positive sense. He didn't deserve to have María take care of him or Jesús look up to him, but he'd gotten that love anyway.

But again, it was never too late for José to change, which began by making up for his behavior to the person sitting to his left, his wife María. He started by passing her the doobie after one more puff for himself.

"I'm sorry, María," José apologized as he transferred the doobie. "You deserved better."

"I know," María agreed, with no hard feelings, the past being the past.

The hardworking young woman from Los Aburridos, who wasn't so young anymore, inhaled her first puff of the doobie and reminisced at how far she'd come. She'd worked so hard to achieve her American dream, and she'd held on to her dream for a sliver of time. The husband and the son and the bed of homegrown flowers outside a whitewashed, two-story ranch—she'd had it all, and the entire time she had it, she wouldn't let it go.

"Well, you'll have to let it go," José said, unprompted, "because we can't go back now."

That didn't matter to María, she realized. She'd lost America, but she still maintained the dream. Because all she'd needed in the first place to enjoy the whitewashed, two-story ranch at 11 Main Street was the very same people sitting around her right then. In truth, the view from the mountaintop offered a slight improvement over her American home, as long as those closest to her shared the experience.

So María puffed the doobie one more time and smiled at those around her, appreciating everyone for the best of their traits. But she appreciated nobody more than the son to her left, who received both a smile and a motherly hug, along with the doobie slowly reducing to ash.

"I love you, Jesús," the mother told her son as she handed him the doobie.

"Stop embarrassing me," replied the self-conscious twenty-year-old, who then pulled his hood over his head. "And for the last time, it's called a *joint*, not a doobie, you old farts."

Jesús' self-consciousness disappeared in an instant as he took his first puff of *Zerojuana* in quite some time. A savior to so many in the country of his birth, the young man from Dullsville deemed himself unworthy of the title, and felt satisfied knowing that everything worked out for the best. All he ever wanted was for those around him to relax. Well, his dream was coming true for his closest acquaintances. And in the bigger scheme, the rest of his compatriots back home in the United States would now have the chance. Those hecklers back in Dullsville sure needed to relax. Heck, maybe even the President would take a puff of the green stuff and settle down a bit.

"Don't count on it," said some-kind-of-Agent Stan DeVille, the only one in the group who'd met the leader of the free world in person.

"I can still dream," replied Jesús.

But to move forward, he realized, he needed to let go of the past, just as his mother recommended. And letting go of the past began with forgiving the man who harmed him the most. Rather than make a formal declaration of forgiveness, he took his second puff of the *joint* and passed it to Stan DeVille, who'd been patiently waiting for his turn.

Jesús was right—both in direction relative to Stan, and in what he thought about the state of the country. Stan knew it too, even before taking his first puff. The President would certainly benefit from a moment of relaxation; so would Plant Inc's CEO, along with more than a few other nameless individuals. But at that moment, puffing on that doobie, Stan couldn't worry too much about them, mostly because he couldn't worry too much at all. He simply felt thankful to have been introduced to the green stuff himself.

Stan had spent so much time telling people what not to do, he'd forgotten to find out whether the activities they undertook were truly that bad to begin with. The *Zerojuana* in the doobie didn't seem that bad. He wondered how many more bad things could actually be good instead. Or, good things could be bad, he reasoned. Regardless, that was a lot to think about right then, so he took a second puff of the doobie and passed it to the last person in the circle. Stan didn't know whether the Guy to his left was a good Guy or a bad Guy, but passed no judgment either way in view of his recent revelation.

The golden-eyed Guy took a big ol' puff of the doobie and looked around. The scenery had barely changed in two decades; not that it felt the same either. In the beginning, he couldn't have imagined a better place to be than at the top of his secret island, with the sun beaming down on his face, and the fresh ocean breeze gusting through his beard. But now that he shared the mountaintop—the very same mountaintop where he previously stood alone some two decades earlier—the circumstances were much better indeed.

It felt good to let others share in his wealth. Actually, it felt *really* good—so good that he didn't care how the President's third Executive Order would affect TH Corp's profits. With all forms of cannabis now legal in the United States, his particular monopoly on *Zerojuana* held less importance. Not only that, but his monopoly on *Zerojuana* would be short-lived. Back at 11 Main Street in Dullsville, a secret garden would be discovered at some point in the not-too-distant future. And off Main Street, *Zerojuana* relatives were beginning to spring up in other parts of town, thanks to prevailing winds perfect for pollination.

But Guy didn't care about any of that. He knew nothing about pollination and prevailing winds to begin with. He was a businessman, not a botanist. The point was that he wouldn't have cared even if he understood the science of it all, because everyone should be allowed to feel as good as he did right then.

So in the end, a dozen men and women sat in a circle, passing a doobie in the same direction that the hands of a clock count hours and minutes. And once everyone puffed, a long silence followed as they lost themselves in their personal revelations. Eventually, someone needed to say something, of course, and the self-proclaimed leader of the island thought himself the man for the job when that time finally came.

A man of few words, Guy perfectly summed up the *Zerojuana* cannabis, the circle of enemies-turned-friends, and the overall mood on the island, when he said:

"This is super dope," and everyone agreed.

THE END

Thanks for reading The Super Dope American Novel,

and please pass the doobie.

---

[1] Studies have shown that only 40% of roosters adhere to a strict morning routine, making the species significantly less reliable than their digital counterpart in the context of a morning alarm.

[2] The phrase "elbow grease" is a figure of speech typically used in the context of performing manual labor, especially vigorous polishing or cleaning. Some scientists have suggested, however, that it's not the actual "grease" fueling the labor, attributing more effect to the laborer's effort.

[3] The University of Miasma in Ohio, not to be confused with Miasma University in Florida, at that time boasted of the nation's third-ranked olfactory (informally, "smelling") undergraduate program, behind only the University of Notre Odeur and Pennsylvania State University.

[4] *Happy Gilmore*, a 1996 comedic film starring funnyman Adam Sandler as a misfit golfing professional, became Sandler's second hit success, following the previous year's *Billy Madison*.

[5] The National Sleepyhead Association (or "NSA") recommends for adults aged 18-55 to receive a minimum of eight hours of sleep per night to significantly reduce the risk of developing

Cranky-Pants Syndrome.

[6] Most experts agree that knives have varying levels of sharpness, leaving some doubt as to the meaning of the phrase "sharp as a knife" unless appropriate context is provided. Butter knives as one example are not known for the sharpness of their edges, while steak knives as another example add serration to the simile.

[7] Hyperosmia generally refers to the condition of having a greater than average ability to smell, usually caused by a lower threshold for odor.

[8] Footnotes can be distracting when used improperly, doing nothing but interrupting a story's flow.

[9] There are over 391,000 vascular plant varieties, according to scientists' estimates, of which about 94% are flowering plants. Understandably, it would take a great deal of time to discuss each variety, with the discussion likely plainer than most people prefer.

[10] Cryostorage generally involves the use of cryogenic temperatures to preserve biological elements over an extended period. Most famously, American psychology professor James Bedford became the first cryopreserved human in 1974; he logically remains the longest-preserved human to this day.

[11] Though there are no hard and fast rules on applicability, "Esquire" (abbr. "Esq.") is typically used by attorneys to denote their status. Contrary to use in the industry, however, the term has no legal significance.

[12] Though most famous for the phrase "Pleading the Fifth," the scope of the Fifth Amendment is much broader than guaranteeing every citizen the right to due process of law. Quietly tucked behind that promising statement is a lesser known section referred to as the "Takings Clause," which enables the federal government to take private property for public use, as long as the federal government provides "just compensation," whatever the government decides that to be.

[13] Penned by Sonny Curtis of the Crickets, *I Fought the Law* became one of the first recorded songs to allude to police brutality. Strangely, a mere six months after the song debuted on

the Billboard Top 100 chart, Curtis died of asphyxiation in his mother's car. The Los Angeles Police Department declared the death an apparent suicide, but many believed Curtis to have been murdered.

[14] Specifically, the President said: "When I was in England, I experimented with marijuana a time or two, and I didn't like it, and I didn't inhale, and I never tried it again."

[15] The phrase "bump in the road" generally refers to a minor setback or obstacle. In most instances, it's questionable whether the driver should've been watching more closely and avoided the bump altogether.

[16] "Breaking the ice" is generally used to describe an act which causes someone to feel relaxed and comfortable. Interestingly, the actual act of breaking ice doesn't always result in a relaxed and comfortable state for everyone involved, particularly anyone standing on top of the ice as it breaks.

[17] Produced by Ford between 1957 and 1979, the Ranchero was a coupe utility vehicle combining a station wagon's cab with a pickup truck's cargo bed. No description could do justice to the vehicle, however, and anyone unfamiliar with the model should view a photograph.

[18] Effective beginning in 1994, the North American Free Trade Agreement (or "NAFTA") created a trilateral trade block between Canada, Mexico, and the United States, reducing barriers to trade and investment between the three countries.

[19] In 1995, *Billy Madison* became funnyman Adam Sandler's breakout hit due to his eye-opening portrayal of a 27-year-old disabled man's journey through the public school system.

[20] The phrase "bury the hatchet" derives from the 17th-century Native American practice of burying weapons such as tomahawks during times of peace. Of course, the planter could always return to the location and retrieve the artifact during times of war, rendering the actual act of burying relatively meaningless outside of securing the hatchet in a safe location.

[21] 1981 marked the first year a member of the Screen Actors Guild served as the President of the United States, with Ronald Reagan holding the position until 1989.

[22] Refer to Footnote #17, which recommended for anyone unfamiliar with the vehicle to view a photograph. Why would a photograph have been mentioned if it didn't matter?

[23] A serape is a long blanket-like shawl, typically brightly colored and fringed at the end. The length may vary, but the front and back normally reach knee height on an average person.

[24] A sombrero is a large hat intended to shield from the sun, distinct for its high-pointed crown and extra-wide brim slightly upturned at the edge.

[25] In 1917, the Mexican Constitution first introduced a one-month parental leave period, which increased to twelve weeks in 1975. In comparison, the first United States federal protection began in 1993 with the Family and Medical Leave Act mandating twelve weeks for new mothers.

[26] To "create from scratch" generally means to create entirely without the aid of something already in existence. Logically speaking, however, everything is created from something in the absence of supernatural powers.

[27] Ketchup, also known as catsup, is a sweet and tangy tomato-based condiment typically recognizable by a blood-red color.

[28] Although every location on Earth experiences darkness at some point in the year, the area north of the Arctic Circle has been known to experience up to six months of constant sunshine due to the tilt of the Earth's axis.

[29] Aquatics experts have long debated whether it's better to be a big fish in a small pond or a small fish in a big pond. Essentially, the question comes down to delusions of grandeur versus likelihood of survival.

[30] "Off on the right foot" generally means to obtain a favorable start, while "off on the wrong foot" generally means to obtain an unfavorable start; though it may often be difficult to tell the difference without the benefit of hindsight, since the right and wrong feet tend not to be labeled.

[31] The Oval Office is the official office space of the President of the United States, located in the West Wing of the White House in Washington, D.C. Although the modern Oval Office

has only been the working space of the President since 1909, the shape of the room dates back to 1790, when George Washington used bowed walls for a ceremonial space at the President's House in Philadelphia.

[32] The State of the Union Address is an annual speech delivered to Congress by the President of the United States at the beginning of each calendar year, giving the President the chance to laud past accomplishments and offer optimism for the future, though traditionally the President isn't held to anything said.

[33] In 1998, two years after California paved the way for cannabis legalization through voter support, Alaska, Oregon and Washington followed suit to legalize medicinal cannabis through similar ballot measures.

[34] The state of Maine followed its predecessors by legalizing medicinal cannabis through a ballot measure in 1999; Hawaii became the first state to legalize medicinal cannabis through state legislature in 2000.

[35] According to most theological experts, states of being with the suffix "iness" are generally ranked as follows: (1) godliness; (2) cleanliness; (3) holiness. Though there are those who believe that happiness and luckiness are arguably more relevant, but have been improperly disqualified from the list due to arcane qualification guidelines.

[36] Referring to drug use, the President said: "When I was young and irresponsible, I was young and irresponsible."

[37] In 2000, both Colorado and Nevada legalized medicinal cannabis through ballot measures.

[38] Some so-called linguistics experts believe that the term "whip," in the phrase "smart as a whip," refers to the political party official appointed to maintain discipline among its members in Congress or Parliament. Understandably, the phrase "smart as a whip" is generally used more in jest than in seriousness.

[39] Vermont legalized medicinal cannabis through state legislature in 2004; Montana through a ballot measure the same year; Rhode Island through state legislature in 2006; and New Mex-

ico through state legislature in 2007.

[40] Referring to drug use, the President said: "When I was a kid, I inhaled frequently. That was the point."

[41] In 2009, the Justice Department issued the Ogden Memorandum, which advised U.S. attorneys to only prosecute cannabis providers who violated state law, improperly assuming that the U.S. attorneys would respect the advice.

[42] Michigan approved a ballot measure to legalize medicinal cannabis in 2008, followed by Arizona with a similar vote in 2010. New Jersey used state legislature to accomplish the same result in 2010, followed by Delaware in 2011 and Connecticut in 2012.

[43] Although Washington, D.C., first passed a ballot initiative to legalize medicinal cannabis in 1998, implementation of the measure fell into limbo until the Council of the District of Columbia passed a bill with the same intent in 2010.

[44] In 2012, Colorado legalized recreational cannabis through the passage of Amendment 64, while Washington accomplished the same outcome with Initiative 502, becoming the first U.S. states to enable their citizens to have a little fun with the product.

[45] Massachusetts approved a ballot measure to legalize medicinal cannabis in 2012; Illinois and New Hampshire followed with legislative decisions in 2013; Minnesota and New York came next in 2014.

[46] In 2014, Alaska and Oregon became the third and fourth states to legalize cannabis for recreational purposes, using ballot measures to objectively prove the support of Alaskans and Oregonians. Washington, D.C., home to the U.S. President, passed a similar ballot measure during the same election.

[47] In response to increased raids on cannabis providers following the Ogden Memorandum advising against such raids, the U.S. House of Representatives passed the Rohrabacher-Farr Amendment in 2014, explicitly prohibiting the federal prosecution of individuals acting in accordance with state medicinal cannabis laws.

[48] On December 16, 2014, the President signed the Rohrabacher-Farr Amendment into law. The Amendment didn't affect the legal status of cannabis, but was still perceived by cannabis advocates as a historic victory on the federal level.

[49] The late-1990s saw a significant rise in the popularity of oversized, loose-fitting denim trousers amongst youth in the United States.

[50] An Executive Order is a directive issued by the President of the United States which does not require approval by the legislative branch to have the full force of law. In layman's terms, an Executive Order represents the President saying, "I can do whatever I want, and Congress can't stop me."

[51] Although his time far preceded the establishment of the DEA in 1973, Earnest Stoppit is often referred to as a pioneer in the art of prohibition, being credited with the first drug bust in the history of the United States for shooting his neighbor, Samuel Quiet, for smoking a tobacco pipe in 1791.

[52] When someone is "worth his salt," the phrase generally means he is competent at his profession. The phrase was coined, however, before experts understood the health effects of a high sodium diet, raising doubt whether a person should wish to equate with so much salt to begin with.

[53] The typical lifespan of a Chihuahua is twelve to twenty years, making the breed not only one of the longest-living canines, but also the perfect species for a story spanning approximately the same amount of time.

[54] The Gregorian calendar, named after Pope Gregory XIII, altered the calculation of leap years in 1582 to place Easter on the day that the Catholic Church celebrated the holiday. Due to the popularity of the Catholic Church, Pope Gregory XIII forced the majority of other religions to adopt the same schedule, regardless of whether they celebrated Easter.

[55] A mango is a juicy stone fruit from a tropical flowering plant believed to have originated in South Asia. The mango is the national fruit of Haiti, India, Pakistan and the Philippines, while the mango tree is the national tree of Bangladesh.

[56] Statistically speaking, the odds of a predetermined group of people being alive twenty years after selection of the group are below 100%, with age making the eldest member of the group less likely than the rest to still be around at the end.

[57] A peter pepper is a rare type of heirloom chili pepper best known for its unusual shape, often described as phallic when fully grown. No description could do justice to the physical characteristics of the peter pepper, however, and anyone unfamiliar with the variety should view a photograph.

[58] The grim reaper is generally recognized as a personification of death, often as a shrouded skeleton wielding a scythe, which is an agricultural hand tool for mowing grass or reaping crops. Some have suggested that other weaponry may be more appropriate for such a bringer-of-death, but it can be difficult to adjust an image already embedded in the minds of a majority.

[59] At the time of its release in 2004, *50 First Dates*, one of many romantic comedies starring Adam Sandler and Drew Barrymore, became the first motion picture in almost ten years to feature a penguin in a central role. Not since the 1995 film, *The Pebble and the Penguin*, had a major Hollywood studio taken a chance on the species. After the success of *50 First Dates*, however, the movie industry followed with *Madagascar* (2005), *March of the Penguins* (2006), *The Farce of the Penguins* (2007), *Surf's Up* (2007), and *Mr. Popper's Penguins* (2011).

[60] At one time, the United States Department of Agriculture (or "USDA") recommended 6 to 11 servings per day of bread, cereal, rice and pasta.

[61] An Academy Award, also known as an Oscar, is the most important award an actor can earn based on the per-film pay increase which typically follows receipt.

[62] Most telephonic experts agree that Sharp introduced the first camera phone in 2000, though others argue that Kyocera released the first version several months earlier. Regardless, the concept of a camera in a phone is so well-known today that every person in the modernized world should expect to be recorded at all times.

[63] It is generally agreed that the concept of pausing live televi-

sion began around the turn of the 21st century, enabling homebodies to be lazier than previously thought possible.

[64] The concept of "social media," which may be broadly defined as any computer-based technology facilitating the creation and sharing of information, dates back to the 1840s introduction of the telegraph. While the broad definition has stayed relatively constant for well over a century, the specific definition of the "information" being created and shared has grown to encompass far more than ever envisioned with the telegraph.

[65] The Presidential Medal of Freedom is an award bestowed by the President of the United States to recognize an especially meritorious contribution to the security or national interests of the United States, world peace, or cultural or other significant public or private endeavors. Recipients of the President's highest award include politicians, religious clergy, athletes, judges, and even a musician named Elvis Presley.

[66] Historians have often wondered whether a chicken or an egg appeared first on Earth, since one seemingly cannot exist without the other. Scientists would note, however, that neither the chicken nor the egg came first, with the original chicken resulting from a mutation of a non-chicken through some form of change in DNA.

[67] To experts in the art of prevention, John Adams is often referred to as the "Original Prohibitor" for his signing of the Alien and Sedition Acts in 1798. Broadly speaking, the Alien and Sedition Acts enabled the President to imprison and deport non-citizens deemed dangerous or from a hostile nation, while also restricting speech determined to be critical of the federal government.

[68] Richard "Dick" Nixon declared the "War on Drugs" in 1971, placed cannabis on Schedule I of the Controlled Substances Act that same year, and then ignored a 1972 commission recommendation to decriminalize cannabis. In other words, Dick really disliked the green stuff.

[69] At the turn of the 20th century, Theodore Roosevelt built the White House's West Wing on the site of extensive greenhouses

after deeming the current floor plan insufficient for his six children and staff.

[70] To "pull the wool over the eyes" generally means to deceive someone, with the phrase dating back to the 17th century use of wool wigs, which when worn the wrong way would obstruct the wearer's vision.

[71] In 1919, the National Prohibition Act, also known as the Volstead Act, established alcohol prohibition in the United States. Although Woodrow Wilson initially vetoed the Act, Congress overrode the veto the next day.

[72] In 1933, Franklin Roosevelt signed the Cullen-Harrison Act, legalizing the sale of beer with an alcohol content of 3.2%. Upon signing the Act, Roosevelt famously said, "I think this would be a good time for a beer."

[73] Moby Dick, the 1851 novel by American writer Herman Melville, is widely agreed to be among the greatest of the Great American Novels. Too bad it's 600 freaking pages.

Made in the USA
Monee, IL
13 July 2020